"A Harrowing Picture of New England College Life in the 1970's!"

—*People*

Billy waited in a blue plastic chair in the otherwise empty Amtrak lounge. When the train finally came, first a pin of light, then thundering in, Zizi was among the first to hit the ground. Heart beating like a drumroll, Billy started toward her, both knees liquefying at the joints, until he thought they might give way, spastically, beneath him. His stomach quivered. His palms sweated, his throat was dry as wool, his shoulders doubled as ear muffs, and a voice in his head said: *Turn around. Run for it. Idiot, what are you doing? Oh, for Christ's sake. Turn arou-ound.*

"Zizi. Hi, I thought I'd meet you and walk you back." She stood there for a second, just looking at him. Billy stood his ground but barely, slouching toward her in his best approximation of someone being cool.

"BY NOT TRYING TOO HARD TO BE HIP, HILARIOUS OR TOUCHING, EPSTEIN WINDS UP BEING ALL THREE!"

—*Saturday Review*

Jacob Epstein

WILD OATS

PUBLISHED BY POCKET BOOKS NEW YORK

POCKET BOOKS, a Simon & Schuster division of
GULF & WESTERN CORPORATION
1230 Avenue of the Americas, New York, N.Y. 10020

For my mother and father,
My sister, Helen,
And my friends
Will Goetzmann and Laura Wagner.

1

HE ATE DINNER FIRST—SOME KIND OF GREASY HAM,
"baked ham," the old lady who served the food told
him when he asked her what it was, "with honey glaze.
It's very nice," she added hopelessly. He said "Okay,
I'll have some of that," as a favor to her. He also ate
some peas that were pale and filmy and made him
think of fish eyes. Then, after dinner, Billy called his
mother collect from the pay phone in the basement of
the dormitory.

"Hello?" Her voice is like purring, whiskey and
cigarette smooth. She sounds as if she has emphysema,
Billy thinks. She is the right age and has led the right
kind of life for some kind of cancer. The operator tells
her it's Billy calling and asks will she accept the
charges. "Oh yes. Of course," she says.

"Billy? At last. Oh, I'm so relieved. I didn't know if
I'd speak to you in time. I've been trying to get you
for two days."

"I'm in the middle of exams, Ma."

"Well that's what I figured. I didn't want to disturb
you. I just wanted to be sure you knew about Henry's
birthday party. It's the day after tomorrow. Remember
I wrote you about it? I thought if you could get home
in time, we could all go out to dinner, just the four of
us, maybe Markie too, if we can arrange it with the
doctors. Then there's going to be a party here afterwards."

1

"I don't know, Ma. I'm probably not going to be able to get there. I'm sorry, you know. Tell Henry 'Happy Birthday' and everything . . ."

"Oh . . ." She pauses, being brave about it. "Well I think that's too bad. I . . ." She considers starting something, changes her mind. "You can't get away, or what?"

"I don't think I can be home in time."

"Who are you talking to? What's 'too bad'?" Billy hears Henry in the background.

"It's Billy," he hears her tell Henry. "He says he doesn't think he can get here for your birthday."

"He doesn't, huh?"

"Hey Ma," Billy says into the mouthpiece, "who are you talking to?"

"Henry just came home . . . what? Oh Henry, come on . . . Just a minute. Billy, hold on a second, okay?"

Billy is sure that Henry is steaming now that his birthday plans have fucked up. "I get his meaning all too clearly," Billy can hear Henry saying—"I get his meaning" is what Henry always says—"I knew he was going to do this. All right, Catherine," he's saying, "the ball's in your court. What are you going to do about this?"

Billy's mother and Henry have been "going together" for almost a year, since last December, and Billy thinks they are about to marry. She wants to go out to a restaurant the night of Henry's birthday—herself, Billy, Billy's sister, Abigail, maybe a couple of Henry's kids, if she can convince the doctors to let Mark out of the sanitarium for the occasion—and in the course of it, announce that she and Henry are engaged. Billy and Abigail hate Henry, and the case they have against him is ironclad.

Article 1: Henry is a drunk. This isn't so bad in

2

itself. Most of the adults Billy knows are drunks to one degree or another. It's a fact of life. Billy doesn't doubt that when he gets to be Henry's age, he'll be a drunk also. And he'll die of cancer. He figures it's environmentally conditioned and there's no fighting it. But Billy doesn't want a drunk like Henry marrying his mother.

There was one night early in the spring of this year when Henry came over, turned the record player on full blast, and yelled and argued and drank some more with Billy's mother. Later he went into the kitchen to make some coffee and there he had found Abigail, months short of her sixteenth birthday, in her nightgown. In Abby's words: "It was so weird. He just stood there in the doorway all sweaty-looking. Like, out of breath. At first I thought, 'Oh no, he's having a heart attack.' I was sitting at the kitchen table eating this sandwich, and he was just staring at me, you know. So I smiled at him, 'Hi, Henry, nice to see you,' but he just kept staring. I didn't know what he was doing. I thought maybe he wanted me to go to my room so he wouldn't have to think I could hear them fighting. So I got up and tried to get past him. I said 'Goodnight, Henry, I'm going to bed.' But he just stood there, in the way. 'No kiss?' he said. I was scared shitless. I wasn't going to kiss that old freak. So anyway, then he grabbed me and he started saying, 'Oh you're so beautiful, you're so sexy,' and all this stuff. So then he said, 'Hey, Abby, listen. Will you meet me later tonight? Will you meet me in the kitchen, right here, say at two in the morning? Set your alarm clock or something. She'—he motioned with his eyes in the direction of the living room, where Ma was—'won't like it, but she ought to be fast asleep by two. She falls asleep fast.' " Abby had been too afraid to say anything. She went to bed, but couldn't sleep. She said she kept thinking she heard him coming down the hall. Once, she said, she thought she heard him

3

turning the doorknob, and she just lay there, all set to yell, but nothing happened. Next morning, on the subway to high school, she told Billy what had happened.

"You got to tell Ma about it," Billy had said, "that'll do it if you tell her. She'll get rid of him."

But it didn't do it. She didn't get rid of Henry.

"He was teasing you, darling. He was just being silly."

"Ma," Abby had said, "I don't know how to tell you this, but I don't think he was teasing."

So at dinner that night Abby worked up the courage to confront Henry. And Henry had said, "I must have been smashed last night. I'm sorry if I scared you, honey." When that didn't seem to work, he said, "Anyway, hahaha, what kind of a place is this where a guy can't get blotto and joke around? Huh?"

Article 2: Henry has been married twice before. Both of his ex-wives are dead. Both died in what were called tragic climbing accidents. Both were alone with Henry, high atop mountains. The first one got it in Washington State, the other one in New Hampshire. Both "accidents" occurred miles away from any witnesses. Billy has heard certain rumors about these tragedies. The inevitable rumors: Henry is a psychopath. He took those women high up in the mountains and God knows what happened up there, but when he was through, he just flipped them over the side.

But the thing is, it's not so much that Billy has heard these rumors. It is how he heard them; and who passed them along to him in the first place. It's very strange. Two years ago Henry and a girl friend had come over for dinner, with three or four other couples who were friends of Billy's parents at the time—this was when Billy's mother was married to her second husband, Jim —so they all had dinner together and then the next day Billy's mother described the party to him, saying it had gone on very late, and everybody had gotten very drunk and so on and so forth. Then she had said, "There was a man here last night who I must have known for twenty years. He was in college with your father and now it turns out he's got some business with Jim's firm. And I tell you, he's always given me the shivers. He always has." And she had proceeded to tell Billy that she thought Henry was a murderer and how she had always had this feeling about him, even before she had heard anything about his dead wives. "I wonder if that nice girl he brought with him last night knows what kind of a man he is. Last night I asked Jim if he thought I ought to call her up and warn her. Poor thing. I hope she knows better than to ever go mountain climbing with that weirdo."

But fate has a way of happening. There Henry was, two years later, visiting one night after a cocktail party in honor of one of the assholes Billy's mother knows. There he sat on the sofa, tense in his suit and tie while Billy's mother adjusted the record player and got him something to drink.

"Billy, I'd like you to meet an old friend, Henry Gould," she had said when Billy wandered into the living room. Billy had shaken Henry's sweaty hand. Later, when Billy reminded his mother of those rumors about Henry's previous marriages, she had said, "I've heard those horrible rumors and I think they are ridiculous and malicious."

Articles 3, 4, and 5: Henry is crazy. He is unreliable. He is a fool. Sometime in July he decided to take an extended leave from his job at the city desk of the newspaper. He had decided that he wasn't getting enough out of his life. He was "disillusioned," "turned off" as Billy's mother explained, apologizing for Henry, as she often has had to. The newspaper world was a "racket," a "swindle," so Henry decided he'd be his own boss for a while and he bought a pottery wheel, a kiln, rented a studio in SoHo and then announced, when his weeks of vacation were up, that he felt better about himself doing this, making lopsided vases and ashtrays, than he did sitting in a swivel chair, in a depressing office, eating fattening lunches that are high in cholesterol, a sure cause of cancer, etc., etc. Billy's mother got in the spirit of things. She went out and ordered a $100 bag of genuine Georgia red clay. She had it sent to him all the way from Georgia. Henry was so happy making pots that he told his editor he wanted to take a leave of absence. He said something about being at work on an independent project and needing time to pull it all together.

Henry's pots and pitchers and goblets began to fill in spaces on the bookcases, on tables in just about every room in the house. In fact, because the rent for his studio was so expensive, Henry tried to talk Billy's mother into allowing him to move his entire factory into the guest bedroom—the lathe, the pottery wheel, the huge kiln. She even consented, at first, and they set a day when Henry would surrender his studio, rent a van, and move in.

A few nights before he was to move in, Billy's mother threw Henry out. Billy never found out what happened—though he could have imagined a number of things. Something got her going.

"Get out of here," she had screamed at Henry that night. Billy and his sister were watching TV.

"Wow!" Abby had said, "listen to that. It's going to be a good one."

"I mean it. Out. I don't want it anymore. I want you out of here." Smash went several of his pots that he had crafted so lovingly, presenting them to her in almost daily ceremonies—Henry worked fast—with his initials, HG, carved on the bottom of the mug or dish or ashtray. She had been, he said, his muse. He

6

wouldn't leave that evening. Even with her shrieking at him, even with Billy and Abigail both "in for the evening." He just followed her around, broken, plaintive, beseeching her to "just listen to my side" (whatever that was); when he wouldn't go, and even followed her into the bathroom, holding the door open with his foot and saying, "Where are you going? What are you doing?" ("I'm going to the bathroom," she had said, trying to trick him), she became hysterical. "You crazy son-of-a-bitch! I don't want you in my house! Get ou-out!" She held the bathroom door shut with one hand while she looked around for something, anything, to throw at him. She settled on the blue soap dish, the very blue soap dish he had made her a few weeks earlier. She had at the time gushed over his artistry—"Oh Henry, gosh it's good," she had said, calling it "darling" and saying she knew just where to put it. She had even listened fascinated while he explained how he had gotten the fluted edges just so—but none of that mattered to her now.

"All right," she had said, and let go of the bathroom door, letting Henry pull it open. She must have looked at him so fiercely, her arm cocked to throw the soap dish, that Henry backed off a few steps. And then they stood looking at each other, surprised at themselves and out of breath from all the yelling.

"I want you to listen to me, Catherine," Henry had said. It was a bad move. Without another word, she had flung the soap dish at him. It clonked him solidly on the side of the head, skipped off and shattered against the wall.

Billy had been following the fight, unnoticed, as the action wound its way down the hall, into the kitchen, out of the kitchen, down the hall again and finally the bathroom. He followed them like a cameraman, thinking all the time of the Loud family on TV. Billy thought that if she yelled at him and said, "What do you want, Billy?" or "Can't you see we're in the middle of something?" he was going to say, "Abby and I are trying to listen to TV. Can you keep it down?" One thing he hoped was that his presence might make them stop, that they might see him, get grips on themselves, thinking "This experience must be terribly upsetting for Billy."

Henry slumped to the floor and rubbed his head. Billy's mother locked herself in the bathroom.

"Oooh Jesus," Henry had said, "ow that hurts." He raised his eyes and looked at the bathroom door. Billy had never seen such a pitiful expression on anyone's face before. "Oh Catherine," Henry said, quietly. Then he noticed Billy standing nearby and it was too much for him. "I'm sorry, Billy," he said, rising shakily to his feet. "I hope you can forgive me."

"It's all right," Billy had said, trying to sound reassuring. After all, poor Henry. Billy tried to imagine him giving those two women the old heave-ho over some precipice. It just didn't seem possible.

"I want you to know that I think you're a great kid. I know you and I never really saw eye-to-eye about everything, but I just want you to know that I always respected your right to your own beliefs . . ." And so on, until at last he disintegrated into a pathetic, teary, "I'm sorry." Then the front door slammed and that was it. Henry was gone.

Billy's mother has had a couple of other good fights with Henry, and one was almost as good, but the time with the soap dish was clearly their best all-around effort.

Henry didn't stay gone. In fact he came back in less than two weeks, acting as if nothing had ever happened. But he still had that big bruise on his forehead.

The Monday after the fight, Henry went back to his office and began writing a series of articles on the city's fiscal crisis. Then, in Sunday's issue of the Color Supplement, a story under his byline appeared entitled "The Thrills of Weekend Mountaineering." He sent flowers twice and called up Billy's mother a couple of times late at night. So Billy was hardly surprised when Abby opened the front door for him one evening when he'd forgotten his keys, and said:

"Henry's back."

So he was.

That night at dinner, oiled with a bottle of red wine, Henry told Billy that on the basis of the articles he had written, "an old buddy of mine, fellow by the name of John Rosenbloom—heard his name around? Bigshot in the old Lindsay administration. Ran into him the other day at a restaurant and we started talking and he tells me, 'Christ, Henry, you're the only guy who really knows the way the city works. You're the kind of guy we should be pushing for mayor.' He thinks I'd be a hit with the voters because I'm not a politician. They'd say, 'Hey, here's a guy who's talking about substantive issues, not a lot of bullshit'—pardon my French—"the old asshole interjected, "Rosey got me thinking. I'm meeting with him later in the week and we're going to toss some ideas around."

So, when Billy set off for college a month or so later, his mother was serious about Henry again, and he about her, and about running in the Republican primary for mayor of New York City.

Article 6: Billy is obliged to call Henry "Henry" to his face. This is something Billy has avoided doing as much as possible. Billy has avoided talking to Henry in general. But Henry gets a big kick out of talking about the issues of the day with Billy. He would wander into the living room when Billy was sitting around while dinner cooked and he would expect Billy to talk to him for a while. When Catherine came into the living room to say "Dinner's ready," Henry liked to be able to say to her, "We'll be there in a minute. I'm just flushing out Billy's views on federal welfare subsidies." He always began these discussions with "So William," or "So Bill," which was worse, "what's new with you these days? Happen to see the column this morning?" Billy had to read Henry's column every morning so as not to hurt the old idiot's feelings.

Furthermore, it made Billy feel ridiculous to see his mother having an affair, acting neurotic, jealous, confiding her hurts, anxieties, disappointments and frustrations in love to just about anybody—her girl friends on the phone, her therapy discussion group, the butcher at the corner meat market. Abby said that she had even overheard her telling her problems to the elevator man. "I love Henry, Louie. But after all the disappointments I've had with marriage and men—I don't want to make another mistake. Do you see?"

"Main floor, Mrs. Wieseltier," Abby said Louie had said.

Billy's mother was serious about Henry. Talking about loving him. Talking about marrying him. "Henry is a very brilliant man," she would say, "and very lonely and misunderstood. He's had terrible luck all his life . . ."

"Oh Ma, you're so fucked up," Billy wanted to say, but instead he ducked out of the room. Because if he didn't, she wouldn't have stopped. She would have told him everything, no matter how embarrassing. Billy did not like discussing his mother's experiments with various contraceptive methods. He wished she would leave him out of it. After all, it was not his affair.

"Hey Ma," Billy says into the phone. But she doesn't answer him. Billy can hear Henry talking about what a horrible day he has had at the office, how incompetent his secretary is, how the typesetter got his column all fouled up in the Early Bird edition, "and then to come home and find out about this . . ."

All that summer he had been attentive and polite to Henry. He had tried to be friendly and to listen generously to the bullshit and bluster as Henry toiled, trying to establish himself as mentor and buddy. Poor old Henry. After all, how was he supposed to know that that wasn't going to work? But poor Billy for that matter. What in the world was he supposed to do? How in the world was he supposed to feel in the morning when, walking down the hall to the bathroom, he passed the door to his mother's bedroom, heard the doorknob turning, the hinges squeaking, knew it was one of two possible people back there, neither of whom he was very eager to see, knew also that he wouldn't get away in time before that door opened? Then there, trying on his tie, wearing his black suit (Henry had even gone so far as to move his clothes into the closet—he was suits-in-the-closet serious about her), out would emerge the old rogue himself, heading to the kitchen for some orange juice. One morning Billy had passed his mother's room a little earlier than usual, when his mother was still in the shower. The door was open and he caught the old fart in his underwear doing push-ups.

This old creep? This jerk is going to be Billy's new stepfather? Billy can just imagine the wedding ceremony, the clumsy groom standing there with the two gray-colored, wiry wings on either side of his otherwise hairless head. His mother in her white veil, and all her sisters and brothers, her nieces and nephews, Billy's fruity, Jesus-freaky cousins, all assembled to bestow their blessings on this, the third of Catherine's marriages. Then he imagines the minister, or rabbi or

11

whoever they get to perform the ceremony, as he snaps shut the book of prayer and entreats the bride and groom to kiss each other. Oh God! What a nightmare!

What then is Billy supposed to do in the mornings, meeting Henry coming out of the bedroom on the way to his office? It was better before, when Billy would sometimes hear the alarm clock go off down the hall in his mother's bedroom at 6 A.M. and he'd know Henry was getting dressed and sneaking out. What was he supposed to do now? Give the fellow a sly wink, a nudge with the elbow? "Hey Henry—Hank. How'd it go, buddy?" Or was he supposed to play it courteous, innocent, as if he had no idea what went on all those nights behind the closed door? Should he have turned on the old charm, saying "Good morning, Uncle Henry—" almost singing it, "didya sleep well? I hope! Or are you just here so bright and early to deliver the newspaper?" What a mess.

Furthermore, Billy's mother is a brittle woman. Cracks and fissures run through her personality and it will not take much from Henry to split her, or chip her. Billy does not want to be around the day Henry suggests a honeymoon hike along the Appalachian trail, for example. He does not want to have to say, "Ma, remember what happened last time."

He really does not want to have to worry about his mother, and he wishes that, at forty-seven, she had learned a little more about taking care of herself. The affair reminds him so much of *Midsummer Night's Dream.* As he leans against the dormitory wall, holding the phone to his ear, listening to his mother tell Henry to "make yourself a drink. Go into the living room and unwind, Sweetie. I'll be in in a minute," he thinks that Shakespeare really knew everything. Because what has happened to his mother is that she has fallen in love with a jackass.

12

2

"BILLY? . . . STILL THERE?"

"Yeah."

"That was Henry."

"I know."

". . . And I explained to him that you still had some work to do and so you might not be able to get here for the birthday party. And he's a little disappointed that you can't be here"—she loads her gun—"and frankly I'm disappointed—but we understand."

Billy winces. "Gee I'm behaving terribly," he thinks. "What's gotten into me?" But all Billy says is, "Yeah, well."

"When do you think you'll be home?"

"I'm not sure." Billy isn't sure. He'd been thinking about not going home at all. He'd been thinking about going to California and never coming back. He'd thought about it a lot. He'd even called up the bus station and found out how much the trip would cost and how long it would take. But that scheme has fallen apart.

He sure doesn't want to go home to face Henry. And his mother. And the Christmas tree with the winking lights and the cranberries. Drunk birthday revellers sprawled all over the house. Billy's mother would tell them to put their coats in Billy's room. And Billy's little sister walking around the apartment in her hiking boots, those two enormous shoes that re-

13

mind Billy of half-track trucks the army used in World War II. Not that Abby doesn't get a lot of use out of them. It's a treacherous hike from the bathroom to the rugged terrain of the kitchen linoleum. And she wears them when she has to walk the dog.

"Well you'll call us when you've finished what you have to do, won't you? And let us know when you're coming?"

"Sure. I will." Billy does not like the sound of his own voice and wishes he could think of some upbeat way to round out the conversation.

"Then I guess we'll see you when we see you," Billy's mother says. And after saying "good-bye," they hang up.

He climbs the stairs and then down the dingy hall-way to his room, whistling in the loneliness. To some-one hearing him coming, his whistling would sound totally tuneless. But Billy has a song in mind and he thinks about the words.

Ev'ryone says "I love you,"
The goose and the gander and the goslings too
And even the rooster who says "cock-a-doodle-doo"
Says "I love you."

Ev'ry one says "I love you,"
But what they were talking 'bout I never knew—
It only causes trouble for the poor sucker who
Says "I love you."

There are more words to this song, but Billy can't remember what comes next. He tries to think where he heard the song, but he can't remember.

Billy's mother had written him a letter, dated the third of December, which is two weeks earlier, and Billy still has it, somewhere under papers, or in one of his pockets. It had been addressed in her large, loopy handwriting and had begun "Dearest Darling—"

She wrote this letter in an effusive and enthusiastic style, with little forests of exclamation points after her not-too-astounding notes of family gossip, and with little faces drawn in the margin, smiling or frowning to illustrate the goodness or badness of her news. She had written that she had "something very important to talk over with you, something that will require a great deal of maturity on your part, Billy, and also compassion. But it could turn out very wonderfully for us all and I want your opinion before I take another step. No more now. A mystery and a secret this will all remain until you're home for vacation."

And it was this, this paragraph in her letter, these several sentences that, when translated from Mummyese into English, read: "Henry and I want to get married. I know you can't stand the old idiot, but I hope you aren't going to make a big deal out of it. Come on, be a sport. You're away at school, you're going to have your own life pretty soon, so what difference is it going to make?"

Billy opens the door to his room with a key. The sun is setting and the room is dark, cast with blue and heavy shadows—some chairs and a sofa bought from the Salvation Army during the bright, hot first days of the term. Now they're torn apart, ripped, billowing cotton from seams. Billy turns on the light and stands in the doorway. Empty liquor bottles have been set up on the floor like bowling pins. Bunched up clothes, tossed onto chairs, sprawl their arms and legs over the sides. In the corner there is a tall floor lamp whose swan neck has been snapped and then bandaged back together with electrician's tape (this lamp was the only piece of furniture, besides a nonallergenic pillow, that Billy had brought with him from home). A few records have been left out of their jackets, on the rug, in the lap of chairs, dribbled with beer, scratched, ruined.

"Slobs," Billy says to himself. He shuts the door, gives an empty tequila bottle a kick, skittering it into the corner, and walks into his bedroom, which is also a mess, with his roommate's suitcases and sweaters and coats and clothes all over the desk and both beds. Randy is going skiing in New Hampshire tomorrow. Or maybe the day after if they don't fix his car in time.

Billy tosses all that is not his, as well as all that is his—a Chinese-English, English-Chinese pocket dictionary, some dirty socks—off the bed and lies down. Then, thinking of something, he gets up again, goes to his desk and goes through some papers looking for that letter his mother sent him. Billy finds the letter inside his copy of *Midsummer Night's Dream*.

"For Christ's sake," he thinks, reading through it as he lies back on his bed, "it's obvious. There's no question. 'I have something very important I want to talk over with you . . . very important . . . very wonderful . . . an important decision . . .'" Combine this with the coyness—"a mystery and a secret this will all remain" —and there you have it. The magic words.

Billy's mother has already had two husbands. The first was Billy's noted father (of all the people in the world to choose from! She had to pick that guy?). Billy's father has long since moved away to the West Coast. Billy never sees him. His father sends him letters every month or so, and makes no sense whatsoever. He has a new wife ("Half his age," Billy's mother has frequently observed). Actually Grace, the new wife, is nearly thirty by now and Billy's father is somewhere in his late forties. Grace was his student when they first met, and now they have a son, named Charles. Billy spent a few weeks one summer with his father and his father's new family, when Charles was two. He must be about five or six now. Billy had the

16

feeling when he was visiting, that he had never been in a more nervous household in his life. Everything went wrong. All the appliances broke down. Grace cracked up the car in the supermarket parking lot the day she took Billy and Charles shopping. And one night, midway through a very tense supper, the oven caught on fire and Billy would never forget how his father panicked and hiked Charles out of his high chair, his little baby booties getting stuck coming through the tray, and dragged the kid, Charles screaming, towing the high chair behind him, out the back door to safety.

"Call the fire department! Call the fire department!" Billy's father whooped through the neighborhood. Billy wanted to call out after him, "Hey—how about me, Dad?" After all.

Billy and his stepmother put out the fire with Kosher salt. Of course Billy's father has had some rough experiences with ovens and fires. He tried to light the oven once when he still lived in New York with Billy and Billy's sister and mother and he ended by blowing up the whole kitchen and knocking himself unconscious in the bargain. Anyway the question is, if Billy's father, this father had stuck around, would Billy really have come out much different? Who's to say.

Billy's mother later married a guy named Jim, who is best forgotten, as far as Billy and his mother and sister are concerned. Once Billy overheard her talking on the telephone to her lawyer, Benjamin, in Reno, Nevada, where he was letting the ink dry on a few divorce pacts. Benjamin is an old family friend and he gives her a discount on the wheeling and dealing, advising and red-tape cutting that she requires to straighten out her life. Car accidents, five hundred dollars in overdue parking fines, letting the bathtub overflow and flood the expensive art collection of the people in the apartment downstairs . . . Benjamin takes care of it. The night she called him in Reno he was probably just settling down in his motel room, pulling off his shoes and socks, having been signing papers and seeing people all day.

"Oh Benjamin," she had said to him without a trace of irony, "oh Benjy," she had said with a sigh, "I guess I have a pretty lousy track record." "Track record?" Billy had thought. What a fucked-up thing to say.

Billy gets up, letting his mother's letter drift off the bed onto the floor. He wipes the mirror above his dresser clean with a sock. He looks at himself, staring steadily as the wry little twist of an expression, that Humphrey Bogart "brother—what a world" smirk, melts away. He remarks that the swelling is going down. The skin around the eye is still discolored, but not as discolored as it was the day before. Yesterday he looked as if a car had hit him. If he has to go home for vacation, he doesn't want to go until his face is healed. He doesn't want to have his mother ask him, horrified, "What happened to your eye?" He doesn't want to confess to her that he got punched in the face. "Who hit you?" she'd want to know. "I want to know the name of the person who hit you." She'd fear that Billy was having problems "relating to his peers." He was having problems "relating to his peers." But it wasn't one of Billy's "peers" who had popped him in the eye and had laid him out unconscious, sprawled on a snowbank near Webster Avenue. The punch had single-handedly ruined Billy's life. "Billy, I want you to tell me what happened to you," his mother would press. How could Billy begin to tell her? "Well, Ma, it's sort of a long story. And I'm not even sure I understand how it happened myself."

Billy stares and stares at that glum countenance and at those two frightened eyes, the right eye puffy and black and blue. Those eyes surprise him. Surprise and scare him. That is what he looks like. And much as the mirror reveals about the outside of him, he reads

18

in it no clues, no clues at all about what is going on inside. That is him—his hair, his eyes, his beaky nose. He tries to leer at himself, to see what he looks like "in action," but the mirror jeers back at him. "What are you doing? What the hell are you doing?" it seems to say. He realizes at this moment that he will never escape that face in the mirror. And he had better start getting used to it.

Not for a couple of minutes, not until he hears the voice of his roommate, Randy Rolfe, outside the door, and the stamp as he kicks the slush off his boots, does Billy abandon this dismal posing in front of the mirror. He lies down on the bed, face downward on the pillow.

"So fine," Randy says. For the most part, Randy says about six to ten things—phrases, words. "So fine" is one of them. The door slams shut. "I can't believe I don't have to see this shitty room, or you assholes, for three weeks. I'm so psyched," he goes on, exhausting his vocabulary.

Randy hails from Los Angeles. He and Billy were supposed to share their room with a third kid, but whoever that guy was, he'd either been killed sometime during the summer or else he'd said, "The fuck with college. I'm going to stay home." So Billy and Randy had shared a two-room suite.

Randy's father is rich and dying. He is still vigorous and hearty, at least for a man in his condition. Emphysema—the big E—combining forces with cancer of the rectum, diseases going after him from both ends, and there is not much doctors can do for him, except cobalt and chemotherapy, which don't seem to have any effect on him. He is still, according to Randy, "playing golf and everything. He doesn't even use the carts." On business in New York one day, Mr. Rolfe rented a car and drove to Beacham to take his son and a couple of his buddies out to dinner. Billy found himself

19

sitting next to Mr. Rolfe, who asked him how he was getting along and what courses he was taking and so forth. Mr. Rolfe just said "Yup, yup, yup," agreeing with whatever Billy said. Billy spent most of the meal watching him, watching and listening and marveling as the old man laughed and gagged, wheezed and coughed his stomach out, shaking the dinner table and sending water in the water glasses sloshing. Mr. Rolfe had a big red face like Randy's. He had lost most of his hair to the chemotherapy, and so his skull was red too, and pointy, and speckled with brown liver spots. By the time dinner was over, Mr. Rolfe had downed four martinis, "straight up with lemon peel," filled the ashtray with cigarette butts, ashes and two spent books of matches.

Mr. Rolfe was worth over fifteen million dollars. Billy found out one night when Randy came back to the room drunk and talkative. Earlier in the day, Randy's father had seen yet another cancer specialist, presumably the foremost rectal authority on the West Coast, and Randy had been trying to call his dad all evening to get the lowdown. After his call rang and rang, nobody home, Randy sat down and told Billy how deeply he admired "the old man." That was the night he told Billy that his father had been indicted, that charges were still pending against him for illegal contributions to the Committee to Re-elect the President—Nixon. "It's so fucking unfair," Randy had declared, his fingers swollen in two angry fists, his face sweaty and twisted, his voice high in frustration, "there was nothing they had on him. He admitted he gave the money. He thought it was all legal. He's given money to political candidates all his life, Democrats and Republicans. 'It's politics,' my dad says. Like the McCarthy witch-hunts. Only now it's his turn. Why don't they clear him? That's all he wants. I think . . . I think all the worrying is what gave him cancer. He

20

never had anything like it before all this stuff started happening to him. They're killing him. I'm sure. It just makes me feel really bad . . ." Billy could understand that. For a second he wanted to go over and put his arm around Randy's shoulder and say "C'mon, Tiger. Things'll work out. You'll see." Just the same, he wished that he had known about this beforehand, so that the night when Randy's father came to take them out to dinner, he could have paid more attention. After all, the old guy was living history.

"Here he is," Randy says, hanging his head around the door frame, looking in. Randy's best buddies, Ron and Pete, appear behind him and the three of them stare in like three drunk gargoyles.

"Hey Pedro," Randy says to Pete, turning on his Mexican accent. This accent has been the big joke making the rounds of the freshman quad for the past three weeks. "Bring up de blade. We cut this mother . . ." Pete pulls a black switchblade out of his pocket. He bought it a few weeks earlier when he and Randy took the train into New York for the day. Randy said they found this store on Forty-second Street that had hundreds of switchblades, billy clubs, kung fu equipment and even phony FBI badges. Pete grew up in Randy's neighborhood in Los Angeles. They attended the same high school, played in the same rock and roll band (Randy played the guitar and sang, Pete was the drummer), ran on the same track team (Randy ran the 440 and the hurdles, Pete was a long-distance man)—so Pete knows about as much about switchblades as Billy's mother knows.

Randy stands there. Billy rolls over slightly, to watch out of the corner of his eye. He lies very still studying the situation. He does not move, except his left arm, which he slithers down the crack between the bed and the wall. Is it still there?

"I got an idea what we can do to him," says Ron. "You gotta hold him down, Randy . . ."

"Yeah. Yeah. I'll get him."

"If he kicks me, man . . ."

"He won't kick you. I guarantee."

"Banzai," Billy screams. He jumps to his feet.

"He's got the goddamn machete. Billy, you're such an asshole, you know it?" Billy swings the rusty sword through the air a few times. His own day trip to New York, an Army-Navy store in Greenwich Village. Once Randy and his friends had come in late at night when Billy was asleep. They were all drunk and started to play the record player at full volume. When Billy shuffled out, bleary, to ask them to be quiet, they had tackled him and tried to take his pajamas off and drag him down the stairs, wriggling naked, like a big pink worm, and then lock him outside the dormitory, in the rain. That was the night Billy sent Ron to the hospital. He knocked Ron out cold with the handle of the machete. If it had been the blade, Billy'd have gone to jail, or reform school. (Is he too old for reform school? He's eighteen years old, can drink and vote.) When he hit Ron, it was only the second time he'd ever seen someone unconscious.

"You were supposed to get rid of that thing. What'd the dean tell you?" Ron says. He's not kidding, either. The nurse at the hospital had told Billy's dean about the machete, and the dean, in his blue blazer and red and white spotted bow tie, had called Billy into his office to "discuss the incident." He told Billy all about the history of the machete, how his uncle had brought one back with him from Japan after World War II. Then he said the machete was a very dangerous weapon, and while he knew Billy wouldn't mean to hurt anyone with it, it would bring him "peace of mind" if Billy would get rid of the machete: "Take it home

22

with you over Thanksgiving break and just leave the thing there."

"I'll get the dean over here so fucking fast if you don't put that thing down . . ."

"No, hey, don't call the dean. Call up the hospital. Call Mental Hygiene . . ." "Mental Hygiene" was the euphemism for the corps of campus psychiatrists. Pete goes off to pretend to use the phone.

"Yeah, call the hospital. They'll take care of him there. Maybe they'll give him something for his eye. When you gonna tell us who gave you that black eye?"

"I know who gave him that black eye," says Randy. "That girl he's always chasing around. What's her name?"

"Zizi," Billy says.

"He tried to kiss her with that ugly face of his and she slugged him."

"I would too," says Ron. "I don't blame her." Ha ha ha.

Billy lunges at Randy with the machete. Randy snares his arm and the machete goes flying loose. It lands on Ron's head, and then clatters to the floor.

"You fucker," Ron says. He dives at Billy's stomach. He throws Billy against the wall and Billy sees shimmering skyrocket colors. His head is coming apart. The dull thud of plaster against Billy's skull frightens Randy.

"Hey . . . You all right?"

"He's faking."

"Hey, no. I know a guy who got a concussion like that . . ."

Later, when Randy and Pete have gone to the basement to play the final game of the season in the Ping-Pong World Series, and Ron has gone back to his room to pack his bags, Billy goes to the window, opens it, and hangs his head out. He gazes listlessly, unthink-

23

ingly, out into the quadrangle. He watches his classmates, some just now returning from dinner or setting
off for Christmas concerts and plays. They look fat
in their puffy ski parkas, like hamsters on hind legs.
They stand at the doors of the dormitories, exhaling
smoke, rubbing mittened palms together, or burrowing
bare hands in pockets while they discuss their grades,
and next semester's courses, and vacation plans, reading the notices tacked on the walls and doors of the
buildings to find out where to go for a movie or a play,
or the room and building where the Christmas carolers
are supposed to organize and prepare for the Christmas
caroling that goes on, caroling down the snowy, misty
avenues of the campus—"Come out, come all"—with
their long scarves and hearty baritone voices, all
smiley and spirited. Fruitcakes. If they weren't in college, Billy thinks, they'd be in the Hare Krishna line
clapping their hands and swaying in their saffron gowns;
to Billy it seems like the same impulse.

No one's singing now. They've just all gathered,
standing around. Down the snowplowed gray walk
come the Chinese twins—Howard Wang and his
brother Stanley—identical twins, except that Howard's
black hair goes to the left—or does Howard's hair go
to the right? And Stanley's the left? In any case, Stanley's hair has been trained to go the opposite way from
his brother's. That is how you can tell them apart. And
coming from another direction is Archie Greenfield,
who's nobody special—just someone Billy knows. And
now comes a girl named Brenda, who always argues
with the professor in Billy's philosophy class. Brenda
objects in class all the time, and though Billy most
often can't follow her, she paralyzes the professor who
sits there at the end of the table winding his watch in
frustration, or chewing his nails, trying to get up some
Socratic quip. He is sixty-ish, an old fellow, and presumably thinks deeply, but not too fast.

And then there, directly below his window, is a boy named Mark Wiseman, the class Marxist. Billy has wound up eating dinner with him a few times. Although Wiseman had grown up in Newton, Mass., had attended private schools all his life, and had never really met anybody from the working classes except maybe his mother's cleaning lady, he nevertheless spent most of the semester hanging around the unemployment office after class and trying to crash union meetings. Twice during the semester, Wiseman had been mugged in working-class bars. And twice he had tried to organize a campus protest, declaring in a letter to the school newspaper his contempt and shame for his un-callused, lily-white yet "bloodstained" hands.

"You just got to think what this college *is*," Wiseman had said one night, a few days after his student strike had fizzled, "like when you think of the foundations this place is built on—I mean, like the corruption and the rot . . . The bedrock of this institution and places like it are the corpses of the oppressed." Billy had sat opposite at the dinner table, munching on a roll. He had wanted to be judicious, to examine all the issues, from every aspect. A clash of dishes while Billy had prowled his mind for something socially responsible to say. All he had been able to think of was: "Well, you have a point there."

Tonight Mark Wiseman is talking to a girl named Francine Palmer, Frankie Palmer, about whom Billy knows little, except that she looks rich and he has seen her carrying a squash racquet around. Mark is gesticulating wildly, telling her a few things.

The gathering below him reminds Billy of a play his mother had once dragged him to, or maybe it was on educational TV. Anyway, a Shakespeare play, and a certain crowd scene where the villagers or citizens congregate and chatter, and everything's chaos, everybody's talking at once and going "Ho ho ho" while off in the corners of the stage, or above, on a balcony, where the hero is, the real action is taking place.

Billy stays at the window for some time and is just about to turn back inside, pull the window closed and start to pack away some of his things when he sees Zizi walking gingerly across the patches of ice that had formed from puddles frozen on the walks.

3

THE FIRST SUNDAY OF SEPTEMBER.

Billy's mother started off all bustly—everybody up at seven, breakfast bubbling and sizzling and toasting in the kitchen—but she came on vague and spiritual in the car, sitting in the back seat of the rented station wagon, with Abby and the typewriter, looking out the window through dark sunglasses, her hair held down under a scarf.

"I so hope you'll be happy here," she said, and after a nervous hug from her, a handshake from Henry— "G'luck, Bill"—and a wave from Abigail—"See ya"—Billy watched them drive down the street, signal for a turn, and head for the interstate highway. His suitcases and boxes lay like rubble on the curb.

Then, after standing in a long line of freshmen, waiting for half an hour to register and get his room assignment, finally reaching the end—a counter with a gray-haired woman behind it who checked her list with a pencil when he told her his name and then handed him a key: in exchange for five dollars—Billy crossed the quadrangle, overrun with families lugging boxes and bags and suitcases, and climbed the stairs of his dormitory to his room. He shared two rooms on the second floor with two other kids, one of whom had already arrived by this time. Randy Rolfe was not there when Billy got the door open. But his boxes were. Randy had not unpacked except to hang a sports jacket in the closet he preferred and to dump a suitcase on the upper of the two bunks. In the living room, the outer room, were all of Randy's cardboard boxes containing stereo components and clothes and books. Leaning against the wall, a bag of golf clubs, colored green plaid. The heads of the clubs had on red and blue covers, like sweaters, or socks, with pom-poms on the tops.

Billy hung his coat and jackets in the other closet. He put his socks in the socks drawer, hung his pants up neatly on hangers, folded his shirts and sweaters into squares and tucked them away in the bottom drawer. Several mimeographed notices had been left on his desktop and he read through them carefully. One letter was from the laundry and it proposed a freshman discount on the first month's dry cleaning. "This is a real bargain. I'm going to need dry cleaning," Billy said to the letter. Another letter was from the fire marshall. It began cordially enough—"Welcome new students!"—but wasted no time coming to the point. No mollycoddling. Ted McGarret came down very hard on students overloading electrical outlets. Billy made a mental note of this. And then: "Forewarned is forearmed," the letter read. In capital letters: "THE PENALTY FOR UNWARRANTED DISCHARGING OF FIRE EXTINGUISHERS IS 75 DOLLARS!"

"Brother! That's a lot of money," Billy thought.

Various student unions and organizations, groups, and magazines had left him flyers. He got a letter from the Afro-American Brotherhood, a letter which began

27

"Greetings, Brother," and ended with a Muslim name. "Why did they send me this?" he wondered.

After he read these through, and subscribed to the newspaper, he had no idea what to do next. Where was his roommate, Randy Rolfe, whose boxes were all over the living room? Where were his own boxes that he shipped weeks and weeks earlier, sometime in July in fact so that they would be waiting by the time he arrived? He wanted nothing better than a box of his books to organize quietly on his shelves. Where, for that matter, was his ready-to-assemble bookshelf that his mother had said she bought for him, and shipped along with the floor lamp from Bloomingdale's? Where were his clothes and blankets, where was his non-allergenic pillow? These things should all have arrived. Were they waiting for him at the post office? Where was the post office?

A man and his daughter were trying to carry an armchair up the stairs; it was hard work and the old fatty was struggling with it and sweating. "Whew! Let's take a rest," he said as Billy went by. Outside, a large clan of Chinese had assembled, half of them clucking in Chinese, the other half arguing in English, and, led by a tearful woman wearing a blue sweater over her shoulders, was bidding farewell to a set of uneasy twins, who wore matching blazers. The Wang brothers, Billy later learned. Water sprinklers spun their radii of water on the grass. Billy asked directions to the post office from a hippie who shrugged his shoulders and said he didn't know.

The post office was closed—Sunday—but Billy found the dining hall and had some lunch—a greasy grilled cheese sandwich and chocolate milk in a container—and when he returned to his room, Randy was there, standing in the middle of the floor with a golf club in one hand, and a golf ball in the other. Before Billy said anything, he was quick to realize that the boxes that had seemed at first scattered carelessly around the floor had really been carefully arranged to create obstacles on the golfer's indoor golf course, make-believe sand traps and water hazards.

"How you doing? You're my roommate, right?" The roommate moved the putter from one hand to the other and strode over, his hand extended. "You're William, right? You like to be called William? Bill? Will? What?" Billy had to think.

"It doesn't matter." It sounded weak and he wished for a little more time so he could have tried out the options. Then he stood there for a second.

"You met Mel? Guy across the hall?"

"No."

"He's taking a shit right now. Just came back from lunch with him. Says he's some hot-stuff golfer." Randy winked.

Mel soon returned from the bathroom, wearing aviator-style glasses, short pants, and sandals. Mel shook Billy's hand and said, "How's it going?"

There was nothing else for Billy to do except sit on a box against the wall and watch as Mel and Randy played their game. Randy set the ball down on the floor and then putted toward the mouth of a drinking glass. The ball grumbled slowly along the wooden planks, veered off course, and stopped underneath the radiator.

"Jesus. Look at the curve in the floor," said Randy. And Billy found himself studying the floor to see what it could have done to derail his roommate's golf ball.

"What am I doing?" he thought to himself.

There were no classes that first week. The upper-classmen would not arrive until the next weekend and those first few days—Orientation Week—were dedicated to explaining to the freshmen how to get around campus and what they were supposed to do. There were a couple of things that happened during those early days which Billy could vividly remember.

One afternoon Billy and Randy went to the library for a guided tour. They were taken up the elevator, guided through the stacks—shelf after shelf of musty books—taken back down the elevator to the basement, to the microfilm room, humming with machines and fluorescent lights, and finally brought back to the circulation desk. Their guide, a library frump in a black skirt, handed each of the tourists a slip of paper on which to practice signing out a book. There was a right way and there was a wrong way. Billy filled out his card perfectly and the guide singled him out and passed his card around to the twenty others by way of example.

"Now this is the proper way to take out a book," she said. "You'll notice that the student's ID number is written neatly and legibly in the corner, then his name, the book's title, author's name, last name first, and the call number . . . Very good . . ." And she handed the card back to Billy to keep, or frame on his wall if he wanted to. Billy flushed with pride—he couldn't help it—and thought of the way he used to feel when Mr. Hoar would read his history essays aloud to the class in high school. Randy, standing beside, poked Billy in the ribs with his elbow, as if to say, "Way to go." Randy was impressed with Billy. A number of times he had spoken deprecatingly of his own high school student days.

"I was never really what you would call into academics. Mostly I fucked around a lot. You know, like an underachiever. This summer, though, I got a lot more serious. I read a lot . . ." Randy admired Billy's seriousness.

Through his post office box later that week, Billy was invited to meet the president of the university,

30

who wrote that he was going to be standing outside his house for an hour Thursday afternoon, greeting the new students. "Hope you'll drop by," was the way the mimeographed letter closed. So at 4:30 Thursday afternoon, Billy found himself in jacket and necktie, hair wet and combed, at the end of a long, long line of new students, talking in gaggles of two's and three's, dressed up and shuffling forward, steps at a time, toward the front porch of the president's house. It had started to drizzle and the line stopped for a few minutes while the president went inside the house to get an umbrella and a mackintosh.

"Billy Williams," Billy said, when his turn came, taking his lead from the boy in front of him who had given the president his name, shook hands and moved off.

"Nice to see you," the big red face pressed it home, looming out from under the umbrella, between the two wings of the turned up collar of his raincoat, "glad you could make it."

And then, on Sunday, the freshmen were required to attend a speech given by the school minister, who pondered aloud the question: what does it mean today to be an educated man (or woman)? (This parenthetical aside brought a titter from the audience.) Beacham University had been, for nearly a hundred years, an all-male liberal arts college with a reputation for being second-rate. It was not a place where students wanted to go, but where they ended up. Billy had not been accepted anywhere else, a fact his mother said she could not understand, despite his disastrous SAT results; Mel, the golfer from across the hall, had said one night that he had chosen Beacham over Princeton and Brown because he wanted to go to someplace small, not someplace "humongous," he said, "and impersonal." Billy wasn't so sure.

31

Times however change, and while Beacham was still second-rate, it had started admitting girls five years earlier and everyone was still acting very coy about it. In the first issue of the *Beacham Bee,* the campus daily, Billy had read an editorial by an angry feminist who complained that women at the college were in a state of what she termed "parenthesis"—e.g., men (and women).Women were not treated as human beings, were always asked for the feminine point of view in the classroom and so on. Evidently the minister hadn't read the editorial, because he greeted the nervous sniggering with a pleased pause and looked around the room, grinning as if to say, "I haven't lost it. I'm still the funniest guy in town."

He went on with his address, issuing wisdom and advice, peppering his remarks with personal reminiscences and anecdotes about the school's history. Then:

"For some of you, I am sure, the old myth dies hard: college is a stepping-stone, a place to pick up credentials, a head start . . . you know what I mean . . ." And here the minister wandered away from the podium evidently to extemporize and to wave his arms. ". . . the notion that a college degree guarantees a good job, a certain social standing. But"—and he raised his forefinger—"I refer you to an article in this week's *New York Times* . . ." He reached inside his pockets for reading glasses and a newspaper clipping and began to read an article describing the difficulty recent graduates had been having trying to find work. When he was through reading, he paused, put away his glasses and the clipping, then faced the audience, looking close to tears, heartbroken.

"It's terrible," he said, "it is all . . . so . . . terrible." What, Billy wondered, was happening? Was the minister coming apart? He looked around at Mel, who shrugged his shoulders when Billy caught his eye. Randy, next to Mel, had gotten bored and was read-

ing a letter from home. "Have we," the minister re-
sumed, "as educators, failed to teach our students the
right things, failed to prepare them, or prepared them
inadequately? For myself, I don't believe this is true.
If anything—and this is something more depressing
—today's graduates enter a world of dwindling resources and opportunity, or so we read in the papers.
Your families, your teachers, and I look on you with
anxiety and hope—not because you will follow in our
footsteps—but because we see in you the promise, or
at least the possibility, of climbing beyond us. We leave
behind for you a very imperfect globe: poverty, strife,
race hatred, violence, torture, civil war, persecution,
corruption, crumbling institutions and ideals that have
gone bankrupt . . . How, you may well ask, are you
supposed to deal with them? I for one have no
idea . . ." He expanded on his gloomy message for
twenty minutes or more, then wound it up with:

"As I look out among you and see your bright,
eager faces, I feel strangely hopeful. Or is it hope that I
feel? Could it simply be relief that I'm not eighteen
years old today? . . ."

After the speech, Billy had spaghetti and watery
tomato sauce with Randy and Mel and Mel's roommate, Simon King, a hulking black guy from Cincin-
nati, Ohio. Simon sat in silence, ate three portions of
the spaghetti, as well as an impressive number of slices
of buttered bread. Of the four who had been forced
into this commune, Simon was clearly the least happy
about being considered a member. He hated Mel; that
was plain.

At dinner Mel announced that he was aiming for
law school. Billy thought that the confusing and depressing lecture by the minister had had a lot to do
with Mel's decision. Billy and Randy said they didn't
know what they wanted to do with their lives; when

pressed, Simon said he wanted to be a lawyer, too, and sprinkled more grated cheese on his spaghetti.

To end the week, the freshmen in the complex of dormitories where Billy and Randy and Mel and Simon lived were invited to cocktails at the house of the college master on the Sunday afternoon before the Monday when classes were scheduled to begin.

The master and his wife stood by the front door, a reception line, greeting the students as they entered. "Ed Moss," the master said to Billy, "how are you?"

"Fine." Billy said. They shook hands. The master's hand felt like wax.

"Who are you?"

"What?" Billy said, surprised that he was supposed to introduce himself; surprised that he had forgotten. "Oh . . . Billy Williams."

"Glad you could come, Billy," the master said, still smiling.

Billy passed on to the wife.

"Hello."

"Hello." She gave him a sad, half-witted smile.

"Alcoholic," he thought, then moved on, into the hallway, through a door leading to a crowded living room. Randy and Mel had already arrived. Billy weaved a path through the clusters of the jacketed and be-necktied, the long-dressed and be-sandaled to the bar.

Mel was there, drunk, talking to Randy about how hard it was to live with Simon King. "I try to talk to him, you know? I say, 'Good morning, man. How did you sleep? If I may be so bold . . .' I don't know what his problem is. Maybe I should say to him, 'Hey, look. We have to live together in this room for a whole year and I think we should both try to get along.' Think that'd work?"

"I don't know," said Randy, scooping a handful of pretzels from a bowl.

34

"I was thinking about this last night. What about this? What if I moved across the hall with you two? . . ." Randy looked at Billy. Randy had hinted a few times that he didn't like Mel. "I just think he has fucked-up ideas," Randy had said to Billy. Billy hadn't thought about it that much.

"I don't know, Mel. I mean you got a bad deal, you know . . ."

"Hey—look—if you don't want me to move in, you should just say so . . ." Mel looked down into his plastic cup, swishing the ice cubes around the bottom.

"Hey, what is this," Randy said, "Peyton Place? Come on. I just think it would look bad."

"Look bad? Like how?"

"I don't know. It'd just look bad."

"You mean, like racist."

"Yeah. I don't know. Maybe."

Zizi was there. It was the first time Billy had seen her in nearly three years. He was sure it was her, leaning against the wall. She was talking to a girl with red hair who was agreeing with whatever it was Zizi was saying with emphatic uh-huh, uh-huh nods of her head, as if to say, "Yeah, I know—I know just what you're talking about." They laughed, Billy watching, and when Zizi's laugh subsided, she sipped first from a plastic cup that she held with one hand, then from a cigarette held in the other, exhaling with a quiet sigh. At first Billy was so grateful to see a familiar face, even that familiar face, that he started across the room to her. He stopped himself when he realized that making his way through the crowd from another direction was some guy in a blazer, holding two plastic cups. He had a mustache and handed one of the cups to the girl with red hair. He came on all jocular, said something so funny that the girl with red hair had to spit the ice cube she had been chewing on back into the plastic cup. Zizi smiled. The boy with the mustache and blazer showed his teeth.

"Greaseball," Billy thought to himself.

IT HAD BEEN THAT STRANGE SUMMER, THE SUMMER his mother remarried, promised everybody she would stop drinking, stopped going to the psychiatrist. Billy was most relieved about her quitting the lousy psychiatrist, more than the drinking, more than marrying Big Jim. So many times at dinner he had sat alarmed while his mother, stoned and careening in her chair, waving her arms about in drunk despair, made him the audience as she recounted her latest psychological progress and breakthroughs.

"Dr. Dupee says I have this complex, like a need to fail, you see, and oh, I don't know, maybe he's right," guzzle of wine, "oh baby, Mommy is such a mess." Mommy was. Billy didn't need Dr. Dupee to tell him that.

Jim wasn't so bad at first. He was big and tall and didn't say much, which gave Abigail the impression that he was dumb. Billy remembered defending Jim from her a couple of weeks before the wedding.

"No, Abby. He's not dumb. He's a pretty smart guy." But just why this was, Billy couldn't say. Billy had really tried to get along with Jim. He even considered at one time playing the fucked-up kid from the broken home, the brooder, the loner, the troublemaker in school so Jim could sit him down and give him a gruff man-to-man talk. And that would make his mother happy and she'd think she'd married a reliable, decent (if somewhat dim) man. Billy couldn't really pull this off, hard as he tried. One day in May, he made up his mind to steal two dollars from his teacher's desk, imagining he'd get caught and that they'd suspend him or something and then Jim could do his stuff and straighten him out and that would get the marriage off to a great start. It would be his wedding present to them. He stole the money, but Mr. Lyons never noticed it was gone. The two dollars went for an airplane model.

Billy spent the summer with the newlyweds in a house Jim rented for them on Cape Cod, by a lake. They moved into one of fifteen cabins, called "Vacation Bungalos" in the brochure, which were spread out around the shore. Billy remembered that the cabin they stayed in had a dishwasher and garbage disposal. The newlyweds seemed to be doing all right, going on long handholding walks through the paths in the nearby woods. Billy remembered them always cuddling in the living room, on the sofa, and how they'd jolt up and rearrange themselves when he wandered into the room. And that had been hard to take. Billy's sister was lucky because she spent the summer away at camp from where, lucky or not, she wrote miserable letters home. One postcard which eluded the Camp Riverview censor read:

Dear Ma,
    If you don't get me out of this fucking place, I will kill you.

                                        Love
                                        ABBY

P.S. I hate this place.

37

"Hate," underlined. Abby was thirteen that summer, and hating every minute of it. Billy was sixteen. The night her postcard arrived, Billy's mother came into his room and asked him for advice. Would it be good for Abby to be taken out of camp? Was she as unhappy as she said she was? She had been the one who had wanted to go to camp in the first place. The money would be forfeited, but oh, the hell with the money. That wasn't what was important. But it might be best for her to stick it out. It would teach her the importance of commitment, make her feel she had accomplished something, seen it through. Maybe it would get better for her. In her letters, Abby had said it did nothing but rain. Well, maybe July would be sunny. Would it, on the other hand, be a good idea for her to come straight home and get used to living in the same house with Jim? What do you think, Billy? He had no idea.

The summer had been so hot and endless. Billy went for long walks and bike rides into town because there wasn't anything else to do. There was a hamburger stand along the road to the ocean beach called "Mr. Deelish" where he used to stop, get a cheeseburger and a Coke and sit on the wooden tables, under the sun umbrellas, just hanging around. After a few weeks he got the idea that he should introduce himself to the manager and ask for a summer job. He was in luck. The manager knew Jim's family who owned property farther down the Cape and he gave Billy a job working the soft-ice-cream dispenser on Thursday and Sunday nights. He made thirty dollars a week this way, and it gave Jim something to talk to him about during dinner. When Jim was Billy's age, well, maybe a little older, he had been a short-order cook at a Howard Johnson's in Maine. "In some ways, the worst summer I ever spent," he said, "but I learned a lot from it, from the other cooks and waiters.

And I don't mean about cooking and waiting tables. About life. It was a real education." So there they were.

It hardly rained at all that summer, that was part of what was so strange. The shore and the garden seethed with insects, mosquitoes in his room at night, humming in his ears, settling on him. They'd go quiet until he shook his head, then they'd start humming again. Wasps jazzing outside, dragonflies darting on the water, among the reeds. Waterbugs skated on the lake surface, their legs spread out like the oars of crew boats. Bees bumbled inside the house and banged against the windows, panicking Big Jim who was allergic to bee stings. His mother was afraid of them, so when a bee got in, Billy had to come to the rescue to kill the bee or to try to nudge it back out the window. He thought of himself as The Bee Squad, and when Jim or his mother sounded the bee alarm, he'd come running out of his room, a siren crying in his head. In July and August bright white flowers grew out of the hedges and bushes and weeds along the driveway; in the hot sun, they seemed to blaze, incandescent and blinding.

One day Billy served ice cream to a carload of Zanzibars—Dr. Z, Mrs. Z, Zizi, and her older sister Muffin. They were driving back from a day at the ocean beach. He remembered how Zizi looked that day, her face red, some skin on her nose white and peeling, her hair wet and tangly. She did a little jig to the counter because the pavement and tar were hot and burned her feet. She had ordered from him, his Zizi, a Banana Barge. (Why, Billy wondered, so many years later could he so clearly remember things like this?)

Another day he was resting on the shore in front of the cabin, his legs and feet splattered with clay and ooze, and he saw Dr. Zanzibar and the two girls sailing across the lake in a Sunfish with a red sail. There were other Sunfish that sailed the lake, but the Zanzibars had the one with the red sail. Billy stayed down at the shore that day for more than an hour, watching them glide back and forth, hearing the sounds of the sisters' shrieking carry across the water as the boat jibed and came about. Billy marked the red sail and always looked for it when he came down to go swimming.

There was another boat on the lake that he used to look for. It belonged to a Broadway actor Jim had known in New York who had not had a stage role in two years and who was making TV commercials. He was the little man found bobbing up and down in his dinghy when a lady comes to look inside her toilet bowl. He represented the product, a toilet-bowl cleaner, and the idea was that, wearing his blazer and captain's hat, he was navigating the perilous toilet-bowl waters making sure things stayed fresh. Billy had seen the ad thousands of times. He could do a pretty good imitation of the captain's voice.

"Ahoy there. Nothing to report. Everything's ship-shape in here."

"It was an ingenious campaign, Jim," Jim's friend said one evening when he came over for drinks. His name was Jerry. Billy recognized him right away—Jerry was the first famous person Billy had ever met. Jerry said that the ad had made him thousands and thousands of dollars, more than any of his show roles had paid. He also said that to show its appreciation for the successful campaign, the company had given him a sailboat just like the one from whose deck he had pitched the toilet freshener. It had the product's name in big colorful letters on the sail.

"Wow!" Billy said, he couldn't control himself, "they just gave you a sailboat?"

"Yeah," said Jerry, "that's something, isn't it? It's sitting in my driveway, on a trailer. I won't take it out on the water until I can get a plain sail fitted for it. They want me to be a symbol for the product, you know, represent that crap wherever I go. And that's where I draw the line. That's something I just will not do."

Jerry had had no offers for jobs that summer, either on stage or on television. "It seems I'm typecast," he had said, so he had sublet his apartment in the Village, was living off the rent and the residuals that continued to come in from his commercial, had rented a Vacation Bungalo, and was trying to write a novel, or some poetry, or his memoirs or something. He never made it clear. "I'm trying to write," was all he said. Billy never saw the book, if it ever came out. Writing had made the actor heavy and melancholy and that night at dinner he got very drunk and sloppy.

"Catherine," he said to Billy's mother, "that was the most delicious meal I've had in so long. It was so wonderful, so kind of you to have me over, to dinner, in your house. You're such a lovely . . . wonderful . . . cook . . ." Billy thought he was going to break down and cry from gratitude. After dessert, and after they got some coffee into him, Jerry pulled himself together and tried to talk about his problems.

"I've just got to face it, Jim," he said, "I'm through as a serious actor. I'm getting old, not the leading man type anymore. I'm overweight. After all those years and years of summer stock and repertory and all the crap trying to make it, watching out for the big break —now to have this happen to me . . . To have this be my big success? Do you know that my ad goes on in Germany and Japan? They dub it, but there I am, that's me in the sailboat, trying to get the Japs to care about 'maintaining good hygiene in the tank.' Threatening them that their toilet is going to stink if they don't do something about it. My God! When I think about it, when I think that that's what I accomplished

in my life, that that's what I'll be known for best, if I'll
be known at all . . . I don't know what to think. It's in-
credible. My face means hygienic and happy shitting
all around the globe. My face is going on the label
next year.

"It's funny, sure. It's funny for a while. It's funny if
you can get away from it, see it from a distance. This
thing had me in analysis all winter, Jim. And that sure
ate up all the residuals . . ." Jerry was carrying a
heavy load that summer and the several times Billy
ran into him, either at Mr. Deelish, or at the mail-
boxes where the road forked, leading down to the
cabin, he never made a big deal out of it, he never
said more than "hi."

What a start. It seemed to Billy as if that summer
would never get over with. Here he was now, sixteen
years old, and had no idea, simply no idea what he was
doing most of the time. One day he decided that he
hated his new stepfather not because he was cruel, or
had failed, or was stupid and despotic, but because he
was dismissable. Then the next day he'd come into
the kitchen and see the big ox standing on a stool trying to replace a lightbulb in the kitchen and his heart
would go soft, and he'd say to himself, "Aw, good old
Jim. He's not so bad."

One morning, after working late at Mr. Deelish,
Billy got out of bed around eleven o'clock and when
he got to the kitchen he found the Zanzibars gathered
around the kitchen table while his mother made coffee
for them on the stove. What were they doing there that
day? How had they gotten there? It seemed pretty mi-
raculous. Billy remembered eating breakfast in front
of these people, ashamed when his mother asked him
what he wanted—scrambled eggs, pancakes or what?
—wishing he could have ordered lunch instead, not

feeling hungry anyway, just sleepy and sheepish, figuring a plate of food would at least give him cover,
something to do, time to think. Dr. Zanzibar, a short
man with hairy arms coming out of the short sleeves of
a green polo shirt, his head mostly bald, except for a
few patches of wispy gray, was doing most of the
talking. This was the first summer they had spent in
the area, and though they were dismayed by the cost
of everything in the summer, they were seriously
thinking of buying a summer house. They had been in
touch with a few real estate agencies and you guessed
it, prices were sky high, but it was so beautiful in
this part of the country, and so on. The Zanzibars
came from Washington, D.C.

"Oh," Billy's mother had said when she heard
that, "now that must be interesting." Billy's pancakes
were ready halfway through Dr. Zanzibar's State of
the Nation Address. "This country's going to get rocky
with this Watergate thing. But I think we're just going
to have to have faith in national institutions and let
justice be served. I mean, you've got to give Mr. Nixon
credit," he said, clapping his hands together, "you
can't get vindictive. He got us out of Vietnam. And
he's done great things with Russia and China. But
about this Watergate thing, I think he's got to come
forward and tell people the truth . . ." Later, Billy's
mother tried to get Billy to talk about his job at Mr.
Deelish.

"Hey, maybe you girls could get a job like that,"
Dr. Zanzibar proposed. Zizi tossed her hair and
looked at him, as if to say, "Oh fuck," and then, when
her father started in on the kinds of summer jobs he
had had in Michigan, where he grew up, she reverted
to her former expression: blank-faced and bored.

The Zanzibars didn't stay that long. They stayed for
their coffee and for a quick tour of the cabin, culmi-
nating in Billy's room—quite a shock, with newspapers

43

and magazines and socks all over the floor, a half-eaten bag of Cheez Waffles and the bed unmade, the sheets and blankets sprawling over the side. Billy wished Zizi hadn't seen it, but what the hell.

"Billy, I hope you're a better businessman than you are a housekeeper," Dr. Zanzibar said. Ho ho ho.

"Really, Billy," his mother said, "you've got to do something about this." Yeah, yeah, yeah. And Mrs. Zanzibar looking at him like a dumb maternal cow, as if it was all very cute. She knew, she had her own little ones.

The Zanzibars took their time saying good-bye and climbing into a brown station wagon; all four doors closed and they drove away.

A few days after the Zanzibars' surprise visit, it was "Matthew Zanzibar calling . . . We were planning to have a barbecue picnic tomorrow night on the beach and you and your parents are invited to join us if you'd like. There's plenty of food . . ." So they had all gone off to this barbecue at the beach, which lasted until it was late and cold. There was a big fire going, a couple of other vacationing families, friends of the Zanzibars, everybody in sweaters and bare feet, hamburgers, five big lobsters that Dr. Zanzibar grilled over the fire. And Zizi. And then, that weekend, it was another outing, and then a dinner party at the Zanzibars' cabin half a mile around the lake. After dinner that night, Billy's mother and Dr. Zanzibar sat outside and talked about Watergate and the end of the Vietnam war. It was 1973 and Billy remembered sitting outside on the grass with Muffin and Zizi and hearing his mother from the porch getting very sincere and heartbroken (very drunk) and eulogizing Bobby Kennedy. Eulogizing Bobby Kennedy was something she'd been doing for years.

"He would have made a marvelous President," she said, "and now with him gone, this country seems so

44

strange to me, so crazy. I mean with all these things being tied to Nixon, I'm certain he was behind the assassination. I'm sure he killed President Kennedy. I've always thought that." Dr. Zanzibar said he thought that that was a little rash, there was no evidence, Nixon had his faults, but he wasn't a murderer. Later in the summer, Billy remembered watching the Senate Watergate hearings in the cool evenings on the Zanzibars' screen porch on a black-and-white TV that got only one channel.

Billy spent nearly every day after that at the Zanzibars'. Some days they would go sailing on the lake in the Sunfish with the red sail that they found, pulled high up on the sand of the Zanzibars' beach. There was an island in the middle of the lake and they often sailed out and landed on it—Billy and the two girls—while the parents stayed ashore, indoors, and had no idea what the kids were doing or where they were, and hardly thought about it. They would take picnics out on the island and go swimming, diving from a rock (on the surface, the lake was warm, but down deep, to the depths of one's dive, the cold hit as hard as a hammer and all you wanted to do was to get to the top and climb out). Or they'd just lie there, no one talking, just the three of them breathing, the girls in their bikinis, with their smooth stomachs and ribs; just lying there. Green and blue dragonflies flitted around their heads and in the reeds; the clouds hardly moved; across the water, Billy could see the top of the steeple of the church in town. And on days like that crickets beat and bullfrogs burped and they spent hours there, like that, and nothing changed and nothing happened.

At first the two sisters together made him nervous. He always had the feeling that when they were alone they made humiliating fun of him and of things he had done or said. They seemed much older than he. But eventually he became convinced that, like him, they were just wasting the summer and didn't really care. He continued to watch himself carefully when he was around them.

And then, around the end of July, beginning of August, Muffin went away to an art camp in Maine where she was going to work on sculptures. Billy wandered over after breakfast and found Zizi sitting in a lawn chair looking at the lake wearing a T-shirt over her red and peeling shoulders and her bathing suit. Her legs were slick with sweat and suntan oil. She told him that Muffin and her father had driven up to Maine and Muffin was going to spend the last month of summer in art camp.

"So what do you want to do?" he finally asked. She was looking away, squinting out at the lake. "Feel like going sailing at all?"

She looked up from the lawn chair at him with the most exquisitely bored face, which read: "We could, I guess. Or you could go by yourself. It's all the same." Nevertheless, she shrugged and got up. "Let me go inside and get my sunglasses," she said, and when she came back, she was wearing them, plastic sunglasses she had bought at the drugstore in town.

While they walked to the boat and tugged it into the water and set the sail, he tried to think of something to say to her, but whatever he thought of came out too quickly.

"What?" she kept repeating.

"Huh?"

"What did you just say?"

"Nothingnothing. Nevermind."

She left him with the tiller and he steered them to the island. She helped him pull the boat high up on a rock and they let the sail clank down. Zizi spread her towel on a rock and lay down on it. She was looking up at the sky, once in a while visoring her eyes with her hand to look in the direction of the cabins and far shore. But she was studying him also, watching what he was going to do. It was as if she knew what he was thinking and by lying there, being there, she had acquiesced. She scratched her knee and waited.

Or did she? She had come across the water with him to this place where no one else was. Did this mean anything, or did people do this all the time? Before lying down next to her, he tried to think what Zizi thought of him, but could come up with no answer, not even an opinion.

As he lay back and shut his eyes, it became very grave and tense and formal. His stomach hurt. Slowly then his fingers began to crawl across the hot rock toward her, like a pink crab, stopping at the fringes of her towel. It took a lot of work. Zizi twitched and scratched her nose. She said she wished she hadn't forgotten the suntan oil back at the house. Billy let it go. He pushed his fingers closer and closer, the whole of him along with those fingers until he grazed something. A rock? Sunglasses? He looked out of the corner of his eye. Her hand. He pretended he wasn't aware of it, or of anything.

Later, a hand touched his arm and that was all. Time passed and the cool limbs never moved, neither toward him nor away. His courage grew. The two o'clock bell. She said she was getting cold and sat up, about to say, he was sure, that she wanted to go back. He wouldn't have gambled fifty cents on his chances. On the other hand, you never knew, so, flushed and trancelike, he reached out, turned toward her. She didn't seem too crazy about what was happening to her.

On the other hand, she didn't appear to mind. Covertly, he looked at her face: it included clenched eyelids, parted lips, smallish forehead wistfully furrowed.

What he wanted, what he really would have liked, would have been to be magically transported back to his room for a couple of minutes, no more than five, to have a think and figure out what to do.

"Let's go back," she said, and that settled it.

Every afternoon that week they sailed to the island. Zizi was pretty sluggish and often didn't get out of bed until after one o'clock. Billy tried to think of other things for them to do, like going to the ocean on their bikes. But the ocean was too far for her and she found his other suggestions boring. "It's too hot to do anything else," she said, "except sleep and sail around and go swimming." On the island, they kissed so much that by five o'clock when they sailed back, their lips were red and swollen. One time Billy was sure he saw Dr. Zanzibar standing on shore, looking across the water at them through binoculars. By the time they landed, however, he had gone back inside.

On days when Billy had to go to work, Zizi bicycled over after dinner to Mr. Deelish to keep him company. Sometimes she talked with Mary who took the hamburger orders. But most of the time she just sat there and waited on the wood benches, her head propped on her elbows, reading the back issues of magazines that were lying around the employees' lounge in the back of the store, in the dim neon light of the yellow Mr. Deelish sign.

When there was only a week or two left of summer, Billy suggested that she meet him by the sailboat at midnight, or when she thought her parents would be asleep. It would be better, "cooler" she said, if they met up closer to one, "cause some nights they stay up late."

That afternoon Billy stole a bottle of whiskey from one of the cartons full of liquor that Jim and his mother stored in a cupboard in the dining room. He hid it in the socks drawer of his dresser. And that evening things could not have worked out better. Jim got inspired to take them out to a restaurant and Billy's mother got a bad clam and afterwards was so sick and "woozy," she said, that she was in bed at nine. Jim stayed around and watched TV for an hour, had a drink, smoked a cigar; then Billy heard him sigh, click off the TV, and shuffle down the hall to bed.

All set. He had not seen Zizi since the morning, not since noontime, which was morning for her. Billy's imagination, quickened by a strange feeling of distance, stranger anticipation, and an almost palpable feeling of ceremony, found it hard to wait the hours it took until he could leave.

He set out a little after twelve-thirty, the whiskey under his sweater. The night was cool and clear and very dark and he waited by the boat. Sometime later, after very long waiting, he thought he heard a screen door squeaking.

"Billy?"

For a second, as she rolled up the legs of her blue jeans, baring her white ankles and walking into the water, she was so beautiful that it knocked the words out of him. The boat slid easily down the sand into the water and when the sail was up, and she was on, holding the line, he headed the prow toward the island, gave the boat a running start, and then climbed on.

The island was cold and dark. A few houses on shore still had their lights on, some people on the far shore were having a party, and they could hear the laughing and yelling, and then every couple of minutes the sound of cars starting, going home. Lights stayed off in the Zanzibars' cabin, and in his own.

What a night. There was not much he could remember, and even that only vaguely. All that year Dr. Dupee would work him over, telling him how important, how essential it was that he remember how things were, what happened that night, so that he could then face it. He remembered showing Zizi the whiskey, trying to drink some.

"This is terrible," he had said, wiping his lips with the sleeve of his sweater. "Want some?" He passed her the bottle, still scowling at the taste. After a brave swig, she said, "I've got something too. I don't know what you'll think." He expected, when she said it, that she had brought apples, or oranges, or something simple and sweet. That was how much he knew. She reached into her pockets and took out a wood pipe with the stem removed, a box of matches, and a plastic baggie rolled up into a tube. From another pocket, she pulled out a square of aluminum foil, which, as he watched over her shoulder, she began to unfold, revealing four white pills.

"I got this from Mary at your restaurant."

"You did? When did you see her?"

"She has an apartment in town. I've been there a couple of times. I went with Muffin once." She had? They did? When?

And then what? He remembered how Zizi looked without her clothes. He remembered how he felt walking around the island without his clothes. He remembered being very cold and chattering, the moonlight on the water and seeing shooting stars and wondering if they were hallucinations. And Zizi crying, for no reason, her mouth pulled down, grimacing and holding on to his arm, her grasp so strong, digging into him. And then her stopping, as strangely as she had begun, and then being pulled down on top of her with a remorseless, reedy strength. But the drugs seemed to blur everything.

How they got back across the water, what happened to his clothes, he couldn't imagine. Did they swim back across? Because the next day, the town sheriff and his deputy found the Sunfish lying on its side on a beach on the other side of the lake, its sail fluttering and ripped. As dawn broke, he somehow made his way back to his house, having seen Zizi safely home. He believed, as he banged loudly on the cabin door, that he had been summoned to this remote cottage by Secretary of State Kissinger, that Kissinger himself was inside, waiting in an armchair, with Ho Chi Minh and the Vietnamese delegation with beards, pointed hats and black pajamas. He was late, and inside Kissinger was embarrassed and angry.

"What? Who is it?" a woman called from behind the closed door. Her voice was shaky and scared. She had been awakened.

"It's Billy Williams," Billy had said, trying to sound authoritative and cool.

"What? Billy?" She opened the door. "What? What is this—? Where are your clothes? What happened to you?"

"Ma," he learned later that he had said with surprise, "what are you doing here?"

"What am I doing here? I live here. I was in bed."

"With Henry Kissinger?"

As he sat in the living room, while his mother sobbed and Jim sat across from him in his bathrobe, his hair standing on end, rubbing his chin and looking very confused, Billy worried that they would call the police. Drug penalties, he knew, were harsh. In their horror, they would allow him to be put away, come visit him in prison every Sunday, tell him how Abby was doing, that his old friends were calling up, asking for him. Would they tell lies about it? "Billy's in California visiting his father. He'll be home sometime within five to ten years, Arthur. Don't forget to say hello to your mother for me when you see her . . . Good-bye, dear."

He waited for his mother to pull herself together so he could see what she would do about him. Would she say something like, "Whatever happens, Billy, I want you to know we're on your side. That what becomes of you will happen because we care, not because we don't"? At that moment, a jail cell didn't seem that bad. The punishment, the hardship, the waiting to get out would doubtless make him a stronger, better person in the end.

She didn't call the police. She waited until eight o'clock ("a reasonable hour") and called Dr. Zanzibar, sobbing over the phone.

"Matthew, this is so frightening . . . What can we do?" Dr. Zanzibar said he wanted to talk to Zizi and said he would call back.

"Dr. Zanzibar asked me to ask you if you have any idea of the name of those pills. Do you think they were some kind of LSD?"

"I told you. I don't know."

"Well where did you get them?"

"I don't know. I don't know."

After Dr. Zanzibar called back, half an hour later, and after he had talked to Billy's mother for some time (Billy was sent out of the room) and then to Jim, whom Billy overheard saying, "Uh huh. Oh yeah . . . absolutely," in a very hard, threatening way, Billy came out of his room to ask if they were going to call the police.

"No, darling," she had said, her eyes wet with tears, hugging him. Shit. He knew right then and there what would happen. They were going to send him to a shrink. That was what Peter Baldwin's parents had done to him after he'd been caught cheating several times in school, and then finally got sent home for stabbing a kid in the hand with a fork one day at lunch.

"I don't see why you had to tell them, Billy," Zizi said. She had bicycled out to Mr. Deelish.

"Hold on," Billy said. He was serving a station wagon full of kids. "I don't know what else I could have done. I didn't have any clothes on, I wasn't making any sense." She was hard and separate as she stood in front of the counter, behind her bicycle.

"You could have lied."

"What kind of lie was I going to tell them? Really. I've been thinking about what I could have said to get out of this for the last three days." He had called her house constantly during those three days and finally she had consented to see him. "I mean look— I was banging on the door at six-thirty in the morning and I got my mother out of bed and I was stark naked, just standing there. She's crazy anyway. I told you she gets hysterical even when there's nothing wrong. You don't see that under the circumstances, there were no lies that fit?"

"Well what I don't understand is why you couldn't have kept me out of it. I was fine, except for the boat, and they would have let that go, figured it was kids from town."

"Oh Zizi—"

"What do you mean, 'Oh Zizi'? 'Oh Zizi' nothing."

"I didn't know what was happening. I'm sorry. I'm so sorry—" When she looked down at the ground, he thought to say, "I've missed you." It wasn't smart.

"No," she said simply, "no," and sure of her power, "oh look, I know it's not really your fault and I'm not angry and I'm probably much guiltier than you, but it really wouldn't be a good idea if you came around. All right? I mean things are really hard—" A Volkswagen bus pulled in and the doors opened. Three ten-year-old girls and a father slid out and made for the counter.

"Wait for me to finish. I'll be through in forty-five minutes."

"No."

"Zizi, please."

No chance. She had started to cry and she left him at Mr. Deelish glopping vanilla sundaes. "No!" was the last word she said to him, a second "no!" spoken so angrily and fiercely, so well-timed to coincide with the first orders for ice cream, so heartbreaking and embarrassing as the little girls at the counter opened their eyes wide and gave each other funny looks, that he didn't dare follow. He watched her drive out of the parking lot on her bike, stop before entering the highway traffic. He watched to see if she'd look back, if she'd give any sign, but she didn't.

"That's a dollar eighty,' he said to the father's silent inquiry, as if the performance of that small act would numb the pain.

He didn't see her again, although one afternoon he stood a hundred yards down the beach, watching Dr. Zanzibar sitting on his lawn chair, his feet sticking out from under the Sunday paper. Some days later, Jim rented a U-Haul trailer and drove to New York, stopping at Abby's camp to pick her up. That fall, they made him see Dr. Dupee as he had feared, and expected.

A week before Christmas, the Zanzibars sent a card with a family photograph reading "Best Wishes for the Holidays." Billy left the card with the others, scotch-taped to the wall over the fireplace until just after New Year's, when, afraid his mother would throw it out, he took it away and buried it in his socks drawer. In the picture, Zizi was sitting on the sofa in a velvet dress, looking glum. Dr. Zanzibar was smirking. Inside it read "Greetings from the Zanzibars, Matthew, Louise, Mary (Muffin) and Elizabeth (Zizi).'"

It took a year to get over her, if he ever really did. He thought about her all the time. In June, he wrote her a ridiculous letter which she never answered.

5

"SHE LOOKS JUST THE SAME," BILLY THOUGHT. SHE and the greaseball and the girl with the red hair laughed and bantered and kidded and seemed really to like one another, on the whole, as tall and slim and healthy people will when things are new and going all right for them. Billy left the party with Mel and Randy. He was almost out the door when he was bumped by someone whirling away from the bar with drinks held high. Billy stumbled out of the way, stepping on and crushing the paw of Master Moss's dachshund, and the pitiful yelping, the shrill series of yipes, brought a hush upon the room. Everybody turned to look at Billy.

"Sorry," was all he could manage, and even that was a mumble, addressed to the dog. The dog whimpered, trembling, tail between its stubby legs, and cringed across the floor to Master Moss, who hoisted it into the air.

"I'm sorry," Billy repeated, a little louder.

"It's all right, sweetie. It's all right," Master Moss said in baby talk and Billy couldn't tell whether his apology had been heard, or what. The master puckered his lips and smooched little kisses to the dog, who recovered quickly and kissed back with pink happy licks of its tongue.

Billy spent the next day visiting classes. Earlier that week, he had read through a catalogue of course listings and he had written down the four or five that interested him the most. On Monday he went to a Chinese language course, taught by Professor Bill Fong. And by the end of that introductory hour, Billy was surprised, and a little thrilled, by how much he had picked up. He had already learned how to write and pronounce the date, according to both the Chinese calendar and the Christian one, and also his professor's name, all in Mandarin. Billy figured that studying Chinese was a pretty shrewd idea. It would take a lot of work, probably years and years of study, but that was all right because in the end, Billy would know something hardly anyone else knew, except for several hundred million Chinese people.

After lunch—hot dogs and some moldy baked beans—Billy went to a philosophy seminar taught by an old man named Mr. Lewis who talked very slowly and densely about pre-Socratic philosophers. Billy had never heard of any of them, so he figured it would be a good course to take. He hadn't even known that they had philosophers before Socrates. In fact he didn't know anything about Socrates, either. So Mr. Lewis's course seemed like a great place to begin.

And then, later in the afternoon, Billy followed Henry's advice and sat in on an introductory economics lecture. Henry had been a big help, overseeing Billy's preparation for college. "Economics—that's the big field these days," Henry had said, as if, like everything else, he had the inside word on this, too. It turned out that Henry was right. Billy got to the classroom a couple of minutes late. The room was enormous, as big as the gymnasium in Billy's high school, and every chair was filled. Billy had to stand in the doorway, and he could barely hear the professor, Mr. Springfield, a little sprite in a black suit, scurrying around behind the podium. Billy didn't understand what he was talking about, but after class he managed to copy down all the diagrams Mr. Springfield had made on the blackboard. Billy vowed to look them over in his notebook later in the evening until they made some sense.

And the next day, Tuesday, after another Chinese lesson, Billy walked into a biology class that met on the top floor of the futuristic science tower. He didn't want to close off any doors; he liked the idea of himself as a doctor, making important diagnoses, giving shots, prescribing prescriptions, getting to act curt and overworked. After that class, and after two donuts for breakfast at a nearby donut counter (a place that stayed open all night, serving coffee and donuts for late-night crammers), Billy found his way to DeWitt Street, and once on DeWitt, to Duckworth Building, for an English survey course taught by Professor Russo. Though he had never thought it worth telling Henry, who would have overreacted (and that would have meant having to talk to him for an hour or more, or worse yet, having to go downtown to Henry's office and get taken out to lunch, to "talk this through"), Billy planned on being an English major. He had always been pretty good at English in high school. He figured he knew more about it than any other subject, although a visit to his dentist a week before school started had raised doubts.

"What do you think you'll want to major in when you get up there?" Dr. Weintraub had asked, looking in the little mirror at the reflection of Billy's molars. Billy knew his dentist very well. He knew him so well because he had been coming to Dr. Weintraub's office six times a year since he was ten so that Weintraub could put in, adjust, rewire, and at last, two years before, when Billy was sixteen, finally remove all the lousy braces, retainers and other crap with which he had tried to reroute Billy's teeth. Weintraub's first name was Dennis, so Abby referred to him as Denny the Dentist. Denny was a family favorite. Henry, who had bragged that he hadn't seen a dentist in twenty years, "since the Navy," went to Dr. Weintraub with a toothache and severe gum rot, was fixed up in three visits and came away saying, "That guy is a genius. Best dentist in New York." Dr. Weintraub's office had all the newest, most awesome equipment, including a retractable space-ship sofa chair that levitated the patient high in the air by remote control.

"You're not considering being a dentist, I take it."

Billy shook his head. "Unh uh."

"Well I'd think about it some more. Don't laugh it off, you know. There's a lot of rewards in this business. You get to meet some great people. So what are you going to be studying up at Beacham then?"

"Ingwah."

"Oh, liberal arts. I guess I should have known."

"Uh huh."

"What period interests you? I ask because my brother-in-law is in English grad school up at Cornell. He's all caught up in Middle English. Chaucer, that stuff. Don't ask me why."

"Whuh pewiuh? Whuh duh uh—" The dentist took the mirror out of Billy's mouth and polished the glass on a white cloth. "What do you mean, 'what period'?"

Mr. Russo's English course was held in a small seminar room in the basement of Duckworth Building, one of two new classroom buildings. Russo's course sounded very impressive in the catalogue: the Bible, Homeric epics, Dante, Spenser, Milton, Shakespeare, Marx, Freud, Pynchon—just about everybody you'd want to

58

read. Just about everybody Billy had ever heard of and then some.

Billy arrived in Russo's classroom a few minutes early. There was a long metal table in the middle of the room with metal chairs arranged around it. Billy sat down. He cleared his throat, looked around. He reached into his pocket for his pen, clicked it open, spread his new notebook apart to a clean first page and, after scribbling some zigzags at the top to see if the pen was working, he wrote:

"English literature, Mr. Russo" and then,

"First class."

He had never taken good notes in high school but he was determined to start doing so for college. He envisioned holding onto his old notebooks for the rest of his life, to have them ready if he felt like refreshing himself with something he had once learned. Billy frequently thought toward the future. Besides taking these thorough notes, he was resolved to read all the books, to do all the suggested outside reading, to speak up in class and to find interested friends with whom he might continue the discussions begun in class. He clicked closed his pen and put it back in his pocket.

Hanging from the ceiling on two thin rods was a fluorescent light with a plastic cover like a honeycomb. It buzzed above his head, one of the bulbs flickering.

"That bulb needs replacing," he thought to himself.

Well this was a lot of fun. He looked at the blackboard, at the pieces of broken chalk lying in the ruts.

About six or seven students had taken chairs by this time. Several of them had begun little buds of conversation. One girl knew somebody's older sister from prep school. There was a brief general discussion on the topic of why the books for the class cost so much. Billy didn't know he was supposed to have bought any books yet. Then nobody talked and it reminded Billy of the way he always felt in crowded elevators.

"He's five minutes late," the girl who knew someone's sister announced. Billy had a mild stomach ache. Three new classmates came in, one at a time, and selected chairs. Everyone sat and waited. They sighed or searched in their pockets or handbags for things.

When Mr. Russo finally arrived, he burst through the door, hoisted a black attaché case onto the table and began to take off his sports jacket, very "okay, can't wait to get started, lots to do, let's get going," and all that.

"I'm sorry I'm late," he said breathily, and gave a nervous laugh. "Right. Let's not waste any more time. We've got lots to do."

Billy had been expecting an owlish, balding don type. Somebody about to retire, a cranky old wheezer who'd be very aloof and depressing, who'd give a little address before class about how nobody knew anything about literature, but they were all going to learn, thanks to him. It would be a tough road, they'd work hard, but dammit, they'd learn something and thank him for it. Billy had seen a movie on TV where the English professor said something like that. But Mr. Russo looked around thirty years old, with wire-rimmed glasses and a greasy black mustache that swept across his face into his muttonchop sideburns.

"Well—" Russo said after he had reached into his briefcase to get a piece of paper. He looked at the paper, exhaled and laughed. "So—good morning, one and all."

"Good morning," the class answered in disunison. The voices sounded heavy and confused.

"Are we all here? Actually that's a foolish question, because how could any of you know. I'm the one with the class list." Mr. Russo pulled a handkerchief out of his pants pocket and he sniffed, pinched and wigled his nose in it. "All right. Now we have to do a little necessary housework. I have to figure out who's taking this course and who isn't. I have this tentative list sent over by the English department. So let's see where we stand. Call out or something when you hear your name . . . Armstrong? . . ."

"Yes. Here," said a girl, signaling it by wiggling her fingers. She was the girl whose sister had been the friend of the other girl.

"Okay, good," said Russo, checking her off on his list with a pencil. "And what's your first name? Or your nickname? Whatever you like to be called."

"Jane."

"Okay, Jane." Russo continued down the list. The students responded and gave their first names. Tom Brown, Lucretia Green, Hennessy . . . When no one responded to the name he called, Russo looked up from his list. "Where's Mr. Hennessy? Or Miss Hennessy? Anyone know him or her? . . . No Hennessy? Well, too bad for him." Billy thought Russo acted a little hurt. And so on, until the W's.

"Wang?" Russo asked.

"It's Wong, sir." A Chinese boy pulled himself upright in his chair.

"Wong? With an 'O'? No 'A'?"

"No sir. It's with an 'A.' And it's pronounced Wong."

"Okay." Russo did not ask for the Chinese boy's first name. It turned out to be Stanley (rather than Howard). "White?" and Jack White identified himself. "Williams?"

Billy was all ready for it, air in his lungs, his mouth was opening, ready to go, when he heard the door open behind him. Everyone's attention diverted.

A girl peeked her head in, around the door. She winced coyly and said, "Sorry."

"Okay. It's okay. Nothing's happened so far. You're who? Hennessy?"

"No. I'm Elizabeth Zanzibar. I don't know if I'm on your list."

"Here you are. You're in. Okay. That's it. That's everybody. I'm glad that's out of the way. I have a terrible block against remembering names, so you'll have to bear with me. It'll take me a couple of classes. Okay . . ." Russo handed out the class syllabus, then went to the blackboard.

"Mr. Russo?" Zizi asked.

Russo wheeled around, chalk in hand. "Yes? Miss Zanzibar?"

"Can I get another copy of the syllabus? This one's all smudged."

"Okay," said Russo. Once she had her syllabus, he raised chalk to the blackboard and began to write.

"I have a different address on weekends. I'd better give you everything. Now this is my address in Beacham. And my phone number. You can reach me there most weeknights. And if I'm not there, then my son is there with a baby-sitter, so there ought to be somebody to answer the phone. But I warn you now, ahead of time, I don't want anyone calling me at eleven o'clock the night before a paper is due asking for an extension. That's happened in the past and I know from experience that I'm a bastard if somebody gets me out of bed. And I have a young son who wakes up . . . So, in fairness to me, if you're going to call me, and by all means call me, do so early in the evening. Now I have an office, but I'm usually never there. I'll just write down the number there anyway. I'll want to hold conferences with each of you every couple of weeks, and I suppose that's where we'll have them. Now. Finally. On weekends I leave for Vermont where I've got a house. I'm trying to finish a book out there, and my silence and privacy are very valuable to me. So don't call me out there unless it's really a crisis."

Russo returned to his chair, and in the next fifteen minutes went on to describe what he expected of the class. He wanted everybody to try to keep up with the reading, which, he said, was going to be a "tough row to hoe" at first. And he expected three papers, the first one due in ten days' time "so I can see how you've been taught to write. So I can see what I've got to work with."

After answering Tom Brown who asked how long he wanted these papers to be ("As long as it takes to say what you're saying") and giving the first reading assignment—the first two hundred pages of *The Iliad* —and a paper topic, Russo dismissed the class.

PHILIP RUSSO WAS GRATEFUL WHEN CLASS WAS OVER. He had dreaded it. He had dreaded having to return to Beacham. In fact, he had told several of his friends and neighbors in Vermont that summer that he was going to give up the lease on his apartment in Beacham. He wasn't going to go back. And he had even thought very seriously about what he would say in his letter of resignation to Jack Dewey, the head of the English Department.

Dear Jack,
    I want to write you now before you leave for Europe to give you a chance to find a replacement for me next semester. I know this may surprise you, that a junior faculty member should quit on you, two years before he even comes up for tenure—two years before you get the chance

to fire him, in other words. But I've thought about it, and I don't want to sound ungrateful to you and to Charlotte for all that you did for me last year, but . . .

Russo had been very serious about quitting, even though he had never gotten around to figuring out how he was going to earn enough money to support himself and his young son. He never actually mailed the letter, although he must have outlined the rest of what he was going to say to that son-of-a-bitch Dewey a dozen times.

He thought the first class had gone all right. They looked a little dull, but what could you tell from going down the class list the first day? When he saw Kennedy and Levine, he'd tell them he had a good-looking girl in his class for a change. He and Kennedy and Levine always liked to talk about the good-looking students they had. Kennedy was living with one of his former students. Cindy'd be a senior this year. Russo remembered that last spring Kennedy had said he was getting sick of Cindy, and he was trying to promote her for a Rhodes Scholarship in England so he could get rid of her.

At least the table had been filled, not like the year before when he had arrived for the first class meeting to find only four students interested in taking his Dickens seminar. That class had met at 8:00 in the morning, and the early hour necessarily limited enrollment, but still . . . The lack of interest—to say nothing about the lack of enthusiasm from the four students who had enrolled, or, as Russo liked to say, "signed on" (he had originated the expression three years before during a senior seminar he was giving on Melville)—had been very depressing, a bad start to a very bad year.

Russo unlocked the door to his office and turned on

the overhead light. The room had a funny smell. He had only meant to dump his briefcase behind, then pick up his son, Thomas, age five, and take him out to lunch. Thomas hadn't started school yet, and wouldn't begin until the twenty-third of September. So until then, Russo would have to find baby-sitters to stay with Thomas while he taught his classes and went to meetings, or went out. Russo was not an experienced parent. He'd left the mothering up to Thomas's mother until recently, and he tended to be as lazy and irresponsible about straightening out his son's life as he'd been about straightening out his own. Faced with the problem of what to do with Thomas for the hour and a half of class this morning, Russo had called Mary Townsend and asked if Thomas could stay with her in her office. Mary had been a student of Russo's a few years before. When she graduated she got a job in the Beacham admissions office. "Sure," she had said, "sure, I'd be delighted to take care of Thomas." So that was the plan. Eventually, something else would have to be worked out.

It was terrible, sure, but Russo had found himself thinking seriously that Thomas had to get away, out of his father's hands and into the hands of someone who knew what he was doing. Thomas's mother wasn't the answer. She had a hard enough time taking care of herself. Besides, she was in Japan, living under the impression that she was Anna Karenina. She was acting more like Erica Jong, Russo thought, and he had told her so in his final letter to her, written about a week before she left the country. She was in Japan with Leon Fortas, or L. C. Fortas, a pudgy, middle-aged minor poet who had taught creative writing at Beacham for a year. Fortas was about five feet four inches tall and somehow Ellen had concluded that this pompous little gasbag was Count Vronsky—at last.

Russo could never ship Thomas to live with his maternal grandparents. Ellen's father was a retired Air Force colonel, second in command at a military academy outside of Wheeling, West Virginia, and there was no way on earth that Russo was going to let Thomas within a hundred miles of that madman. As for his own sad parents—that was out of the question.

Russo had not been back to his office all that summer.

Last term's books were all here, last term's lecture notes, last term's grade book. Also odd bills and scraps of paper scattered over the top of his desk. There was the receipt from the garage for replacing the generator on his car, with the home phone number of one of his associates on the back, a copy of a poem by W. H. Auden that he had run off on the ditto copier and handed out to his class; another poem, an original, mailed to him, in fact, dedicated to him, by a girl who had been his student two years before. Also a bill from the shoe store for a pair of sneakers for Thomas. Had he taken care of all these things? Called the friend? Discussed Auden's poem, giving the class a bit of Auden's background, his politics, his hatred of the English class system, his homosexuality, the dominant themes in his verse? Russo had met W. H. Auden once. It happened at a tea given in honor of the poet at Princeton—they had "meet a great man" teas every other week at Princeton—when Russo was in graduate school. Had he told the class about the time he met Auden? Probably. Russo always bragged about it, even though the exchange had been nothing more than his saying to the poet, "It's an honor to meet you, sir."

Russo sat down in his chair. The mess was his own. It seemed to bear his signature in some way; it reminded him of himself, or of a part of himself he had forgotten about. There was something about it and Russo stood for a second, wondering if this weren't a moment full of meaning, in the hope that some meaning of his life, some epiphany, some poetry, would come to him; but nothing did, force it though he tried.

He hadn't had much sleep the night before. Anxious about the new term. Anxious that he'd have to spend the term with only four students again, or maybe fewer; maybe none. But it was more than that. Teaching seminars made him nervous. It used to make him nervous to be in a seminar during his student days. It would have been a lot easier for him if the department had given him the Victorian novel lectures. If he was giving the lectures, all he'd have to do would be to grade the papers and read from a script. He was so fucking clever about those Victorian novelists, he really had worked up some great stuff. He'd already published one book on the subject and at one time, which seemed like very long ago, he had written a number of crushingly condescending reviews of books by other people in his field. Now, he was working on a book about Charles Dickens which tied in the same material. The Victorian novel was supposed to be his specialty, but Kennedy had hustled the Victorian novel lectures for the second year in a row. Kennedy was readying his own book on the Victorian novel.

As if it made any difference.

Russo was anxious that the class go well. He wanted the class to "take off," to come together, everyone looking forward to the next meeting; he wanted to be friends with his students, to get to know them outside the classroom. Maybe that would straighten things out.

Russo had begun psychoanalysis the winter before —he had taken a break from it for the summer while he was in Vermont, a breather—but he had had enough of it to find himself hopelessly indoctrinated

67

by now. Why hadn't he been able to sleep well the night before? Why had he shown up late to his class? It was obvious: he was terrified. He didn't want to do it. He hated it. Why was he so fucked up? The question interested him and he thought about it for a while. He often examined himself like this, as if he were a dense, opaque object, as if he was not himself but someone else whose motives you could only guess at.

"I wonder if those crazy letters are still there," Russo said to himself. He opened the drawer of his desk and found three envelopes inside. Over a period of weeks before Russo's wife had left for Japan, and after she had moved in with Fortas—or "Fat Ass," as Russo had always referred to him—she had written him letters: explanations and explanations of explanations, and explanations of that. Her last letter, twelve pages long, had detailed just what the trouble with him was, just why she could no longer stand to be in the same house with him.

Screwball. Russo closed the drawer without reading any of the letters.

"Better not reopen that can of worms," he said to himself.

Russo left his office to pick up his son. He walked down DeWitt Street, sidestepping a sprinkler twirling water off the grass onto the sidewalk. He stopped for a moment to talk with a former student of his. The student's name was Bernie Gould, and Russo remembered him only vaguely. He did remember having written Gould a recommendation to put in his file. Bernie had taken Russo's Melville seminar. That was in the good old days when Russo was considered, or considered himself, the student's pal, the kind of junior faculty member who'd play basketball in the gym with the kids on Saturdays and who'd go out drinking with his undergraduate friends. Russo remembered that he'd given Bernie Gould a praising recommendation. In those days, he hadn't wanted to feel responsible for Bernie's not getting a good job and missing out on a happy life. Bernie Gould said he was in his second year at Beacham Law and that he was pretty busy, but that he'd really like to call Russo up one day and have lunch. Russo said, "That'd be great," and they had exchanged phone numbers. Then, Russo crossed DeWitt Street when traffic was clear and walked to the junction of DeWitt and Chapel to the admissions office.

"Hello. Hi, Thomas."

"Here's your father," Mary said, moving back from the papers she had been working on at her desk, taking off her glasses. Thomas was sitting in a blue armchair by the window. "How did class go?"

"I'll tell you about it at lunch. You hungry?"

"Starved."

"You hungry, Thomas?"

"No."

"What did you do here all morning?"

"He was great," Mary said. "I want him to come and sit with me every morning. It's great to have him here. You can help me interview students when all that starts . . . Want to?" She was grinning at Thomas with a big toothy grin, big unblinking pop-eyes, trying to be so friendly. Hers was a difficult position to be in, of course. But so was everybody's. "We had a very pleasant morning," she went on. "He sat in that chair, we talked for a while, he told me all about his summer, he told me about catching that great fish, and when I said 'I have some work to get done if we're going to lunch with your dad' he didn't bother me once. What were you doing over there all the time you were being so quiet? Did you try to read that book I brought you?"

"Yes."

"How far did you get? I brought him Maurice Sendak. I had it at home. I was going to bring him *Wind in the Willows,* but I didn't think he could really read that, and besides I figured if I brought him that, I'd spend all morning reading it myself . . ."

"You probably would," Russo thought. He could picture her doing it, her legs curled under her in her chair reading about Ratty and Mole.

"Do you remember what happened in the story?" Thomas didn't answer her. "What happened? How far did you get?"

"I don't know," said Thomas. Russo watched his son squirm.

"You don't remember what happened?"

("Enough!" Russo wanted to say, "Mary, don't do this.") "Let's each lunch," he said. "Come on." Thomas slid down from the chair. Mary excused herself to the bathroom.

"How about you, Thomas?" she wanted to know. "Do you have to go?" Thomas said no. "Good boy," Russo thought.

"Did you get much work done on your book this weekend?" Mary asked. The waitress had just brought her lunch, cottage cheese and lettuce. Russo and his son were having cheeseburgers and sharing an order of fries. Russo didn't answer.

"You know what you're eating for lunch? You know who used to eat that very combination every day for lunch? Probably still eats it?"

"What?"

"Lettuce and cottage cheese. You know whose lunch that is?"

"Whose?"

70

"Nixon's. He used to eat it every day. He put ketchup on it."

"Why are you telling me that?" She really seemed confused.

"No reason. It just struck me." She gave him a funny look, as if she didn't know what he was getting at, then looked down and put her fork in the cottage cheese.

"No, but how did you do on the book?" she said, her mouth full, chewing.

"I don't know. I didn't do anything on it last weekend. I had to prepare for classes."

"Are you going to make the deadline?"

"I don't know. I could. I've been considering just giving up on it. I really haven't got much interest in it anymore. Well, that's not true—sometimes I get interested . . ." Russo looked across the table. He could clearly trace the boundaries of chalky white powder that Mary patted on her face to cover the acne on her forehead and chin. She sat stiffly, churning the curds of her cottage cheese with her fork, thinking no doubt, worried. Lipstick smeared the rim of her water glass. Russo felt queasy and looked away. "I don't know . . . I go to bed at night and I say to myself, 'Okay. Tomorrow you're going to get moving—you're gonna get up at six and go jogging or something, then you're going to write a letter to your wife and get her back, or at least, you know, ask how she is, try to be nice, and then once that's done you're going to sit down every day for the next two months and write that book until it's just right so it can be out by next fall. You're going to do everything that needs to be done. You're going to butter up everybody on the committee so you can get tenure and keep your wonderful job. You're going to do it. Starting tomorrow.' So I go to sleep, bristling with resolve, making notes to myself. Then it's morning and I can hardly crawl out of bed when

71

the alarm goes off at six, and I say, 'I'm fucked if I'm going jogging.' I think to myself while I'm lying there, 'Forget it. There's nothing you can do. It's out of your hands.' Anywhere from two to five hours later, the day begins."

"Oh Philip—come on . . . ," said Mary. She sounded concerned. Thomas looked up.

"It's all right. Things'll work out. They always do."

"Well . . . well what if you give up on the book? Have you got any better ideas?"

"Yes and no. I have plenty of ideas. I doubt they're any better. I think about writing a novel, but then I think that's what everybody does when life just stops. I can be more original than that."

"I think you could write a very good novel."

"About what?"

"Philip—" She started to say something, but changed her mind. "I'm surprised you're so down on the Dickens project. I thought you had all that new material from Harvard."

"Mary, there is no new material on Dickens. Everything that could possibly have been written about that man has already been written. By everybody. From every angle. There have been enough books about him. And I wouldn't read one of them if it wasn't my business. The only ones I'd ever be interested in reading again are the ones Dickens happened to write himself."

7

"I CAN'T BELIEVE YOU'RE HERE," ZIZI HAD SAID AS they walked up the stairs to the street. "I was really flipped out to see you there. I mean, talk about thinking you've seen a ghost, right? . . . So it was you at the master's house. You were at that party on Sunday, weren'tcha? Cause I said to my roommate, 'I don't believe this. I think I know that guy,' but I wasn't sure it was you . . ." When he didn't say anything, she added, "Old Billy Williams. I can't believe it. Are you going to stay in that class?"

"I think so."

"I probably will too. What did you think of Mr. Russo?"

"He seemed pretty good."

"Is he what you expected?"

"No, I was expecting some old guy."

"With sort of an English accent? Right? That's what I thought he'd be like too." They had climbed the stairs and reached the outside, a warm September day, leaves rustling on the trees that grew equidistant out of the sidewalk. The upperclassmen had arrived and the campus was filled. Classes were getting out up and down DeWitt Street. Parked and double-parked Audis, BMWs, a few old Volkswagens lined both sides of the street; bicycles glided past; those on foot moved up the slope of DeWitt Street toward the dining hall and lunch. Billy and Zizi had turned left, joining this flow, when Billy heard from behind, "Elizabeth!" shouted with an accent. Zizi turned around.

"It's Francisco," she explained to Billy as Francisco loped up to her. The red-bow-tied greaseball from the party—now sporting white tennis shirt and a tweed sports jacket over his arm.

"Oh good. He brought his teeth," Billy thought, for there they were, glinting.

"I came to take you to lunch."

"Great. This is Billy," she said, "and Billy, this is Francisco." Francisco nodded.

"Nice to meet you."

"Nice to meet you too." Hands shook.

"How about it, Billy," Zizi said, squinting at him from the sun, "want to get some lunch?"

"No. I have to be somewhere."

"Oh . . . okay," was all she said.

Billy walked with Zizi and Francisco as far as the corner. Zizi was explaining the origin of her nickname to Francisco, how when she was a baby she had tried to say "Elizabeth" but "Zizi" was what came out. Billy had already heard this story three years before. Whether Francisco—from his accent, Billy decided he was Hungarian—found this story delightful, Billy didn't know, because by that time he was out of earshot, heading back to his room.

He did not run into her for a couple of days. He thought about how strange it was that he should see her again at Beacham. He'd get to spend the next four years with her. He wondered what she thought of seeing him there. Whether she felt at all sorry for him when he walked off alone while she and Francisco went to lunch. He wondered whether she told Francisco about him. He wondered what she had said. "Oh he's just a little jerk I used to know. My parents kind of know his parents." Christ.

74

On Saturday, Billy telephoned his mother and sister and gave them his report. He did not say anything about meeting Zizi again because it was none of their business, and it felt like bad luck to talk about her. He gave his mother the rundown on the courses he had signed up for. When his mother said, "So, you sound happy and well," he was able to say that he probably was so.

By that time, he had read nearly 150 pages of *The Iliad* on which a paper would be due that coming Friday. He had not learned much from his economics professor and Mr. Lewis had failed to intrigue him with his lengthy explications on what the pre-Socratics were really all about, but on the other hand, Professor Fong's Chinese class was paying dividends. Already Billy had learned several key phrases and words—some of which he practiced on his sister over the phone.

"Good morning, sister Abigail . . . My name is Billy (Son of Eric) Williams . . . Mr. Bill (Son of Wong) Fong is the instructor of the course . . . ," and so on.

"How would you say, 'I'll have an order of egg-rolls'?" Abby wanted to know.

Billy told his mother that when he had gone to check his mailbox earlier in the week, he had found a threatening letter from the bursar, who said that the bill for his tuition, which should have been paid by September 1, was still outstanding. He asked his mother what he was supposed to do about this.

"I'm writing to your father this very minute," she said. "You should write him yourself. It'll shame him if you write him. Frankly, I'm appalled. It just makes me furious that he can be so careless and thought-less. I mean, really, Billy, that man thinks of no one but himself . . ." She was often furious with Billy's father. "Don't worry about it, though, lamb," she assured him, "but what you must do is sit down and write him a letter explaining the situation. You better make a Xerox of the bursar's letter and mail that to him too in case he says he forgot how much the check was supposed to be. How much is the bill for?"

"Thirty-five hundred dollars."

"God, that's an expensive school you go to . . . But that's what things cost. Anyway, I hope you realize by now how hopeless your father can be at times . . ."

"Dear Dad," Billy began, "I've been here almost two weeks and so far things are going well." Billy crumpled up the paper.

"Dear Dad, this morning when I went to the post office, I got this letter (see enclosed) in which the bursar says that my tuition bill is way overdue. What about this?" No.

"Dear Dad. Well, here I am . . ."

"Dear Dad." Forget it. Do it later.

Billy collected all his dirty clothes, from two weeks of school—the dirty sheets, the ten pairs of dirty, crusty socks, the underwear, pants, shirts—and stuffed them all into the pillowcase. Allergic to the school feather pillows as he was, and with the nonallergenic Dacron-polyester pillow lost in the mails, Billy had slept without a pillow, so the pillowcase was very clean. Billy took his copy of *The Iliad* with him to read while he waited for the laundry to go through the machines.

There was a laundromat a few blocks from the dormitory. Billy had never had to wash his own clothes before, but he found a helpful list of instructions tacked on the wall over the detergent dispenser. Following these instructions, he put in two briquettes of detergent and got the machine to start. Soon soapy water was sloshing inside the glass window and Billy felt pleased with himself. He sat down on a wooden bench and began to read *The Iliad*.

He had been there about twenty minutes—the machine was on rinse—reading and marking down the important parts with a pen, when he had the feeling something was going on. He looked up to find Zizi standing over him.

"Hi," she said, "whatcha reading?"

"Oh, *The Iliad*. See?"

"How far are you?"

"Book Five."

"You read really fast," she said. "I'm just up to Book Three and I read for five hours all yesterday. It's really hard."

"I'm marking everything," he said, and for no good reason he turned the book around so that she could see the pages, marked with blue ink.

"I don't see how he expects us to be finished by Friday *and* write a paper. You know?"

Billy agreed with her.

"Look," she said, "I'm supposed to be back in my room waiting for my parents to call me. Would you keep an eye on my clothes till I get back? I'll get them all sorted out and in the machine and everything."

"Sure."

"Okay, look. If I'm a long time, like if they don't call when they're supposed to or something, could you move everything into the dryer? If you're finished before then, then never mind. Here, I better leave you some money," and she reached into her pocket for some coins. "Excuse me," she said to the woman at the machine next to Billy's, "the dryers take dimes, right?"

"Dimes, that's right," said the woman, whose jowly features came to life as she spoke, "yep, dryers take dimes, washers takes a quarter and a dime."

"Thank you," said Zizi. The lady looked about to

say something more, then seemed to think better of it, and slumped back on the bench. "Billy, here . . ." Zizi slipped two dimes, warm from being held, into Billy's hand. "I'll try to be as short as I can."

When she had gone, he looked at the two dimes she had given him. He tried to remember what he had been reading, but all the time Zizi spent stuffing her clothes into the washer and measuring detergent and bleach, he had been unable to concentrate. Three pages had skimmed by and he couldn't think of what had taken place on them. He turned the pages backward until he could find a page he remembered having read before. He would have to spend hours every night reading this if he was going to finish by Friday and write a paper. The assigned topic for the paper was "The Homeric Man." Billy had been trying to figure out what it could mean.

Every time the bells clattered above the door, he looked up from his place, thinking it was Zizi. When her clothes stopped churning, he took out his own two dimes, wanting to keep for himself the two dimes she had given him. Tribes in Africa attribute certain powers—it has something to do with voodoo—Billy remembered, to one who holds an item of another's property. It was not exactly that Billy held on to the money to hold power over her. It was hard for him to know why he wanted them. But this learning, gleaned from an anthropology course in high school, and probably the only thing he remembered from that course, recalled itself to him. And when he opened the hatch of her machine, he felt strangely as if he had opened a secret vault. There were all her clothes, soaked, clinging to the sides of the drum. She had worn these, the underwear, the socks.

He took out the soggy clothes in bunches, staying calm, and stuffed them in the mouth of the dryer. He was worried about the woman at his neighboring machine. She had tried to talk to him a couple of times, but he had pretended he hadn't heard her, he had to read this book for school, you see.

When his own clothes had come to a stop in the dryer, he rubbed them with his fingers and judged them "still damp." He put another dime in the slot and let them dry some more.

Half an hour passed and she still had not returned. But her clothes washed and dried. He opened the hatch of the dryer to check them. Nice and dry. His were still going. Her shirts were dry, so were the pants, the socks, the frilly panties. Very good. He pulled the panties out of the dryer. It was just then he heard the bell ringing over the opening door and he felt sure it would be Zizi. He tossed the panties inside.

"Just checking. They're getting there," he prepared to say. But it was not her. Instead the manager, a fat man in a T-shirt, smoking the remains of a cigar, waddled down the corridor between the benches and machines, toward his office at the back.

"Hello, Mr. Rigoletto," the lady Zizi had asked about the dryers greeted him as he walked by. Rigoletto nodded, mumbled something and then—uneasy lies the head that wears the crown—went into his office, shut the door, and closed himself in.

Billy wanted the panties and he reached in and took them, panties and one of her socks, and he hid them both deep within his pillowcase. Afterward, he felt very strange about it.

Sunday, the next day, Billy slept late, Randy up at nine for a shower, breakfast, and some touch football. Billy spent most of the day in the library, determined to read *The Iliad* all day and all night if that was what it took him to finish. He was going to get the damn book read.

But by Tuesday's class, the damn classic had not

been read. He had flipped the pages of twenty books' worth, but he wasn't entirely sure what had happened in them. He was, as it turned out, not alone. Russo did the best he could with the dumb and silent class, talking fast when he thought what he was discussing would interest them, giving page references—"Okay, let's turn to the pages where Hephaistos comes into this—that's one thirty-five in my edition." Books open, pages shuffle. "Who can tell me what he's all about? . . ." Nothing. "All right, who is Hephaistos? What does it say about him? . . ." Many of his questions dying in mid-air. Zizi tried to describe Hephaistos—"Isn't he, like, the carpenter?" she volunteered, and then confessed that she had only been able to read up to Book Thirteen. So at that point, Russo asked who in the class had been able to finish the assignment. A few hands went up, but only a few, and Billy's among them.

Russo plunged on. Class was half over. There were moments when he seemed not to know what came next himself. And when he did get going, several of his more complicated sentences fell apart with long, sinking "um-m's." There were several of those moments when the class seemed to slip into the void, everybody hoping that somebody else would please say something.

"What do you think about the theory that *The Iliad* was written by a woman?" asked Kranepool, the boy sitting on Billy's left. The question made the professor furious. He said that Kranepool should get into the habit of thinking about what he was saying before he opened his mouth, that that wasn't what the class had been talking about, and that what Kranepool had said showed that he was going about literary scholarship all wrong—he should not be discussing theories of authorship when he had admitted twenty minutes earlier that he had only read eight books of the poem. He let

Kranepool have it. Toward the end of this tirade, Billy was sure he noticed the professor glance at his wristwatch to see how much longer he had to go. Kranepool slouched sullenly in his chair, whispering a humiliated "geez" which Billy, seated next to him, could plainly hear.

Zizi made a point, her second of the hour, about Tiresias, the old seer who had been both man and woman. Russo thought it was an important idea. Or at least important enough.

"All right," he said, "good! Now see if you can take off with that."

"Huh?"

"Take it a step further. Embellish it a little." Unfortunately Zizi had taken it as far as she was able. For the rest of the hour Russo did the embellishing. "So what you're getting at . . . ," he _filled_ in, and even went to the blackboard and drew some diagrams. But as far as Billy was concerned, the good idea had died with Zizi, and although he copied down what Russo had written on the blackboard, he couldn't figure out what any of it meant. It was very abstract and very strange.

Because Billy couldn't finish _The Iliad_ in time he was also having trouble writing his paper on "The Homeric Man." Lying in bed that night he remembered having heard an expression: Clothes Make the Man. Maybe that was the way to do it. Write about how clothes might represent—how clothes might "symbolize"—character in _The Iliad_. Billy was very excited—having had his first breakthrough, after all—and he got out of bed, turned on the light and scribbled a few ideas in his notebook. The next morning, when he looked at the notes he had made, he wasn't sure that the idea was as good as he had first thought. But the paper was due in a couple of days and he decided to go ahead with it. He'd pick some article of clothing that didn't appear very often in the book. Something that had a good chance of not coming up in those last six unread parts. Finally he settled on the theme of shoes and worked out a five-page paper on this subject—typed between wide margins—and slid it under the door of Russo's office Friday afternoon. He was pleased with it, all things considered. He had used quotes cleverly—"I like it, I like it," he could almost hear Russo whispering in his ear as he typed on the title page, *The Shoes of the Greeks.*

Billy's other courses were going less well. He had dropped his biology course—too competitive. The class intimidated him, his colleagues scurrying around the laboratory with their test tubes, protecting the results of their experiments like Top Secret. When Billy tried to borrow a second set of lecture notes to match against his own to see if he had missed something important, no one would lend them to him. So one day Billy went over to the dean's office, waited for the dean to see him, then signed a slip of paper. Let the other guys be doctors if they wanted to so badly. He left them to their films about cells and their dissecting of animals.

Chinese, too, had been less rewarding that second week. Billy had spent hours and hours at his desk, practicing squiggles on a piece of paper in preparation for the first of weekly quizzes. He was sure he was going to fail it.

To make matters worse, Billy's birthday was around the bend; he would be nineteen in a few months, and to Billy nineteen seemed very old. When Billy was twelve, his cousin Andy was nineteen. Six feet tall, blonde hair, muscles, running track his freshman year at U. Mass., swaggering good-naturedness. Because why not? At nineteen what was there to worry about? Billy was coming out all wrong. When Shakespeare was nineteen did he have these problems? Freud? Karl Marx? Mickey Mantle broke into the majors when he was eighteen. Bob Hope was already telling jokes. Frank Sinatra wasn't bullshitting around even then. Young painters were painting, young scientists analyzing through their microscopes, young tycoons were wheeler-dealering—Onassis had two ships in his fleet before he hit twenty. It was a busy world. So? So here now was Billy Hedgecote Williams and just who was he? and what was he going to do? Dropping biology class because it was too hard and writing a five-page English paper about shoes.

When Russo's class met on Tuesday, Russo said that he had started to read some of the papers and hoped to get through them all by the end of the week. He said he wanted to hold conferences with everyone in the class about the essays. He handed a sheet of paper around saying that everyone should write down his name and a time he'd be available for a conference. When the paper came to Billy, he saw that the appointment just before Zizi's was free, so he put himself in the slot.

By this time, the days of the week had settled into a pattern. Billy got to know where all his classes were held, in what building, what room in the building, what day, what hour, all without thinking about it, without having to consult his schedule or a street map. On Mondays he had three classes: philosophy, economics, and Chinese. On Tuesday: English and Chinese. And down through the days of the week. By this time, three, nearly four full weeks after his arrival, there were several new people whom he knew more or less, some only by sight. There were all of Randy's friends, Pete and Sam and Ron and Rick and Toby. There was the boy Billy saw every clear evening after dinner wearing spiked saddle shoes who stood in the middle of the quadrangle with a golf club and a cotton ball practicing his drives into the sunset. There were Mel and Simon across the hall, and all Simon's friends, Kevin and Willie and Fred, black guys. There were frisbee players and touch-football players, the freshman woman tennis sensation whom everyone knew from photographs in the back of the *Bee,* kids he recognized from classes, or from the dormitories. Weekends there were always parties, all kinds of parties. There were everyone-get-dressed-up-and-stand-around-and-make-conversation-with-oldsters parties, usually Saturday afternoons, usually in honor of one of the oldsters, and then Saturday nights there were parties and dances, beer and lights flashing, loud music and everyone jumping up and down or smoking hash in the corners; the noise and happy yelling climbing in through the window made Billy's room seem cold and very dismal. Sometimes he played Randy's records on the stereo. Randy didn't mind, he'd said, so long as Billy put all the records back in their jackets and didn't leave the amplifier on all night.

Sundays, Billy slept late, sometimes past noon, too late for breakfast in the dining halls. He'd try to do some work in his room, unless Randy was there and had brought his friends around to spend the day lounging, breaking things up with a round or two of living-room golf, in which case Billy packed himself off to the library.

He was not working nearly as hard as he was supposed to and had promised himself that he would, merit and happiness not coming, as he knew, to the lazy. He never once thought whether it weren't impossible to "figure out" Homer, or Plato and now *The Aeneid* in a little more than a weekend. Billy's eyes had skated over two thousand pages in those three, nearly four weeks of school, but his eyes had scarcely had time to inform his brain of what they had seen. It had nothing to do with the tireless underlining that he did, that didn't seem to help. He sat there endlessly in an overstuffed leather armchair in the C. Douglas Dalton Room in the library.

"What are we supposed to read for next week? I hope it's not Chaucer—I'll never be able to do that one," he worried. He reminded himself to get a new copy of the syllabus from Russo next class; the librarian disturbed him from his concentration, rattling by behind a cart returning books to their shelves.

Billy had his conference with Russo at 4:15 on Wednesday that following week. The night before he had been kept awake with the fear that the part of *The Iliad* he hadn't finished was crammed with references to shoes. Russo would look at him sternly as he came through the door; "Ah yes, come in, Williams. Now I'd like to know why you left out Homer's description of Achaian footwear that appears in Book Twenty-two. The passage is—to me, at least; you may think otherwise—one of Homer's most lyrical passages. So, Williams, what about this? Hmm?"

What Russo in fact said was:

"Gee, Billy, I don't know what to tell you about this essay. It wasn't badly written on the whole, you seem to know how to present an argument. But why did you choose the topic you did? I thought maybe you worked at a shoe store over the summer . . . ," and Billy could see his professor was trying to be nice, so he did his best to smile. "Well? Why this interest in shoes? I find it very funny. I showed it to one or two people in the department—I hope you don't mind—and we had a laugh about it. You see, what I assigned was your basic first assignment in freshman English, no more than an exercise, you know. Anyway, nobody in the department had ever seen a paper like yours. I mean, your title here, what was it?"—and he picked up the

paper from his desktop—" 'The Shoes of the Greeks,'
I can't tell if you were making fun of this, of me for
asking you to write on something as . . . well, irrel-
evant, really, as I did . . ." Billy didn't know what to
say. He was grateful for the praise. "Anyway, shoes
or no shoes, whether you were putting me on or not,
this was one of the more interesting papers I got. There.
Conference over. It wasn't so bad, was it? Don't look
so worried." And as Billy got up and made for the door,
Russo said, "Hey, I hope you don't mind that I showed
your paper around. I really got a kick out of it."

Zizi was sitting outside the door on the floor with her
back to the wall.
"That bad, huh?"
"What do you mean?"
"You look as if he really tore you up in there."
"No. Not really. I don't know."
"I'm scared. Jesus. Wish me luck."

A LETTER FROM HIS SISTER, DATED OCTOBER 11.

Dear Billy,
   How is college? Are you still taking that
Chinese course? I told some of my friends that
you were taking Chinese and they said, "He
sounds really weird." I had to admit that when it
comes to being weird, my brother is the king of
weird. Anyway, are you having a good time?

You're really lucky to be away at school. I'm going crazy. I hate it here. Just tonight I was watching TV when who should come barging in but Henry. He said he had just had these campaign buttons made up and he gave me a whole shopping bag full of them. I'm supposed to pass them out to kids in my class. The buttons are so stupid! You know what they say? They say "Good as Gould" on them. That's his slogan. Can you believe anyone could be such a total asshole? What am I going to do? I can't start handing these crummy buttons around. I'd be ashamed to tell any of my friends that my mom goes around with that fascist.

. I've been thinking of getting my own apartment. Do you think Mom would let me? What if I tell her that if I don't get out of this house, I'm going to have a nervous breakdown?

And then, in different color ink, red instead of blue:

It's three hours later and I've got to do this stupid homework. I'm supposed to give this report tomorrow in Astronomy about black holes. I just got through having dinner with Mom and Henry. I wish I knew a place where you could buy poison, the kind you can put in people's food and they can't taste anything different. Because then I'd put some in Henry's soup. He got drunk again tonight and he started picking on Mom. They're still fighting because I'm all the way in my room, with the door closed, and I can hear them from the dining room.

Well, I guess I have to finish this homework. Write soon!

Love,
ABBY

A letter from his father, dated October 13:

Dear Billy,
   Sorry about all this business with your bursar,
but as I tried to make clear to your mother, I've
been up to my ears in money hassles of my own.
Don't worry. Between us, your lovely, if slightly
hysterical mother and myself, we've worked
things out for you. Hope you're working hard,
things are going well.

Love,
POP

"Since when," Billy thought when he had finished
the letter, "have I called the guy 'Pop'? Where did he
get that crap?"

A letter from his mother, five pages, both sides, on
yellow sheets of stationery with scalloped edges and
with "From the desk of Catherine Wieseltier" em-
bossed in black at the top, dated October 19:

Billy Dear,
   I've been on the phone all morning with your
father and I think we've finally settled this tuition
thing. Finally. If another letter comes from your
bursar let me know. I hope things are going well
for you, dear, that you're finding the work interesting and rewarding. These are very important years for you . . .

"If I do get another letter from that bursar," Billy
reasoned, "then that means Dad didn't pay up after all,
and that means she'll send a lawyer after him." She
had sent lawyers after Billy's father before, a couple
of times, for one thing or another.
She went on in her letter to say that the dog had

some doggy flu and she was worried and had made an appointment for later in the day at the vet's. She wrote that Henry was working on an important series in his column, on budget cuts and the ramifications in city and state, and, inevitably, the nation. Just the same, Henry had taken time out from his research and muck-raking to send Billy his "best wishes." She felt as if she hadn't seen him in weeks. She had gone to the movies one Sunday with Abby, who was fine, and Henry had taken her to see Baryshnikov at the ballet, an experience she described as "yummy." She had also spent an afternoon with an old friend of hers, a woman named Frieda Burger. Frieda Burger and her family lived, at one time, down the hall from Billy and his family. That was when they still lived on the West Side with Billy's father. Billy's father hated Frieda, and especially Frieda's husband, Jon, a huge Swede, and he wouldn't allow them in the apartment. Frieda and Billy's mother arranged rendezvous when their husbands were at work. Frieda had a son named Horst, Billy's age, or a year older, and when Billy was small he and his mother and Horst and his mother would sometimes spend Saturdays together. Most of the time, they'd drag through department stores, downtown to Macy's, then uptown to Saks and Bloomingdale's, taking taxis everywhere, the four of them filling up the backs of Checker cabs. Sometimes they went to movies and other times they went bowling. Horst and Billy bowled while the mothers talked and, in the end, paid. Once, they all went to *The Nutcracker* around Christmastime and in the middle of the performance Horst threw a tantrum, got angry about something—some chocolate his mother refused to buy, having to sit still through the boring ballet—and started to cry. Frieda hauled him out of his seat, towed him away, up the aisle until they were in the lobby, where she slugged him. As late as intermission, Horst still bore the red imprint of her fingers on his arm where she clamped on to drag him off. That, as far as Billy could remember, was his last and most vivid memory of Horst Burger, the son of his mother's friend.

. . . I saw a dear, old friend of mine the other day, Frieda Burger, who remembers you from when you were a child—I hadn't seen her in several years, she and her husband went back to Sweden for some years, so I was just delighted when she called me and asked me to lunch.

I don't know how to begin to describe the shock I received. Abby was too young to remember the Burgers so I thought it best not to tell her about my visit. But I think you might be interested to hear. I rang the doorbell and a young, tall, somewhat statuesque woman opened the door, her hair in curlers under a scarf, wearing those flip-flop type sandals, you know, like the kind Abby used to wear, a very tight pair of shorts and a blouse with the ends tied around the middle. Well, I had no idea who this young lady could be, so I asked if this were Frieda Burger's apartment. "Oh yes, Mummy's in her bedroom," the girl told me. Her voice was very strange and deep and that should really have tipped me off, but honest to God, you know, it just didn't register. I still remember so clearly the way this person turned around and sort of sashayed down the hall, saying, "Mummy! Company!" Well, I found Frieda in her room, talking on the telephone, and she motioned for me to sit down, which I did. And when she got off the phone, we chatted for a while, she talked about Sweden, and I must say I was so happy to see her that I totally forgot to ask about the girl. So I did a terrible thing: I asked her, "Where is

90

Horst? I'd love to see him," and she said, "You just did. That was him—or it used to be him—who answered the door. He's changed his name to Eileen . . ."

"How fucking funny," Billy thought when he read what had become of his old friend. He was not all that surprised to learn what had happened to Horst Burger. Over the years Billy had heard many horror stories, men hurling their wives to rocky deaths on climbing trips, divorces, cancer, nightmare drug trips, unwanted pregnancies and abortions. He was grateful—and certainly, no less so was his mother—that at eighteen years of age, nothing much had ever happened to him. He hadn't succumbed to any perverse sexual demons, never seen or heard God, never gotten a girl pregnant, never run away from home, never had a head-on car crash, never been kidnapped or raped or gotten cancer.

ONE DAY, WHEN BILLY WAS FOUR OR FIVE YEARS OLD—however old, he had not yet begun going to school—his mother took him out for the day to the movies, or to the museum. Abigail had a cold, and so she stayed at home with their father. They were all living in the West Nineties then, in a small apartment a few blocks from the Hudson River. Billy's father was an assistant professor of creative writing at New York University. Three mornings a week he took the bus downtown to his classroom, taught for an hour and a half, sometimes stayed around for conferences and meetings and then came back home, usually around two in the afternoon. He was working on a book of short stories, and after lunch and a shower he would disappear inside his study and close the door.

"Shhh now—your father is trying to work," Billy's mother always implored him when all he was doing was coming into the kitchen to get something to eat. The house had to be dead silent. No screaming, no fighting, no loud TV. Even when Billy wasn't making any noise and Abigail was just sitting in her room drawing, or maybe watching TV quietly, his father would come storming out of his study, slamming the door.

"For Christ's sake, Catherine. I'm trying to work in here—" he'd start screaming at Billy's mother, "isn't there some way you can keep those kids quiet?" So what she would do was take them out for as much of the day as she could. They went to the movies and ice skating and to museums. Billy, who was nobody's fool, had the feeling that his mother was as eager to get herself out of the house when his father was closed up in his study, typing and smoking cigarettes and balling up typing paper and tossing it around the floor, as she was to have the children out of his way. They would all stay out until dark, buy groceries on the way back, and come home to have dinner.

"What did you do all day?" Billy's father would ask. And most of the time, after dinner, he was very agreeable.

That day, Billy was standing in the hallway, outside the front door, waiting for his mother to find her housekey. "I know it's in here," she had said, digging in her handbag, "I hope it's in here so I don't have to ring the doorbell and disturb your father." Billy could hear his sister crying. "Oh no. What's wrong with her?

What is the matter with your father? How could he just let her scream like that?" she asked impatiently.

Abby was kneeling by the front door and when she realized that her mother was home, just fitting the key in the lock, about to open up and ask what was the matter, she began to wail louder and more hysterically. How long she had knelt there, crying, no one could tell. It could have been hours.

"What is it? Oh baby—what's the matter?"

"Mommy. Oh Mah-hah-hahmy."

"What is it, sweetie? Please calm down and tell me . . ."

"Dad's dead."

"What? What do you mean, 'Dad's dead'?"

"He is—he's dead in the ki-the kit-the kitchen."

"The kitchen? . . ." And she ran to the kitchen. Billy followed her like a little man.

"Oh!" she cried, standing in the doorway, her hand covering her mouth, blocking Billy's view as he came up behind her to see what had happened. She turned around and Billy ran into her hips, blocked and smothered, blinded from whatever lay behind. Before he could take a step backward, she had grabbed him fiercely by the arm and was pulling him away. She picked Abigail up where she had left her, crying in a squat by the front door, taking her by the hand and dragging them both into Abigail's bedroom, where the television was.

"What is it? Is Daddy dead?"

"No, Billy. Daddy isn't dead."

"Well, what is it?"

"He's all right. Just please, both of you, stay in here. Please, Abby, don't start crying again. My nerves won't be able to take it anymore. Turn on the television for her, Billy." She closed the door.

Abby soon settled down, sucking her thumb and watching cartoons. Billy went to the keyhole and looked out. But all he could see was the white wall across the way. Was his father dead? What was the story here? He could hear, very muffled and faint, his mother talking on the telephone. Ten minutes later, he heard the doorbell ring and so he turned the doorknob and was about to say "I'll get it!" on the premise that he had heard the front doorbell and was going to see who it was.

"I told you to stay in there, Billy. Now come on." Billy pulled the door shut behind him.

"Wow!" he told himself. He didn't want to get her angry with him on top of everything else. They both had enough to worry about if his father was dead. One thing Billy thought, while he waited for his mother to tell him about whatever had just happened, was: no hockey game. His father had said something a few days earlier about getting tickets to a hockey game. If he was dead, that was the end of that. Billy heard some men's voices, saw the blue of his mother's sweater and slacks walk past the keyhole once or twice. The men left, the house was silent, and at first Billy thought that his mother and the men had all gone out together.

"How are you two?" she said, opening the door for them. "Are you all right?"

'Where's Daddy?" Had the men come to take him to the cemetery?

"Daddy had an accident and he had to go to the hospital. He's all right."

The story of what had happened, as she later told him, was that his father, feeling restless and finding his writing going slowly, had decided to go into the kitchen to make himself some lunch. He turned on the oven, not knowing that the pilot light had gone out, and went back to see whether Abby, who was watching television, was hungry. When he got back to see if the

94

oven was warm, he didn't smell the gas that had seeped poisonously around the room.

"He must have caught your sister's cold," was how his mother explained it. He realized, however, that the pilot light was out and without thinking he struck a match and the explosion knocked him out, threw dishes off the racks onto the floor, and shattered the kitchen window. (It must have been a terrifying thing for her, Billy thought, to have gone into the kitchen, Abby squalling behind her, and then to have seen her husband lying there on the floor, bald, half-naked, surrounded by broken china and glass.)

Billy's father spent two weeks in the hospital. They went to visit him almost daily. He was lying there in bed, very feeble. Billy and Abby would climb up on the bed and crawl around. Billy still remembered, years later, how his father looked with his hairless, slightly pointy skull and no eyebrows or eyelashes.

He stayed in bed when he came back from the hospital as well, at least for the first week. He seemed perfectly cheerful, though, and made jokes about his hairlessness. "Hey, Ab—Want to find me my comb?" he'd say, gliding his hand over his bald skull. Abby would squeal, and it became her favorite joke. And soon—it was the holidays by then, a few days before Christmas—he was getting up frequently, making a trek to the kitchen, or shuffling along the floor in his bathrobe and slippers just to say hello.

He was better and some of his hair grew in, little black bristles like a toothbrush, and he went back to work in time to prepare for the second semester of classes. But he gave up on his book and possibly because he no longer had the book to occupy him and fret about, he fought a lot with Billy's mother.

"I can't live like this," he'd menace, "in this pig-sty. I hate this house, this dump, this city. The whole thing really stinks, Catherine."

"Well then, why don't you just leave?" Billy's mother would yell back in her *nyah-nyah* style of debate.

But he didn't leave just then. The term was soon over, and with summer he calmed down and spent a lot of time doing some work in his study. In August, they rented a house on Long Island, and then, in September, Billy's first days in school, his father went back to work.

Until one very cold day just before Thanksgiving when he came home and announced that he had quit his job.

"Oh my God!" Billy's mother said. "Children, go into another room please."

"No, now there's no reason why they can't listen to this. It makes perfect sense." He said that he had walked down the corridor to see the head of the department—"that fake, that prick Harry Bloomberg"—and told Bloomberg, "That's it, that's it for me—I've had just about all I can stand of this pointless, ridiculous job. Take it and stick it up your big fat ass," and before Bloomberg could say anything, he had run out of the office, down the hall, then downstairs and out. "I stood on the corner, waiting for my bus to come, and I can't tell you, I've never felt so good, so clear of bullshit in my life . . ."

"What have you done?" Billy's mother said in a whisper, and she started to cry. "I can't bear this."

"Hear me out, Catherine. Please stop and I'll explain, I'll tell you what I've got planned."

"What?"

"I've been in touch with Father Fergus . . ."

"That madman? Oh no! Children, go, please go to another room." So once again Billy and Abigail drifted off to the television, heads bowed, not knowing what to do or say or think. Billy realized that if his father wasn't working at a job, he wouldn't be earning any money. The arguing and crying was so loud and serious this time that they were sent down the hall to stay with Horst Burger. They only stayed there for a couple of minutes, talking to Horst and watching Mrs. Burger do the dishes. And when their mother came to collect them, looking very tired, their father was gone (although not quite gone for good).

Billy's parents had a reconciliation the following March. It was very brief and very minor. One day, Billy's father came to the house with flowers and toys. He had been working on the Bowery in a soup kitchen run by the Salvation Army. Father Fergus, in charge of the Greater Bowery Crusade, had helped find him this position.

"I'm feeling on top of the hill," he said, "just great. Alive, healthy, vigorous. I look good, don't I?" he asked, sucking in his belly and running his hand down it. "I wish you could see it, Catherine. For the first time in my life, it's as if I'm doing real work, as if I'm helping someone, doing something useful. I can't explain to you what it's like." Perhaps he had come that day in the hopes of bringing his estranged family downtown to live with him. He had rented an apartment. (Billy already knew about this through Henrietta, the woman who came Mondays and Fridays to clean the house. Henrietta had told him that she was cleaning for his father as well, that he had "a nice little place way downtown," and she said that as far as she could tell, he seemed "jus fine. He axed how you all was, an I tole him you all seemed jus fine . . .")

"Will you three come down to meet me this Sunday? There's something special going on in the community and I'd like to have you with me. Catherine, it would help me out a lot if you could make some effort to understand why what I'm doing is important to me. Will you come?"

So, the following Sunday morning, Billy and his

mother and sister climbed into a taxi, gave the driver an address—a street without a number—and set off downtown to meet Billy's father and see what he had found for himself in the months he had been out on his own.

They reached the apartment at a few minutes after ten.

"Oh good," he said when he opened the door, "you're a little late. I was starting to get worried that you weren't going to come . . ." He gave everybody a kiss and then, before Billy had unbuttoned his coat, his father was putting on his sweater and then pushing them back out the door.

"I have some place I want to take you to. We may be a little late but come on anyway." They walked a few blocks through the cold, Abby complaining first that she was too cold and then that she had to go to the bathroom and Billy watched his father smile slightly at that, as if he was just so happy to have his family and little family problems back again.

He led them up some steps to a church, pulled open some heavy wooden doors and waved his hand, signaling to them to get inside fast and not make any noise. A priest—Father Fergus—was reading the Gospel to rows and rows of unshaven, grimy, solemn-eyed men. Billy's father led them to an empty pew. Billy sat between his mother and his father. He remembered Father Fergus finishing his sermon with an angry "Amen," then the organ winding up and everybody rising to his feet. Billy looked covertly at his father booming out the hymns lustily on one side of him, and then at his mother trying to sing while she took it all in. He imagined her thinking to herself, "You better not cry, or get hysterical, but maybe you should call Eric's parents in Wisconsin, after all, you're still married to the screwball . . . or, better yet, I'll alert Dr. Dupee." Dr. Dupee had treated her husband for depression.

The hymns were led by a Negro minister in a white robe who waved his arms in the air and swayed left and right as he belted it out. All around him, to the left and to the right, above him in tiers in the balcony, an army of bums raised their heads and made a loud, collective moan. The bums reminded Billy of the Disney seven dwarfs, only now there were many more than seven.

After the service, as the bums filed out, and as his parents talked to Father Fergus, Billy watched a church deacon slap awake a bum who had just wandered in to get out of the cold, and heedless of the singing and sermonizing and praying (fearless of the wrath of God by this time—reconciled to the fact that he had sinned so often and so badly that nothing now could make up for it, even make a dent in his spiritual debit, so why bother? why get neurotic about it?) had lain down in a corner of the church, pulled a rug over himself, and gone to sleep. He glared at the deacon, but collected himself slowly and hobbled out the door and down the steps.

Outside, still talking to Father Fergus as he locked the door to the church, Billy's father caught sight of three bums who were sitting on the curb, debating the meaning of the morning's sermon.

"Come over here," he said to Billy's mother, "bring the kids. Excuse us, Father . . . Catherine, kids—there are some people I'd like you to meet. Come on . . ."

The bums stood up when they saw him coming and dusted some of the dirt off their coats and trousers. The one man who was wearing a hat doffed it. Another adjusted his tie.

"Mr. Schwartzbach, Mr. Tannenbaum, Mr. Burns— I'd like you to meet my family. This is William here—" And he pushed Billy a little forward, wanting him to shake hands all around.

"How do ye do, young fellow. Who would have suspected Mr. Williams would have himself a family, especially so proud an example of a young son as this? Now tell me something, young lad. Why haven't I seen you around here before?" said Mr. Burns, the one with the hat.

"They live uptown, Mr. Burns," Billy's father explained.

"And who are you, pretty little girl?" said Schwartzbach.

"This is—she's shy, come here, Abby, say hello to the nice men—well anyway, the little girl hiding behind my wife is my daughter, Abigail."

"What a doll," said Burns.

"And I'd also like you to meet my wife. Catherine." She said, "Hello," but no sound came out. It might have passed for shyness.

"It's a pleasure to meet such a lovely lady," said Mr. Burns. There was a silence after the introductions. Tannenbaum went down on one knee to tie up the laces on his sneakers.

"Well, Mr. Schwartzbach—have you been taking your medication? Have you gotten over your cough?"

"Oh, thank-you-very-much-for-inquiring, Mr. Williams," Schwartzbach said quickly, "all better, sir, all better thanks to you, sir."

Divorce proceedings were begun that night.

10

BY LATE OCTOBER, THE WINDS GREW HARSHER, LEAVES turned, fell off the trees dry as paper and skipped across the concrete walkways around campus. Some days the students wore scarves and ski jackets; other days it would be warm again.

Tuesdays and Thursdays after Russo's class, Billy would dawdle, scribbling bogus summary notes—"Just hold on, just want to make sure I've caught that last point, that was a sensational windup, really put the Middle Ages in perspective, sort of"—finishing with a flourish and a sigh—"There! That's got it"—waiting for Zizi to collect herself, her books, her cigarettes, her pen, her coat, and get ready to leave. After seven weeks of this class, Billy had read: two-thirds of *The Iliad,* most of *The Odyssey, The Bacchae, Oedipus Rex, Prometheus Bound, The Aeneid,* two-thirds of Dante's *Inferno,* and the first sixty pages of *The Canterbury Tales,* as well as Genesis and The Book of Job.

After class, if he timed it right—there were times when he committed himself too early, and times when she stayed around to talk to Russo—Zizi walked down the hall and up the stairs with him and there they were, chatting just like friends about other classes and their roommates and other things that concerned them for as long as it took them to get outside the building. Once outside, however, they always encountered Francisco. There he'd be, greasily lounging across the hood of a car, or if Russo let them out early, he'd come bounding down the street before they'd gotten very far, after them like a poodle. One sunny Indian summer day, he showed up all in white—white shirt, white pants, white shoes—with a blue sweater tied around his neck by the arms in a stylish embrace; dark sunglasses settled securely on his hooking, Roman nose. Billy thought: "Christ almighty. He looks like an ad for something." And after Zizi introduced the two of them for the third or fourth time, Billy left them to each other. "Okay, bye," he said in a voice that didn't carry, was probably unnoticed, and in any case went unacknowledged, before he scuttled away like a crab going up the street.

But then, a week or so after the final hot spell had broken, Zizi grabbed Billy's arm in the hallway after class and said to him: "Hey, listen. If Francisco is out there, you know, that guy who sometimes waits for me after class, will you stick around and go have lunch with us? Just this once? Please?"

It was raining that day, rain splattering down in wind-whipped scurries. The street was filled with rushing lunchtime traffic, kids who had had classes all morning, who had set off at eight before the rain, dodging from store awning to store awning along DeWitt Street to keep from getting soaked. Junior professors in stylish, belted trenchcoats covered their heads with newspapers and trotted to wherever they had to get to. Francisco was there, sheltered under the awning of a shoe store a few numbers down DeWitt Street. He was struggling with a black umbrella which had evidently blown inside out. He was bending it back, but took time out to give Zizi one of his smiles when she came up.

When he had finished his repairs, he said: "How about some lunch?"

"Sounds great," Billy said eagerly, and they set off down the street in formation, Zizi on the inside, Francisco in the middle holding the umbrella over her. Billy tried to wedge himself under the umbrella at first, but there was no room. He was forced to take to the outside, riding the curb like a balance beam, hopping with one wet shoe in the rushing gutter and dodging trees and parking meters.

They had hamburgers at a table surrounded by several of Francisco's friends: Carlos, Eddie, Juanita and some others whose names Billy couldn't catch. Most of them talked to each other in rapid Spanish, laughed and seemed to be having a good time. Billy sat next to Francisco at the long rectangular table. And Francisco sat next to Zizi so Billy couldn't even see her through Francisco's hair, which had frizzed up in the rain and blocked the way.

"How did I let myself get into this situation?" Billy asked himself. Francisco was relating some anecdote to one of his friends across the table. He leaned forward over his plate to deliver the evidently off-color punchline, and Billy stole a glance at Zizi whose face appeared briefly over Francisco's shoulder, gazing dreamily in a world of her own, smoke twirling from the tip of her cigarette, a hamburger daintily half-nibbled on her plate.

After some minutes had passed, Billy said to himself, "Well, I think I'm going to get myself another hamburger." No one had said anything to him so far, not even to ask what he was doing there. He pushed back his chair and stood up.

"Oh good, are you going to the kitchen?" asked Francisco, turning toward him. "Would you get me a hamburger too?"

"Certainly," Billy said cheerily, as if to say, this is great, all of us having lunch together like this, isn't it? On his way back from the hot and crowded kitchen, balancing the two plates, each with a hamburger and a sprig of parsley on the side, and as he maneuvered through the lunchtime throng, shoving his way through against the backs of chairs, he felt like some Negro waiter, the kind who wears a red jacket and bow-tie and says, "Here yo is, suh, yo hamburger, medium rah, just the way yo likes it." Old Black Joe. "Jesus," he thought. When he got back to the table, setting Francisco's plate down before him, saying, again cheerily, "There you go!" he noticed that several of the lunchers had left, among them Zizi. "Wonder where she went?" he said to himself, and decided to eat his hamburger as fast as he could, say "Thanks for lunch, we'll have to do this again some time soon" to Francisco, and then get the hell out of there.

"So Billy—I'm glad we finally get a chance to talk," Francisco said after he had salted his hamburger and recapped the top bun.

As it turned out, Billy stayed around to talk to Francisco for nearly an hour. The rest of the table soon emptied, gone off to study, or to classes or to the gym, and an old hag in a blue smock, sweeping a damp cloth over the grimy tops of the lunch tables, had to tell them twice to move along, she had better things to do than to wait on them to finish gabbing before they finally took their lunch trays up to the conveyor and left the dining hall.

Francisco supplied his personal history: his father had been one of the richest men in Cuba before Castro. He was one of the first civilians to be imprisoned there. When Francisco was three years old, his mother and his governess had smuggled him out on a banana boat bound for Miami. A few months later, Francisco's father paid somebody off and was allowed to join his family in exile.

"What did Castro care? He had stripped us clean, impounded all our land, taken both houses . . ." Forced to start life all over again in a new country, at forty-five, speaking no English, Francisco's father sold what few holdings he had in U.S. interests and, with the capital, bought a supermarket in Miami, which he stocked mainly with Cuban staples, those foods rarely found in Florida markets.

As for himself, Francisco planned first on going to law school. He eventually hoped to run for national office, using Miami as his base, where, he said, there was a large community of exiled and bitter Cubans, several of whom were already counting so heavily on him that they'd contributed what little money they had to help pay his college tuition. "For many of these people, I am one of the few hopes they have that they, or their children, may someday go back to Cuba." As Congressman, or Senator, Francisco hoped to legislate for a full-out invasion of Cuba to restore popular democracy. "That is my purpose in life," he said, "that is my destiny."

"Wow!" Billy thought. As they sat there, drinking coffee, Francisco described to Billy all sorts of hideous tortures which—he said he had proof—were routinely inflicted on innocent Cubans by the communists to keep them in line.

"The image of Cuba in the American press is so wrong. When people here think of Castro, they think he just has everybody playing baseball. Well, that's not so. He had your President Kennedy killed, you remember."

"He did? I didn't know he was behind it."

"Oh yeah. Everybody knows it," said Francisco, matter-of-factly.

He seemed to enjoy very much impressing Billy with his background, goals, and ideals. "Here, wear this," he said, reaching into his pocket for a button which he then pinned to Billy's shirt. It read: "Cuba Libre."

"Thanks," Billy said. Later, walking through campus to his room, he thought to himself, "That guy is really something." He had a depressing vision for an instant

105

of the two of them, Francisco and Zizi, arriving at Kennedy Airport, surrounded by flashing photographers, microphones shoved under their noses. Francisco would be the youthful, daring, democratically elected El Presidente, much beloved by liberated Cubans, a hero for the modern age. Castro would be a shrunken, bitter, Nixon-like creep, holed up in Venezuela, counting the million dollars' worth of Cuban currency (whatever that was) that he had smuggled out with him as his regime collapsed. And Zizi there, smiling for the photographers, on Francisco's arm would, of course, be the lovely first lady of Cuba. "No wonder she hangs around with him," Billy thought.

On his way up the stairs to his room, Billy ran into Randy going down.

"Late for class," Randy said, rushing past, then stopped one landing down, and called up. "Hey, Billy. Some guy just called you. Just five minutes ago. I left the number on your desk."

"Okay. Thanks."

"Okay. Oh, also, my dad might call. If he does, tell him I'll be back by four, okay? That's real important."

Earlier in the week, Randy had gotten a letter from his father, the one saying that the cancer was too far advanced, that there was no hope, he was dying. He had known about the cancer for months, but kept going to new doctors who claimed they had some great new treatment, a treatment found successful in ninety percent of the cases when tested on rats, never before used on humans. In this recent letter Randy's father had said, "They keep telling me to have hope, that maybe the cancer will stop with this medication or that . . . Who are they kidding? A man knows certain things. The show is over." So Randy had talked to his father three times in the past week trying to convince him to go back to the specialist, the new man in San Diego, to just "give it a shot."

"Since when do I have a quitter for a father?" Billy had overheard Randy saying over the phone.

It had been a very depressing letter that his father had sent Randy. Randy had left it out on his desk and Billy had read it one afternoon when Randy was at class. Five typewritten pages. The first two or three were very philosophical, all about the meaning of life and the importance of getting a good education and having a goal and working hard and being kind to others on the way up. The last couple of pages were instructions for Randy once the old man's light went out for good. He wanted to be buried in such and such a cemetery, next to Muriel, his beloved wife of thirty-three years: "Bury me in Our Lady of Lourdes Cemetery, next to your mother, Muriel, my beloved wife of thirty-three years . . ." He didn't want a big funeral, "nothing showy," he said, just a few of his nearest and dearest friends, and he enclosed a guest list (among whom Billy was surprised to find the names of several celebrities—Jerry Lewis for one, and Sammy Davis, Jr., and Peter Lawford, all presumably among the old man's nearest and dearest buddies). His will was in the lower left-hand drawer of the desk in his office. The key to the drawer was on his key ring. He was leaving everything to Randy. The letter ended, "God bless you, son."

The second Billy had returned to the room on the day the letter arrived, he sensed something was up. Randy was at his desk, sitting in the dark. Billy sat down on his bed, sighed, said he was exhausted, had had a long day, tried to appear sensible and approachable, a good friend, full of Ann Landers wisdom, but with no result.

Billy found the note Randy had left for him on his

107

desk. "Billy—call Bernie Gould" and then, below, the phone number. But instead of picking up the phone and calling Bernie, who was Henry Gould's son, the off-spring of his mother's boy friend, Billy picked up the phone and dialed the first six digits of the number of Zizi's room. Although he had never used the number, he had called "student inquiries" within a week of finding out she was at school and it had been easy to memorize.

Armpits sweated, head buzzed. He hung up.

"She's probably not even there." He dialed again.

"Hello?" She was there. What now? Think fast, stay calm. Hang up.

"Phew," he said out loud. That was a close shave.

11

WHILE BILLY WAS TRYING TO MAKE UP HIS MIND ABOUT which college to go to (make up what mind? his decision was considerably simplified in May when Billy found out he had been turned down at every college except one, Beacham University in Connecticut), he had called Bernie Gould to ask, among other things, for some pointers on how to file an application, and how to comport himself during an interview. He also asked if Bernie would mind if Billy came up to Beacham and stayed in his room so he could see first-hand what living away at college was like. The visit had been Henry's idea. He had been chasing after Billy's mother only for a month or two at this juncture, and the old rascal clearly saw a way to make a few points with her, knowing how desperately she needed and wanted a "take charge" kind of guy to straighten out those two kids of hers. Through Billy, he saw a chance to create new intrafamily ties (his son and Catherine's boy) as well as to reinforce the existing ones; if he took an active interest in Billy's search for the "right" college, that would really please old Catherine and she might then overlook the fact that he was a drunk, an old lech, a creep, and, very conceivably, a murderer. She might let it go, might say to him, "Hen —you may have your faults, but you're the only man for me," or something like that.

"Now look, Bill," Henry had said one night during dinner, "what you've got to do is just get up off your duff and stop expecting your mother to do everything for you. Call up Bernie, I'll get the number right now, and get him to put you up for a few nights. That's the only way you'll find out what Beacham is like." So Billy called from the phone in the hallway while his mother and Henry drank coffee and talked in the dining room in low whispers, his mother doubtlessly admiring the masterful way Henry had handled things.

"Uh—hello. Is this Bernie? Hi, you don't know me, but my name is Billy Williams and my mother is a friend of your father's and uh—" Anyway, one weekend Billy took the bus up to Beacham and spent two nights camping out in a sleeping bag on Bernie's floor.

Bernie was the eldest of Henry's two sons. Mark, the younger one, had been instrumental in getting Billy's mother and Henry together in the first place. Henry had shown up at the hospital one day to commit Mark to the mental ward where Billy's mother was doing volunteer work on a part-time basis (Dr. Dupee, her psychiatrist, had convinced her that a job would boost her self-confidence and since she had had so much experience dealing with maniacs in her life, the job at the mental hospital seemed right up her alley). She had known Henry from before, although never very well, and when he walked into her office one afternoon to talk about his son, it was the first time she had seen or heard anything about him in over a year. ("Henry? Henry Gould? Is it you? I can't believe it. How are you?") They soon started going to dinner together, and to parties and to movies, and the rest, as they say, is history.

Sometimes when he got drunk, Henry would start bragging self-pityingly about how screwed up all his kids were, all except for Bernie, who, Henry liked to say, "seems to have pulled himself together." But Henry also liked to say that Bernie hated him, that he was glad that Bernie had finally decided he wanted to be a lawyer, but it broke Henry's old heart that Bernie never seemed to appreciate all that his father had done for him. "I never said 'no' to him. I remember after graduation he was all excited about being a filmmaker. Well I knew he didn't have any talent at that. But I never discouraged him. I gave him five thousand dollars as a graduation present, figured I'd let him make his own mistakes. I don't know. What's with these kids? I gave him everything he's got. I never had any of his opportunities. My father died when I was nine years old. I've had to make money all my life. It just isn't fair that the kid should hate me like he does." And when Henry would go off like that, on and on, whining sometimes for two hours, three hours about the same old stuff, the same list of grievances, Billy's mother would reach across the table and put her slender, blue-veined hand over his gray, liver-spotted one, and she would say to him sweetly, "Oh Hen—I'm sure Bernie doesn't hate you. That's just the way kids are."

Henry's two other kids, Mark and Ruthie, came from Henry's second wife. "And God only knows what Ruthie's up to," Henry would moan, "Hare

Krishna, or some kind of thing. It would have just killed her mother to hear what's happened to Ruthie. The girl tells me she doesn't want to go to college, I say 'Okay, if that's not what you want, then don't go.' So she goes to California, lives in a commune, good neighbors of the Charles Mansons before they got thrown in jail—Manson used to come over to borrow their hatchets and kitchen knives. They're like Indian tribes out there. One big happy valley, Manson, Ruthie, crazy drugged-up hippies. I don't know, I don't understand anything. Well, at least Ruthie loves me, I'm her dear old Dad, she's always sending me these spaced-out postcards on Father's Day. 'Greetings from planet Earth,' she wrote me one time. I must have been a terrible father to them."

But Mark caused Henry the most pain. Henry and Billy's mother always talked about Mark, about what they could do to make him well again. She was the social worker and he was the kook's father, after all. They had arranged a day pass for Mark one day the past spring. They brought him over to the house for lunch, and they sat him down next to Billy, hair all over his face, smelling like urine, catatonic and strange. After lunch, Mark said he wanted to look around the house, and Henry had looked at Catherine, and she had said, "Well, sure, Mark, if that's what you want to do." Billy walked in on him in Abby's room, threatening Abby's hamsters, Frank and Francine.

"I ought to choke you, you disgusting rats," he was saying. The hamsters weren't doing anything, Francine was sitting up in the corner trying to crack a sunflower seed, and Frank was jogging along on his exercise wheel.

"Uh, Mark, I think your father wants you for something," Billy had said. Mark broke into a crazy grin and said, "Thank you!"

Billy had heard Henry's story about finding out his

111

son was a loon so many times that he knew all the details by heart. According to Henry, Mark was the real writer in the family. He, Henry, was just an old newshound. Markie was the artist. "He put together some great stuff for the literary magazine at that prep school he went to," Henry attested, as if he was any judge. But after prep school, Mark decided he didn't want to go to college. He had heard from somewhere that you couldn't learn anything about writing at college, so he told Henry he wasn't going to go, and Henry, strict disciplinarian that he was, had said, "Well . . . sure, uh, what do you think you might like to do instead?"

"Write a novel," Mark said.

Mark had locked himself away in his room, working very hard, Henry knew, because he could hear his son banging away on his typewriter. Henry was a light sleeper and he said the noise kept him up all night, sometimes until after 4 A.M.

Then, three weeks after he had begun, Mark emerged and said he had completed the first draft of his novel. "It still needs some work, Dad," he had said, "but see what you think." And Billy could readily image it as Henry, with trembling and proud fingers, had turned to the dedication and begun to read:

"Dedicated to my mother, Madeline Greenburg Gould, 1925–1972." (Old Mad was the one Henry flipped off Mount Washington.) And then, page 1:

Here is Edward Bear, coming downstairs now, bump, bump, bump, on the back of his head, behind Christopher Robin. It is, as far as he knows, the only way of coming downstairs, but sometimes he feels that there really is another way, if only he could stop bumping for a moment and think of it. And then he feels that perhaps there isn't. Anyhow, here he is at the bottom, and ready to be introduced to you. Winnie-the-Pooh.

"Winnie-the-Pooh?" Henry must have thought, "what the hell is this?" He turned back a page and read the title.

WINNIE-THE-POOH

And then:

A Novel, by Mark Gould

"Oh shit," Henry must have said.

One thing rapidly followed another. There was a confrontation (Mark at first denied that he had plagiarized, but when Henry said, "For God's sake, Mark, you can't do this. Do I have to drag you to a bookstore to prove this thing to you?" Mark ran down the hall and locked himself in his room and wouldn't come out). There followed the obligatory suicide attempt, ambulance ride, stomach pump, the works. Henry was in Billy's mother's office by Monday morning.

Thus it should not be surprising that Billy was of two minds about having Henry's children, the Gould kids, joining the family as his stepsiblings. It was not that he was entirely unsympathetic. Only that he felt that his family had enough troubles of its own.

Billy spent most of that weekend at Beacham visiting Bernie playing pinball in the game room in the basement of Bernie's law school dormitory. The other law school students were a jocular crowd, not above unwinding on the pinball machines after a hard day's studying. There must have been twenty or thirty of them, jostling and carousing, racking up the points, tilting out and arguing about whose turn it was to play next.

Bernie had had to work hard that weekend, preparing for some oral presentation he had to make. In fact, one of the things that impressed Billy most about Beacham was that both nights, while he lay awake in the corner of Bernie's small room, cocooned in his sleeping bag, Bernie stayed awake at his desk, poring over his case books, back hunched, reading by a Tensor lamp. The scurrying of Bernie's pencil across the pages of his legal pad kept Billy awake until after two in the morning with curiosity and admiration and excitement and envy. How he wished it was himself there at the desk in the middle of the night, doing important work and smoking cigarettes; how he wished there was someone else watching, pretending to be asleep on the floor. Finally Bernie flopped onto his bed and fell asleep in his clothes. And in the morning, when Billy woke up, he had to go to the crowded dining hall by himself. Bernie didn't wake up until sometime after one that afternoon.

Billy remembered the weekend he had spent with Bernie very well. He remembered how the walls of Bernie's room were lined with bookshelves crammed with books. It was the most impressive private library Billy had ever seen. Taped to the base of the shelf, underneath the books, was a Dymo label that read: Modern German Literature, or Drama, or American Colonial History, or Anthropology—like a bookstore.

"Hello?"
"Hello? Is this Bernie?"
"Yes."
"Hi. It's Billy Williams. I just got your message."
"Oh . . . Billy, how are you?"
"Fine."
"I called to see how you were making out. I'm sorry I didn't get a chance to look you up earlier, but I've got to pass my bar at the end of next year. I've just been run ragged. I thought we could get together some day and have lunch."

"Sure."

"This week's tough for me. But how about next week? How is next week for you?"

"Same as this week, as it so happens," Billy thought of saying. "Next week's fine," he said.

"Great. Let me check my date book here . . . hold on . . . Monday's no good, how about Tuesday? Say arround twelve-thirty? In the Law School cafeteria?"

"Fine."

"Great, Billy. See you there."

"I better not forget all that," Billy thought after he had hung up. "I'd better write it down." So he sat down at his desk and wrote a reminder to himself on a sheet of paper, and while he sat there, gazing pointlessly at the wall, he got an idea. "I think what my big problem is," he said to himself, "is that I waste too much time. I've really got to get on the ball . . ." So he pulled open his desk drawer and took out a second sheet of paper and drafted a schedule for himself, a timetable for studying. Because he was going to have to get going. Exams were only weeks away and he was weeks behind in Chinese already, and chapters behind in the economics textbook. Plus, Russo had assigned another paper and there was no way Billy was going to risk it again, writing a paper without having read the book. So he decided that what he would do was to move into the library where it would be quiet and see how that worked. Randy made too much noise, had people over all the time, played the record player, etc.

"Tuesday—" Billy wrote, "read *The Canterbury Tales*. Two hours study Chinese vocabulary lists. One chapter in Samuelson . . ." This last, his economics textbook.

"Wednesday—complete *The Canterbury Tales*. Two hours Chinese. One chapter Samuelson."

"Thursday—resume Dante's *Inferno*. Finish. Two hours Chinese. One chapter Samuelson."

"Friday—finish *Inferno* if not finished Thursday. Chinese. Samuelson." At the bottom of the page, he wrote "Stick to this!" and underlined it. He considered adding to this regimen a morning jog, or a dozen laps in the pool, but decided, "No, come on, I'd never do that." Billy was getting better about this. He frequently invented artificial challenges for himself. The summer before he had tried to teach himself Greek. He had paid twenty-five dollars for the books and had puzzled over them stupidly for a few days, before giving up.

Billy spent most of the next week at the library. He sat at a desk by a window where the sun found its way to him around three in the afternoon, and sedated by its warmth on his shirt, he often found himself staring off into space, or pointlessly at some word on the page, or at the wall. His mind would go black for a minute or two and he would close his eyes and sigh with gratitude. Once he fell asleep and had to be awakened by the janitor who said it was closing time, "It's twelve midnight, the library's closing."

He cultivated a careless, distracted and overworked appearance. After Tuesday, he didn't shave again for the whole week and by Sunday he had developed impressive patches of itchy, uncomfortable wool along the cheeks and under his chin. Twice Randy asked him if he was growing a beard, adding, "I think you'd look cool with a beard," and "Maybe I should grow a beard ... Ya think so?"

"No, no, no," Billy wanted to explain, "I'm not trying to grow a beard. I'm just too preoccupied and busy and there's nothing I can do to stop it from growing. I've been studying really hard—can't you tell?" So he didn't shave. Or shower. Or change his clothes. Every morning when Billy climbed out of bed (at 7:30 so he would have an hour's time to bone up on his Chinese vocabulary—Professor Fong's course met every morn-

116

ing of the week at 9:00 A.M.) he found his old clothes rumpled and waiting for him on the floor. By the weekend, his socks were particularly crusty and smelled like cheese, and he was very pleased with himself.

A COLD NIGHT, WET AND DARK IN A CITY. WATER DRIPping from awnings, stoplights winking along the intersections of the avenue, green to yellow to red, green, yellow, red. A car comes, its tires hiss on the wet asphalt, an old car, a big American bomb, a Pontiac, maybe with tail fins. Inside, two black men. They're cruising down the street, cruising, drunk resentful, nothing fucking better to do. Get outside, drive around. Unemployed. No family. Bitter. Alienated. They're sharing drinks from a bottle in a brown paper bag. Late at night. Two A.M. Then one sees her, says, "Hey, Willie," blonde hair dancing in the nighttime city breeze, waiting at a street corner, crossing at the light, walking down the deserted avenue, no cops anywhere, no cop cars, no one. "Check it out . . ." They slow down and glide.

They stop the car, both doors fly open, they come running out, the driver grabs her. A flash of knife is all she sees, and the smell, the men's cologne and the hot, sweaty stink of the whiskey or the Thunderbird or whatever they've been drinking. "Hey baby—heh heh heh. All right . . ." And they take her down an alley and throw her down on the ground, garbage cans all around, the alley of a restaurant she thinks incongruously.

At that point she seemed destined to become just another statistic in the daily log of the city's mayhem. Somewhere—at the morgue or at the Howard Avenue police station, or at the office of the district attorney—it would be recorded that she was nineteen, unmarried, a student at Beacham University. He stands over her, reaches down to his fly and tugs out his dick. She screams and Billy hears her. He'd been unable to sleep and had gone out for a walk, unshaven, beat, tough, thinking to himself, "Who gives a fuck," like Humphrey Bogart. "Somebody's in trouble," he thinks to himself. "Well, it's not my business." She screams again and he comes to the alley and peers down it, through the gloom, sees the black silhouettes, hears one of the men hiss, "Scream again, bitch, and you're dead."

"Hey, motherfuckers, get the fuck out of here," Billy says into the alley. The two men swerve around, their shadows. Then the smile of white teeth grinning in derision in the alley dark.

"Hey man, don't come looking for trouble."

"I'm not looking for trouble, man. Just take off. Leave the girl alone."

"Hey man—" (chuckles) "why you want to play fucking hero?" and he adds, "Chump." Comes toward Billy, flashes his switchblade. Billy stands still. The black guy lunges, Billy grabs his hand, digs his fingers into the bony flesh. "Aye—" The knife clinks on the alley floor and Billy kicks it into the street with his foot. They reach for each other's throats, jostle, struggle, teeter over, crashing into the garbage cans. Billy's got him, strangling, adrenaline, can hear the bones cracking, hear the man choking, he's got him. But the other rapist comes over with his knife and he stabs Billy, first in the leg, and the pain is so severe that Billy has to let go. They stab him again in the side. "Willie, hey, you

118

all right?" he hears whispering before he blacks out. The rapists, one nearly dead from strangulation, hobble off (to leave the city, to stay away from alcohol, to look for work, lessons learned) leaving Billy collapsed on the alley floor in an expanding red pool of blood.

The scene: A hospital room. He awakens, surrounded by all the people he has ever known or cared about. He has been unconscious, near death for days. Ten days in a coma. Those who had sold him short, there would be tears in their eyes. They had not known the actual size of his heart. (Like most people, Billy believed he was a better person than the circumstances of his life had given him a chance to show.)

"Oh Billy, thank God."

"We're so proud of you."

"You were so brave."

Finally a doctor with a white coat pushes his way through the crowd around the hospital bed and shoos everybody out.

"Just one more picture, Doc," a photographer would say, wearing a gray hat with a cardboard PRESS sign tucked in the brim.

"Let's see a smile," and the flashbulb would pop and Billy would sit there, blue spot swimming hazily in front of his eyes, dazed, bewildered. What was all this?

"Get well, Billy."

"Hurry on back to class, Billy. Professor Fong doesn't know whom to call on anymore to conjugate those verbs."

"We'll be back tomorrow. Anything you want us to bring you?"

"Hey, take it easy," Randy would say.

"Well, I won't lie to you." the doctor would say, "I'm surprised that you pulled through. We all consider it something of a miracle. There were some tense moments when we thought we'd lose you. You lost a lot of blood. Fortunately, you're young and strong, and that was a big advantage. Also, the girl you rescued rode in the ambulance with you that night. She provided the pints of blood you needed."

"The girl—is she all right?"

"She was a little shaken up, but she's all right now. You managed to frighten the rapists away."

"And the men? The rapists?"

"They turned themselves in, Billy. You see you've become something of a hero around here. The community's been inspired by your courage and example. The rapists confessed. Apparently they couldn't live with the guilt. I was here the day they came to look in on you in the hospital. They broke down crying and later confessed everything . . .

"The young lady you helped that night is outside now and asked if I would let her see you. I said I'd ask you."

"Sure. She can come in."

And Zizi would come in then. Then it would all be all right.

"Yeah," Billy thought as he lay in bed late Monday night, "that would really be something." He played the fantasy through his mind's projector a couple of times more before finally falling asleep.

The next day Billy had Russo's class. It was a disaster, even though Billy had so thoroughly prepared, had raised his hand and learnedly (he thought) answered several questions. Part of the problem was that five of the ten students failed to turn up. Russo delayed the start of class for fifteen minutes. Everybody sat in silence, Russo frequently looking at his watch and saying, "We'll give them another couple of minutes, then we'll get started." Finally, broodingly, Russo closed the classroom door. Billy felt sorry for him and tried to help.

"I think it's very interesting what Chaucer has to say on page two-sixteen," he announced before Russo had even gotten back to his chair, "in fact I think the whole passage is emblematic of a major theme in *The Tales* . . ."

"Well, elaborate on that, Billy," Russo said.

"Well what I found sort of provocative was the whole question of dualism . . ." And Billy carried the discussion for the next couple of minutes, explaining what was so provocative about page 216 of *The Canterbury Tales*.

After class, Billy met Zizi at the door and commiserated with her as they walked down the hall about how uncomfortable and depressing the class had been.

"God, that was so awful," Zizi said as they left Russo behind in his classroom, restuffing papers and notes and books into his briefcase, "it makes me so sorry for him. He really puts so much into this class. I didn't know what to do. I had a really hard time reading Chaucer." Billy fought the impulse to sit Zizi down someplace and tell her just what he had decided *The Canterbury Tales* was all about. It was one of the few books he had managed to finish for Russo's course and he felt a little cheated that he'd missed his chance to expound. And next week they'd be doing Spenser's *The Faerie Queene*.

Billy was halfway up the flight of stairs that led to the front door and out onto DeWitt Street when Zizi grabbed his arm and said, "No. Wait. Let's not go out that way."

"Why not?"

"I'll tell you later. Come on. Let's find the back way."

The back way let out onto a parking lot off Jermain Avenue. Zizi led him through the lot and as they maneuvered through the labyrinth of parked Datsuns and Volvos, Billy had time to observe her.

She wore black cowboy boots that made her tallish, nearly Billy's height. And a black wool coat. Mid-length gold hair framing strong features and lustrous skin. Black mittens, a green plaid scarf, several silver bracelets, a couple of rings. Contrasted with Billy who was wearing a blue button-down shirt, a moldy pair of blue jeans that were too tight and too small, mismatching socks, one black, the other red, sneakers and his blue winter coat with the artificial fur hood that he'd worn every winter since ninth grade; in other words, the same ensemble he'd had on the day before, and the day before that, and the day before that—since last Wednesday, in fact.

Once out of the parking lot, they crossed Jermain Avenue to a donut counter, a place called Super Do Nut. Super Do Nut stayed open all night long so that the neighborhood bums would have a place to stay warm in the winter, the same way a bird feeder works for birds. Also, Super Do Nut was the place where students would go for coffee at four o'clock in the morning during exam week to sit bleary-eyed in the buzzing fluorescent light and munch gummy donuts, taking resuscitative breaks from their notes and textbooks and take-home finals. But in the daytime the place was empty. Zizi had asked Billy to have a cup of coffee with her. At first she had asked him to have a whole lunch, but Billy had said he couldn't, much as he wanted to. He said he had already made plans to meet someone at the Law School. Billy was a little pleased that he could say that he was busy, that he had to meet someone for lunch in a quarter of an hour, someone who would probably be a lawyer and make lots of money someday. And also, though he would never admit it, not even to himself, he was relieved to have an excuse. What would he be able to say to Zizi, after all?

Where could he begin? Especially as she had taken him by surprise, and he was so badly prepared. His brain was still teeming with leftover explications of *The Canterbury Tales* to which he had been unable to give a proper airing in class.

As they sat there at the Formica counter, on swivel stools, waiting for the waitress to come, a fragile-looking woman in a pink uniform and white shoes, with big, bulging psychotic eyes, Billy wished that he were somewhere else. He didn't want to forfeit the opportunity entirely, of course. But he wished that time might somehow stand still, give him a chance to go back to his room and think, clear his head, make some notes on a piece of paper, prepare for all this. Then come back.

"So what have you been up to?" Zizi asked him. "I hardly see you."

"I haven't been up to anything. I've . . ." He thought of telling her a story about himself and his roommate, Randy, but decided it was too long and too stupid. "No. Nothing. How've you been?"

"I've been okay," she said, eyes averted, looking down at her napkin and knife and fork. Signs clearly read: "Of course I haven't been okay. But I'm going to pretend I don't want to burden you with my problems."

The waitress came around to them and stood there, rustling her order pad. Billy ordered hot chocolate. He thought that this was a smart move. It would impress Zizi that he didn't take himself too seriously. Sure he was going to see some guy in the Law School, but that didn't mean that he wasn't a down-to-earth, ham-and-eggs kind of fellow, still had a lot of the kid in him. Zizi asked for tea with lemon.

"And do you have artificial sweetener?" she asked in a little-girl voice. The waitress went away and Billy's eyes wandered around the store, occupying time until he could figure out something to say. He scanned the

123

menu and was about to say something idiotic about the inflated price of jelly donuts when Zizi asked, "How's your mom?"

"She's okay."

"I really liked her. She was really nice to me that summer. I felt really bad about what happened. That was really crazy."

"Yeah."

"I heard that your mother got divorced."

"Yeah. It happened a while ago."

"Any idea why?"

"I don't really know. He left her for some tootsie. They weren't getting along at all."

"That's terrible. Were you, like, really upset?"

"No. Not really. I didn't like Jim much. I mean he was about the stupidest man I ever met."

"That's what my mother thought, too," Zizi said.

"Well he was. He was really dumb. You can't blame him for it, I guess. And I think my mother kind of liked how dumb he was. He was so dumb he sort of had to be stable . . . How's your family? How's Muffin?"

"Oh it's so great," Zizi said, excited, her eyes widening, her teeth white and perfect, "she got married and she's got a baby. And she's really happy. They live in California now."

"Oh yeah?"

"Yeah. It's great."

"Do you ever go to visit?"

"Yeah. In fact I spent last summer there."

"You were in California last summer? What were you doing?"

"My brother-in-law has a farm. And he manages a health food store in Berkeley where he sells all his produce."

"That's great. So you got to live on the farm?"

"Uh huh. But mostly I was just hanging out. It was

124

really great to get away from my parents. They almost disowned me."

"Why?"

" 'Cause I went out there with this guy I knew. He'd gotten into the University of California at Berkeley so I spent the summer with him. We all lived on the farm." Zizi looked wistful. The waitress brought over the tea and hot chocolate. Billy watched Zizi's slender fingers as she held the packet of Sweet N Low by the corner and wagged it a couple of times before opening it and pouring it in her tea.

He could imagine the scene. The boy friend, good-looking and tall, wearing blue jeans, probably reading *Steppenwolf* and really "digging it," and Zizi and Muffin and her husband and the baby. "I bet they sat around and played guitars all day," he thought. For some reason, Billy could very vividly imagine them all having breakfast together around a big wood table. Fresh eggs and milk and Zizi'd make pancakes for everybody. There'd be a big dog sleeping on the floor. Everybody acting happy. And Muffin breast-feeding the baby right there at the table. Billy wondered why he'd never met a girl who liked him enough to take him across the country to her sister's farmhouse so he could have an idyllic breakfast. Life had passed him by.

Billy found that he had lost his appetite for the hot chocolate. His stomach was upset.

"Francisco said you guys had a long talk the other day after I left."

"Yeah, we did. He told me all about escaping from Cuba and everything. I think he's a pretty interesting guy . . ."

"He is interesting," Zizi said quietly (what was wrong with her?), "he told me he liked talking to you a lot."

"Well, I liked talking to him."

"Francisco's . . . I don't know. Francisco's really . . ."

125

"Really what?"

"He's a really nice guy and everything, but he's got a lot of problems."

"He does?"

As it turned out, in fact, Francisco was falling apart. Heartbroken, lovesick, was hobbling around on a broken leg, crying all the time, following Zizi everywhere.

"I'm just sick of seeing him all the time, every time I turn around. That's why I wanted to take the back way out. I know he was there, waiting. I just really don't want to see him anymore. I can't take it. I mean, like it's not just this class he shows up at and waits for me. It's everywhere I go." Two weekends ago, she said, a friend had invited her away for the weekend. They left late Thursday evening and she didn't tell Francisco where she was going. First of all, she didn't think of it; second of all, there was no reason she should have told him. It was none of his business where she was going, with whom, or even that she was going away at all. This was something Francisco had been unable to understand.

"When I got back, my roommate told me he'd called up maybe fifty times. So I call him right away to tell him I'm back and I get this 'where have you been? how could you take off like that without telling me?' and all this. I mean, he was acting worse than my parents. So then he told me he got so worried about me that he called my parents, he called my fucking parents to see if they knew where I was. I couldn't believe that. He said he thought maybe I went home for the weekend. He got them all worried and upset. It took three hours with them on Sunday to get them off my back. 'Where have you been? You had us worried sick,' " she mimicked.

For the next couple of days, she had tried to be nice to Francisco, but he kept accusing her, yelling at her.

She explained that she had invited Billy to lunch that day to take the pressure off. She had dreaded walking with Francisco all the way to the dining hall. Because she just couldn't have gone through another scene with him at that point. He said she was making him miserable. Well, he was making her miserable, too! It was a huge mess. She refused to tell him where she had gone. "He thought I had gone away with you," she said. Billy perked up, flattered. She shook her head, as if to say "isn't that ridiculous?" caught her breath and recouped. She tried to explain patiently to him that where she went, whom she saw, what she did was none of his business and he appeared to understand. Then five minutes later he burst into tears. Cracked.

The rest of the week things had gotten even worse. One disaster after another, all of them, he claimed, her fault. One night she refused to see him when he called, begging, saying he had to talk to her. Frustrated, bewildered, Francisco borrowed his roommate's car and went speeding off down the highway and smashed into the concrete divider, going seventy-five miles an hour. He broke his leg in the accident. Two days later, when he was released from the hospital, he burst into her psychology class halfway through, streaming with tears, tripping over his crutches, disrupting everything, and just stood there crying.

"He says I led him on. I said, 'I'm sorry, Francisco, I'm sorry about your leg and I'm sorry you say you haven't been able to work, but I really don't think I had that much to do with it.' He was in the hospital for a couple of days, getting his leg set, you know, and it was so great, it was a relief to come and go as I pleased. Of course, then he started calling me up in the middle of the night. He's on crutches now and they slow him down, because when he had both his legs— you saw him—he was all over me. I couldn't shake him. I don't know, Billy. He keeps saying he's going to kill himself. I know it's only for effect, but it makes me feel so awful. I wish I knew what to do about it."

"Jesus Christ," Billy thought. "So much for the revolution." In his mind's eye, he pictured a crowd of exiled Cubans assembled outside a storefront—Francisco's father's supermarket, with placards in the windows advertising cane sugar and cigars and tortillas, or whatever Cuban people bought at Cuban groceries—all of them unsmiling, bitter, disillusioned. They'd never see their homeland again. "She might as well be an agent for Castro," Billy said to himself.

When Zizi had finished her tea and stubbed out her second cigarette, Billy paid the check and they left without leaving the waitress any tip. They were walking up Jermain Avenue together, chatting just like friends, when something got into him. What was it? What made him do it? Hadn't he just had this nice conversation with her? Hadn't she told him a few of her problems? Trusted him? Laid the foundation for more talks, more conversations in the donut shop? Why did he feel it again, that same feeling he'd had just as strongly three years before, on the island, that the time was now or never, that claims must be staked? Old alley cat yearnings. Nothing ventured, nothing gained. They walked a hundred yards or so in silence, Billy assembling his words in sentences, thinking, "Okay. Any second now, I'm going to begin. Ready, set, okay, here I go . . ." and his mouth opened and he squeaked.

"Look," he warbled, "what are your plans this weekend? I mean if you wanted to we could go to the movies . . . I don't know . . ." These were, sure enough, the words he had worked it out to say to her. His tongue had gotten it out right. The words had formed a sentence, asked a question, which had meaning and sense. Quite a lot of meaning, in fact. Why then did he wish, once they were irretrievably spoken, that he had just kept his big mouth shut? Nothing ventured, nothing lost. Why hadn't he included an easy refusal clause, such as "unless you have something better to do." She looked smugly at him. Pleased with herself, with this unforeseen opportunity for a display of power.

"Oh Billy," she said poignantly, "I can't." And his face fell, corners of his mouth weighted down as if with lead sinkers. His face shimmered with humiliation. "I'm going away for the weekend."

"Oh well."

"But next time, okay? I promise."

"Sure. Great," he said.

"Bitch," he thought to himself as he turned the wind-swept corner and headed towards the Law School cafeteria where he was supposed to meet Bernie Gould, the son of his mother's boy friend. "I wonder what she's doing going away all the time on these weekends."

13

MEANWHILE, OR MAYBE LATER IN THE DAY, IN THE sanctum of his office, the door locked, the window shades drawn, Philip Russo sat at his desk cooling from his anger and humiliation and confusion, jiggling a paper clip. Resting on his lap were two student essays.

Things had not been going right for Mr. Russo. Not that they had been going all that badly. His classes had been disasters—he was clearly no teacher, no Mr. Chips—but other things compensated for that. Sort of. Besides, he had decided a few weeks earlier that he would give up teaching after this year. And that was a relief: at least there was some end in sight.

Still, a vague feeling of unease, a presentiment of very bad things to come, had been following him around for the past several days. It had almost come to a head, boiled over in the classroom that morning when none of his students showed up. And why should they show up if the stuff bored them? It was boring. It bored Russo. But anyway, all right, he had gotten through it.

If he were to think about it, he would conclude that he was in a better mood now than he had been in over a year. The reasons behind this mood change were suspect, perhaps, but so what? If it worked, why not?

Not that things were bad, just that they were on the brink of being so. All that he had done, he had done because he wanted to—so he had decided, along with his psychiatrist's help and guidance, administered twice a week for the past two months. And the doctor said he was making progress in the battle against his demons. Well, Russo hoped so. He hoped it was so, but he wasn't sure.

After a very good patch on the Dickens book, he found himslf at his desk in Vermont the past weekend unable to commit a new word.

Thomas had stayed behind—Mary Townsend had taken him. Russo had the first five chapters of his book. Good chapters. Nearly a hundred pages. Since then, blocked. He had had those chapters for weeks. They had been good chapters the first time he drafted them, no better the second time, and just as good the third and last time he had gone over them. Now he had forgotten what he planned to say in the rest of the book.

And as for his classes: twice in the last ten days he had fought with the urge to stand up in the middle of class and say, "Forget it. No one cares. I sure don't. This is all shit. No one's prepared," and walk out.

Besides the Introduction to Great Books course that Russo was teaching the freshmen, he was teaching a senior seminar on Dickens. This class was the real disappointment. The freshmen were dumb (ten blockheads), but at least they weren't as competitive (and dumb) as the seniors (seven blockheads, and two neurotics who chain-smoked and talked all the time). Of course the seniors were worrying about their grade point averages, about getting into law school and things like that . . .

And that would account for the two papers on Russo's lap. A few weeks before he had assigned to the seniors their midterm paper, ten pages. The papers had all been handed in, more or less on time, but the two now on his lap had come in identical. Same topic, same title—"The Specter of Technology in the Novels of Charles Dickens"—every idea, every sentence, every word, even every punctuation mistake—the same. Everything about them—except the names on the title page, Ross Joyce and George Katzenbaum respectively, of the students who claimed to have written them—the same.

Russo stood up, put the papers on his desk, and walked over to the filing cabinet by the window. He pulled open the middle drawer, then flipped through several folders until he found what he was looking for. A third ten-page essay. The title? "The Specter of Technology in the Novels of Charles Dickens." The date: April 1970. "Unbelievable," Russo thought to himself. The author (for so he had claimed) of this essay had been a boy named David Solomon, thrown out for plagiarism in October 1971. "Unbelievable."

These three papers, he knew, had all been written by a computer in New Jersey. It was no coincidence that these three students had plunged deep into the works of Dickens on different weekends and emerged to write exactly identical accounts of what they had found

within. Russo knew the racket. An agency, probably
a couple of college kids behind it, a couple of hustlers,
had thousand and thousands of these essays on file—on
Malthus and Plato and Rousseau and Homer and
the Russian Revolution. They solicited college kids in
ads placed in the back of underground magazines to
send in checks, with a description of the essay they
wanted written, how long they wanted it—ten pages,
fifty, a senior essay, even a dissertation—all they had
to do was identify the subject. Obviously, the agency
was a little short on Dickens essays because this was the
third time in six years that Russo had been handed
this particular one.

"Well if I ever get stuck and need to make a couple
of dollars, I sure know how to go about it," Russo said
and sighed. Because after all, what a world.

What was he going to do about this? It was very depressing. If he turned the kids in to the department,
they might get suspended for the rest of the term. But
they'd come back, if they felt like it, in September. Who
was he to say they couldn't? The school needed tuition, they were both paying customers. Russo had seen
Katzenbaum driving around in a fancy sports car, hanging around with a set of identifiably rich kids, wearing
mirror sunglasses. Katzenbaum wasn't going to learn
any lessons from this. The world was corrupt. Why not
try to get away with as much as you can? Katzenbaum
was a smart kid. He'd done good work up until now,
the days he had bothered to show up in class at all.

There was nothing the faculty or college administrators could do about cracking down on cheating rings
like this. Such operations were doing a very good trade
from the look of things. "Oh well," Russo thought, and
sat back at his desk. He would have to leave soon to
pick up his son at kindergarten, take him home, get
him some lunch. He put the two Dickens papers in his
desk drawer, then picked up the phone.

"Hello?"

"Alice? Hi, it's Phil Russo. Is Zizi around?"

"No, she hasn't gotten back from lunch yet. Do you want me to have her call you?"

"Yeah, okay, would you do that? I just want to know if she feels like baby-sitting for a couple of hours this afternoon while I go to the library. Tell her it's no emergency."

"Okay."

"Okay, thanks, Alice."

Walking down the street, on his way to meet his son, Russo was thinking: "Who the hell am I to set myself up as some moral paragon, as if I know right from wrong. The hell with it, the kids are desperate to get good grades, they want to please their parents and get into law school, be rich guys. I might not have done something like this in my undergraduate days, but the world was different then. Priorities aren't what they used to be. Kids don't believe in the kinds of things I used to believe in." He stopped at a traffic light, stood still as cars and vans rushed past. "Now come on, Phil, don't be too charmed with your own cynicism, for Christ's sake," he said to himself, recognizing the self-congratulation behind that recognition and the self-congratulation behind recognizing that recognition.

And in the end, Russo decided not to turn in the two students who had cheated. He gave them both failing marks with no explanation, no comments in the margin. He was very surprised, nevertheless, when both Joyce and Katzenbaum waited their turn after class to speak with him, saying there must have been some mistake, and when he said no, there was no mistake, both were exasperated and took up ten minutes each, protesting their bad marks.

14

"Ah, Billy. Sorry I'm late," Bernie said, unbuttoning his camel's hair coat and unwinding a fringed scarf from around his neck. "Have you been waiting long?"

"Only about ten minutes." More like half an hour.

Bernie looked a lot like his father, although somewhat less stooped, less fat, less miserable. Being thirty years younger than the "old man," Bernie didn't have his father's jowls, sagging paunch and horseshoe baldness; otherwise the resemblance was remarkable. Henry's sideburns were white, Bernie's a sort of rusty, monkey orange. For a second as they waited at the tail-end of a long lunch line to get their plates, Billy thought of those photographs he used to see in certain scientific and medical journals. Billy's mother always subscribes to all sorts of magazines which she never reads. She leaves them out for a few weeks, lying conspicuously on the coffee table, then throws them out in time for the next month's shipment. When Billy had nothing else to do, he used to take a stack of them into the bathroom or to his bedroom and kill a few hours flipping through the pages: *AMA Journal, The Smithsonian, Modern Bride, Guns and Ammo.* Henry and Bernie, his son, reminded Billy somehow of those photographs that accompany articles on cancer research placed next to each other for shocking before-and-after comparison—a photograph of a cancerous lung, scabby and black, as if someone had barbecued it on a grill, and opposite that, a pre-cancerous lung, pink and clean and healthy. That was about the way Billy imagined photographs of father and son next to each other: on the left, a cancerous Gould; on the right, Bernie, the pre-cancerous one.

"So, how are things going?" Bernie asked when they had settled their trays on the table and sat down. Lunch was macaroni and cheese, bread and butter, a carton of milk, dessert was red Jell-O, plastic silverware and a napkin, all on a red plastic tray.

"I'm doing okay."

"I figured you'd be having a good time. Freshman year is wild. Bet you spend the whole time partying. Right? When was the last time you cracked a book?"

"Oh a couple of weeks ago," Billy lied, "I can't really remember."

Bernie laughed, his mouth full of pasty macaroni and cheese. When he had swallowed, he said, "You sound like me, man. I remember when I was a freshman I did nothing but fuck off. Partied, got stoned, got laid. I mean every night, you know. It got a little heavy after a while. Like I did some crazy things. Like drugs. I was heavy into drugs for a while, and I kind of regret all that now because sometimes I think it sort of ruined my brain. Like even now, I haven't tripped or anything for two years and like I still have trouble thinking. Like last year my grades just weren't as good as they should have been. I got kind of scared that I'd done some real damage. But I think I've straightened things out. I don't want to sound like your father or anything, but maybe you should take it from me. Get drunk all you want, smoke hash, get stoned, but stay away from chemicals. I mean I'm assuming you want to go to law school or medical school someday. Cause chemicals can mess up your future."

"How are you doing this year?" Billy asked, gen-

135

uinely concerned. "Are you still having trouble thinking?"

"No, like I say. I've worked things out. But at law school there's no time to fuck off. You really have to work so hard. Cause the guys with the best grade point averages are the ones who are going to get snapped up by the big firms. Good grades really translate into money. I mean suddenly it's your fucking life, you know? Cause the guys who can't handle it aren't going to get diddley-squat when they get out of here. I mean, who'd want to hire a dumb lawyer, right? It's terrible and materialistic of me to say, I guess, but you get to be my age—I'm almost twenty-five—and you begin to see things a little differently. It's the law of the jungle. It's not much fun—there aren't as many parties—but there you are. What are you going to do about it?"

"I bet you've still managed to have some good times since you've been here," Billy said, one-of-the-guys.

Bernie grinned. "Yeah, it's not as black as I paint it. I'm getting by. I've got this chick and . . ."

They talked for a while more about college and law school life, Bernie regaling Billy with his favorite accounts of early 1970s undergraduate hi-jinx: lacing with LSD the Jell-O that was going to be served to the ROTC; the time a kid hit the president of the university in the face with a cream pie to protest the university's large holdings in Dow Chemical, the company that made Napalm; the night they burned Nixon in effigy in support of the Vietnam Moratorium, and so on.

Bernie paused to concentrate on tearing apart a slice of bread, then on buttering one of the segments. He poked the bread into his mouth, chewed, his forehead flexing, then swallowed.

"So what are your plans for vacation? Making the Thanksgiving dinner scene with your mother and 'the old man'?" Billy assumed that he was referring to Henry.

"I probably will. How about you?"

"If I can get through with my work. I talked to Dad the other day on the phone. I think he's getting pretty serious about your mother. I think they're going to get married. What do you think? You're around there more than I am."

"I don't know," Billy said. He was going to add, "I sure as hell hope not," but refrained from saying this. He knew from hearing Henry whine about it that relations between this son and that father were strained; just the same, holding back on what you thought of other kids' parents (who might be drunks, or lunatics, or ex-cons) was a code from childhood. Besides, Billy was used to checking and often swallowing back down the things he could have said about Henry. After nearly a year of having the old sucker around the house, it was a reflex action.

"I only met your mom once," Bernie said, "and she seemed all right to me. I don't think it'd be so bad if they got married. Dad's getting old—can you believe he's fifty-five? I mean he looks good and everything, he's in good health, but when you get old like that it's hell if you don't have somebody around all the time. It keeps you from going crazy. I mean I'd hate to have to put him away in a nursing home in a couple of years, right? I know he's not that old yet, but he's getting there. Another twenty years . . ."

Billy thought about what Bernie was saying. In another twenty years Henry would turn into a palsied, drooling seventy-five-year-old man. Bernie, in his early forties, would be busy with his own life—alimony payments, orthodontia for his kids (ugly little Goulds in miniature)—and he'd be too caught up with his lawsuits to nurse his feeble father. He'd have to stuff Henry in a nursing home. Unless Henry married Billy's mother, in which case Bernie'd be off the hook. Twenty years from now, Billy's mother would still be in her

137

wrinkled but chipper and energetic and kindly sixties. She could take care of Henry and all Bernie'd have to do would be to come uptown for dinner every couple of weeks and make small talk; advise Henry on his will. Billy would be in his late thirties. He tried to imagine himself at that age and had no idea what he would be like, what kind of person he would be, what kind of job he would hold, what kind of woman he would be married (probably unhappily) to. He could imagine paying a visit to his mother and stepfather, however: she, white-haired, varicose-veined; Henry, trembling in his wheelchair with a shawl wrapped around his knees, mumbling insanely to himself.

Across the table, Bernie was lighting an after-lunch cigarette. "So anyway, Billy," Bernie said, shaking the match until it was out, "what kind of courses are you taking?"

"An English course."

"You going to be an English major?"

"I don't know. Probably."

"Oh man. Don't make that mistake. Liberal arts are such bullshit. I was going to be an English major for a while, but I bagged it. I wound up doing political science, which is bullshit too, only less bad. And it helped me get into law school. But anyway, I don't want to discourage you or anything. Who's the teacher?"

"Professor Russo."

"That asshole? I had him for a course. He's terrible. He's like the worst teacher in that whole department."

Billy was going to say, "I don't think he's so bad," but decided to say nothing. For all he knew, Russo probably was the worst teacher in the department.

"The guy is such an asshole," Bernie went on, "I have no respect for him. I mean I used to know the guy pretty well. Actually I was better friends with his wife. She was a really hip woman. Finally it was too much for her. She split. Moved in with this other guy. I think she's in Europe now."

"Really?" Billy said. "How about that," he thought.

"You should have been here last year. It was like fucking Peyton Place. What other courses are you studying?"

"Economics . . ."

"Oh God," Bernie winced, as if to say "So predictable!" "That's a lot of bullshit . . ."

". . . And philosophy . . ."

"That's all right," Bernie said; "and what else?"

". . . And I'm trying to learn how to speak Chinese . . ."

"Far out!" Bernie said, delighted. He said a few sentences in Chinese, not a word of which Billy could interpret, then said, in English, "That's really far out of you, Billy. That's really aware. I've been studying Chinese off and on since high school. It's a really expressive language. And the society is so together. I mean the society in Red China really works. Like the educational system is so much better. Like you take a test, right? When you're twelve years old or something, and if you don't do well then that's it, you don't have to go to school anymore and they find something else for you to do. It's not like in America where every guy who doesn't have a job calls himself a student and wastes four years of his life learning a lot of uninteresting bullshit in a classroom. There's no waste. And if you fail the test, well that's cool, you don't feel bad or anything because being smart is like being tall over there, some guys are and some guys aren't and it doesn't make one person better than another. One guy's smart, the other guy's dumb but he's a good cook and makes terrific eggrolls. Everybody's happy and feels important. In China there's this whole joy-of-learning thing they're into. 'Let a thousand flowers bloom,'" Bernie quoted Mao's Red Book. "American education is really life-denying. It just makes you passive so when you get older you won't mind taking orders and you won't ask any questions. I'd really like to go to China someday. That's kind of my dream. Maybe teach law over there."

They sat and talked about China for a while, then Bernie poked the nub of his digital watch and said, "Christ, it's one-thirty. I've got a class." He rebuttoned his coat and rewound his scarf. Before he left Billy he said, "Look, feel free to call me if you need some advice, or if you just want to sit down with a friend and get your head clear."

While Billy was zipping his coat and hunching his shoulders, getting ready to push open the heavy wooden door out into the cold, he wondered, "'Get your head clear'? What did he mean by that?"

For most of the afternoon, Billy worried about some of the things Bernie had told him. All the courses he had signed up for were bullshit. His English teacher was bullshit, too, the worst in the department. Being an English major, as he had always assumed, albeit for no good reason, that he would be, was bullshit, too. Beacham was bullshit. Education was bullshit. America was bullshit, although China wasn't. Going to law school was bullshit, but making a lot of money once you were a lawyer was not bullshit.

Well, maybe Bernie was right.

At around three-thirty, sitting at his desk, Billy had an acute consciousness-of-existence attack. "What am I going to do with myself?" he asked himself. "I can't be an English major. That won't look good when I apply to law school." Up until that moment, Billy

140

had never even considered applying to law school. But he had already dropped biology, so he couldn't go to medical school. Or graduate school, because there weren't any jobs for teachers. He thought about going to law school some more and then realized that he probably wouldn't get into law school anyway. Too stupid. So what was he going to do when he ran out of college and his parents stopped paying for him? What kind of job could he get? Nothing physical because of his asthma. Besides, he was too uncoordinated, he'd screw everything up. He'd get another hernia. Maybe he could drive a cab, or a bus. Except all those jobs were already filled. Companies were laying off their workers left and right. They would never hire him over all the other men who were really unemployed and had eleven children to support. It wouldn't be fair and Billy wouldn't accept a job under those conditions.

"I suppose I could work as a waiter in a restaurant," Billy thought, "or deliver groceries." Suddenly it all seemed very near and very frightening. Responsibilities closing in. Big decisions to be made. Pretty soon he'd be too old and his mother would stop paying for him. She'd shut off his allowance and let him sink or swim.

Billy sat at his desk and brooded on the bleakness of his prospects. Career, family, kids, the whole process, life renewing its sickly self. He'd probably have some lousy job and be broke all the time and buy all the furniture in installments. He'd live in a slum neighborhood and probably have to marry a fat ugly woman because no slender, beautiful one was going to be interested in him. If only Grandma Louisa had been rich after all. Everybody had figured she was until she died and left behind, after taxes, $50,000, one-third of which the crazy old bat bequeathed to the dog pound, another third to her church, and the rest to Billy's father, who was her son, after all, so it was only fair. But the ditched daughter-in-law and grandchildren never got a dime.

A home, a garage, a mortgage, bank loans, phone bills, roaches all over everything, crawling out of the drains. His wife and her food budget, TV dinners, canned ravioli. Up to their ears in hock. Chicken maybe once a month. Maybe once every couple of weeks Billy could still call his mother up and she'd take him downtown to Schrafft's the way she used to when Billy was small.

Sweltering in the stinking apartment in August, taking the family to Jones Beach, stuck in traffic for three hours both ways, having to shell out ten dollars for parking, water full of sludge. On the way home his fat, ugly wife, uglier still with sunburn and peeling, wearing sunglasses and a scarf over her hair, her fat white legs spreading over the Naugahyde front seat. The kids in the back, his daughter, eleven years old, wearing blue eyeliner and red nail and toe polish, screaming and punching her brother in the back seat of the car. (And what car was this anyway? How was he going to be able to afford a car on $125 a week, a delivery boy's salary?) And he, meek little dad, keeling over at forty-five from a heart attack, providing for his family's well-being with a fat insurance policy.

"He was just a delivery boy," the reverend would say from the podium, Billy stretched out in his casket, wearing a new suit for the occasion, "but that doesn't begin to tell the whole story." Billy's mother, dressed in black for the funeral, and Abby in her mountain-climbing boots. And his father and his family, the three of them bleary with jet lag. And Henry.

"Oh hell," Billy thought.

15

"GOD, LIFE IS COMPLICATED. IT WAS SO MUCH SIM-
pler when I was little." But then he thought about it
some more, thought about what his life was like when
he was little, with his father going crazy in his apartment way downtown with the bums and his mother
going crazy in the old apartment on the West Side,
mostly in her room, taking pills and drinking behind
the closed door, and he decided, "No, it wasn't so great
when I was little, either. Thing's were pretty screwed
up back then, too, as I remember."

What it was like "back then" was still painfully
clear. He remembered how his mother tried to play
everything as normal: "Don't worry about me, I can
make it on my own . . . We don't need your father.
I'm perfectly . . . all right . . . Really." He remembered how she used to patrol the house in her furry
slippers, fixing breakfast, dressing Billy and Abby,
then sending Billy downstairs at ten minutes to eight
to await the yellow school bus which stopped in front
of the building; then, an hour later, slipping a coat over
her shoulders, often over her nightgown, she'd take
Abby to experimental kindergarten in a cab; then,
coming back home she'd shut the door behind her, in
the silence of a husbandless, temporarily kidless house,
and Billy imagined her letting slip—for all her courage—a groan of exhaustion, or a pained sigh. Home

from school, Billy would eat the tunafish sandwich she had made for him and covered with a membrane of Saran Wrap, drink chocolate milk which he made for himself, and he would hardly see her until dinnertime. She had become a gossamer-nightgowned figure, occasionally to be glimpsed through a crack in the bedroom door, propped up in bed, reading from enormous thousand-page or multivolumed books, like Painter's biography of Proust, or *The Collected Works of Sigmund Freud*.

Billy spent the days that followed working in the library. He took few breaks. He read his books, studied his notes; he practiced Chinese calligraphy until his hands shook and he could no longer control the pen. His fingers slipped, and the character for "moon" became the character for "bean sprouts." He steadied himself, put pen and paper to the side, sighed and opened up Spenser's *Faerie Queene,* which of the several books he had tried to read for Professor Russo had him buffaloed the worst. He couldn't figure out two consecutive stanzas of the stuff.

The weekend came and went without Billy's noticing. It was Tuesday evening, around dusk, when he got the letter his father had sent him. The post office was closing, the janitor was getting ready to lock the doors for the night when Billy got there. Wedged inside his mailbox was a yellow, manila packet, the kind with a metal clasp. Inside was a letter and a copy of a magazine called *The Sequoia Review: a magazine of the arts.*

Dear old Billy Goat,
　　Hope this letter finds you busy and well, your mind expanding, your awareness growing. These are good years. The young years. I am enclosing

my latest story hoping that you will read it and enjoy it. It is about fathers and sons, generations, and people trying to cope, generally. I suppose you could say it is about LIFE. All in all, things go well out here, the campus dull but the life rewarding just the same. Kind of a mellow time. Reflective. Grace and Charles send their love to you, as do I.

POP

Billy turned to the contents page of the magazine and scanned the list until his eyes fastened on his father's name. Sure enough:

HARK! The Pterodactyl, a new story by Eric Williams 12

He ate dinner first, declining Randy's and Pete's invitation to go to a bar and get drunk, saying he had work to do. He got around to reading his father's story lying in bed that night a little before midnight.

HARK! THE PTERODACTYL!

The narrator is in Chinatown, a guest at a party in honor of Buddha. Buddha's a good fellow to those who know him, but a little pompous. You could say he's got charisma.

Buddha assumes this form and that form—a camel for one instance, a toad for another, as does the narrator, each competing with the other in originality and speed of transformation. At this moment in time, Kierkegaard appears to sort things out, restore the lost order. Kierkegaard's dentures are in sorry shape and need repair. The narrator, moved by suffering, becomes a dentist, a switch which takes the Buddha by surprise and throws him off. Way off, but not, as they say, for

145

long. For Buddha, fat and reclining as he is and much resembling a couch or chair, transforms his skin to the substance of imitation leather and so serves as Kierkegaard's dentist's chair. Buddha's chubby fingers double as the dentist's tools, his thumb, the drill, his index finger, the novocaine syringe.

The next day, a Sunday, the narrator goes out by himself for his testimonial and meets Richard Nixon, sticking up the liquor store on the corner of 116th Street and Amsterdam Ave. His henchmen are several other Kierkegaards, H.R. Bob Kierkegaard (The Brush), Jeb Stuart Kierkegaard, John (The Big Enchilada) Kierkegaard, Howard Kierkegaard Hughes. To punish them, the narrator pulls their teeth which he strings together as Voo-Doo. (Hint: "Hoodoo the Voodoo man.")

Back home, Jesus Christ is back from church, first in his infant, and later in his adult manifestations. Buddha wheels him down the boulevard in a baby carriage.

Christ, Buddha and several other ancients like Helogabulus take part in a race. Buddha wins handily on the principle of total inertia. Jesus Christ, the odds-on favorite, had the race in the bag, but unfortunately he ran afoul at the Soviet-Red China border to catch a night owl as a love token for the narrator.

Sadly, the world learns that Kierkegaard has died. He is buried with Mrs. Nixon, not Pat, but The Saint. There are signs, scratching earth, muffled, inhuman growling that the two are trying to dig their way out. In due course mole hills appear on the way to Prague, indicating that the process is under way.

The narrator mourns. He continues to assume other forms. He becomes an English school-girl, whose nanny reveals herself to be Kierkegaard's long-lost mother. "I don't believe it," the narrator says. Lonely, abandoned by Mrs. Nixon, spurned by Brezhnev and the Czechs, Kierkegaard marches to London to see his mother one last time before she expires. He is so crazed, so torn by Oedipal mixed feelings that he nips her breast with the dentures. Mother K. gasps and falls to the floor, spurting blood like a geyser.

"I have reached her heart," Kierkegaard laments, "too late. Damn." The narrator realizes that the dentures are still clamped to the withering woman's breasts and the offenders are pried off in the emergency room of the hospital. The offenders do a clattering, chattering castanet dance on the newly waxed floor. Kierkegaard and the narrator are thrown out. Police come to interrogate the woman, alleging several perpetrations.

Later, we get a glimpse of Kierkegaard as a boy, digging up a radish. The radish turns out to be his own head (Get it? Ed.) who turns Kierkegaard in for grave robbing.

Then Kierkegaard enters a hospital for treatment, having mastered the secret of life. "The secret of life is to get through it," he confides in a friend. A spell in an old folks' home follows and Kierkegaard keeps fit by forwarding the causes of those advanced in years.

Klugemeyer, lying in the void, has been working along similar lines. He, however, predicts a dangerous uprising of the old, a 1000-year-old Reich. He consults Tarot cards and calculates the rise of the old, but their eventual downfall, due to death and dying, but their ultimate triumph and glorious vindication.

Klugemeyer, an eccentric, writes his works at the bottom of the sea. He ignores Kierkegaard, who undergoes a sobering weakening of faith, and is forced to recant and annul everything.

Kierkegaard's doctor sums up the rest of the story. "It vass hiss desire to enrich der voild," he says.

Billy read the story, shook his head clear, then started reading it again. "This is a little like *The Faerie Queene*," it occurred to him.

When he had finished reading the story through this second time, Billy found himself alarmed, hot, sweating. He was certain his father had started taking hallucinogenic drugs again.

Billy reached across and turned out the light, rolled over, buried his face in his pillow and tried to go to sleep.

16

BILLY LAY IN BED FOR WHAT SEEMED LIKE A LONG
time. He lay there, on his back then on his stomach,
then on his side until his arm fell asleep. On the pillow, without the pillow. In the dark, his eyes were still
open as the midnight chapel bell went off—twelve
gongs—"If I don't hurry up and get to sleep, I'm going to be dead to the world all day tomorrow," he
thought. He had set the alarm clock for 6:30 the next
morning. His professor was giving a big quiz on Monday on the last five chapters of the economics textbook. Billy had studied the first three of those five
chapters but he still had two left, fifty pages of charts
and graphs, supply and demand curves and profit
margins to read, re-read, and underline when something seemed important, or didn't make any sense.
And he lay there, his mind still going when the bell
went off again—one gong—one in the morning. "It's
one already? I've got to get to sleep!"

Insomnia. He was exhausted, but his mind was still
jumping. Bits of everything, nothing making any sense.
Memories of his childhood. It was like a dance floor,
jazzy music being played, Chinese characters with big
white cartoon eyes dancing swing-time with each other,
supply and demand curves writhing and swaying and
waving their rubbery arms around, figures from his
boyhood—his mother of course, his sister, his stepfather, his father, his stepmother, his old teachers,

enemies from school in a long, happy conga line, hands on the hips of whoever was in front, snaking through a crowd of stiff knights in armor and ladies in long gowns, characters from Spenser's *Faerie Queene,* who had no idea what was going on, and just stood around confused. Walt Disney presents: Billy the Teenager in "Going Nuts." An all-new animated feature.

The radiator was hissing and clanking. The alarm clock was humming. And through the walls came the beat of music from Simon King's record player across the hall. A guitar playing like a locomotive interspersed with piano. Then, a smoky black voice:

> *"Who's the black private dick that's a sex machine to all the chicks?"*

CHORUS: *"Shaft!"*

> *"Damn right . . . Who is the man who would risk his life for his brother man?"*

CHORUS: *"Shaft!"*

> *"Can you dig it? . . . Who's the cat that won't cop out/When there's danger all about?"*

CHORUS: *"Shaft!"*

> *"Right on! . . . They say this cat Shaft is a bad mother—"*

CHORUS:
(cuts him
off): *"Shut your mouth!"*

> *"But I'm talkin about Shaft!"*

CHORUS: *"We can dig it!"*

> *"He's a complicated man,/But no one understands him but his woman . . ."*

CHORUS: *"John Shaft!"*

More tommy-gun guitar until fade-out in a triumphant organ hum.

"How many times is that guy going to play the same song?" Billy said out loud. Simon King had played the song five times in a row. There was silence for a moment, just the hum of the clock, then the song began once more, a steam locomotive pounding down the rails at high speed.

When Billy's father left New York for California, he took a train. Like Woody Guthrie. Probably hanging around with all those hoboes on the Bowery gave him the idea. Being free and easy, having no ties, no responsibilities. He'd said that he'd gotten a commission from some travel magazine to write an article about traveling across the country by train. He never wrote the article and got in big trouble with the magazine, which had paid for his train tickets, and he never came back East, back home. Never. He stayed in California. He was thirty-seven years old, busting loose.

Other than his family (which apparently wasn't much of a magnet) there was nothing to hold him. He realized after he'd worked for fifteen months for Father Fergus and the bums, that what he had done to himself and to his family was totally ridiculous. He kept his little apartment downtown after he quit because Billy's mother didn't want him back (well, sometimes she did, sometimes she didn't—it was complicated, she said). He went back to his old campus and tried to apologize to the head of the department, Mr. Bloomberg, who, instead of being happy to hear from him, Billy's father said to Billy's mother, "tried to humiliate me. He tried to make an ass out of me." Billy never found out what Mr. Bloomberg had said. He couldn't get his old job back. He was out of a job and running out of money, trying to write another novel, so Billy could understand now, years later, why his father had left, although he hadn't understood at the time.

Things might have worked out down on the Bowery. Billy's father often called up on the phone and told him how he was doing, and how some of the bums were being rehabilitated. He talked about them very fondly, very fatherly. "Do you remember Mr. Schwartzbach, Billy? The one I was telling you about who lost all his money in the stock market crash? Remember you met him once, the old man with the beard? Well he had to go to the hospital last week and we were very worried about him, but he's back with us now and he says he's never going to drink another drop of whiskey as long as he lives. That's wonderful news, don't you think? I hope he sticks to it, don't you?" Yes, Billy did. He, alone, not his sister who was too young, and certainly not his mother who was seeing a psychiatrist and not making much sense, and who was very angry with Billy's father anyhow; only he, Billy alone, took an interest in what his father was up to. He got very interested in his father's stories about the bums he was trying to help. He knew most of their names, what they looked like, what they used to do before they became bums.

And then one day Mr. Schwartzbach pick-pocketed Billy's father and spent a week in a motel across the bridge in New Jersey spending $500 on liquor, paying for everything with a stolen Master Charge card. Father Fergus urged Billy's father not to press charges against the old bum. Schwartzbach apologized, vowed to pay back every penny, he was sorry, he'd lost his head. But by this time, Billy's father had had enough and he tried to put the bum in jail, but Schwartzbach got off because "the old guy got some shifty lawyer from Legal Aid."

After that, Billy's father couldn't go back to work.

He told Billy he would never be able to "reestablish lines of meaningful communication."

Billy's father frequently invited Billy down weekends to stay with him in the apartment and keep him company. They went out for walks, spent afternoons together sitting on benches, talking, sometimes watching some of the old bums in the neighborhood arguing or snoozing on the sidewalk or just wandering around. Once Billy's father took him to a street corner where they saw the bums earning drinking money, waiting for cars to stop at streetlights where they would stumble over and threaten to wipe the front windshields with rags so dirty that the drivers paid them off with quarters so as to avoid having their windows gunked up with filth and snot and grease. Billy remembered his father telling him that some of the bums used to wipe the rags in dogshit first before they started work. He, Billy's father, had cracked down on that. But now that he was gone, who could tell what was going on. "Father Fergus spends his whole day in his office, behind a desk. He doesn't know what the hell is going on out here . . ." Not once did any of the bums come over to say anything, to ask Billy's father how he was getting along, what he was doing. They were giving him, he said, "the silent treatment." Billy suffered for his father the times when they would pass one of the winos, one of the filthy, stinking old creeps to whom his father had been very kind, whom his father had tried to help, and his father would say, "Hello, Ed," or "Jeff," or "Sam," and the bum would avert his eyes, wouldn't say anything back, pretending he didn't exist.

"It's like they've got a union," Billy remembered his father telling him once.

"What's a union?" Billy had asked. He was the only kid in his first-grade class who knew what a union was. He remembered that Miss Butterworth was very impressed when she asked if anyone knew what a union was, and Billy raised his hand and answered her. And how did he know? His father had told him. But then his father went away to California, got a job teaching creative writing, got remarried. And Billy never surprised his teachers with the things he knew after that. Year after year, he was one of the dumbest kids in the class. Remedial reading, remedial math, almost remedial fifth grade. They told him if he didn't go to summer school, if his mother didn't shell out a thousand dollars so he could get special help, they would make him go through fifth grade all over again.

It was 1965 when Billy's father left for good. For the next couple of years he only telephoned, always cutting short the conversations before they got started, with "I've got to get off, Billy, this is going to cost a fortune. Let me just say a word to your sister . . ." He wrote letters for Billy's birthday. Billy had practically forgotten all about him until he was thirteen or fourteen and got interested in him again (no doubt in adolescent reaction to his mother, whom he decided he hated at that time). In 1967, Billy and his sister flew out to California to see their father marry one of his students. She was a quiet girl with round metal glasses, who held on to a bouquet of flowers, wore a red-checked gingham dress that reached all the way to the ground, with just her bare toes sticking out. A few days later, back home, Billy told his mother that he thought his father's new wife was "strange looking." Billy remembered that she had baked the wedding cake herself. It was crunchy and had a lot of nuts in it. It was made with honey and granola.

Grace meditated and wrote mystical poetry, samples of which Billy's father had sent to his old family back East printed up as obscure holiday greetings, as Christmas cards. And once, along with a letter from his father and a new masterwork by his stepmother,

Billy found a photograph, clipped from the *Marin County Alternative,* a small California newspaper. The photograph was gray and grainy and it was hard to make out what it was a picture of. But after looking at it a little closer, and under a light, Billy could see the photograph showed two people sandwiching a huge, gray bulk which Billy determined was the trunk of a tree. Closer inspection revealed his father's balding head on one side of the tree trunk and a glint of metal granny glasses led Billy to assume that somehow his parents and this tree had made the newspapers. At first he was very excited and wanted to run off immediately to show his mother, but he knew that even just mentioning his father to her could make his mother mad. In the end, he was glad he had curbed his enthusiasm.

He studied the photograph some more and saw that his father and stepmother had joined hands around the tree, to create a ring of human arms, as if they were each hugging the wood, one on each side. The caption below explained a little of what was going on:

"EMBRACING NATURE"

And hidden within the folds of his father's letter, which he had not as yet opened to read, Billy found a second clipping, the accompanying story. His parents were protesting "the rape of the forests by unscrupulous lumber operations." The tree was going to be cut down by some lumberjacks and Billy's parents had been handcuffed together, creating "a protective shield of human flesh" around the tree. The protest, it appeared, was symbolic. An entire forest of hardwoods, of which the tree in the photograph was only a part, had been bought by a conglomerate with vast holdings in the building industry, and they wanted to chop down the trees immediately and put up some houses and make some money.

Billy's father and his father's wife were not protesting all by themselves. According to the article, several other sympathetic couples joined hands around different trees. The story said that the brave crusaders were joined each day and night of their three-day vigil by concerned townspeople and friends who brought baskets of food, sang "All We Are Saying Is Give Trees a Chance," trying to drown out the shrieking chainsaws. "Tuesday morning," the article stated, "Mr. Williams's students hitchhiked down from the State University campus and gave public readings of their recent work."

As an addendum to this story, the newspaper printed that on the morning of May 11, 1969, the third and final day of the protest, the lumberjacks had come along with bulldozers, ignoring the protesters and their chants and placards, and chopped down every tree in the forest except for those protected by Billy's father, his wife, and their friends. When the work was done, the trees felled and dynamited and loaded up onto flatbed trucks, the lumberjacks ignored the boos from the crowd and went home. Handcuffs were unlocked, everybody went home, except for Billy's father, who stayed around to have an interview with the reporter from the paper. Billy's father told the reporter that he thought his actions had been of great "symbolic importance" and that he hoped that "what we have done here today will be an example to people that they can make a difference, that they must stand up now, before it's too late, that they can change the world, that they can put a halt to some of the stuff that's coming down if they want to." Then there was some stuff about the Vietnam war.

Billy was old enough to know that his mother, for

156

everybody's sake, should not be shown the newspaper clippings. It wouldn't do her any good.

"Oh that fool!" she would say, "he is making the worst fool of himself." She wouldn't understand. So when she asked Billy what his father had had to say in the letter that had arrived that morning, Billy had replied, "nothing much."

THE LAST TIME THAT BILLY HEARD THE CHAPEL BELL go off that night, it was 2:00. He didn't sleep very long before he had to get up again, but he did have time to have a bad dream.

It started with him at the bottom of a rickety staircase, watching a girl climbing up. He watched her, his heart pounding, not wanting to be seen, watched to see what she would do, where she would go. She reached the landing, opened a door, went inside. "I shouldn't be doing this," Billy told himself, "but . . ." And he climbed upstairs, following her.

The room was dimly lit, except for a crisscrossing set of winking Christmas lights. There was music playing, long, low notes from a clarinet. The room was crowded with girls, beautiful girls like fashion models in glamour magazines. They were gliding and sashaying around the room as if they were modeling clothes, their faces made up, painted, gleaming, shiny, their gowns swirling about their legs as they turned around, like graceful sailboats coming about on a quiet lake. A girl drifted past, skin tanned dark and oily, like wood stain, or mahogany, as if she had spent Christmas vacation in the Bahamas. Billy recognized her.

"Hi," he said, "how are you?"

Her name, he remembered, was Christine Kelly and he had seen her picture in a copy of *Penthouse* magazine that Randy had bought and left lying around the room. Christine Kelly. How his eyes had devoured her photograph, how many times, her lovely arms and legs and breasts, spread out between his legs, her skin the color of quicksand, his bare feet cold on the bathroom tiles as hotness grew. And spread. She had been photographed in blue underwear and silk stockings, lying on a bed looking sleepy and gentle and fertile. He had sat there on the toilet, late at night, pushing and pulling, his eyes sweeping over her slender, naked limbs and skin. "I love you," he had declared, ". . . I love you . . . Oh God, you are so beauti . . . ful . . ."

And here now, in this dream, she stood before him. In the magazine she had responded to the question of what turned her on the most, by saying "I suppose you could say I have a fetish for boots and shoes. High boots especially make me feel wicked and dominating, like a lion tamer." Billy wanted to ask her a few questions about that. It also said that she was trying to launch a singing career in the Lake Tahoe area. What was she doing on the East Coast? At Beacham? Billy wanted to ask her how she was getting along, whether she'd met any big producers, was having any luck. He wanted to be friendly and to talk to her, to warn her that a beautiful girl like her had better be careful. There were a lot of creeps and hustlers around, men who would use her, take advantage of her, not appreciate her. She needed looking after, he thought. Of course she probably knew how to take care of herself. Judging by the way she was looking at him, sneering at him, hands cocked on her hips. He tried to think of something to say to her.

"So," she said, "we meet again, eh, Billy? Only this time things are a little different. The ball's in my court, wouldn't you say." She looked at him sarcastically and bulged her left cheek with her tongue.

"Uh-oh," Billy thought, "she's mad about something."

"Well I'm glad to have this chance, Billy, to really tell you what I think of you. I think you're the lowest kind of person, you know that? The lowest of the low. You're sick, you're disgusting. You need help."

"Hey, Christine, who's that you're talking to?" The girl Billy had followed in the first place, the girl who had gotten him into this mess, reappeared. It was Zizi. "Oh," she said, when she recognized him, "how did you get in here?"

"I just came up the stairs," Billy said, hoping she wouldn't press it. Other girls, distracted from their gliding, came over to rubbberneck the confrontation. The clarinet stopped.

"All right, you know, so what? So fucking what?" Christine went on, talking loudly. Billy wondered if she was drunk. ". . . So maybe I did pose for those pictures. I needed the money. I couldn't get any gigs. I was broke. Tahoe's deadsville. No one goes there anymore. So is that a crime? Does that make me somehow less of a person? Does that give this little creep the right to jerk off all over me?"

"Oh no," Billy cringed, "not so loud, not in front of Zizi. Have a heart."

". . . and I had to lie there and pretend to like it. I had to keep smiling, looking sexy. But not anymore. I'm through with that cheesecake bullshit now. Yes sir, you better believe it."

"Kick his butt," one of the black girls called out from the back of the crowd.

"Give it to him, Christine," said another. But Christine just shuddered with haughtiness and revulsion and said, "You gross me out." She spat on him and turned away. The other girls stayed where they were, they wouldn't break up, staring at him, talking and muttering among themselves, buzzing angrily like a lynch mob, or a swarm of bees.

"Come on, girls. Don't worry about Billy," Zizi said, "he's nothing to get worked up about. There're bigger fish to fry." She started pushing the crowd apart and broke them up. Before she went off, Zizi looked at Billy, shook her head as if to say, "I don't understand you, Billy. I don't know why you do the things you do sometimes. It's like you just ask for it."

"Whoooo . . ." Randy made a ghost sound. A girl tittered. Zizi? "Billy? Hey, Bill . . . You asleep?"

"What?" Billy raised his head slowly off the pillow, his eyes bleary, glued together with sleep. He drew a deep breath in through his nostrils. "What time is it?" he asked.

"It's uh . . . Saturday night already. You slept through the whole day. I wanted to get you up for dinner. Thought you might be hungry."

"What?" Billy sat up in bed. The girl couldn't control herself and started to laugh.

"Come on, Randy. Don't be mean to him."

"Okay, naw, it's only around three." Billy could see them both in the gray light. The lights were on brightly in the outer room and shone through the open door.

"Why'd you wake me up?" The girl giggled again.

"Carol wanted to meet you . . ."

"I did not! . . ." Carol hit Randy on the arm with a slap denoting mock outrage.

160

"Hey cut it out, willya?" Billy rubbed his eyes. There was a confusing silence.

"So anyway, did my dad call tonight?"

"No."

"Randy, come on. Let's just leave him alone. We can go somewhere else."

"Yeah, okay. Sorry, Billy. Look, go back to sleep. Didn't mean to wake you up."

"No problem. Goodnight," Billy said. What did they mean, they didn't mean to wake him up? They just walked in and started talking to him. What did they mean to do?

"Nice to meet you," said Carol. She pulled the door shut behind her.

"Well that didn't work," Billy could hear Randy saying through the door, "now what are we going to do?" Billy listened to their conversation until he fell asleep. Carol noticed Randy's stereo and said "Oh wow! Is that yours or your roommate's?"

Randy said it was his and gave her the rundown on the list of features.

"See this? This is the pre-amp," he said.

"What's the pre-amp do?" And Billy listened while Randy explained.

"So that's what that thing does," he thought to himself. It was very interesting.

They played Stevie Wonder records for a while. Randy talked over the singing, talking solemnly about his father.

"That must be so tough for you," Carol sympathized.

"Boy, Randy's gonna get her," Billy thought. After that he fell asleep.

"Hey, Billy. You still awake?"

"No . . . I mean, yeah. Now I am. What do you want?"

"I got sort of a favor to ask you."

"What is it?"

"Carol wants to stay here tonight." Was that all? It was fine as far as Billy was concerned. He'd try not to wake her when he got up early to start reading economics. He'd just leave her alone, snoozing on the couch. Did she want to borrow a pair of pajamas? That was all right with him, too.

"Mind if I turn on the lights?" And before Billy could say anything the light was on. He visored his light-shy eyes with his hand.

"So is it okay with you if Carol stays here?"

"It's fine. I don't mind at all."

"Good. Great. Thanks, man." Randy went over to the door.

"See you in the morning," Billy said.

"Wait a minute. No, you don't get it. If Carol's gonna sleep in here, then you can't, you see."

"Oh. Where do you want me to go?" A hotel? This late? Who was going to pay?

"Just sleep on the couch in the living room. You know, take your pillow and blanket and stuff. Just for this one night. Carol has to be back at Fritter in the morning . . ." Fritter College was a two-year girl's college situated in a town ten miles to the east of Beacham. The girls who attended this college didn't have much to do while they were there, so they were always getting picked up by the more gregarious Beacham boys, in student bars and at mixers, even on the street. "You don't mind, do you?"

"No." Well, there really wasn't much of a choice. It would have been too complicated to say he didn't want to move. "Just a minute. Let me get my pillow . . ." (A few weeks earlier the package had finally arrived from Bloomingdale's with the big, fluffy non-allergenic pillow. Before the pillow had arrived, Billy

162

had improvised, stuffing sweaters and sheets and underwear into the pillowcase and sleeping on that.)

"Hey, take a blanket too. The heat's off and it's cold as a bitch tonight. Might snow somebody told me ... Hey, Carol," he called.

"Yeah," Carol called back, as if she had just been waiting to see how negotiations would proceed, just sitting there, reading a magazine. She looked up. "Yeah, Randy?"

"It might snow tonight. Didn't we hear that?"

"We heard it on the radio . . ." Well, that was proof enough. Billy walked into the living room with his pillow under his arm and his blanket wrapped around him like a toga.

"Goodnight, Billy," Carol sang sweetly before she closed the door, "sleep well. See you in the morning."

Billy lay down on the sofa and tried to put his bed together. He flopped the blanket toward his feet. He set his head back on the pillow and sighed. It was brightly moonlit outside the window, and for a while he gazed out at the navy-blue sky, and at the hulking chapel bell tower, clock face glowing at him from across the quadrangle. It looked very impressive just then. It would have looked attractive in the pictorial catalogue of the school, he thought. There was little else to admire other than the sky and bell tower. No snow as yet. The living room was cold and dark, except for a crack of yellow light shining out from underneath the bedroom door. And he could hear them within, quiet at first, then giggling, and squirming, then shoes hitting the floor. And soon it was worse.

What is that door made out of? Plywood? Oh this is awful. It's just like at home, with Mom and Henry. At that moment, he would have made, if he could, all casual sex a capital offense. For one thing, it was discriminatory against the shy and the ugly. For another, it was going to keep him awake.

163

So he spent the remaining few hours until daybreak in the closet. It was warm in there and quiet. He thought the hard floor would be good for his back. He found the closet door in the dark, pulled on the light string. There before him were all his roommate's clothes, jackets, and overcoats, smelling of camphor mothballs. Randy's blue suit had slipped off the rack and slumped to the floor. Helpfully Billy put it back. In one corner of the closet Randy had tossed his dirty laundry, old handkerchiefs and socks, a mud-stained sweatshirt from playing touch football in the rain. Also a towel stained with maroon blotches of blood from the morning a few weeks before when Randy had cut himself shaving. And in another corner, against the back wall of the closet, was Randy's golf stuff—his golf bag and clubs, and arranged neatly on the floor were the golf shoes with the spikes. Billy threw down the pillow and blanket after roughly clearing the floor for himself. He turned off the light and pulled the door closed, but not all the way. He didn't want to get locked inside. Randy and his girl friend were probably drunk. They'd wake up sober and realize, "Hey, Billy spent last night in the closet. What a good sport that little guy is!"

The dust from the floor excited his asthma—he must have sucked whole dust balls right down his windpipe and he could only sleep for two or three hours before the clog of his wheezing woke him up. Nevertheless he did sleep for a while. Beneath Randy's ski parka and dry cleaning, even cuddling one of his roommate's golf shoes, Billy managed to get some sleep.

Sometime during the night, a necktie slipped off the bar and fell down on his head.

18

THERE WERE MOMENTS THAT MORNING, WHEN BILLY, struggling to breathe, feared he was going to die. "Oh," he drew in breath, ". . . God." He crawled out of the closet on his hands and knees, then sat in the middle of the room. Morning outside the window was a freezing blue velvet. The air passed through his clenched lungs, went in and came back out in long, involuntary groans. He sat on the floor and thought about the trouble he was in.

About twice a year he came down with bronchitis —the doctor called it bronchitis, his mother called it "his condition." He knew it was asthma. It struck so regularly that Dr. Prothero had prescribed medicines for him to take with him everywhere. He made a special "crisis package"—antibiotics, epinephrine, steroid cortisone inhalants—to carry around and ward off death during April and August, those months when the disease struck, regular as clockwork. But this particular attack was five months early. It was only November. His conventional weaponry—some pills and a spray he could shoot down his throat like oil squirted on seized-up gears to free the mechanism—were in his dresser drawer and his dresser was in his bedroom and in the bedroom was Randy with the girl he had brought back.

What, he wondered incongruously, would he do in bed with a girl if he had an asthma fit?

"God—what's the matter with you?" she would ask, alarmed, "your chest is making all these funny sounds. You look like you're dying or something."

"Yes—hee—well—nothing to—hee—worry about. Don't worry—hee. I've never—hee—failed to sur —hee—vive an attack yet—gasp—hee. Of course, there's always a—hee—first time—ha, ha—gasp. I'll be—hee—all right—once they—hee—get me in the —hee—oxygen tent—hee." His lungs whistled and wheezed at every inhale and exhale as he squeezed air from them, then drew new air in, heavy as sucking liquid.

He couldn't barge in and get his medicine. He was going to have to go to the hospital. That was all there was to it. Except what was he going to do about clothes? All his clothes were hanging neatly in his closet or sitting in his chest of drawers. All his clothes were in the bedroom.

"Reaally—hee—" he thought, for even his thoughts had fallen into the rhythm of his wheezing, "this is— hee—hopeless." What was he going to do? Go to the hospital in his underwear? Wearing the blanket like a poncho? Cut a hole in the middle? "Oh—heee—for Christ's sake." What had he done to deserve this? Why did things always have to get worse, never better? "Why—hee—is this happening—hee—to me—hee? Why am I—hee—dying—hee—here?" He thought about Job and human suffering. People starved to death, were tortured, mugged, robbed, their kids were kidnapped, their houses burned down. Life was miserable. Millions and millions of Jobs. It wasn't fair at all. "Calm down—hee," he told himself, "think of what to do . . ." and then, "no—hee. I'm sick of this—hee. I'm sick of taking—hee—this. God—hee—I've had enough now. You've kicked—hee—me around long— hee—enough. If you want me to have any confidence —hee—in you, then give me a break. Give me—hee

—a sign. Let's not play—hee—games. Cause you're going to drive me over to the—hee—devil in a minute." It was a bluff of course, but a chance he would have to take.

Billy found some clothes in Randy's closet. They were dirty and way too large—a pair of itchy trousers, a pair of loafers that slipped off his feet as he walked, slow as an old arthritic, down the stairs.

The sun silvered the horizon. It was a little after six and the cold air was like a knife, slashing at his lungs, no easier to breathe, but hurting. He could hardly tell if he was walking in the right direction. He was so weak and tired and sick that he could hardly walk. He was so sick he could hardly breathe. All his faculties were quitting on him one at a time. He was going to collapse in a minute and be found around nine when someone on his way to breakfast would recognize him.

"Hey, isn't that Billy Williams curled up on the ground?" Stone cold. Dead.

Then, crossing DeWitt Street, he saw a police car parked against the curb halfway down the block. The light was on in the interior. There was a policeman inside.

"Hey—" But he lacked the breath to shout. His lungs were so clenched that no words came out. Just gasps. So he put his head down, looked down at the pavement, at his feet as they made steps, counting off to himself, "In a hundred steps, I'll be there . . . one . . . two . . . three . . ."

The cop took his sweet time refolding his newspaper and setting it down on the front seat of the patrol car, then rolled down his window after Billy rapped on the glass.

"I've got to—" he gasped, "go—hee—to the hos—hee—pital." It was all Billy could say. He swooned and had to brace himself against the police car.

167

"Hold on there, son." The cop reached behind him and swung open the rear door for Billy to slip in. The cop started the engine. He lifted his radio transmitter off its hook and pressed down on the red lever on the side.

"All right, this is car six ninety—over . . ."

"Go ahead six ninety—over."

"This is Sergeant Rankin. I've got a sick kid . . . something's wrong with him, taking him over to the Beacham infirmary—over." Billy sat behind a wire grill which caged him off from Sergeant Rankin in the front. He had never been in a police car before, although he had seen a thin black man get arrested, the handcuffs slapped on him, then led by two tough-looking detectives to sit between them in the back seat of the police car, behind the wire grill, taking him down to the precinct house to be booked. The black man had tried to hold up a grocery store around the corner from where Billy lived. It had been Billy's turn to walk the dog the night of all the action.

"You're going to the university hospital, am I right?" the policeman asked, looked at Billy through the rear-view mirror before putting the car into gear. Billy nodded, then gasped.

"Yes please."

"So—what are you studying over there at the university?" the cop wanted to know as the car raced through the streets of Beacham, the siren whooping, piercing the dawn still of the college town.

A nurse came out to the squad car and helped Billy into a wheelchair. She wheeled him up a ramp, through some glass doors that swung open electronically. She wheeled him into an examining room to wait for fifteen minutes, to watch the thin second hand of an electric clock glide smoothly past the numbers. Finally the doctor came along, in an open white coat, with a tongue depressor and a stethoscope. He listened to Billy's wheezing. The stethoscope was cold against his back and chest:

"That's terrible. My God, you should hear yourself," the doctor said, "you got mucus, all kinds of crud down there . . . What have you been doing?" He smiled, as if it all wasn't so serious, he got a big kick out of kids, he was having some fun. He had on thick glasses. Ash hair, speckle-backed toady hands. Big yellow teeth, robust gums. He shook his head. "Well, don't worry. We'll fix you up," he said and disappeared for ten minutes more.

"He's probably looking up what to do in his medical encyclopedia," Billy muttered. The doctor came back and brought the nurse carrying a syringe on a white towel in a white pan. He asked Billy to roll up his sleeve, took the needle and administered the shot, saying, "That should do the trick, loosen up those old tubes," in a very jaunty way that inspired no confidence whatsoever. The skin where the needle had gone in swiftly swelled up and itched, a little red button.

"I think we better keep you here for the next couple of days. Keep you quiet, rested. You'll be over this in time for vacation." Thanksgiving vacation started Wednesday. Five days in the hospital. The nurse wheeled him to the elevator and then to a sunny room on the fifth floor of the hospital. There were three beds in the room; one was empty, the remaining one had a black kid sleeping in it, his leg in a plaster cast like a big white bootie, suspended in traction.

"Maybe you've heard of your new roommate," the nurse said, indicating the bed with the boy with the broken leg lying in it. "That's John Bokku. Do you know who he is?"

"No," Billy shook his head.

"He's the great soccer star. Leading scorer on the team. He's out for the season now. A bus ran over his

169

foot. It's a shame. The big game's today and he can't play in it." The nurse left after drawing the curtains across the window by Billy's bed. She said there were some pajamas in the locker, then she went out. Billy slept until five o'clock that afternoon.

Billy stayed in the hospital until Friday. He called his mother and told her he would be unable to get home in time for Thanksgiving dinner. She was disappointed, she said, so he said that if he felt well enough he'd try to take the train home and spend the weekend.

"Oh that would be wonderful, darling," she said.

It wasn't half bad in the hospital, just lying there, resting, feeling sick and feverish and wheezy and not having to do anything. He didn't care that he would have to take a make-up quiz in economics, or that his other assignments and studies had all outdistanced him. He was sick. He couldn't think about it. Had to concentrate on getting well, that was the important thing. He put Professors Russo and Fong far from his mind and thought instead about other things. He talked to the soccer star sometimes, although John Bokku was feeling pretty low. The team lost the big game that Saturday afternoon, 8–2. After the game some of Bokku's friends from the team came over and sat around his bed. Some of them wandered over and talked to Billy and looked at his fever chart on the clipboard fastened to the end of the hospital bed.

"Hey, Jerry, come here and look at this. This guy has a 105-degree temperature."

"No shit. Hey man, what's wrong with you?"

"I had a bronchial infection, but I'm getting over it." The soccer players had a great time wising off to the nurses and cranking the beds up and down. Randy came to visit one day and brought over Billy's clothes. He sat by Billy's bedside on a metal chair and acted just like the relative of someone who was dying, trying to make small talk, but unable to think of anything to say.

"Got a fucking C on my math test . . ."

"Oh yeah?"

"Yeah, fucking bastard dicked me, you know."

"Yeah, too bad."

"Hey, anything you need?"

"No, I'm okay."

"Books or something?"

"Yeah, you could bring me that Chinese book if you get a chance."

"Sure thing," Randy said, but he never brought the book.

Billy talked to the young interns on the floor. They were all very impressed with his high temperature. One of the interns, named Biff, talked to Billy for about an hour in the coffee lounge at the end of the hall. They talked about asthma, Biff saying that as far as he was concerned, asthma was a psychological disease rather than a physical one.

"The suffering is physical. And I don't want you to think I'm saying it's not a very dangerous condition, because it is, very. But studies really bear me out on this, that chronic asthma is induced by stressful situations. It's repressed rage, really, that's all it is." And after their talk, Biff took Billy walking around the hospital in his floppy white pajamas that were at least three sizes too large, down to the third floor to the in-patient library where Biff showed him several texts about asthma and bronchitis and the latest pulmonary research with regard to psychosomatic complications.

"Can I take this upstairs with me?" Billy asked. It was a book about diseases, a pictorial encyclopedia with pictures of people with elephantiasis and skin cancer and Silver's syndrome and cleft palate and asthma. The pictures were fascinating. Biff said, "Sure, go ahead," and Billy spent most of the next two days familiarizing himself with all the sicknesses. It was a lot more interesting than *The Faerie Queene* or any of that other boring crap. It was better than *People* magazine, for Christ's sake, or TV. He was thinking again about taking biology when the new term started after New Year's.

ON TUESDAY AFTERNOON BILLY WAS SURPRISED WHEN Zizi came to visit him in the hospital. He was lying in bed, rolled over on his side, back to the door, to the hallway, to the nurses pushing carts of medications and walking back and forth busily. He was reading through the M's in the medical encyclopedia: malaria, meningitis, mononucleosis were some of the better-known diseases he had read about since morning. Monday night, he had stayed up until past one reading about the different forms taken by venereal diseases. When a picture was really interesting, or disgusting, he would call out, "Hey, John. You want to see something?" And Bokku would say, "Yes. Sure. Bring it over to me," and they'd look at the pictures over by Bokku's bed and comment appropriately. "Oh that's horrible," John would recoil at the full-color sight of an old woman with a cancer bulb the size of a lemon growing off her nose, "that poor woman. Take it away, Billy—ugh—" he shuddered. "It makes me sick."

"Billy, you have a visitor," the nurse said. Billy pulled blotchy face out of the medical book and rolled over: Nurse Thorpe in her white pants suit and name tag, blue sweater riding her shoulders like a slipcover, white nurse's cap, old wrinkled face . . . and Zizi standing a little behind her.

"How are you feeling?" Zizi asked, sitting down at the edge of the bed after the nurse had left.

"All right. I'm getting better."

"You missed a terrible class today. We only had five people show up again. I bet you were the only one who was really sick."

"What'd Russo do?"

"He got furious. I mean, can you blame him? Like, he works really hard to prepare and everything for this class, and then when no one shows up that must really be a drag."

"So what was class like?"

"Well—we didn't really have class. He was really mad. He canceled class. He said 'Tell your friends . . .' He says he's going to start lowering our grades if anybody cuts his class anymore."

"Damn. I bet he thinks I was just goofing off. I bet he doesn't even know I'm sick," Billy thought. "Oh hell." He poured himself a glass of ice water from a plastic pitcher. The nurses came by to put in fresh water and new ice cubes every couple of hours.

"I really like your pajamas," Zizi said. "When can you get out of here?"

"I don't know for sure."

"Are you going to have to miss vacation?"

"I don't know. My fever has to go down first."

"That would be terrible if you had to stay here over Thanksgiving. I know I'd go crazy if I didn't know I was gonna get next week off for vacation. And then Christmas break after that."

"Are you going home? Are you going to Washington?"

"No. I'm not," she said poignantly.

"What are you going to do?"

"Stay with some friends."

"Oh . . . Well I guess I'd go home if I could. But look at my chart. I had a fever of a hundred and five two days ago."

"You're really sick." Zizi was as impressed as everyone else had been with Billy's statistic. "Let me feel . . ." And she put her hand on his forehead.

And then her hand was so warm and soft and moist and he shut his eyes, smelling the wool of the sweater, and for the brief seconds that her hand rested on his clammy forehead he knew such peace, such dreams of happiness.

They would live in a white house, a big white farmhouse on a river, a dirt road winding out of the gate, lush soft grasses leading down to the lazily flowing water. In the back, behind the house, the pasture with sheep and goats and dairy cows. Dogs sniffing the ground, wagging their way around, sniffing the air and barking, bounding out the gate to meet him.

"Hi, Red, old fella. Hiya, Petie." Cats curled up in the rafters, on the hay bales in the barn. His children playing quietly in the garden, a boy and girl, running out to meet him.

"Daddy, Daddy. Bring me anything?"

And she, his love, coming to the door, wiping her hands dry from cooking dinner, her hair pulled back, and he'd walk up the path and up the steps to her and softly kiss her, secrets in eyes, Zizi his wife and love.

In the summer, the acres plowed and from everywhere fruits and vegetables swelling, ripening on the vines, flowering, and they'd spend some Sunday in August on a picnic, a chicken barbecue sponsored by the local Jaycees. The children would run around and the men would gather after lunch and play softball. Hitting a home run over everybody's heads, into the high waving branches of a maple tree.

"Way to go, big Billy!"

"What a smash!" Whistle, whistle, whistle. And Zizi holding the son, his legs splayed around her thrust-out hip, joggling him—"Where's Daddy? Huh? Do you see Daddy, Junior?" Driving home in the old Ford, children asleep in the back seat, headlights on the road, his wife beside him tired, talking quietly.

"I love you, Zizi. More than anything. I am so happy." Just this simple life of love. Happiness without end.

Zizi didn't stay long, just a couple of minutes. She seemed nervous, asked if he knew what time it was twice in the short time she was there. She said she doubted she'd see him again until after vacation, but "anyway, have a good time. Say hello to your mother if you ever get home." She hoped he'd get better.

Billy was not discharged from the hospital until Friday morning, the day after Thanksgiving. He called home Wednesday night to tell his mother he was still not completely recovered. She said that was a shame as Thanksgiving was going to be "so special this year." She said Henry had rented a car and they were all going to leave very early in the morning—herself, Henry, Abby, the dog—and drive and spend the day with Henry's mother, who was, apparently, "a marvelous cook." So it was a shame Billy was still sick, she said, because she thought the day would have been a lot of fun for him.

"Oh yeah," Billy thought, "I bet it'd be a blast." He was surprised that Henry still had a mother. Henry was fifty-five years old, therefore his mother would have to be at least seventy-five. He tried to picture Grandma Gould. An old lady with a face like Henry's, only more shriveled.

"Will you be able to salvage any kind of break, Billy?" his mother asked. "Do you think you'll be able to come home for the weekend? Naturally we're all dying to see you." He told her he'd try, he'd have to see what the doctors said. You just don't take chances where your lungs are concerned.

So Billy gave thanks in the hospital. At a little after five in the evening Nurse Roberts wheeled her food cart into the hospital room, said, "Happy Thanksgiving, fellas," to Billy and John Bokku, whose leg had been taken out of traction, the wires unfastened, the pulleys and the clamps removed, but who still had to stay in the hospital for a couple of days more to rest and undergo a few tests.

So the two fellows ate rubbery turkey, gummy stuffing, and apple pie, and while they were eating, John Bokku asked Billy to explain to him the origins of the holiday they were celebrating. Bokku had arrived in America for the first time in August. Billy explained to him about the Pilgrims and the *Mayflower,* how they had all sailed over from Europe to escape religious persecution and how they had struggled through the first harsh winters in the New Land and how the white men had been aided by their Indian brothers who instructed them how to grow corn and other vegetables.

"So at the tail end of the harvest season, when everything had been harvested and gathered and stored for the winter, these Pilgrims threw a big banquet to celebrate that they had made it, you know, survived. They'd taken a big chance and now they were

176

going to be all right. They had a new home. So they offered 'thanks' to God, and they invited the Indians over and had a big feast."

"Marvelous," said Bokku, evidently touched. He clapped his hands when Billy was through.

"Maybe," Billy thought, "I should think about teaching kindergarten." He had enjoyed the explaining, liked hearing himself speak.

It seemed that Bokku himself might have to seek asylum on American shores from persecution in his native land. Bokku came from a small country in Africa along the northeast border of Swaziland. The region had been delivered from colonialism after World War II and political power had been transferred back to the ruling tribes. Bokku stood third, at the moment, in the line of succession for the largest tribe's chieftainship. But of the two tribesmen who came before him (his two cousins), one had already been thrown in jail for having displeased the king, their father (John's uncle, Walter). Politics was a dangerous business in the land where John Bokku came from. "As least I am safe in America." But you could never be too careful, and he confided in Billy that he suspected a few of the campus blacks—two in particular —of being agents, informers, planted by his uncle. Three earlier pretenders to the kingship had all been brutally executed within the last two or three years, among them Bokku's oldest brother, Bob. But Bokku was his uncle's favorite, the pet. The most formidable warrior-athlete in the village, and now a college student in America, where he was the fleet center-halfback on the varsity soccer team.

Unfortunately, Bokku was having a hard time at Beacham otherwise, and his grades were all very poor. All D's. Grades were not final, of course, and he still had a few weeks to improve his scores before the registrar folded up his transcript, slipped it into an en-

177

velope, and mailed it to Bokku's uncle, via Swaziland by way of Uganda and The Congo. Bokku said he had begun to have nightmares and to fear for his life. The pressures on him were considerable.

"When Uncle sees my transcript," (his big eyes popping with fear) "he'll have my throat cut for sure. On the spot."

When all his friends from the soccer team had come over to visit him, to cut up and write their autographs on his cast, Bokku had smiled and laughed and had seemed very happy, well liked, well adjusted. Contrary to appearances, Bokku said, this was not the case. He was lonely in America, missed his younger brothers and sisters (there were twenty-four of these scattered in various huts around the capital city; or half brothers and half sisters, bred as they were from a number of combinations of village elders. Bokku claimed kinship when either his mother or prodigious eighty-seven-year-old father was involved). The only true friend Bokku had in the U.S., he said, was his country's delegate to the United Nations, another one of his cousins. But Sidney was miles away in New York, and many years older. Besides, there were generational problems, matters which Sidney could not comprehend. Bokku coped with this loneliness by telephoning his best friends in Africa every couple of nights. He had gone to boarding school with the sons of princes and kings and witch doctors from all over the continent, young Ugandans, Dahomeans, Nigerians, little Pygmy princes and princesses. So when he felt like talking things out with an old friend, John called long distance and he billed all the calls to his home phone—in the royal palace—and his uncle ripped up the bills when they arrived. The telephone company had been nationalized since 1963.

Later that night, or early Friday morning, Billy was

awakened by a poke in the ribs. It was Bokku in his bathrobe, jabbing at him with the tip of one of his crutches.

"Billy—I need you for something. I'm sorry to wake you up, but it's very important."

"What? What is it?"

"Just keep quiet and follow me." Outside the door, the hospital corridor was dark. A red exit sign glowed by the stairwell, and at the far end Billy could see the light on in the nurses' station.

Bokku led him to the phone booth by the elevators and drinking fountain.

"Wally—you still there?" he said into the mouthpiece. "Okay, I have your proof for you, mon . . . Here," he said to Billy, "talk." Billy took the phone and put it to his ear.

"Hello?" The phone wires whistled and crackled.

"Who is diss?" asked the voice on the other end, sounding very fierce.

"My name is Billy Williams."

"Oh—you are John's friend in de hospital?"

"What? Oh yeah. We're in the hospital together. We share a room."

"Ah—good. How are you? Do you enjoy going to college?"

"Well—yes and no."

The voice, African, laughed. "Yes, that is what John says, too. Tell me, Billy Williams. You have lived all your life in de U.S.?"

"Yes, I have."

"And do you like it?"

"Well, I guess so. I've never really thought about it. I've never lived anywhere else. I don't know. Yeah, I guess it's fine. I'm sorry, I can't really think clearly about your question. I'm very tired. You see I was fast asleep. I don't know what time it is for you, you sound wide awake, but here I think it's around four in the morning." At this, Bokku wrenched the phone receiver from Billy's hand and said, "I have you, you see, Wally. I win the bet."

Later, back in bed, Bokku explained. Wally was his uncle the king's eldest living son, hence, a prince. He was thirteen years old and being groomed by the king to take over. Having grown up in the palace all his life, being waited on and feared by the other members of the tribe, even by the old men, and being thirteen, a spoiled age regardless of nationality or social standing, Wally tended to be on the arrogant side, and too stridently proclaimed that he was right about everything, could not accept the fact that he did not know everything. John liked to tease him. Tonight, John had been unable to sleep. The Thanksgiving meal had given him indigestion, and lying there, trying to go to sleep, he had gotten it in mind to telephone back to the palace and tell his uncle that he had broken his leg and been forced to miss the big soccer final, and to reassure everyone that he was all right and working hard, taking his responsibilities seriously. King Walter had left the palace early in the morning, however, for so John was told by one of his many aunts. His uncle had gone out with a hunting party and was not expected back for two or three days. He had left the affairs of government in the hands of Walter the Second, or Wally, his son. So John had talked to his cousin for a while and told him all that had happened. Wally was jealous of John. Their cousinship was noted throughout the realm for its rivalry and jocular suspicion. As often happened, tonight their conversation had grown heated, and John had caught himself talking too loudly into the phone. He had said, "I'm talking too loud. The nurse will come and catch me not in my bed." And Wally had asked him what he was doing in bed and John had said for one thing, he had broken his leg and was supposed to be resting, for another it was very late at night and everybody was asleep. Wally refused to believe that if it was midmorning in Africa, where he was, bright and sunny, a beautiful clear day, it therefore could be anything other than the same hour in America. John had called him a fool and tried to explain time differences, a phenomenon even he did not fully understand, it never having been clearly explained to him by any of his old professors at boarding school. Just the same, facts were facts, it was black as pitch outside the window. Wally refused to believe him. They argued some more, then made a bet.

Wally had said, "Now give me proof."

And John had said, "All right," and called Billy in as his star witness. After hanging up the phone, he had won the bet from his young cousin, which delighted him. The stakes had been rather large: twenty-five chickens and one of the submachine guns his uncle had bought in a big arms deal with the Soviet Union.

Seven-thirty the next morning. Nurse Wilson came in with Billy's breakfast on a tray, cold cereal, milk and juice, set it down on his bedside table, put a thermometer in his mouth, did the same for Bokku, went away, came back, told Billy his temperature was normal. If he checked out normal again by noon, he could be discharged.

He was normal the second time and they let him get dressed, gave him a bottle of pills to finish off the infection, and said he could leave. Billy went back to his room, packed his bag—one shirt, one pair of pants, underwear and socks, toothbrush, and then piled on top ten pounds of books. He called the train station for the time of the next train to New York, called home sometime after one o'clock, got Abby on the phone—he woke her up, she had been out late the night before, Mom was out—told her he was taking the next train, he'd be home by nine that evening.

20

DURING THE FOUR-AND-A-HALF-HOUR TRAIN JOURNEY, *The Faerie Queene* lay unopened, unfinished, dogeared at page 80 (as it had been for the past week) upon Billy's lap. He was shaken, nervous, apprehensive about returning home (what would that be like?), and still wheezing a little. His fever had broken, but his lungs were still gunked up with ooze; the seventh day. Twice Billy staggered up the train car, smacked back and forth, seat to seat as the carriage rocked and swayed, to pop down a pill in the men's room and drink water from a paper cone. Discarded newspapers. *Time* magazines, suitcases blocking the aisles, potato chip bags, Coke cans, sandwich halves in cardboard fold-out cartons. The stick of spilled beer on the floor. Children running back and forth, fighting. A baby a few seats back screaming until walloped by his teen-aged sister (mother?). A woman sitting by the door with a cat carrier on her lap, the cat yowling in terror. A quintet of college kids, rugby shirts, Adidased feet. And a blissful Moonie sitting in the seat next to Billy, trying to strike up a conversation.

"What the hell happened to my wallet?" Billy found himself asking out loud, later. He was standing at the bus stop on Eighth Avenue and Thirty-third, the bus arrived, waiting for him, door open, engine chugging, the driver having issued an ultimatum ("C'mon kid, you coming or ain'tcha'a?"). He couldn't find his money. He checked all his pockets. "Could I have left it on the train?" Worse yet, "Did I get pickpocketed?" In either case, his wallet was nowhere to be found. He stood there, frantically patting all his pockets when the bus driver, fed up, flipped the lever and the big doors closed with a pneumatic hiss.

When could it have happened? The train station had been crowded, the travelers piling against each other waiting to board the "up" escalator out to the street, shoving, jostling and bumping their suitcases into each other's legs. Someone might easily have lifted the wallet in that jam.

What was he going to do about it now? There was nothing he could do. Report it to the police when he got home. Gone was his driver's license. (He'd had to take the driving test three times before he finally passed. On his second road test, he ran the car into a fire hydrant. Fortunately the car belonged to the driving instructor who was up to his ears in insurance policies, so it could've been a lot worse. Until Billy hit the curb, it had been smooth sailing—he had parallel-parked, executed a three-point U-turn, all without a hitch.) Gone too was his college identification card (a mixed blessing—the picture made him look ridiculous), and while these two might be returned to him by the considerate thief, the twenty-dollar bill he had been carrying would never be returned. Write it off to experience. He considered himself lucky. He could have been stabbed. A bomb might have gone off in a locker.

"Tragedy rocked the city tonight as a bomb exploded in Penn Station, killing and maiming thousands," the news anchorman would begin.

"I guess I'll have to walk home." Cars, taxis, buses clogged Eighth Avenue, backed up from a broken traffic light. Assorted Turks and Slavs huddled over the stoves on their carts to keep warm, rubbing their hands together in the steam that curled out from under the pans of pretzels and chestnuts. Further along the avenue, the neon lights from the dirty movies and peep shows that stretched uptown beyond Forty-second Street grew brighter. Junkies, drunks, street freaks of all kinds. Black pimps, thin and elegant and cunning-looking as weasels, clopped past him on their high-heeled shoes, swanking and strutting up and down the strip where their hookers were soliciting. Green velvet suits, red velvet suits, alligator skin shoes, diamond rings, floppy hats. A police car from Midtown South was idling by the curb, an officer looking out the window, and it didn't seem to worry the pimps or their hookers in the slightest.

He had almost gone off with a whore once. It happened that past spring. A few weeks before school let out Henry and Billy's mother had decided it might not be a bad idea if Billy got a job for the summer and made some money. Henry was a big believer in kids getting work experience, and Billy was too, for that matter. So they tossed suggestions around for a few nights at dinner, and then Henry said that maybe there was some opening at the paper where he worked. "There are always a few openings for bright kids in the summertime. That's how I started, Bill. I was no older then than you are now when I got my first job. I started out being the copy editor's gofer. You know, he'd send me out for coffee and candy and stuff. But I just hung around and watched him, and it was great experience." And a year later he was covering the Battle of Britain, having been promoted to London correspondent. Sure, Henry. Sure, sure, sure.

"I'll talk to Howard Mitcham at personnel today

and see what he says about taking you on in some capacity," Henry promised at breakfast the following morning. And he did, and Howard Mitcham thought about it, and talked to the head copy boy, who said there were too many copy boys working at the paper as it was. (After Woodward and Bernstein dozens of rich kids were hustling their fashionable parents into pulling some strings and getting them started in the newspaper game.) Finally Mitcham called up Robert Middlekauf, who was in charge of the city desk for the midnight to morning shift, and Middlekauf said, yes, he might be looking for an assistant. So when Henry came back from work that evening, he made it all sound very promising. The next afternoon, after Billy got home from school, a little before six, the hour when Henry called it a day, and also when Middlekauf had promised he'd turn up at his office, Billy would take the bus down to Times Square for an interview.

Billy had been shown into Henry's office by Henry's secretary. He'd been in Henry's office once or twice before. A desk, a couch, a window looking down on Forty-second Street, newspapers with his articles stacked up in piles in the corner, yellowing; photographs along the walls featuring Henry and an assortment of bigwigs: Mayor Beame, Nelson Rockefeller, Golda Meir and Barbra Streisand.

Henry shook his hand, told Billy he looked nice in his tie and jacket, but "shouldn't you comb your hair?" and handed him a comb and the directions to the men's room, where Billy tugged a comb through his mop. Later, putting his arm around Billy's shoulder, Henry walked him down the carpeted office hallway, past the clacking typewriters, ringing phones, water cooler surrounded by distraught and overworked, scraggly reporters and proofreaders; then took him around a corner, pushed the button for the elevator which took them to the fourteenth floor, where Robert Middlekauf's office was.

The interview didn't go badly. It was short, and Middlekauf seemed friendly. Billy sat in the chair in front of Mr. Middlekauf's desk for a couple of minutes, no longer than five minutes at the most, then Middlekauf showed him to the elevator and said he'd call Billy within the week to let him know.

Billy had agreed to meet a girl named Lulu, to go to the movies with him after the interview. Lulu was "crazy about Al Pacino," so they were going to see *Dog Day Afternoon,* where Al Pacino plays a fag who holds up a bank so he can pay for the sex-change operation of his boy friend. Lulu had already seen it before, three times, in fact, and she had told Billy the plot, and even acted out some of her favorite scenes. But she wanted them to go so Billy could see it for himself. The movie was playing on Forty-second Street, two blocks from the offices of Henry's newspaper.

He felt it was an idyllic situation really, he felt so grown-up! Striding into a newspaper office to be interviewed for a job, then, afterwards, meeting a girl to take her to a movie, maybe for a bite to eat later. Well, idyllic on the face of it, sure.

The movie didn't start until seven-thirty; Lulu had said she would meet him out in front of the theater a few minutes before showtime. So Billy had over an hour to kill, and being a normal youth, or more-or-less normal, or normal enough—with more-or-less normal curiosities and a healthy sexual instinct (or, anyway, not much more fucked-up than most of the other boys Billy knew, although that wasn't saying very much, it was true)—he thought he would wander around Forty-second Street and look at the dirty marquees advertising the porno movies, look at the whores on Eighth Avenue, see what they were up to, maybe put a quarter into a peep show, what the hell.

Next to a movie theater that was showing the triple-feature *Teenagers on the Loose, Elsa, She-Wolf of the S.S.*, and *Discharge*, the buzzing neon of a sex emporium urged him in.

FEEL FREE TO BROWSE.
SALE ON 25 MM FILMS.
YOU MUST BE 21, OR BE GONE.

The place was packed. Discriminating shoppers perused the racks and bargain bins, leafed through material, stroked their chins. Men of all kinds—old, young, black, white, all of them on their own. Lone wolves. All of them except for one black man who had brought along his wife or girl friend. They appeared to be pricing a display of vibrators, leather dongs, and other sexual hardware.

A pockmarked youth was scanning the rack of magazines featuring women with huge breasts. He picked one out and leafed through. Billy saw the cover: a fat woman with black hair, flat on her back, peering through false eyelashes like a sniper out over her tits rising up like bunkers out of her potbelly. A businessman in a suit was at the counter talking to a fat black man, trying to purchase as discreetly as he could an inflatable rubber woman. The display model was taped to the wall over the counter and cash register. A cardboard sign by her left leg introduced her as "Sexy Suzy"; a last resort for the lonely, ugly and the shy.

CAN'T GET A DATE?
WHY WAIT?
DON'T HESITATE.
KINKY OR STRAIGHT.
I'M READY WHEN YOU ARE,
JUST INFLATE.

187

Billy didn't see Henry there until after he put a quarter into a slot and watched a peep show. The cardboard sign over the small viewing window, written with Magic Marker, advertised: "See this luscous [sic] blonde chick really get it on with her well-hung old man. Then with Brutus, her Great Dane. Must be seen to be believed."

"I ought to see that," Billy said to himself. No surprises, the show was called "Animal Passion." A fat blonde woman was sitting on a couch in a living room, reading a magazine. Brutus, the dog, was sprawled in front of a crackling fire. The camera clumsily drifted to the plywood front door; the scene was captioned: "Knock, knock," but the letters appeared reversed, as if in a mirror. Needless to say, it was her old man wrapped up in a big raccoon coat. "B-r-r-r," he said in reverse, "it's cold." The girl said, "Let me warm you up," and she took his hand and led him to the couch where they talked enthusiastically for a couple of seconds, the girl giving provocative looks right and left. One thing led to another, until his quarter ran out.

"Boy," Billy had said. What time was it? He'd spent some time in a luncheonette before coming in, ordering a Coke and reading the newspaper which someone had left behind, folded over on the bar stool. Billy looked around for a clock in the place and it was then that he saw Henry.

It was clearly him, or clearly Henry's back and horseshoe bald dome no less than fifteen feet away, browsing in the "Nymphet" section, the covers of the magazines showing naked little girls, some certainly no more than ten years old, in stretch socks and pigtails but not much else. Hugging teddy bears, for Christ's sake.

"Oh my God. That's Henry. I've gotta get out of here," was his first thought. Billy didn't stop running

188

until he was three blocks away. His heart was pounding. He saw a police car parked on a side street, the two officers in blue short-sleeve shirts interrogating an old junkie who was sitting on the sidewalk where she had collapsed. Billy wanted to go up to them, tell them what his mother's boy friend was doing. "He's in there, officer, at this very moment," pointing down the street. "If you hurry, you'll catch him red-handed." "That fucked-up old bastard. I hate him. This is terrible. This is the worst." Should he go home and tell his mother? Better yet, call her immediately and report what he had seen so she could have Henry's suits and shoes and toothbrush neatly packed up by the time he got home? "So long, Henry. This is the end. I'm sure you know why." And had Henry seen Billy in there? What, in any case, could Billy say he had been doing in a place like that? "Well—" his mother would spell it out, master sleuth that she was, "how did you come upon this information, Billy? I mean how do you know Henry was looking at dirty magazines in Times Square this evening? What I suppose I'm getting at is, what were you doing in a place like that in the first place?"

"That dirty fucker." Child molester. "Into nymphets, oh brother!" It occurred to him that his little sister was top priority now. He'd get a lock for her bedroom door from the hardware store first thing in the morning. "That sickie. That pyscho."

He stood on the street corner of Forty-fourth and Eighth Avenue for a couple of minutes, lost in tragic thought, feeling worse than Hamlet, strategizing, conjecturing reprisals, and then how to parry Henry's counterreprisals. All this when an anorexic prostitute clumped up to him in her platform shoes, took his arm and asked if he wanted a date. He looked at her, bewildered.

"What?"

"You wanna go to a party?"

"What kind of party?"

"That depends."

"On what?"

"On what you want, on what you can spend." She smiled. She had no front teeth.

"No, no."

All right, he didn't almost go off with a whore. He ran down the street. He didn't come close. But Billy was self-dramatizing, and when he replayed the events of that evening, he liked to think that he was so outraged, so despairing—so mixed up—that he almost went off with her.

In the end, Billy told no one what he had seen, not Abby, not his mother, and not Lulu, to whom he answered when she asked where he had been—"The movie's already started"—that he had just gone for a walk after his interview, that he thought he had blown the job and had walked off his disappointment. But he had the goods on Henry now. He had evidence with which to prosecute if it came to that. At first his instantaneous loathing for his mother's boy friend had been largely unsubstantiated. He couldn't clearly explain it, even to himself, why he hated Henry as much as he did. But piece by piece, he was preparing an airtight case against Henry. Every article would stick, nail the old creep to the wall. He had the hard facts. He was right about Henry. And had been from the start.

Had Henry seen him? And was he aware of what Billy had on him? Billy watched for signs, prepared for warfare, to lay the cards on the table if that was what the old goat had in mind. He was not in the least bit surprised three days later when Middlekauf called him up and said he was sorry but he had found someone better suited for the job. (His nephew, as it turned out.) Billy took it as a challenge, tantamount to a declaration of war. He played it coolly, let the challenge go by, trying to draw Henry out into the open. To commit himself now would give Henry a chance to throw up his arms at the dinner table, uttering disclaimers. "What's he talking about, Catherine? I don't know what's going on. What am I supposed to have done?"

Henry, however, never made it out into the open. A week later, he took his vacation, caught the potting bug, and was talking about quitting his job. At which point, Billy's hatred deflected to pity and embarrassment.

And so the old man continued to have free reign of the apartment, continued to sleep over, his suits stayed in the closet, the front door key stayed on his key ring, he continued to influence Billy's mother and continued to eat up all the food and drink up all the booze.

21

THE OLD NEIGHBORHOOD. SAME AS EVER. AS BILLY crossed the street, struggling with his book-laden suitcase, wheezing dramatically, he was surprised to find that he felt next to nothing as he came within range of the familiar awning. There was no warming, cheery "welcome back, stranger," to be detected in the winking of the traffic lights—red, yellow, green all the way uptown to Harlem—nor, for that matter, did he infer surly reproach from the stares of the zombie doormen, standing in front of their buildings, ready to rush into action when some rich bitch swanked through the

191

lobby in her sable and expected the door drawn open for her. ("Have a pleasant evening, Mrs. Rockefeller-Kennedy-Onassis-Bitch!") The avenue from Sixtieth Street to Ninety-sixth was an enclave of the well-to-do, guarded by sluggish dotards in fancy doorman uniforms and caps. Wasps and Jews lived inside, lawyers, heiresses, and their families, professional people. Also émigré Russians. There were two complete sets of them living in Billy's building, the Obolenskys and the Droutzkoys, both claiming to be rightful heirs to the Russian throne, all members of both households wishing to be addressed as Prince or Princess. Instead of "There goes Mrs. Droutzkoy walking her dog," it had to be "There goes the Princess Droutzkoy, walking her dog." The Droutzkoys on the sixth floor and the Obolenskys in the penthouse suite, needless to say, were not on speaking terms and even refused to share an elevator ride down to the lobby with one of their rivals.

Billy had expected that the return to the city, the walk up the avenue would bring on a This-Is-Your-Life newsreel retrospective: the Wieseltiers moving into their new Park Avenue apartment, big Jim himself in command. Then, a year later, still in command, big Jim moving out. And other newsreel loops as well: of the listless pubescent taking Bonnie for her nightly walk, who was mugged by a trio of savage Puerto Rican girls, who kicked him and laughed at him and stole his wallet; and of the high school youth, chewing a piece of toast, racing to the subway stop on Lexington and Seventy-eighth Street to catch the train for The Bronx, late for expensive, private high school. But now he dragged himself homeward, exhausted, sick and apprehensive, his childhood nowhere to be found.

"So—home on vacation, huh, Billy?" Louie the elevator man asked him, sealing the elevator door shut with a switch. Louie had worked for the building for years. The board of directors had been trying to force him to retire—Louie was sixty-eight years old, past the mandatory age for retirement—but Louie didn't want to retire, and he had given an emotional speech to prove it to a meeting of the tenants, a speech so affecting, so filled with homely eloquence that it brought Billy's mother downstairs in tears. Louie kept his job. "I'm so glad about it," Billy's mother had said after the board announced its decision, "I just would have felt so awful if that nice old man had been forced to retire. I mean, where could he go? What else could he do?" Billy hated her blither talk about what a sweet old guy Louie the elevator man was, such decency and friendliness—so helpful with heavy packages—so full of warmth and virtue and, well, just plain goodness, a rare commodity in this day and age. And wasn't she wonderful herself, and terribly sensitive to feel this way?

Billy, too, was glad that Louie hung onto his job, if that was the way Louie wanted things. He and Louie had been good friends, once upon a time. Louie always came to work with his transistor radio, which he'd keep in the pocket of his elevator jacket, the earphone stuck in his ear, and he'd listen to baseball games on it. Most of the tenants thought the wire running from his pocket to the plastic plug was part of a hearing aid, but Billy knew better and he and Louie talked about the games. The Mets weren't much, but they were all Louie had after the Dodgers and Giants moved on to California. But then Billy grew older and developed a conscience about such things. He grew up to find Louie a pitiful victim of an unjust social order, a man forced to degrade himself daily with "Sir's" and "I hope the weather stays warm like this, mm-hmm" and "You're welcome, Mrs. Whitney-Astor-Vanderbilt-Cunt!" a man, it seemed to Billy, contemptibly willing to lick

193

any ass in the joint for his Christmas bonus. And when Louie continued to ask him, "Did'j'a see that game last night? That Tom Seaver is one heckuva pitcher, isn't he?" it made Billy feel like an asshole. To answer back, as he had done in the past, "Yeah, but Louie, facts are facts. The team has no hitting," in his private-school diction would have been to accept, if not positively to condone, things for what they were. To have chatted with Louie as usual, elevator parked somewhere between the third and fourth floors, listening to the radio, Mets at bat, bottom of the eleventh, score knotted 3–3 would have been just as hypocritical, and just as fatuous in its way as his mother's bleeding-heart smugness. From then on, he rode Louie's elevator in silence. Soon after, Louie began addressing Billy as "Sir."

"All right now, you take it easy these next couple of days, you hear me? You relax. Eat good. You look like you've been starving up there at that college. No sir, you don't look too good," Louie said. The elevator door rolled closed and Louie went downstairs to the lobby, mission accomplished.

Billy set down his suitcase and went through his pockets until he found his key ring. He unlocked the front door and called out, "Hel-lo-o, I'm home." Yoo-hoo!

"In here," Abby called back, "watching TV." The lights were out in the study where the big color TV was. But there was Abby, his sister, the rainbow colors of the giant 36-inch screen splashing across her face. But wait a minute—had she grown another head? Or, was that somebody next to her? Or under her? She was sitting on someone's lap. Yes, that was it. A gawky hippie swiveled his pinhead languorously to take Billy in.

194

"Welcome home, big brother. How's that old asthma?"

"Not too good. I think I had a relapse walking uptown." Abby stayed intent on the TV. A thirty-ish housewife and her preteenage daughter were arguing about toothpaste. This time daughter seemed to know best, the toothpaste Mom wanted to use was old-fashioned. Abby adjusted her seat in her boy friend's lap, squinted up at Billy for a second, seemed to be shaking her head, thinking to herself, "That kid is my brother. What a disgrace." "Oh—" she said, "Jason, this is Billy, my brother."

Jason nodded, everything was cool, and said, "Hey." Billy sized him up with distaste. Prosperous cowboy's cowboy boots, some kind of Mexican poncho shirt, shredded blue jeans, elephant-hair bangles on his wrist—the works.

"Where's Mom?"

"Out with Henry. They won't be back till late. Pull up a chair if you want. Jason's got dope."

"No, no, I'm too tired," Billy waved her off, trying to sound hip and yet gracious. "I think I'll just go to bed." He faked a yawn. Ho hum. Jason started cackling with mirth. Billy felt foolish and ashamed. He thought of saying, perhaps in parting, "Listen, by the way. I'm planning a short trip to Harlem tomorrow afternoon. Thought I'd try to round up some heroin. How about it, kids? Anything I can get for you while I'm there?" Jason continued to laugh. He could have been crying, for that matter, his eyes squinted, his body jiggling like a steam engine.

"Ho! That fucking Don Rickles, man! Heh-heh-hey. He's rilly insane."

"What the hell's happening around here?" Billy thought, equilibrium somewhat restored. "How can they just sit here and watch the fucking Merv Griffin

195

show? What's this guy doing to Abby?" He asked, "Hey Ab—has anyone walked Bonnie tonight?"

"Bonnie's okay. She's not going to need to go out."

"Why not?" The dog was sleeping on the floor in front of the television.

"She took a big shit on the front carpet. So she'll be all right until the morning."

As Billy left the room, he heard Jason telling Abby: "I really hate that fucking dog of yours, Abby. She's a real turd. Next time I come over I'm going to kill it."

Abby replied, "Jason—" (in a mock-protesting whine) "you're terrible!"

After cleaning up the dogshit with a paper towel, Billy retired to his room. The maid had put everything in order in his absence, stacking his old magazines into piles, making the bed. The room looked to Billy as if a real person lived there.

He unpacked his asthma pills—and walked down the hall to the bathroom where he swallowed four of them.

Back in his room five minutes later, the pills having had no effect to speak of, he was starting to undress for bed when he noticed a postcard, leaning photograph outwards against the mirror of his dresser. The picture showed a giant redwood tree, an immense arching doorway carved out from its trunk through which a road had been routed, and under which a red station wagon, presumably full of vacationers, was passing, dwarfed like a Dinky toy. Billy didn't remember having ever seen the card before and he assumed that his mother had left it there for him; it had come in the mail last week or so, and rather than forward it to him at Beacham, she had thoughtfully left it out on his dresser.

"Maybe it's from Dad," Billy thought, although it

wasn't the kind of card his father was likely to mail. For that matter, why hadn't his father mailed the card directly to Billy at Beacham? "Maybe it's from Charles," his stepbrother. It was the kind of card Charles might send. Cute Charles.

But when he picked the card up and flipped it on its back, it became immediately apparent that the card had not been sent to him by Charles. The purple ink and loopy, crowded script told him that. As close as he could figure out, the card was from Lulu, who wrote:

Have been hanging out in San Francisco for last six weeks. Thought you might like to know. Oregon next stop. Visiting my brother and feeling laid-back. Things were rough in N.Y. with Mom and you and the whole unbelievable scene. Time and change mellows us out. That was quite a number you pulled on me, but I was talking to my brother about it, and I suddenly flashed on it that I was pretty weak about the whole deal. Anyway, I send this card to let you know, no hard feelings, OK?

And then a postscript, letters crawling up along the sides of the card, running into, merging with the letters and numbers of Billy's address and zip code. "It's a wonder that those boys in the post office were able to decode this thing and figure out where to send it," Billy thought.

P.S. I read a story in a magazine the other night that turned out it was written by your Dad. I really enjoyed it.

"Oh yeah," Billy said to himself, "I'll bet you did." Lulu had always labored under the delusion that Billy was too smart for her. She thought he didn't respect her very much because once she let it slip that out of school, now, on her own, she had read maybe a total of two books in her entire life. She had told him she thought he thought all she did was watch TV. True enough, that was what he thought. Because that was all she ever did do, as far as he ever saw. She was well meaning enough: she even dragged Billy into a bookstore one day, and said, "Okay, get me some good books. I mean some really important ones."

"Stupid bitch. Why couldn't she put this inside an envelope where nobody could just pick it up and start reading it? You don't air dirty laundry on the back of a postcard. You just don't do that." Seconds passed before he took a deep breath and read the postcard through a second time. He was slightly relieved to find that it wasn't as bad, as embarrassing, as incriminating, that it was a lot more vague than it had seemed to him at first. Just the same, he cringed at the thought of the mailmen sorting mail, one guy turning to another, "Hey Ralph, here's one for ya," Ralph then adjusting his glasses, reading Lulu's postcard for himself, going "Ho boy! This one's hot." Ha ha ha.

Then, after reading it a third time over, Lulu's postcard only seemed pathetic to him. All in all, well in keeping with her previous patterns. The card still made Billy feel bad, but now for different reasons.

Lulu. First of all, what a ridiculous name. It was not (in fairness to her parents) her given name at birth. That was Lucinda Walters. She picked Lulu out herself. Why? She liked it. "Why," Billy had once asked her, "don't girls get together and do something about those idiotic names they get. Sissy, Twinkie, Muffy, Grumpy, Sneezie. They're bitching about everything else. You'd think dumb names like that would be way up there on their list of grievances." Lulu had agreed.

She didn't think her name, Lulu, fit the category. She once told Billy that she thought it sounded French.

Nearly a year had passed since the day they met. A smoggy freezing December day, Billy's lungs wheezing like an old church organ. Ah yes.

He remembered parts of it all very clearly. Parts of it he had blocked out. He met her on a day when he was thinking about the self-congratulatory essays all high school seniors have to make up to send off to college admissions offices to be evaluated. ("Hi, there. My name is Billy Williams, and I come from the great city of New York and I think of all the Americans in the world today, I'd like to meet Gerald Ford the most because I think he's doing a great job as our President . . ." Pause for the applause, grin embarrassedly, genuinely, waiting for Bert Parks to cross the stage, "Isn't he something, ladies and gentlemen. A big hand for Mr. . . . Billy! . . . Williams!" Deafening applause, shrill whistles.) What agony those applications had been for him. Because just who did he think he was? What did he think he had done that the admissions deans would be interested to hear? "I am a male, five feet nine inches tall, weigh approximately 150 pounds . . . I say 'approximately' because this varies . . ." The most he had accomplished in his life, it seemed, was to age, and even this he had done neither gracefully nor normally. He was seventeen that winter. And when he thought how he had once imagined himself at seventeen, the kind of person he had always assumed he would be by this time, even by conservative estimate, the distance he had somehow failed to travel devastated him. He hadn't grown up at all since he was twelve years old. He was a little taller, but not much, not so you would really notice. Seventeen-year-old boys all had blond hair and played on the football team, had busty girl friends and would end up

199

as rich lawyers, jetting out to the Hamptons on weekends.

Also, there were other times, more worrying times when Billy realized he was already an old man. Middle-aged, with middle-aged worries, middle-aged limited expectations, even a middle-aged sense of humor. An old man already, with no illusions, and besides, asthmatic and too small anyway to play football.

The day had been a Tuesday.

She was wearing an orange ski jacket, tattered blue jeans, and boots for climbing mountains in. On Tuesdays, Billy had two classes in the morning, then nothing again until four in the afternoon. He was out on his own, then, walking around the neighborhood after lunch, thinking of how to go about selling himself to the college administrators. He was simply walking, and as he remembered it, feeling somewhat soulful—it was a day that made you feel like that, windy and raw, trees clogged up by the sewer grates, tree branches long since stripped—feeling as if he was carrying a barrel of poignancy around in his diaphragm, and hoping that in the course of his walk some idea about what to write down on his college applications would come to him.

And that was when it happened. Or something happened. Something—you couldn't call it "love"—struck him soundly, right on the head at approximately eleven minutes after one o'clock, Tuesday, December 1.

"Hey, you." She started it. A voice calling out "hey" behind him, a voice maybe a dozen feet away, maybe half a block. A sharp little-girl's voice.

"Hey—You." But the world, the city, The Bronx were full of you's.

"Hey . . . John. Hey Bob. Robert, hey." She had plenty of friends.

". . . Hey Sam, hey Steve, hey Mickey, hey Donald, hey Goofy . . . uh . . ." As she thought of more names, Billy stopped and turned around.

"Hi," said a girl, sauntering up to him, head at an angle, gnawing on a piece of gum, grinning. As she chewed and grinned, her front teeth, which overlapped, stuck out like the prow of a boat. "What ya doin'?"

"Nothing much. Just walking. Do I know you?"

"I don't know. Maybe. I know I seen you around here before."

"Oh." Okay, now what next? Billy felt flat on his feet.

"That isn't your name is it?"

"What isn't my name?"

"Goofy. Like, you turned around when I said 'Goofy.' "

"Oh . . . right." Billy had no idea what she was talking about. Neither, it seemed, did Lulu, at least at the time. She lowered her head, sort of gulped, tried to concentrate, stumbled around for something to say, shy flower that she was.

"So what are you doing?"

"Walking around."

"Well—like, what for?"

"Nothing else to do." She looked up at him, squinting, head tilted, chewing her gum.

"Why'n'ch'a tell me what your real name is? I know it's not Goofy."

"My real name is . . . Ichabod." Billy's clever spontaneities, of which this was supposed to be an example, were never very spontaneous at all. His impetuosities had all been rehearsed and played over year after year to different audiences. Like a not-very-funny middle-aged nightclub comic.

"What?" She frowned. "What'd you say your name was again?"

201

"Ichabod. Please, I'm very sensitive about it."

"Uh—no offense, but how about if I don't call you either of those names?"

"Suit yourself."

"What should I call you instead?"

"Call me Billy."

Her name was Lulu Walters. At first Billy thought she was making up a joke name for herself, just as he had. Funny girl. Clever, too.

"Which way are you going?"

"This way." He pointed.

"Okay if I go with ya?"

And so it began. She had, it turned out, a brother in Billy's class at school, her brother Jack. Lulu went to a public high school but she had come over to see Jack play basketball that afternoon against Bronx Science. It was the second game of the season and Jack was one of the substitute guards. Billy and Lulu walked around for about half an hour before Lulu began to complain that she was cold; her "fingers were freezing up," she said. Billy was surprised, if not altogether alarmed, to find himself sort of having a good time with her.

"What do you study? Like what's your best subject?"

"German."

"Sheesh, 'German,' he says. Some people like math best, or English best . . . Nazi." She shook her head. "I meet a guy who likes to talk in Nazi. All right, so say something to me in German. Go on."

He said the only German sentence he knew: *"Der wetter ist warm und mild."*

"I said German. Say something in German."

"I just did."

"That wasn't German."

"What do you think it was? Sure it was German."

"What does it mean, then?"

"Uh—" Billy tried to think of something. "It means, 'Put all the Jews in that oven and stuff all the Poles in this one over here and then give 'em the gas . . .' "

"Hey, that's not funny."

"Shit," Billy thought, "I should have figured she was Jewish." He was readying apologies when she said, "It doesn't really mean that, does it?"

"Yes, it does."

"You serious?"

"Absolutely."

In addition to complaining about the cold, Lulu said she had promised Jack that she would show up at his basketball game. If they headed back now, they could probably get to the gym in time for the start of the second half. Jack was a substitute, she said, so he probably wouldn't play until the second half anyway. It wasn't what Billy wanted to do at all, but before he could get out of it, she had him grabbed by the hand and was pulling him, saying, "Come on, let's go." Billy surrendered and walked back with her, attached to her hand like a dog heeling on a leash.

But they never got to the basketball game. That wasn't what Lulu had in mind at all. Fuck Jack. Fuck some boring basketball game. When they got to the gym, she tugged him through some doors, down a stairwell he never knew existed, down a dark hallway he had never explored, left turn then down another hallway, hunching over now under a low ceiling, like two sailors on a submarine. She seemed to know every curve, every door, every bend in the road.

"Wait a minute, will ya? Where are we going?"

"Will you stop worrying and just come on." And then: "This way," and her grip on his hand tightened. She tried the knob on a door, said, "Good, it's unlocked," and when the door opened she pulled him inside.

"It's dark in here."

"Yeah."

"Where are we?"

"In an old boiler room someplace. I think we're like directly beneath the basketball court."

"How did you find out about this place?"

"Jack showed me it one time. He says he comes down here sometimes to smoke dope, like before a game or something." The things that went on at the high school! And Billy had never known about any of it. They sat down on the damp, moldy concrete floor.

Billy and Lulu had reached an impasse on the subject: was Bob Dylan a greater musician than Beethoven or Mozart, "Y'know, cause Dylan's into that whole prophet and social critic thing which like I don't think Beethoven got into." Billy took the apples-to-oranges tack on this one, but Lulu rebutted that he was copping out. What did he really feel? Which did he really like better, "get into more?" Meanwhile Billy did a swift analysis of the afternoon—of modes and gestures —before tilting toward her, breath steaming, eyes thick-lidded, arms spread tentatively open.

He was, as they say, in like Flynn.

It wasn't bad with her. Certainly no worse than the three earlier times which comprised Billy's total experience. But also, in fairness to the competition, not any better. Stripping eyes down, as if for gym class, followed by three or four minutes valiantly struggling not to come . . . Ping-Pong players playing, a lean gray battleship wheeling about, steaming into battle, gun turrets raising, jet planes sweeping off into the sky, trailing chunky gray poison vapors, elephants crashing through the jungle, raising their trunks, trumpeting, monkeys crossing a bamboo bridge, old movies, Keystone Kops, firemen, a school of dolphins . . . anything to keep his mind distracted from the matter at hand, or below him . . . a baseball player stealing second,

Martin Luther King, oh God . . . I have a dream . . . here it comes . . . Little black boys shall walk hand in hand with white girls . . . Stop! Ouch. Nuclear fallout, asthma pills. Where are they? Help! . . . dreading what would happen once he did, then ambushed by the penultimate shivers, stopping straining . . . but too late now. Impossible. Hopeless as getting toothpaste back in the tube. Nothing to do but wait (ten more, five more . . .). Then he surfed down the cresting ripple of the orgasm and there was nothing else to do afterward but lie there on top of her and wish he were asleep, or elsewhere. Time passed. Just lying there. Thinking about his life. Oh my . . .

"Oh well . . . ," Lulu said. It didn't help. He hoped they weren't going to talk about it. "Hey? You okay?"

"Sure."

Seconds ticked away like months.

"Billy?"

"Uh huh."

"What's wrong?"

"Nothing."

More time passed.

"Hey."

"What?"

"You want to get off me pretty soon? You're getting pretty heavy."

Billy cut his afternoon class so he could escort Lulu back into Manhattan on the subway. It was the least he could do. Halfway home, they both ran out of things to talk about and just sat next to each other, reading ads.

He took her all the way to her apartment. But he begged off when she invited him upstairs, lying that it was his mother's birthday, and well, they were having a little party for her, she was sixty years old today and that was a rough thing for her to accept; a quiet little dinner, just the family, would facilitate the rite of passage, you know how it is. More to the point, Billy dreaded meeting Lulu's mother. In the short time he had known her, Lulu had had time to give him the lowdown on her family. Her dad wasn't very interesting—a lower-echelon executive for a greeting card company—but her mother was a drunk and a crazy, full of surprises. Also, Billy didn't want to be around when her brother Jack slumped in, brooding about having ridden the bench all afternoon, pissed off as hell that the team had lost to Bronx Science 84–20, wanting to sit down in the living room and watch N.B.A. basketball on the television.

"Well—good-bye, then."

"Wait a minute . . ."

"For what?"

"Aren't you going to call me?"

"Sure. Sure I'll call you. When?"

"What do you mean, 'when?' "

"I mean what would be a good time to call you?"

"Whenever you feel like it. You don't have to call me at all, if you don't want to."

"Oh I wouldn't do that. I'll call you soon, okay? Good-bye."

It was all as clear as if it were only yesterday. He could even remember that when he got home that day, his mother opened the front door with a towel wrapped around her wet hair like a turban. She said, "Big rush," and ran back to her bedroom. She was going out to dinner with Henry that night and had first-date jitters.

A week passed and he had not called Lulu. It was one of those things that he kept in the back of his head to do, to call her up just to see what was new, but then put off in favor of something less demanding. Another week passed, then Christmas vacation. Then

206

snow. Then one Monday Billy found a letter for him on the front mail table. Green stationery with scalloped edges.

Dear Billy—

I was doing OK until tonight at dinner. I just couldn't eat and so finally had had to ask to be excused and had to go and cry in my bedroom. Sometimes I really think I don't even care. I mean, I don't really even know you. I guess I just gave too much away. I just trusted you to be kind, that's all. I don't know what you must think about me, but I want you to know that what I did I only do with guys I really like. Maybe you don't think of me at all, figure I'm just some sort of stupid kid. OK, I know I'm not Miss Genius or anything, and I go to public school, but so what? I'm getting off the track. That's not why I wrote this letter. I don't know why I wrote this letter. I just think you took advantage of me, that's all. And I don't mean that I was drunk or stoned so I didn't know what I was doing, because I did know. But if you thought so little of me, you just shouldn't have done to me what you did.

LOVE,
LULU

P.S.—I'm sorry for this letter.

That was it. The letter was without crossing out or smudges, and Billy knew that she had spent a lot of time working on it, copying it and recopying. He stuffed the letter in his pocket and took it to school with him. A mistake, because classes were so boring, and he spent so much of his extracurricular time just hanging around that he probably took the letter out of his pocket seven or eight times, reading it through from beginning to end. "I'm sorry for this letter," she had written in a flight of anguish just before slipping the letter in the green envelope. And she was probably sorry that she made him feel guilty for what he had done. She was sorry if he was sorry, although down deep she probably hoped that he would feel sorry that she felt sorry for making him sorry. Billy had a soft heart and was unable even to consider that if Lulu was sorry about anything that had happened, she felt sorriest for herself. He telephoned her that same night from the kitchen while his mother and Henry belly-laughed in the living room and played Fred Astaire records full blast and blew scotch bubble kisses to each other. Abby was watching TV, the door shut. Out of the way. Billy dialed with cold and nervous fingers. What was there to talk about? "Hi, I just got your letter. Good to hear from you. Long time, no see."

Jack picked up the phone.

"Lu-lu-u-u," he yelled, "it's for you." In the distance, Lulu's muted voice said, "I've got it, stop yelling."

He started with small talk. He had sent in all his college essays and he was very anxious about all that. His grades were good, but they weren't really great, maybe borderline. He'd had a lot on his mind, tried to call her up a couple of times but either the line was busy, or no one answered. This worked on her but she gave grudgingly. He tried a few jokes that went lame and finally broke down into craven excuses and apologies, and invited her out to a movie. She accepted. She accepted everything and thanked him sincerely for calling.

"Billy . . . ?"

"What?"

". . . Billy . . . ?"

"What?"

"I just want to say that I'm really happy that you decided to call me."

So it went on for several months. He got a breather over spring vacation when Lulu's parents took her to Florida. She sent him letters as well as a three-month anniversary card to mark their first meeting, which featured a cartoon boy with brown hair and poppy goo-goo eyes holding a puppy. She wrote inside that the card had reminded her of him. And just how was that? She added: "I hope this isn't too dumb." Of course it was.

He never brought her home to meet his mother, but he did spend some time with her charming family. Dad was out of town on business the night Billy came home with her after the movie, but Mom was around. They came across her collapsed on the living room floor, wearing her raincoat for some reason, an ashtray full of cigarette butts tipped over near her head, a drained J&B scotch bottled lodged in the crook of her arm, an overturned glass by her left shoulder. She had been plastered since breakfast. She had been plastered since breakfast since a week ago Friday.

Later there would be the awkward dinners with her father at the head of the table, carving, Lulu's mother to one side, propped up in her chair for the time being, her brother Jack (who was an exceptional belcher) at the far end, and the two lovebirds, side by side. Lulu's parents were all smiles and seemed very interested in Billy's applications to college. A smart boy, they seemed convinced, he would have no trouble going off to any school he wanted. The school that ended up with him should thank its lucky stars to have such a boy.

"I have to get out of this," Billy thought to himself one evening, sitting on Lulu's bed as she gave him a guided tour of two of her most recent high school yearbooks.

"Oh, yeah, see this girl here," she said, tapping her finger at the murky picture of some pig-tailed girl in the third row of a class picture, fifth from the left, "that's Terri Cohen . . ." and then she began another pointless and interminable anecdote featuring herself and her high school friends.

"There has to be something I can do, I've got to figure something out, or I'm going to lose my mind." The task seemed insurmountable. He couldn't imagine what jolt from outside, what event would have to happen before he could get a chance to break free from her. (A war would do it—he could be drafted, ship out to Russia; she'd drop him then, especially if he got killed.) What did other people do? Why was he such a coward? Why couldn't he just go up to her and be truthful? "Look, Lulu, you don't mind it if I level with you, do you? Good, because I've been meaning to tell you that I really don't like you at all. I think you're callow and superficial and boring, an accumulation of simpering affectations. Frankly, I think the only reason I've stayed around until now is because you had me petrified with guilt. There, now I've said it. Still friends?" But the relationship had hung on for months now without benefit of candor. Billy felt obligated to keep lying, if only for the sake of the commitment and energy he had put into all the other lies. No, maybe it didn't make too much sense.

How was he going to get out of it? For that matter, how was he going to get up off her bed and troop in to eat dinner with her family? He'd have to laugh a lot at Lulu's father's jokes, and say "really?" with incredulity when Lulu's mother managed to put a sentence together to the effect that the cost of the dinner steak had gone up twenty cents in one month, and discuss the several major issues of the day. All that seemed equally farfetched.

He got his chance. It wasn't much, just a small crawl space to wriggle through, but he wriggled. It was May by this time. Coming out of school after English class, he was surprised to see Lulu sitting on the grass out in the quadrangle. She was wearing a spring dress and looked less ugly than usual. She was sitting there with her brother and a lanky black kid, Cal Campbell, one of the starting forwards on the basketball team on which Jack had been the sulky third-string guard. The idea came to Billy very quickly. It was risky, and might not work, but anyway, here goes.

Just as Lulu raised her hand to wave to him, to say, "Hi, come on over and join us," he turned around and bounded up the steps to the building out of which he had just come, doing his best to appear heartbroken. He ran out the back way, took a few detours to the subway stop and went home. He didn't call her, and she didn't call him for three days. He dreaded the hall table in the morning because of the letters it might have for him. Besides his letter from Lulu. Billy was expecting the rest of his replies from colleges. Results had already begun trickling in: Harvard, no. Yale, no. Brown, no. There were still seven or eight left to come in, so the verdict was still out. It was the following Friday, in fact, that his lone acceptance came, the letter frrom Larry Lyndon, the dean of admissions at Beacham University.

Dear Billy,

May I begin by telling you that this year presented us on the admissions staff with one of the most impressive applicant pools of recent years . . .

"Sure, Dean," Billy had thought, "you can tell me

211

anything you want. But what I want to know is, do I get in or don't I?"

> . . . For your splendid record alone you already have good reason to feel proud. And I am glad to have this opportunity to welcome you to Beacham University for the forthcoming academic year.

There had been more, a green card to fill out and some literature about the place.

"Well, that's something at least," Henry had said that night at dinner, "I mean you can relax now, a little."

Lulu called over the weekend.

"I haven't seen you in a while," she said.

"I know."

"I thought maybe you had a lot of work or something."

"No. Not really."

"Well, what have you been doing?"

"This and that."

"What does that mean, 'this and that'? Billy, tell me the truth."

"The truth about what?"

"Why you haven't called me."

"Well I don't know, Lool—I guess it started when I saw you with Cal Campbell the other day, and you seemed so happy there, talking to him, I mean you seemed to really be . . ." He paused. ". . . communicating, the two of you. And you know, we haven't been able to talk much lately. I thought, well, if that's what she wants, if she wants to move on I don't want to stand in her way. It was beautiful what we had, but . . ."

"That's crazy. Billy, that's really crazy. Cal's just a friend. He plays basketball with my brother. I was

212

waiting for you. I came all the way out there to see you, and I ran into Jack and then Cal joined us."

"I wish I could believe you . . ."

"I don't believe this. What are you talking about?" Billy breathed deeply.

"I think it was a test for me. You wanted me to see you with Cal that day, you planned it, I don't know why. I'm not clear about a lot of things. I guess I'm not really over it, yet . . . I'm not blaming you for anything. I don't want you to think that. I mean, let's both keep off the guilt-go-round . . ." (a term Lulu had coined herself once before when describing her family). "You just realized we weren't growing. It took me a while. I wasn't there yet, and it still hurts, but I can accept it. I guess you're right."

"What is this? What is all this crap, Billy? I never thought any of—"

"—Don't get angry. All I'm saying is that I've come to terms with the end of this. I thought you'd be glad to hear that. I didn't want you to think I was bitter about it."

"You've come to terms with the end of this, huh?" Billy drew another deep breath then dived back down. This was going to be hard work.

"Do you see what I'm saying?" he concluded.

"I think so. What you're saying is, you don't want to see me anymore."

"No, that's not what I said at all. I mean, yes it is, but—" She hung up on him. And she gave him the silent treatment for the next six months, breaking it now with the postcard.

22

BILLY WAS THE FIRST ONE OUT OF BED THE NEXT morning. He figured out that the rest were still asleep when he opened the front door and found the mail and newspaper still outside. It was around 10:30, he'd been sitting there, reading the paper, numbly spooning cold cereal into his mouth, when his mother flowed in in her bathrobe and nightgown.

"Good morning, darling," she said, "what time did you finally get in last night?"

"A little after ten."

Soon she was making a "real breakfast" for him, eggs and bacon, and had already poured out two mugs of coffee. She asked about his health and asked about college, how were his courses going, what were the professors like, and the other kids, etc. Fifteen minutes later, Henry made his entrance wearing a green turtleneck shirt (probably a present from Billy's mother, picked out of the L. L. Bean's catalogue, or at Brooks Brothers), a pair of white duck trousers, his face ruddy, fresh from a hot shower and a shave, a dollop of shaving cream clinging to the inside of his ear. So Billy had to go over the whole thing again for Henry's benefit about his courses and professors, expanding the talk to include just what he thought he was getting out of college and what he planned to do with his education in the future.

They stayed at the breakfast table for a long time,

drinking coffee and discussing things, Henry talking about the campaign—"Things are starting to pick up," he said, "we'll talk more about it later today; I'd like to hear your views"—and sharing parts of the *New York Times*. Henry got the dog's leash and called Bonnie and took her around the block. Billy had offered to do it, but Henry had said, "You've worked hard all semester. I hardly do anything anymore. You relax, talk to your mother," which in a way was very decent of him. And while Henry was out with the dog, Abby shuffled in for her breakfast at a few minutes past twelve.

"Did you have a nice time last night?" her mother asked her. Abby said nothing, but obviously outraged by this invasion of her privacy raised her eyes ceilingward, as if to say "oh wow!" She pulled open the refrigerator door.

"What's there to eat?" she wanted to know. Billy was curious to see whether Jason would come in next, complaining "What a drag, you guys used up all the fuckin' hot water," to make it a fivesome, but evidently sometime late in the night, or early in the morning, Jason had slinked off home.

That afternoon Billy tried to do some school work at his desk. He gave some thought to a topic for the final paper in Russo's class, due in about ten days, and he crammed some economics. Final papers, final exams, everything now coming to a head.

His mother went out shopping at a little after two, sticking her head in before she left to remind him that they were all having dinner together tonight, sort of a late Thanksgiving dinner for him since he had been sick in the hospital. Henry left the house right after her to go downtown for a meeting with John Rosenbloom, his campaign director, and some media expert who, Henry seemed to think at breakfast, could really help get the ball rolling. An hour or so after him,

Abby went out too. So Billy was alone in the house for a couple of hours and he managed to get a few things done in that time. For one thing, he took a bath, the first time he had bathed, rather than showered, in over two months. He lay there soaking in the water, not moving, just letting the dirt drift off him in the lulling swishes, like a sleepy, lazy hippo.

Abby brought Rosemarie home with her. Rosemarie was Abby's oldest and closest friend. Rosemarie had been coming over to the house for sleep-overs or to play with Abby since the two girls were five years old.

When Billy's mother got home at a little after five, carrying in with her two shopping bags of groceries and a hat box, she asked Rosemarie to stay over and have dinner with them, but Rosey said she had to be getting back, she was going to a party that night, otherwise she'd stay, "Thanks anyway, Mrs. Wieseltier." Billy remembered Rosemarie from the days when she was just Rosey, Abby's best friend, a little girl with buck teeth who used to wear a T-shirt with a Batman and Robin logo all the time, and who used to giggle about everything. But what had happened here? Who was this, this painfully, depressingly beautiful girl riding high atop those fashion-model boots, wearing corduroy golf knickers, tight black turtleneck sweater, and loopy earrings?

"Those clothes must have set her parents back two hundred dollars," Billy thought. He was hardly surprised when Henry drifted into the living room, sat down in his chair, leaned toward Rosemarie, hands folded in front of him, and asked: "So, Rosemarie, how's the modeling business?" It didn't take him long.

Rosemarie said she was doing "pretty good." She had been only part-timing it since her school started in September, "You know—just weekends and stuff." She said that that past summer, the run-around "was

216

just getting too crazy" so she was glad she didn't have to do it six days a week. "I'm making really good money, though, and I've always been into wearing nice clothes." She sat across from Henry on the sofa, gripping a glass of Diet Pepsi in her long, skinny fingers, her nails curving and candy-lacquered red. Her fingers made Billy think of a chicken's foot.

For some reason the topic of conversation shifted to teenage drug abuse in the high schools. Henry, the hard-nosed reporter earthing out the sometimes unpleasant facts, as well as the sober, concerned candidate for the mayoralty, wanted to know if that sort of thing still went on among high school kids.

"All the drug stuff, the LSD and mescaline, the uppers and the downers and the mushrooms and the banana peels, all that stuff went out with the sixties and long hair, didn't it? I mean, I know the kids are still smoking pot, but they're steering clear of hard drugs, aren't they?"

"I don't know if that's true at all, Mr. Gould. I still think hard drugs are like pretty big. Like there's this guy I know—" she turned to Abby, slumping beside her on the couch "—you remember that guy Marty Simmons, right, Ab? That guy I was like sort of balling last summer? The guy with the red Stingray who thought he was so cool?" Abby nodded, then scratched a pimple on the side of her nose. "—well, like this guy was like a total drug fiend. Like he had this drawer over by his bed, you know, that must have had five thousand dollars' worth of drugs in it. His parents were really rich and everything, you know, and I think they really kind of spoiled him. By like letting him have anything he wanted . . ." At this point, Rosemarie must have intuited for the first time Henry's sweaty discomfort at hearing her talk this way, because she flicked looks at Billy and Abby as if to say "Oh shit! You mean he *isn't* cool?" "Marty is a complete jerk, if you ask me," she added sweetly, but it was a case of too little, too late. Less than twenty seconds later, Henry was slapping his duck-trousered thighs and rising to his feet with an old man's groan, and saying, looking at Billy: "Well, I'm going to go look in on your mother and see how she's doing with our dinner."

For dinner that night were Billy's favorites: double lamb chops with mint jelly, artichokes.

"The thing I've always felt is, you have got to have a goal," Henry was telling Billy after the plates had been cleared and slotted in the dishwasher. The tablecloth was stained with food—spilled butter, lamb chop juice, wine stains from the three bottles of red wine that had been drunk (at least two of those bottles straight down Henry's gullet). "A man's life just doesn't mean anything without a goal to strive for. I mean, look at me, I'm an example . . . I hate the newspaper racket sometimes so badly I'd quit in a minute. I'm getting old, I'm no good at it anymore . . ." He paused for a second to get the full effect. ". . . it's exhausting and it pays lousy and you don't get a chance to write what you want, but I also know that I'd commit suicide in a minute if I didn't have it to do. Because the great thing about journalism, and I've been saying this since day one, is that it sets you a series of goals on the short-term. Every day you're working on a story, say, or working on a deadline and that just keeps you going. It's gotten into my blood. It's my life. Some of these other fellas who started out with me, these guys have all gone into other fields, most of them, into publishing, or TV, desk jobs, editing. I'd go crazy doing that, cause it's really so much pushing buttons, isn't it? It's all automatic. There's no feeling for the goals of the work itself.

"I'm not saying you should have a big goal, I'm not

saying you should be wanting the moon, you understand? Just lots of little goals, that's what gives life its sense of direction, of meaning, of getting somewhere. You know, of progress? Do you follow me? Don't try to do everything in one day, or one week or even one year. What's the big hurry, right? Just one foot in front of another, like an old plowhorse, that's what I've always said . . . next time you see Bernie at Beacham, you ask him about how many times I've said the same things to him. One step in front of another, that's the secret. You know what I'm saying?" Billy, tipsy after draining two wineglasses, nodded.

"What you do is, you set your sights high, right, towards some final destination. Not something impossible, not the moon, as I say. Something you want, something that you'll really have to stretch for: it won't be easy. A challenge, that's the only way you'll value it. And then move slowly towards it, one step, one goal in front of another until you get there, your big goal. See? It's like me and this running-for-mayor thing. Okay, I know, John Rosenbloom knows, that I'm no politician. Nobody knows who the hell I am, I'm just some reporter for the *Daily News*. Right? Big deal, right? But right now, being mayor of this city is my objective, my sense of purpose. Who knows if I'll make it. Crazier things have happened in this world, am I right? Who knows? All these other fellows, the slick politicians who've been stealing the people of this city blind with their payoffs, they're getting all the media exposure. They're the rabbits in this race, do you get me, and I'm like the tortoise. The old plowhorse, one step at a time, dealing with the issues and problems one at a time, not trying to curry favors or sweet-talk anybody. I'm trying to deal with the facts about this city and maybe this time the voters will have caught on. Maybe they'll see through all the double-talk, who can tell?

219

"And what I've been saying about my personal philosophy, okay, well the same principles apply to good city management. One step at a time, leading up to your final end-point. I mean, what would be the greatest thing a mayor could do for this city? Ask yourself that. What should be his ultimate ambition? To show a profit at the end of the first term? A profit, like in any other business, like any other businessman. After the decades of deficit spending, to be able to announce a surplus in the city's coffers at the end of my term, money to hire more cops on the streets at night, to build new schools, to reopen hospitals, money to create a viable mental health program. That's what I'd like to do. And I could do it, I think. I really do. First of all, I want to spend the city money not as if it were someone else's money, but as if it were *my* money. Use what little money there is for what we really need.

"I'd look at each problem individually, one step at a time. Like industry. Like attracting industry back into town. About re-establishing a viable tax base. Do you realize that New York has lost six hundred thousand factory jobs in the last decade or so? Sure, New York was once a great manufacturing city. It was a great harbor first, then it became a great manufacturing city. But then a lot of things happened. For one thing the unions got too strong and the cost of living got so high that the wages an employer had to pay his factory workers were way out of proportion. When once they had factories in Brooklyn that would stitch those blue jeans you're wearing, now they have them made in Korea, by Koreans, for a tenth of what it would cost if they were still being produced in Brooklyn. You didn't know all this, did you? That New York used to be a major manufacturing city, did you? You know why? Because you live in Manhattan, all you ever see are the skyscrapers and the banks. You live on Park

Avenue, you've probably never even been in Brooklyn in your life . . ."

"I have so," Billy thought about protesting, "I've been to Coney Island. I went on a trip to the aquarium with my class in eighth grade."

"Well, Manhattan is like the spoiled child of the boroughs. It's where all the big shots live and it's where all the tourists come and spend their money, so it gets all the money, it gets first crack, while the other boroughs —Brooklyn, Queens, Staten Island . . ."

"And The Bronx," Billy threw in, just to show he knew all the boroughs too.

". . . And mostly The Bronx, in fact, they all have to go without. They're starving, those places, those great old neighborhoods are going broke. Manhattan is like the little baby in the family that gets all the attention. Look, I grew up in Brooklyn, and you know if I was the mayor I'd put a stop to it. We've gotta spread what little money there is left all around the city. Manhattan just doesn't deserve all that attention anymore. It's like a kid, a rich kid, right, who's been molly-coddled since birth, you understand?"—Billy nodded—"who suddenly finds out that his parents have gone broke. He's grown accustomed to all that fancy living and he's unprepared for having to go out and earn an honest living. You know what I mean? Take for an example, say, a kid like you and a kid like . . . well, like I was when I was your age. I was poor as could be. My dad drove a subway train and there were twelve other kids besides me. It wasn't poverty, but it wasn't the Hamptons every June either, you get my meaning? Well, it was rough at the time, but you know, now I wouldn't have traded that upbringing for anything in the world. Because being poor, being down when there's plenty of big guys just across the bridge who seem to have everything, that really gives you a cutting edge. You get mad as hell about it. Somehow or another, you develop an instinct for survival which these rich kids just don't seem to have. Okay? I went out, hustled for a buck for a few years, stayed together, didn't crack up like some people I could name . . ." (the reference was probably to Billy's father) ". . . and now I've got to say I've done pretty well for myself. But now take a kid like you, or Bernie if this is going to touch a nerve. Bernie never went without. New shoes, nice bicycle like the other kids', hell, better than the other kids'. He never went hungry for anything. And now he's not hungry and that's his greatest problem if you ask me. He doesn't want anything out of life. He's already had it already, or he thinks whatever it is, if he wants it badly enough, I'll buy it for him. He's under the impression my last name is Rockefeller. It's no such thing.

"I worry about him terribly, Billy, all the time. He doesn't know what he wants to do with himself. One second it's a writer, next second it's a painter so I give him five hundred dollars to buy himself a good set of paints. That lasts two weeks. Now he wants to be a lawyer. I remember when it was an astronaut and he made me go out and go buy him some expensive space suit at F.A.O. Schwartz. It's his problem, you know. He's twenty-five now and he ought to be able to make decisions himself. And he never listened to me anyway. But a fellow like you, Billy, you've got to watch it. Because the way you've been brought up is cursed, it really is. It's got a big hex on it. Money is a curse, unless you have more of it than you could ever possibly need. Which you don't. But you've been spoiled, Billy, kids like you and Bernie. You go to college, take a lot of liberal arts junk that you could be doing at home, after work, if you wanted to read it all so badly. You never seem to give a thought about what you're going to do with your life.

"You've got to want things. You've really got to

want something bad to have even a slim chance of getting it. So few people get what they want in this world. You've got to be hungry, starving, determined. I don't suppose there's anything you feel that way about, is there?"

Billy thought about it. He ran through a list of occupations he had been considering in the last couple of days—airplane pilot, doctor, architect—and felt very "nothing special, nothing to write home about."

"Any more coffee?" Henry turned to Billy's mother, who had been listening quietly from her chair.

"It's all gone. I could put on a fresh pot if you want." Henry deliberated and decided that, ultimately, it wasn't worth it.

"Don't bother," he said, "I think I'll just take the dog out, buy a cigar and go to bed . . . Bonnie!" He smooched the air for the dog to come, wagging her tail, out from under Abby's chair.

Billy helped his mother clear the dessert plates and the coffee cups. They didn't talk about anything special.

"I think I'm just going to get into bed and read for a while," his mother said. "I've been exhausted all day for some reason . . . Oh, and before I forget, are you going to need some money for the train tomorrow?" Billy's face radiated shame as he took the handout. He was grateful that Henry wasn't there to see it.

An hour later, after making a few notes toward his term paper, Billy got into bed. Lying there in the dark he could tell it was going to be one of those nights, keyed up with insomnia. His mind had become a garbled switchboard of anxieties, mostly all old ones—Zizi, flunking out of school, being friendless, the meaninglessness of his life—mixed in now with some fresh ones —his mother's impending remarriage (enjoying a revival, an oldie-but-goodie), his little sister's mental

223

stability (too many mind-warping drugs?), the need for goals in life (the easy, reachable kind, and the ultimate, final dreamed-of destination—he was lacking both at the moment), plowhorses clopping one foot in front of the other, heading down the road toward happiness and fulfillment.

Somewhere down in the street, a police car's siren booped and blared. Seconds later, the coughing fit started. It began with a tug in the solar plexus, imploring him to sit up, then a hollow pressure in the back of his throat. Each coughing rasp clogged his windpipe with asthma fluid until he was left with a strangling, husky resonance in his chest and there was no air left in him to cough out. Squeezes of inhalant failed to clear things up for very long. It drove him out of bed, into his suitcase for all his pills, then out into the kitchen for a glass of water with which to drink them down. Dried-out dog food in Bonnie's dish, water dripping from the faucet, Abby's hiking boots on the kitchen floor, all objects tingling to flayed senses.

Back in his bed, it still wouldn't let him sleep and it made him feel sickly and pathetic, and it made him feel old. The epinephrine herded some of the phlegm up from his lungs and there was nowhere else to store it for the night except in his head and sinuses. He lay in bed until daybreak, nostrils cemented shut, shifting positions every half hour, breathing through his mouth like a bloated fish.

23

BILLY MUST HAVE FALLEN ASLEEP AT SOME POINT during the night, because when he got out of bed and went into the kitchen, the clock next to the toaster said that it was a few minutes after ten. Henry was up, too, and showered and shaved and reading the Sunday *Times*.

"Good morning, Billy," he said. "Did you sleep well?"

"Pretty well," Billy said. "Is Ma up?"

"No, but she should be. We're supposed to be downtown in forty-five minutes. I told John Rosenbloom we'd drop down to his place and have brunch with him. Why don't you go wake her up?"

Billy opened her bedroom door with a squeak. A rustling of sheets, "Henry—?" as she rolled over.

"No, Ma, it's me. I just came in to say good-bye."

"Oh—" she said, getting oriented, "what time is it?"

"After ten. Henry says you're supposed to get up and go downtown somewhere for brunch."

"All right, hold on," she said, getting out of bed and putting on her robe, "I'll make you some breakfast before we leave."

"No, don't bother. I've got to catch an eleven o'clock train. I've got a lot of work to do."

"Oh. Well—" They stood there, still in silence. Then his mother finished tying her robe. Billy opened his mouth as if to speak, but found he had no words. "I'll

225

fix you some scrambled eggs. It takes two minutes. I hate the thought of you leaving this house without anything in your stomach." Billy heard echoes. He had probably heard this one sentence as much as, if not more than, any other single sentence in the language.

They walked in on Henry emptying the dishwasher.

After breakfast, Billy went down the hall to his room, where he packed his bag. Then, back into the kitchen, loaded bag in hand, for good-byes. He shook hands with Henry, shook off Henry's offer to be dropped at Penn Station in a taxi—they were going downtown and it wouldn't take them all that far out of their way—and then kissed his mother, always an awkward performance (how could he manage to do this gracefully, the way it's done on TV?), bumbling feet, hands not knowing where to go, lips brushing the dry, aging cheek. Saying, "Tell Abby good-bye for me when she wakes up," Billy zipped his coat, took the elevator downstairs, and after walking around the corner to the stop, caught the subway to Penn Station. It took three trains, the Lexington express to Grand Central, then the shuttle to Times Square, then the Eighth Avenue line to Penn Station. (Riding the New York subway system was a fine art. The trains were temperamental and arbitrary. Some mornings, Billy would board the B train, expecting it to take him to The Bronx, and to high school, only to wind up a prisoner of the express train to Flushing, Queens.)

He bought a ticket for the train back to Beacham at a ticket window, the only one open. It was only 11:15 and the terminal was nearly empty. Furthermore, it was Sunday. A drunk was just waking from his bed of Saturday's newspaper. He sat up, yawned, rubbed his eyes, then sat back against the corrugated fence that protected a newsstand, closed Sundays. The bum nodded to Billy as he went past, adding: "Good mornin'," with a cheerful wink of an eye and an idiot's smile.

Billy fell asleep against the train window for a couple of hours, but he woke up feeling horrible, when the train stopped in New Haven to drop off some Yale students getting back from their vacations. Billy still felt sick. Taking four different sets of pills four times a day wasn't helping. All the action inside him upset his stomach and he was surprised when he got off the train in Beacham that he hadn't thrown up at least once. Inside him, a war was being waged and it was going to be a long, drawn-out campaign. Germs, viruses, bacteria, sinister little organisms in dozens of unimaginable shapes, sizes, and colors had occupied his lungs and adjacent territory. Very possibly they were plotting an offensive, raids and invasions directed at as-yet-uninfected parts of Billy's system. In the laboratories, scientists, working and experimenting for years, thought they had perfected a sophisticated arsenal of chemical weapons to combat them. Tetracycline, epinephrine, steroid cortisone, some capsules called Bronkodyll subtitled "Micro-pulverized Theophylline" (a hash of other asthma fighters) which Billy hardly ever took. Take them all, Dr. Weiss, the idiot at the Beacham infirmary, had advised; saturate the system, one will surely do the trick. So Billy had been swallowing pills, one after another, for days and days, it seemed now, dropping them like little bombs into his stomach, radiating antibiotic agents to the affected areas. But Billy's germs, apparently, were like the Vietcong—you couldn't kill off the little fuckers no matter what you dropped on them.

Billy imagined that his germs looked like little Vietnamese with their triangular straw hats, black pajamas, carbine rifles slung over their shoulders, running around, firing, retreating, advancing. Then, a bat-

227

tle scene, the germs retreating into the tangled forests and deep cavities deep down somewhere in Billy's lung tissue, while over their shoulders, the mushroom cloud of a tetracycline pill exploded harmlessly in the distance. Extending the fantasy, that made Drs. Weiss and Johnson, the two dunces who had prescribed all these pills, just like the U.S. presidents (Johnson, again, and Nixon—Dr. Weiss could play Nixon, he looked something like him), just a couple of hicks, Sunday golfers in leisure suits, with no idea what they were doing, or what they were fighting.

On the train ride back to Beacham, Billy gave further thought to Henry's lecture of the night before.

The need for goals. The need for a sense of purpose in one's life. Something to dream about, to plan for, to work toward. What did he want that badly? Was there anything? As close as he could come, it was Zizi and him going to live on a tropical island where you couldn't get asthma, a lush, fertile, palm tree, pineapple paradise where no one knew them from before, or bothered them, or made them feel bad, but instead, treated them with unassuming deference and neighborly respect. Life like an Elvis Presley movie, with Billy getting to be Elvis.

When Billy got back to his room, his cheeks red from the cold walk back to campus from the train station, he found Randy giving himself a pedicure on his bed with a silver clipper and file. At first Billy thought he was practicing yoga, his leg twisted up to his mouth.

"Hey, how ya doing?" Randy said, prying off some of the nail on his big toe with his fingers. "How was your vacation? You go home?"

"Yeah."

"When'd they let you out of the hospital?" Randy

228

uncrooked his leg and swept the gray snippings and file dust off the blanket onto the floor.

"Friday morning."

"Oh. So you got home for the weekend. So how was everybody?"

"Fine. How about yourself? What did you do?" Billy sat down on the chair by Randy's desk.

"Oh man, I had some of the most fucked-up experiences of my life."

"You did? Why?"

"Well, first of all, you know that chick Carol, right? Yeah, well, like she invited me home with her for Thanksgiving dinner, right, and I figured, well with her parents there it's going to pretty much of a drag, but then I thought, 'Aw, what the hell, might as well go. Better than hanging around here for Thanksgiving.' So, like we catch a bus and it takes us a couple of hours to get there and everything. And, like, I get inside her house, and everything's all covered with plastic slipcovers, you know, and everything smells of room freshener and her parents were so totally fucked-up, I mean, like I'd heard things about New Jersey, man, but I never imagined it'd be as bad as that. Everything was so totally gross.

"So I stay there for two days, then I catch another bus into New York to meet my dad who's flown in to consult some new doctor he heard about. And so I see him, you know, and he looks really bad—his hair's all fallen out from like this chemotherapy he's been getting. And he was in a really bad mood the whole time. I've never seen him like that. He must be in a lot of pain. He was talking about death the whole time, telling me, 'When I'm gone, you'll be all alone. Nobody's gonna give a shit about you in this world. Family is all you have,' shit like this, itemizing all the stuff he's leaving me in his will. We had lunch at the Plaza. You ever eaten there?"

229

"No," Billy lied.

"So, anyway he goes into this rap about how he wants to die soon, he wishes it would all just stop, he doesn't care anymore, he doesn't want to take any more cobalt treatments. I just told him, 'Dad, you have got to stay with it. There might be something that will work. I don't want you to die,' and then we're both crying, you know, and everybody in the restaurant is staring at us. And, anyway, Dad goes right on bitching, talking about how I don't understand how much it hurts, he even tells me he's dead already and I just couldn't take it. I took off. I said, 'Dad, if you don't quit talking like this, I'm going to leave.' But he just keeps going on, so I got up and left. I caught the next train to Beacham.

"Then I get a call from him and he says, 'How could you do that, I won't ever see you again, you're all I have,' and we're both crying again, and I say, 'I'm sorry for leaving like that, it was a real idiot move,' can he forgive me, and he says, 'Of course, but how can I ever forgive myself for driving you away. I get so lonely and so scared in the big house now alone I guess I can't handle it.' So I say, 'Look, Dad, I'm coming home. I'll quit school to stay with you while you're sick,' and he says, 'You do that and I'll break every bone in your body. You want me to be even more miserable, drop out of college,' and I say, 'I'm doing it anyway, besides, college is bullshit, I want to be with you, Dad. I love you, you're my father.' And all this. He says, 'Don't quit!' I say: 'I'm quitting.' So he says, 'I'm coming up there this minute. I'll be on the next train. I'll call you from the station,' and I say, 'No, Dad, please don't do that, I'll come to New York,' but it's too late, cause he's already hung up. Okay, so I feel like shit all night long because I think he's going to be sitting on some train for five hours so he can come up here and straighten me out. So I don't

230

sleep all night. I'm waiting for the phone call, but it never comes. I even changed the sheets on your bed so he could sleep in a clean bed. But I don't hear from him. So I think he's died, right. I start to cry and then I call the cops, and I call the train station, you know, I'm on the phone to just about everywhere —I called up Beacham hospital, even. I'm going crazy. So finally I decide to call the Plaza, it's like four in the morning by this time, and the guy tells me that as far as he knows, he hasn't checked out yet. He buzzes the room and my dad tells me he went out and got loaded, came back to his room and passed out. He's leaving for L.A. tomorrow morning."

It was about the saddest story that Billy had ever heard in his whole life. He told Randy so. He couldn't think of anything else to say, so he said that.

Randy shook his head. "Yeah, well," he said. "So like I was supposed to get all this studying done over the vacation, and it ended up I didn't do anything. I got two papers to write and three exams. What've you got?"

"I've got a paper and three exams. Actually, I might have four exams. What happens in English classes? Can they give you tests on the books?"

"Sure. How else are they going to find out if you've been reading them?"

"Gee—I don't know. Russo never said anything about an exam."

"Well, that doesn't mean anything. Besides, I thought you cut that class all the time?"

"That's not true. I've been nearly every time. I was sick last week. He might have said something about it on Tuesday . . ."

"You better find out."

"No kidding. I've still got six books to finish. There

231

are two books for that class I'm supposed to have read that I haven't even bought yet."

"Yeah, you sound like me. Why don't you call up somebody in that class, find out what the story is."

"I don't know who'd be back from vacation yet . . ."

"Call up that chick Zizi. She might be around. Invite her over here while you're at it. I'm bored."

"I suppose I could call her to find out about the exam, but, well, I find her sort of intimidating."

"Why?" Randy said in a challenging tone.

"I don't know why. I just do. I suppose because she's beautiful and everything. I just think she's really formidable."

"I don't get it. I thought you said you fucked that chick."

"I did. But that was years ago. She was drugged up at the time. I bet she doesn't even remember that it happened." "Repressed it," he thought.

Randy contemplated him unhappily. Embarrassed, Billy reached down for his suitcase, unzipped it, ready to begin unpacking. "You're fucked up," Randy finally said. "You're acting like a whimpman. What's wrong with you, anyway?"

"I don't know." Billy shrugged his shoulders. "Beats me," he thought.

"Let me tell you something. I'm not an expert on the subject by any means, but I know enough to tell that you got women all wrong. There are tricks to it. Good-looking girl, right, guys are always trying to nail her, they're falling all over her acting nice and giving her things, taking her out to fancy places, listening to all her problems. Beautiful women have it made. They got the easiest lives in the world. People are always being nice to them, always after them for something. You think a good-looking girl has to worry about getting lonely? Or horny? Naw, of course not. All she has to do is walk around outside. Women have the easiest lives in the world," he repeated, as if resigned to it, "next to little kids. If they're cute and all. Except kids can't do what they want. Chicks get all that attention, plus they can do what they want. Okay, so try to imagine what it's like for a girl like Zizi. She's got all these clowns drooling after her, guys in the library, guys in classes, bus drivers, everybody. What would some guy have to do to get her to sit up and take notice. Huh? To be different? I mean, what if he just didn't give a shit? Or didn't seem to? Wouldn't that get her to thinking?"

"Hold on. Let me get this straight," Billy said, "you think I should call Zizi up and say, you know, 'What about this final exam business?' and then, 'Oh, by the way, don't think I give a shit about you, cause I don't.'"

"Oh, man," (Randy shook his head) "naw, not like that. Look, the thing about these chicks, I think, and this is just a theory of mine, is that they're really guilty about being so beautiful and having things so easy for them. They're all fucked up about it. Most of them have egos that work backwards. Most people like to hear compliments, they like people to be nice to 'em. Beautiful girls don't like that. They don't want to hear that they're beautiful, they want to hear that they're not beautiful enough, or somebody else is better looking. That gets 'em worked up, see? You think some fox likes it when there's a dumbfuck following her around writing poems about her? No way. The kind they go for, and I've got proof of this, if you want to hear it, are the kind who don't give a fuck at all, some guy who'll stick it to 'em but he can take it or leave it, it's not like he's going to commit suicide if she cools him or anything, it's not like he can't get something else. Chicks go for that. I don't know, they like to suffer. They're crazy. A buddy of mine in L.A., he's amazing with women. He's not rich or anything special. Average surfer-type kid. He's got this maxim: 'The only way to treat 'em is to mistreat 'em.' So stop sweating it. What's the big deal, right? Who's she, right, to get you all fucked up? Just think to yourself, 'I'm a pretty cool guy here, I don't give a fuck.' Just be cool." Randy stretched and yawned. "I'm going to dinner. You coming?"

"Maybe later. I've got to unpack and everything."

"Okay."

Billy unpacked while Randy laced up his boots and got his coat from the closet in the other room. "I'm going," he said, looking in the door to fix Billy with a pitying "poor kid" look, a look that a stray dog might get. "Aw look, don't sweat it. You'll be all right."

When he was gone, Billy dumped his suitcase on the chair and went to the phone. He managed to dial Zizi's number straight through.

"Hello, Zizi?" he readied the words to begin, "Billy Williams here." But Zizi wasn't back yet from vacation, or anyway this was what her roommate told him.

"Who's this?"

"Uh, tell her it's Billy Williams . . ."

"Oh hi, Billy," this girl said very matter-of-fact, we're-all-friends-here, "Zizi called about two hours ago. She said she's getting in sometime around eight. I could ask her to call you?"

"No, I'll call her. What, she's taking the train?"

"I imagine she is. That's the way she usually gets in. They might be driving. I'm not positive. Okay?"

"Yes. Thank you. Good-bye."

Who were "they"? he wanted to know.

24

WHEN PATROCLUS FELL, ACHILLES THE AVENGER knew what would happen. He'd have to go down there and tough it out with the Trojans. He had no choice, and he didn't complain about it. He could spend a day or two in camp, lamenting and rolling in the dirt and tearing his hair out—psyching himself up, in other words. But he knew he'd have to go down there and kill Hector. He knew he'd never see the green fields of Achaia again.

Billy thought about this, sitting at his desk, trying to outline his English paper. He, too, really had no choice in the matter. He was going to have to meet Zizi at the train station. Otherwise, he'd never get to be a man. He sighed and pushed the pencil and piece of paper away. He was reconciled to it. It was his fate.

Randy had not come back from dinner. It was a few minutes after seven. He'd probably stopped off in some kid's room to borrow notes taken during classes he had missed. Billy put on his coat, turned off the lights, and left.

Zizi's roommate had said that Zizi would probably be taking the train back, getting in "sometime around eight." Of course, someone might have been lying, and Zizi could slip in by bus. She might be in her room right at that minute, for all Billy knew. The

235

girl had suggested darkly that "they" might drive back. And who were the others, or other, who added to Zizi formed the plural? And supposing "they" put their heads together and decided not to take the car after all. Didn't that mean that "they" would all have to take the train in together? All seventeen of "them," qualifying for group rates? Or just two of them? Or would Zizi be there, alone?

What difference did it make? What chance did Billy have, anyway? He tried to figure it out.

Walking down Main Street, having turned off De-Witt Street, and now headed for Jericho Avenue which would run into the road which led to the Beacham train station, Billy saw a rock in his path and picked it up and carried it with him for a few blocks. Good luck. Actually, it wasn't even a rock, just a chip of concrete, a grainy, jagged piece, bits of which crumbled off when he rubbed it with his thumb. Billy passed a dry cleaning store, shut and locked and murky inside, but through the glass window he made out the time on a glowing clock: twenty to eight. A lot of time. He was nervous and had not thought through what he wanted to say to her.

About fifty yards ahead, lit sickly pale by a street light (a buzzing white ball at the head of a tall, gray brontosaurus neck), was a tree with a trunk about two feet wide. Billy stopped, stood still, concentrating, aiming. Not an easy shot. But if he could hit the tree, everything would break his way, there'd be nothing to worry about. He could just be cool and watch things happen. If he could hit the tree with the chip of concrete in his hand, that would be some kind of omen. He threw, and the rock struck the tree and fell apart with a *thock*. He'd hit it. That was a sign. But what kind of sign? Maybe a bad omen. If he got cocky, thought he had it made, everything would backfire, all the good of hitting the tree and it would be a disas-

236

ter. He had hit the tree. What did that signify? What did that mean?

"It means you hit the tree," Billy told himself. Part of him, he thought, was losing his mind.

The streets to the train station were quiet and empty. What would he do? What would he say? "Well, Zizi! What a surprise!"?

Zizi was not aboard the first train that came in. It was the 7:53 from Washington, D.C., via New York, New Haven, from points south. That meant she would be arriving on a southbound train, from Boston and Montreal, points north. If she would be arriving by train at all.

Billy waited in a blue plastic chair in the otherwise empty Amtrak lounge. At three minutes before eight, he put a quarter in the hot-beverage machine and pressed the button for hot chocolate. The machine poured back a Styrofoam cupful of milky hot water, all out of chocolate powder it seemed. And just what kind of a sign was that? At 8:09, the 8:05 train from Boston was apparently late; Billy pulled open some heavy metal doors and walked upstairs, up to the cold night and the platform.

When the train finally did come, ten minutes late, first a pin of light, then thundering in, Zizi was among the first to hit the ground. She emerged from one of the last cars and, listing to one side, pulled down by a heavy suitcase, she walked in his direction, the direction of the stairs down to the terminal. And as she came toward him, hordes of travelers disembarked all around and in front of her, embracing their families, striding swiftly ahead. Heart beating like a drumroll, Billy started toward her, both knees liquefying at the joints, until he thought they might give way, spastically, beneath him. His stomach quivered. His palms sweated, his throat was dry as wool, his shoulders doubled as ear muffs, and a voice in his head said:

237

"Turn around. Run for it. Idiot, what are you doing? Oh for Christ's sake. Turn arou-ound."

"Zizi. Hi, I thought I'd meet you and walk you back." She stood there for a second, the suitcase about to yank her left arm cleanly out of the socket, just looking at him. Billy stood his ground but barely, slouching toward her in his best approximation of someone being cool. She murmured a few words, which he couldn't hear over the chugging engine and hissing brakes. He took her suitcase from her without a fight, and carried it the rest of the way. Just making himself useful.

Downstairs, in the terminal, Zizi said she was hungry, that she had left wherever it was she had come from without dinner. She didn't seem overly annoyed that he had shown up to meet her. But she certainly didn't act overjoyed to see him, either. She really didn't act anything at all, not even mildly surprised, as they walked awkwardly silent through the train station, through the glass doors out onto the street. Did this kind of thing happen to her all the time?

"I just didn't like the idea of your walking back from the train station alone at night," he said. "I called your room to see if you knew anything about Russo giving us a final exam, and your roommate, what's her name? . . ."

"Alice."

"Alice, yeah . . . she told me you were getting in by train, so I thought I'd find out about this exam from you in person. Also see how you're doing. How was your vacation?" One voice inside him said: "Nice work, kid." A second: "You idiot!" Zizi hadn't answered his question about her vacation. "Huh?"

"Huh? what?"

"How was your vacation?"

"My vacation," she said, "was horrible. Like everything else."

238

"Hmm . . . ," Billy thought, "what does she mean by that?"

The only restaurant he knew about that stayed open late on Sundays was a grimy pizza parlor on the corner of DeWitt Street and Union Boulevard. They made good pizza there, but had he been alone and hungry, Billy would never even have thought about going there. It was a hangout for low-level hoods. Crazies with tattoos, and scars all over their faces from knife fights. But with Zizi there, Billy figured, they'd be safe. It was an unwritten law of the street that they wouldn't beat you up if you were with a girl. A holdover from the days when being a mugger didn't mean you couldn't act like a gentleman about it.

They made very good pizza and had attracted a steady stream of college trade. Cops even looked in once in a while to check the bathrooms to make sure no one had been wasted and dumped, and maybe to have a bite to eat, take a break from their rigorous prowling, sitting on the bar stools, joking with the nervous owner, their walkie-talkies whistling and squawking.

Billy and Zizi sat in a booth, ripped red Naugahyde benches, stitched back together by masking tape. Cups, crumpled napkins, pizza plates and crusts obscured the surface of the Formica table, as well as mostly mutually obscuring Zizi on one side and Billy on the other. But a waiter came after a couple of minutes and cleared it all away. He went so far as to mop the table with a few strokes of a wet rag, and afterward he took their order. Zizi ordered spaghetti, even though Billy warned her it would come out of a can, be terrible—"Order pizza here, that's what's good about this place."

"I feel like spaghetti," Zizi said. Billy's stomach was queasy from all the tension and the asthma pills,

239

and getting queasier by the second, so he ordered a glass of milk. A hood pivoted on a bar stool and looked them over, picking his teeth. Billy kept an eye on him.

They stayed in the pizza parlor that night until closing time. When the spaghetti finally came, Zizi didn't want it. Billy couldn't blame her. It arrived on a paper plate, a big red log of solid spaghetti, the noodles running through it like veins, in the exact size, and with all the indentations and ridges, of the can it had come in, like a Jell-O mold.

"You should have ordered pizza," Billy said. "You could still get some. Do you want me to order it?"

"I'm not really hungry," she said. She was terribly upset, he saw, and really had no appetite.

Zizi talked for four hours. She talked so long, and in such detail, about her recent whereabouts and activities, what she did, where she went, whom she saw, that she had to interrupt her story several times, or her side of the story (there was another side, she wanted to be fair, she wanted Billy to know that), to close her eyes, bite her lip and strain to staunch the tears. There were times when tears took her by surprise, swelling in the corners of her eyes, then glinting in the strange fluorescent lighting in that place, they trickled down her cheeks.

She had had a horrible vacation, as she had told him earlier. Everything was such a mess now. She had thought very seriously on the train that she was really crazy, not just "into self-dramatization," but really crazy, self-destructive, "the whole bit." She had brought all her books away with her when she left on Wednesday, she had so much work to do, but things had been so bad that she hadn't been able to get anything done. She had an exam tomorrow, Monday, that she hadn't prepared for, and that was the least of her worries.

She said she thought she was pregnant. She was pretty sure. That was what she had been doing the day she had stopped off in Billy's room in the hospital. She had come in to give them a urine sample. She had been too scared to go see the doctor right away and had just walked all over the hospital, thinking, when she saw Billy's name on a nurse's clipboard and found out he was a patient and what room he was lying in. It had been while sitting on his bed that she had found the courage to get up, walk in to the doctor's examining room and tell him the thing she feared, give them the sample, and go home. The results had been waiting for her since Saturday morning. She could have called them from where she was staying. But she had been too scared. She was certain the test would come out positive, but she just hadn't wanted to have it certified that she was pregnant just then.

She had spent Thanksgiving vacation with Mr. Russo, the English teacher, as she had spent many of the last several weekends, in his converted barn on a hill overlooking "this really beautiful valley" in Vermont.

On Wednesday, on the train to Boston where Russo would meet her in the car to drive her up to the house (he had left the day before, Tuesday, after class because he wanted to get some work done), Zizi had sat and cried to herself for hours. A sailor taking the train back to his submarine base after a furlough had made some bet with his buddies all sitting across from her and he had moved in to sit next to her and kept asking her what she was crying about.

"Well, maybe if you just stop crying and told me what you're crying for, I could help." And she had thought: "I wish I had a gun right now, because I swear to God, I would put a bullet through this guy in a second." But she had just looked out the window,

241

frozen and rigid. "I was just really getting into hating men," she said, describing her thoughts at the time, "just hating being used and treated like shit and being treated like something a bunch of sailors could make bets on, about whether or not one of them was going to score with me, ya know?" As it turned out the sailor had been persistent, but finally gave up. His buddy came over to give it a try, until they all got off the train at Springfield, Mass.

When the train arrived in Boston, half an hour late, Russo was furious. As if it were her fault that the goddam train was late, as if she had had anything to do with driving the lousy train. He had been waiting there for two hours, did she know that? He had thought she would be arriving on an earlier train. Wasn't that what she had said? No, it wasn't at all what she had said.

All right, he wasn't mad at her, but the whole thing, he said, had really thrown him off and he had planned on finishing a chapter of the Dickens book that evening; now two hours of the day had been blown and he was tense and the whole day was shot to hell, a fucking write-off. Furthermore, Thomas had been getting on his nerves and he wished he had left him back in Beacham with Mary Townsend; trying to write anything with that brat in the house was impossible. Would she take care of him, keep him out of his hair? It'd be a big help. Anyway, he wanted to know, how was she, as they sat snarled in a traffic jam for half an hour, trying to get out of Boston.

"I'm okay," she had said in a totally transparent voice, only to wonder minutes later how in the world he hadn't noticed that she wasn't okay at all.

He made her so nervous that weekend, made her feel so neurotic and miserable, that she had never been able to tell him to his face, "Phil, Ive got something important we have to talk about. I just want to know

242

how you feel about this, what you're prepared to do, what you would like me to do. Stay calm, let's both stay calm because the thing is, you got me pregnant, I don't know how it happened, I've been careful, doing everything I was supposed to do, but these things aren't one hundred percent effective, surely you're aware of that, and this happens sometimes." But she was afraid of telling him. She wanted to catch him when he was in a good mood.

When they pulled into the driveway of Russo's house —a beautiful little house high on a mountain—out the window in the living room, you could see the whole valley, the dairy farms and the closest town—it was already dark. Phil went inside to call the neighbor's house, where Thomas had spent the afternoon, and arranged for Thomas to sleep over with Fred and Annie, the neighbor's twins. Then he went into his study saying that he wanted to work something out for a few hours before dinner—he just had to have the next two chapters finished by the weekend. So Zizi had gone up the stairs to the bedroom and fallen asleep. He came upstairs himself after eleven, to ask if she was hungry, he was making some sandwiches, but she had said no, she just wanted to sleep, and he went back downstairs again. When he came back, it must have been after one. She woke up when she heard his footsteps coming up the stairs and lay there, pretending to sleep while he undressed. She said she had been too groggy and too scared to fight much beyond saying "No, please, I don't feel like it, Phil." But he had forced apart her legs anyway and gone right ahead. She figured it wasn't worth making a scene about.

The next day, it got worse. He sensed that something was wrong with her, but when he asked her to tell him what it was, she didn't tell him. She just said, "I don't know, I'm just in a funny mood," so Russo couldn't really be blamed for just letting it go. If she didn't feel like talking about it, he couldn't make her. She said she was mad about the way he had yelled at her when her train was late. She wanted to know, if meeting her at the train station in Boston was such a huge inconvenience for him, why couldn't he just wait around until her classes were over so she could drive up with him? Why did he have to leave Tuesday afternoon, why couldn't he wait till she could join him? She wanted to know if he was ashamed of her. She wanted to see him more during the week. She wanted to go where he went, "to the parties and stuff," to meet his friends, to stop just pretending now, it was about time, that she was just some student in one of his classes who occasionally baby-sat for his son and hung around in his office a lot for conferences about her work. And what had he said?

"You're driving me crazy with this. The same bit. I've explained it a thousand times to you. I'm not ashamed of you, Zizi. That's sick, that's paranoid of you to think that. It's just that my private life right now has to be very private. It's no one's business what we do, don't you understand that by now?"

Zizi started to cry, biting her lip.

"Do you want to get out of here?" Billy asked.

"I'll be all right," she said. "I'm all . . . right." The hood who had swiveled around to talk to the pizza chef, leaning over the counter, swiveled back around to watch the crying girl. They both watched, the guy who made the pizzas and the hood. Billy tried to ignore them.

"I wanted to leave," Zizi said. "I wanted to walk into town, leave my suitcase there and everything, just get into town and take the bus back here. I didn't know, Beacham, back to Washington. I just wanted to run away. I mean, I know Phil was under a lot of pressure with his writing and everything, but I still couldn't

244

believe some of the crap he was laying down, you know. Like, he said I was being too selfish. Can you believe that? I had said, 'If you don't like having to drive seventy-five miles into Boston to pick me up, why don't you just wait around till I'm ready to drive up with you?' and he said that was being selfish."

Thanksgiving had come and passed. She hardly saw him at all. She took Thomas for a hike in the morning, then took the car to town, hoping to buy turkey and groceries for Thanksgiving dinner that afternoon. But all the stores were shut. Thanksgiving dinner they ate out of cans.

Somehow Friday passed, and Saturday too, but then Saturday night, after eating in agonizing silence, she went to bed early and Russo had gone to his books and then early in the morning to his bed, thinking he was going to "fuck me again." He woke her up, but this time, she struggled and kicked him, fighting with everything that had built up inside her: fear that she was pregnant, resentment at having been made to sneak up to see him from campus on the train, and anger at having to keep it a secret so that nobody would know—when she had told her roommate Alice about them, Russo had almost killed her. "Why did you do that? That's stupid. What business is it of hers?" And Zizi had to say, "Alice doesn't care. She's not going to tell anybody. I just want somebody to know where I am in case something happens." She said she had rationalized not telling Russo because she wanted to hear the results of the urine sample first, she wanted to be sure—and she wanted to kill him, in the dark bedroom, pinned down by this disgusting, cruel, sweating man.

She had fought him off and then, as she sat cowering and trembling on the bed when he turned on the light, arms locked around her knees, pinning her nightgown around her, he tried to talk and explain. He was under a lot of pressure, things weren't going well, the end of term was always a crazy time, he was sorry. Yeah, yeah, yeah. He loved her.

Finally he gave up and went into the guest room to sleep.

When she woke up the next morning, Russo and Thomas had gone out. For a minute, she felt abandoned, they had just said "fuck her" and taken the car back to Beacham. But they came back within the hour, just as she was thinking she had better start packing and write a note in case they came back. Thomas ran upstairs to his room. It seemed that father and son, too, had had a fight. Philip slumped into his chair. And Zizi had sat down opposite him, on the couch, both of them there in the terrifying silence.

"Where did you go?"

"To get the papers."

"Where are they?"

"They were sold out." So they sat some more, brooding, until finally Philip said: "This has been a terrible mistake. I've been thinking about it all week. This has been all wrong, from the very start. You see that, don't you? How wrong this is? . . ." She nodded her head. "Why, why, why," he pleaded with the ceiling, "did I have to do this? Zizi, I'm so sorry for everything. I think you're a terrific girl, I really do, but I'm ten years older than you, and I'm supposed to be an English professor and there are things I'm not supposed to do." She heard him out for about half an hour, at which time he had said, he thought, everything to her that there was to say. That was when she told him she thought she was pregnant.

"Oh come on, Zizi," he had said, "don't be hackneyed. I mean how could you be?" Zizi said she had managed to keep cool and she thought he was convinced when he dropped her off at South Station in Boston to catch the train back to school. He had offered to drive her back to Beacham, but she had said, "I couldn't take that, Phil." So he had driven her to Boston where she had to wait around for a few hours for her train.

She had looked up at the huge departure board inside the terminal, at the spinning numbers and letters of trains and times and destinations and tracks and thought that no, she wouldn't go back to Beacham. She couldn't. She'd go someplace else. She had a hundred dollars in traveler's checks in her suitcase. How far would that take her? Not out to California, the first place that came to mind. And she wasn't going to go home. That was the last place she would go. Maybe to Princeton to see her best friend from boarding school who was a freshman there now. Buy some time there, think, come to decisions. Most of all, have someone to talk to. But then she thought that to go to her friend at Princeton would only be a vacation, she'd have to come back eventually, it would be the same world she had always known: her parents, Beacham University, Philip Russo. What she wanted was to find a new one.

Nevertheless, when the Beacham train pulled in, she got on, steeling herself during the long ride to be tough when she got back, to call the hospital in the morning for the results of her pregnancy test, then to go bright and smiling into Philip's classroom Tuesday morning, maybe have coffee with him after class and tell him, "Yeah, the test came out positive, so I guess I'm pregnant after all. It's kind of a drag, but aw don't worry about it, it's not that big a deal. They've got me written down for an abortion the week after exams. Everything's cool. So how are you doing? That's what's important. Did you get any work done on your book after I left? I hope all that fighting didn't throw you off." She had never felt so alone in her life.

Therefore, he could not know, Billy could never know, how grateful she had been to see him waiting

247

there for her. She hadn't been able to believe it was true at first, that he had come to meet her, that he was really worried about her walking back to campus through the dark street by herself.

At a little before one, in the yard in front of Zizi's dormitory beside a statue of something or somebody (nobody could quite determine), there in the cold, Zizi before him a foot or two away, with her hands in her pockets, looking down at the ground, standing there, everything came pouring out of him.

"I love you, Zizi. I always have. I think about you all the time. I'd do anything in the world for you. I just think you're the most wonderful girl in the world."

Several minutes, more frantic avowals which themselves prompted more tears, and one shy kiss later, Billy was back in his room. The lights were out; Randy had gone to bed. Billy stood by the window looking out at the darkened college buildings and spires under the navy-blue sky, reviewing the night's events. He tried to step back from the situation, to look at it coolly and sensibly, "to just hold on and keep from getting carried away by all this emotion." For perhaps the first time, in any case the first time in modern (post fifth grade) history, Billy's life no longer seemed ridiculous to him, no longer someone else's unkind joke, no longer self-dramatizing nor obsessional, governed by hormones and whimsy and what was on TV and how the Yankees did the night before and boredom. This was serious, very serious, in fact—Zizi was in serious trouble and she would need him to be serious and responsible and kind and patient.

"So all those omens and intuitions about what a disaster everything would be, even Randy's first law of women, they all turned out wrong," he thought. How strange. Maybe he had just read the signs incorrectly. Because it was hard to believe that he had just gotten lucky. Unexpectedly he could feel, playing across his face, a wobbly look of hope. Life worked, or it seemed to. Things were still screwed up, but at least he had something to work with now, someone to think about now, no matter how anxiously; at least it was someone other than himself.

Things were making some sense to him now, as he turned away and walked into his bedroom, closing the door behind him.

25

THE NEXT MORNING AFTER THE ALARM HAD GONE off at a quarter to seven, Billy and Randy dressed in the still-dark bedroom in groggy silence. They met Mel Lavender on the stairs and all walked across the quadrangle together to the dining hall for breakfast. Billy listened to Mel and Randy bitch about all the exams they had to take and all the papers they had to write—Mel said he had brought some amphetamines from home to help him stay up at night. His mother had been dieting and had wheedled pep pills out of her doctor. Billy felt oddly mature, older, sober. He was a changed man, even though to look at him, huddled over his bowl of breakfast cereal, listless as ever, he was from appearances the same Billy as always.

He sat through Professor Fong's Chinese class that morning from eight until nine, taking exhaustive notes. Normally those mornings he bothered, or dared, to show up, he took a seat in the last row where it was less likely that he'd be called upon to translate and where the strange-sounding words of the professor and the incantatory echo chorused by Billy's all-too-eager classmates soon lulled him into a state of dazed dreaminess that the Maharishi himself might envy. But today he arrived in a new spirit, got to the classroom early, took pride, in fact, on being the one who flicked the switch for the overhead lights, and selected a prime seat in the front row. The notes he took were so copious and thorough that he even kept at it—like some court stenographer—when Professor Fong decided to sweeten the hour with a somewhat incoherent anecdote (Professor Fong's English was frequently confusing: he was fine with simple phrases and words, like "now repeat" and "you try" and "nice, nice, velly nice," but syntactic sentences threw him sometimes) about his Far Eastern boyhood growing up in the Hung-Kwa Province, 300 miles to the north of Shanghai.

And after class Billy made arrangements with a kid named Jeff somebody-or-other to rendezvous by the Xerox machine in the library with all the vocabulary lists and notes they had individually managed to assemble over the term so that then they could trade off what they were lacking, like baseball cards, making copies of the material on the Xerox machine.

On his way back to his room to get his lists and notes, Billy stopped off at the post office to check the mailbox. Two letters for Randy and a postcard for Billy from his grandparents in Fort Lauderdale, Florida, where they were wintering (and where they also did most of their spring- and summer- and fall-ing). Just a short note with a picture of a sunny, sandy beach, just to say "having a wonderful time, wish you were here. How are you? We're still alive." Billy decided to bring Randy his two letters. He walked across campus, climbed the stairs to his room, and got his vocabulary lists from a desk drawer.

As it turned out, Jeff, Billy's fellow Chinese scholar, had managed to cut or sleep through or to not pay any attention to nearly all the same classes Billy had missed. They made a deal to enlarge the society in order to acquire the missing material and each promised that whoever got somebody with a complete set of material first would notify the other immediately. Fortunes linked, they went separate ways, Jeff to an eleven o'clock class, Billy to go see if Zizi was around.

Zizi's room: First of all, the door was unlocked. "She shouldn't just leave her door open like this," he thought. There had been a lot of burglaries in the dorms all fall, kids from town who slipped in and somehow slipped back out, having jimmied open the doors, taking wallets, expensive stereo equipment and typewriters with them. The campus daily, *The Beacham Bee,* had been plastered all semester with accounts and interviews concerning these thefts; also concerning four rapes. The Women's Student Caucus was threatening legal action if the university didn't do something to beef up security. A spokesman for the administration in an interview with the *Bee* expressed sympathy but thus far nothing had been done by the school, nor had any legal action been filed by the women's caucus that would then force them to do something. The organizers were all too busy. They had getting into law school to worry about. Priorities, first things first.

So what was Zizi doing, leaving her door open like this?

The living room was quiet and sunny, lush with colorful Impressionist posters and prints, potted plants on the windowsill, on top of tables and desks, a four-foot tree growing out of a wicker basket on the floor.

It was so different from the grim, greasy room Billy shared with Randy Rolfe. It was a room where people changed the lightbulbs when they went dead; it didn't stink of socks and beer and vomit (from the time Mel Lavender had come back drunk from a happy hour and thrown up on the rug—nearly a month ago, and you could still smell it, especially when it rained); no three-week-old laundry piled up in corners, or sprawled over desktops and chairs, no dirty magazines, no football posters, no pyramidal beer-can statue. Billy thought the room even smelled of girls, like shampoo and plants, clean. It occurred to him that he wouldn't mind spending the rest of his life living in this room, or one like it.

The bedroom was another story. First of all, he almost tripped over Zizi's suitcase, split open but not yet unpacked, in the middle of the floor, a stewpot full of sweaters and balls of socks, a rumpled dress, assorted underthings, a flowery toilet kit, more girl's stuff. On the two dressers, lined up side by side along the wall, stood all sorts of bottled preparations and prescriptions, shampoo bottles, contact lens solution, deodorant spray cans, a hairbrush with a nest of Zizi's pale yellow hair woven among the bristles: more female junk than Billy had seen anywhere, even in his mother's bathroom, and her private collection was vast. The bunk on top, where Zizi's roommate Alice had slept, was neatly made, decorated with stuffed bears and rabbits and kitties, all sitting up like gentlemen, propped against the pillow or the wall. Zizi's bed was also occupied, Zizi still sleeping in a fetal bundle: blue nightgown, kneecaps for breasts, hair falling over her eyes and nose, bedsheets pulled tightly around her. A stuffed bear, this one Zizi's friend, presumably had been chucked out of bed and lay face down on the floor surrounded by crumpled Kleenexes.

Face hushed and brow creased, Billy watched her

sleep for a while, then woke her. Zizi stirred, rolled over and looked at him strangely. What are you doing here? Then seemed to remember.

"What time is it?"

"After eleven."

"I've got my exam at two-thirty. I haven't studied at all for it."

"You don't have to take it. They'll let you make it up. How did you sleep?"

Zizi got out of bed, looked at herself in her mirror, opened her closet and took out a towel, getting ready to walk out to the bathroom at the end of the hall to take a shower. From a chair Billy watched her prepare. While she was gone, it gave him a chance to examine her room in greater detail, her closet, what her drawers held, her desk, but he didn't find anything very extraordinary.

After her shower, still in her bathrobe, Zizi called the infirmary to learn the results of her pregnancy test. From the bedroom Billy heard her talking.

"Uh huh. I understand. I know that." She sounded very businesslike, her voice steady. She walked back into the room and managed to say, "Well, it's official," before she started crying again. It took Billy half an hour comforting her, holding her shoulders, gushing reassurances before he finally convinced her to "listen to me. You aren't totally fucked up" or manic-depressive or pathetic or a "really hateable, horrible person." Which were all the things she said she was. He finally got her to get dressed.

They almost missed lunch. As it was, all the grilled cheese sandwiches were gone and they had to settle for two of the last hot dogs. There were, however, plenty of baked beans left. Out of the corner of his eye, Billy saw Randy at a far table, laughing and clowning with several of his madcap friends. He didn't think that Zizi was ready yet to sit with that crowd.

At least not for the next couple of years. They sat down instead with John Bokku. John had been released from the infirmary only that morning—the doctors had given him a set of crutches to ride around on until the bones in his foot healed. Bokku had been eating alone, and he seemed delighted to see Billy. So that was good. He complimented Billy on how well he looked, so much better than that first day in the hospital. Bokku told colorful, exotic stories about the dances and rituals his people practiced, describing his village, the palace, his uncle the president (read dictator), the new planes his uncle had recently purchased from the French (six supersonic fighters and two swing-wing bombers), tribal life in general. The dialogue became so animated that it managed to bring out regular smiles and some color to Zizi's full but pallid lips.

After lunch, Billy walked Zizi over to DeWitt Street, to the building where she had to take an exam. She'd done most of the work in the course (introductory psychology) and was pretty sure she could at least pass it. She said she didn't want things to pile up. She didn't want the exam hanging over her head for the rest of the term; she'd have enough to think about in the coming ten days. "Are you going to be all right?" She'd be okay, she said when he asked her, his hands on her upper arms, her hands playing with his jacket button. She said she was going to have dinner with her roommate—she and Alice had stayed up late last night, talking about everything. She'd promised they'd eat dinner. Did he mind that? Did he understand?

"Sure, that's good that you can talk to Alice. I mean, her being another girl and everything." After dinner Alice and she were going to the gym to do yoga until eight-thirty. They'd be back by nine o'clock. He could give her a call then.

"Listen," he said then, "are you listening?" She raised her head, looked a little weak, but nodded. "I'll do anything for you. Honestly. I don't care about anything else. I don't care about this stupid school or anybody in it. Just you. Things'll be all right. Really. Just don't worry. Okay?" She nodded.

"I've got to get inside." He let her go and she walked up the walk, up three steps to the entrance of the building. He thought she might pause to turn around to just catch one last glimpse of him, so he tried to look at once handsome and responsible, checking both ways for two-way traffic before crossing DeWitt Street.

Billy went to the library to work on his paper for the rest of the afternoon. Considering all that was on his mind he managed to get a lot accomplished. He had decided to write about Sophocles. *The Bacchae* was one of the books he had been able to complete and even to understand for Russo's class. And he had read *Oedipus Rex* as a junior in high school, so he could throw in some stuff about that. Things were really falling into place as he sat in a futuristic stall in the recently constructed Star Trek Wing of the library, all glass, space-center leather chairs, and demonic Xeroxing machines.

At dinner, Billy sat down with Randy and some guy Billy had never seen before whom Randy introduced as Ron Finkelstein. Finkelstein talked very fast and Billy listened while Randy tried to bargain with him for a copy of the last year's Engineering II final exam.

When Finkelstein went back to the kitchen for a second helping of stringy roast beef, Randy said: "I can't believe this guy. He's trying to get me to pay twenty-five dollars. Can you believe what a Jew this guy is? Only a Jewish guy'd do something like this.

I'm serious. A normal guy wouldn't try to make some big profit off me. Like if it was me and some guy was going to get screwed in engineering, what the hell, I'd give him the exam if I had it. What good would it do me?" When Finkelstein returned, Randy told him: "Look, Finkelstein, you know I have no way of telling if this year they're going to give the same exam as last year. How do I know I won't shell out all this money only to have the exam be different? Huh?"

"Don't worry, Randy," Finkelstein assured him, "it'll be the same exam." He sounded sure, so Randy looked at Billy, shrugged his shoulders, and after they all put their trays away, they walked back to the room together and Billy watched Randy write Finkelstein a check. Finkelstein said he'd be over later to hand-deliver the merchandise. Billy went back to the library.

He called Zizi from a phone booth at a little before ten. She said she thought she had passed the exam and that right now she was in the middle of "a really good talk with my roommate." She sounded happier. She said he could come over if he wanted to. They'd just be talking.

He closed his notebook when the clock over his head said it was eleven. He stopped in Zizi's room before returning to his own room, but he had the feeling that he was interrupting things. He stayed long enough to drink a cup of tea that Alice made for him with an immersion heater. In that time, they talked about Zizi's exam, Billy's paper (Zizi commenting that she was "really impressed" that he had gotten as far as he had, lamenting that she hadn't even thought up a topic for her paper "and you're almost finished with yours"). They talked about John Bokku, Zizi deferring to Billy to tell Alice all the funny things about him. It seemed that Zizi had already told Alice what little she knew about Bokku; it seemed also that she had painted a cheerful picture, rather than a freakish one, of the lunch the three of them had had just after she had called the hospital "and everything and was really upset." So that was a good sign. Billy felt good, liked, trusted, useful. "Billy was so great to me," he could almost hear Zizi describing it to her roommate, "he's a really old friend of mine. I've known him since I was about fifteen."

Zizi sat curled up in a high-backed armchair, legs folded up inside her blue nightgown. She held onto the white tea mug with both hands, raising it to her mouth from time to time, to sip, gingerly. While Billy was there, no one said anything about anyone being pregnant, or about Russo, or about anything being wrong, anywhere. Billy thought Zizi looked tired, though beautiful—warm-cheeked, nice, lustrous hair. She seemed to be taking things all right.

She even walked him out to the landing when he said he had to get back to his room and go to sleep.

He didn't get much sleeping done that night, but now he was getting used to it. His mind was full of thoughts he hadn't had time to digest during the day. Zizi would have to have an abortion. Or would she? Sometimes girls get mixed up, carry on, get attached to the idea of having a baby. Who cares if it's practical. Billy's mother had worked for about a year as a volunteer for Planned Parenthood. "Abortion on demand"; "Every child a wanted child." Emotional issue. Senseless fetus, nothing more than scraping out baked beans. Or murder? Right-to-life versus overpopulation and dwindling food resources. Black leaders protested it when the government financed abortions for poor women. They said it was genocide. The abortion doctor, wearing a mask and gloves, white bed sheets, metal clamps, stirrups that would spread her legs apart. What happens next? Billy didn't know much about the process. Something about "scraping." His mother had said something about how they stuff a plastic hose into the girl and turn on a vacuum that sucks the baby right out of her. Vacuum the womb. "Zizi, I want to see your womb vacuumed. Also, the bed made, windows washed."

"No doubt about it," he thought, "I got a good deal when I wasn't born a girl." The last time he looked at Randy's radio alarm clock, the vague gray face informed him that it was after 3 A.M.

26

JUST A LITTLE OVER A WEEK TO GO UNTIL THE END OF the term, but what a week!

It was a week of being startled awake at 5 A.M. by Randy's alarm clock radio going off. Billy woke one morning to hear an ad for sanitary napkins. Another morning, to the fast-talking, throaty hustle of a deejay conducting a phone-a-thon for chronic insomniacs and anyone else who had some reason to be awake at that time of the morning. The issues bandied about at that hour included: the energy shortage, food prices, the President's failure to construct a single cohesive policy on anything, the riots that had occurred earlier in the fall between ecologically minded protesters and the National Guard at the site of a nearby nuclear power plant, the race for the next mayor of Beacham, and also some kook who said everyone'd be dead anyway soon because the polar icecaps were melting. "God what a country," Billy thought, lying in the dark, waiting for Randy to roll over, sigh, sweat, get out of bed to turn the radio off, then shuffle out to the bathroom for a shower before starting to cram for his exams later that morning.

It was a week of working for two dark hours at his desk, the only light coming from the Tensor lamp, Randy working under similar conditions in the outer room, both trying to pass exams and make up the work they hadn't done. A week of blearily stumbling around campus, a week when bloodshot eyes, ragged beards, inside-out shirts were badges of honor, of distinction, when amphetamines commanded two dollars a tablet if you wanted some (Billy didn't, but he watched Randy get some). It was a week of hysteria, daring plagiarisms, the week his mother's letter came to tell him "big surprise in store," her "I might be marrying Henry" letter. A week spent trying to take care of Zizi, and a lot of other things.

In that week four important events took place.

One: Russo's first class after the return from vacation. (Less an event, or incident, than a premonition of things to come.) Billy started out on the offensive. He strode carelessly into class ten minutes late, offering neither craven excuse nor apology; he disrupted everything, cutting Russo off in midsentence with the well-timed thump of his books dropping from a height of two feet onto the tabletop; he sat down, asking loud questions of his neighbors: "Hey, what have I missed?" "Hey, how was your vacation?" "Can I look over some of your notes later?" Whether Russo noticed all this provocation or not, Billy wasn't sure. If Russo did, he chose to let it go.

Russo was in a good mood because for the first time in nearly a month most of the chairs around the tables had students sitting in them. Billy was surprised to see all his classmates again too. He figured that since it was the end of term, final exams and grades, they had turned up on their best behavior for the long final stretch. Kranepool was there, and Stanley Wang and Jack White. Billy wanted to ask them, as loudly as he dared, how they all were, "it's been, like, ages, man." It felt like a twenty-fifth high school reunion. Most of the chairs were filled except for one at the foot of the table where Zizi normally sat.

"You dirty son-of-a-bitch," Billy thought, staring murderously at Russo, who, back to the class, was illustrating some point with a diagram on the blackboard. "I'd like to take a hammer and bash your head in. I'd like to . . ." And he enjoyed home movies of his own two hands around the professor's chicken neck, choking him over backward until he slumped lifeless to the floor, tongue hanging out of his mouth, eyes glassy with death, still bulging in terror and throes of agony.

But these visions soon gave way to one far more disturbing.

"I just don't see how Zizi could have done it. What could she see in Russo? All sideburns and acne scars . . ." Billy always had trouble figuring out what women found worth admiring about men's bodies. He could never understand why they weren't all dykes. "With those big eyes and mouth, he looks like a fish I caught once." There was a second while his thoughts almost moved away, on to Russo's lecture, or something about the last chapters of *The Faerie Queene,* or anything. But they didn't. Suddenly he was hit full force with it. Curtains parted and Russo appeared on stage, coming forward into the white harsh light, naked, scrawny, spider-hairy. He bowed. The audience applauded. "Thank you, thank you. Oh, too kind people. Really." Lights lit up the rest of the stage, revealing a bed, a brass-steaded double bed with a girl sleeping beautifully under the quilted covers. Zizi. More applause.

Fiddling a minute, setting an alarm clock, then folding a pair of trousers, Russo pulled back the bedsheets and crawled in beside her. A hairy black hand, a spider's foot, a monkey's paw creeping up her back, over her milky shoulders, over the hump to the other side. Billy was devastated. Zizi would roll over and smile sleepily at him. She'd let him. She'd want to. He couldn't chase these pictures from his mind. He wondered if he had ever felt as depressed about anything in his life. When Russo finally dismissed the class, it was nearly all Billy could do to get out of the chair.

Two: Zizi said she wanted to quit school, or at least quit Beacham. When he asked her what she proposed to do instead, she said she would go to California and look for work. Her sister lived there, she could stay with her. She might work at the health food store her sister's husband managed in San Francisco.

Zizi had spoken to Billy a couple of times about her hating Beacham and not wanting to go back after the end of term. But Billy hadn't taken her seriously, dismissing it as just so much wild talk. She was upset and had every right to be. But she'd get over it.

And then Saturday nght, after studying in his room until ten—boredom teetering on the brink of something worse—he decided to visit her. She had said earlier in the day that she'd just be in her room all night, trying to write her paper for Russo. Billy had finally convinced her not to drop Russo's course. He told her she didn't have to show up at class anymore, and all she had to do to get credit was to write her paper. Russo'd probably give her an A, considering he'd been sleeping with her and all.

Once again, Billy found the front door to Zizi's room unlocked, and when no one answered when he knocked, he just walked in. Zizi's voice, both languid and anxious, came from behind the closed bedroom door.

261

"Alice?" So he popped his head in brightly and said no, it wasn't Alice, it was Billy. "I thought I'd come by."

She was propped up in bed, surrounded by a zoo of stuffed animals—tigers and camels and koala bears, several of whom lived upstairs on Alice's bunk but who now had come down to stay with Zizi until she got better. Wadded Kleenexes littered the blanket and the floor. Zizi was sitting up in the middle of the mess, haggardly chain-smoking cigarettes, the ashtray on her stomach.

He came over, threw the koala bear off the bed, and sat down in its place. He decided to try asking her how she was.

"Fine," she mouthed, averting her eyes. She sniffed and reached over for her cigarettes with an apologetic smile.

She had been, he eventually got it out of her, talking on the phone with her parents. They had called to see how she was, they hadn't spoken to her for so long, they were worried that she was pushing herself too hard, she sounded tired. Was she well? Had she gotten through that backlog of work which had kept her, or so they believed, from coming home to spend Thanksgiving vacation with them?

She had told them—"Hold onto your hats, folks . . . Mom, Dad"—that she was thinking about dropping out of school. What did they think of the idea?

Her parents had been berating her for over an hour, taking turns.

"You pull a crazy stunt like that, Miss," her father had said, "and I'll cut off your allowance as fast as you can bat an eye. I won't give you a dime." And so on, and so forth.

How had she left it with them? She had promised them that she would think it over a little more. Whatever she decided, she had sworn to them that she would finish out the term. She would do nothing rash. But Zizi told Billy that she had done all the thinking she needed, or wanted to do. Her mind was made up. She would have her abortion—she had already made an appointment through the Beacham infirmary to have the operation the day after her last exam. The abortion would be performed, or administered, at the Beacham Medical Center, a large facility in town which had a fine abortion/gynecology/obstetrics clinic. Alice was helping to finance things. Zizi would have the abortion, then get out of Beacham, away from Washington and New York and Boston and what she called "the whole fucked-up northeastern mentality" and take a bus, or maybe even hitchhike, to California where she had heard the mentality wasn't so fucked up.

"It's not like I don't have any plans or any idea what I'd do. It's not like I'm just running away," Zizi explained, "cause I'm not. Like, my older sister—I told you about Muffin? Right? How she's living out there with her husband and their baby, you know, and they own a lot of land in the country north of San Francisco, and they've got this sort of farm and Alfred [Zizi's brother-in-law] manages this big health food store. I worked there last summer. I know I could get a job there for as long as I wanted. Or I could live on the farm with Muffin and the baby. And, like if I wanted to, I could go to school out there. Muffin's taking some adult education courses, like, once a week, at Berkeley. She'll get her B.A. in two more years. You don't even have to pay tuition if you're a California resident. And California's so beautiful. It's sunny and it never really gets too cold. Have you ever been there?" Billy said yes, he had, he had this father, sort of, who lived out there, but he decided not to get too deeply into it.

Billy started out trying to convince Zizi to be what

he called "realistic and sensible." He tried to convince her that education was a privilege, a wonderful thing, she mustn't throw it away. Beacham was a good school. Adult education was, well, for anybody. For truck drivers who had never read *Huckleberry Finn* or *Moby Dick*. She didn't want to do that.

"Billy, wow! Like, that's just so . . . so . . . well, like no offense or anything, but that's so middle-class. I'm not putting you down. But college isn't a privilege unless you like it, unless you're really excited by all the things you're learning in it. And, like maybe that's the way it is for you, but that's really not my experience at all."

Alice came back from the movies at around 2 A.M. By this time, Zizi had gotten out of bed and they had moved to chairs in the living room where the tea cups and immersion heater were, and where they could listen to the record player. Alice sat down and talked with them for a couple of minutes, long enough for a mug of tea, describing the movies she had just seen. Evidently it was Nazi Atrocities Night at the Beacham Film Society. She had been taken to see *Nuit et le Brouillard* about the death camps, showing film clips of the Nazis bulldozing corpses into a ditch, playing on a double-bill with *The Sorrow and the Pity*. She had gone with a morose Jewish sophomore, a philosophy major on top of everything else. The movies lasted five hours. After that, she and her date had discussed the pictures for another hour or so. She said she was exhausted, and that the movies had been "sort of depressing," so she went to bed around two-thirty. Billy made an offer to leave, but Zizi said, "No, please stay up with me just a little more. I really need to talk to somebody about this." She made them fresh cups of tea.

Billy continued to try to talk her out of quitting Beacham at the end of the term. He didn't say so, but the truth was simply that he didn't want her to leave. He had put so much energy into just getting this far. He had a big stake in her staying. As soon as she had her abortion and the new term started, they could go out to movies, and study together, and go out to dinner and go away for weekends. She'd see what a good time they'd have. What a waste if, after all this, she would quit school. Nevertheless, he told her that he was trying to be honest with her, he had her best interests at heart. She told him:

"Philip told me this once. And, like, this really made me think, you know, for like the first time about what college is really about. He told me that if he had it to do over again, like if he was your age . . . or," she caught herself and qualified, "our age, you know, and he knew what he knows now, he'd have stayed out of college. He said he might have been a writer if he'd only had the courage to like resist Princeton when he got accepted by them. He said he almost didn't go, and that, like going to Princeton was the worst mistake of his life, because it's almost impossible to get off that like, higher-education treadmill. He said when he was about eighteen and he found out he could go to Princeton if he wanted, he was really seriously thinking of maybe getting on some freighter and working his way around the world, you know, to like, get experience. And then after maybe five years or so, he said he dreamed about going to the Caribbean to live down there on some beautiful island and write. But he didn't, and now he really regrets it. His parents sort of wanted him to go to Princeton. They were all caught up in the big status thing, you know, like, 'We have a son who goes to an Ivy League school,' and all this. And he won some scholarship. So he went. But Philip said to me once, and I really think it makes a lot of sense, that when you're young, like we are, like nineteen and twenty and twenty-one, you have more en-

265

ergy and more curiosity about the world than you might ever have again. You pick up things faster, it's like you have all this restless, psychic energy and it's a really terrible waste, he says, to hang around in some school the whole time. Because you're young, right? You're restless and more important, you're enthusiastic about things. Philip says that's what college killed in him. Like he went to Princeton and he lost all his enthusiasm for the world because the world he lived in was so controlled. He said he's just been a passive receiver of information all his life. He really wished he had done it differently. Now, he's too old, and he's got a kid and everything, and he's really bitter. He wishes he was a young guy again. That's a big part of the reason why he's so screwed up. You know?"

They stayed up that night, sitting in high-backed armchairs, drinking mugs of tea and talking until dawn broke. They talked about: Zizi's parents, Henry Gould and Billy's mother, why the world was so fucked up, Russo, his house in Vermont, Russo's son and how cute he was, the abortion and what a son-of-a-bitch Russo was, why Billy hated Russo and why Zizi couldn't bring herself to "like, really hate him"; they talked about California and what kind of life Zizi dreamed of living there: enthusiasm, self-confidence, making money, living on farms, the country as opposed to the city. Among other things. Finally, dawn broke outside the window. When he looked outside, Billy became at first aware of an indigo deepness, a color he must have seen so many times, from so many sleepless beds, but which it now seemed as if he had never noticed before. Like some full and rich staining of emotion. Gradually, the indigo brightened, turned translucent, and then dissolved completely.

Billy had started out trying to convince Zizi to stay in school, but by 6:15, he was not only convinced that she should quit school and go to California, but that he should quit school himself and go to California with her. Or at least that was what he said to her, and that was what they discussed excitedly until 7:00.

"Oh Billy, we could go. We really could. And you could work with Alfred on the farm. I'm really excited, this is really great. It really sounds great, doesn't it?" It did sound great, really.

"I wonder how I'm going to explain all this to my mother," was what Billy was thinking to himself as he walked down the stairs on the way back to his room, to take a shower and shave, maybe nap for a few hours, then study economics all afternoon in the library.

Three: Simon King came by to see Billy to ask him for help writing his English paper. Simon King was in jeopardy of flunking freshman English. There was nothing surprising about his seeking help, nor was there anything surprising about his seeking Billy's help, since they lived on the same floor and Simon had doubtless overheard Mel Lavender, or Billy himself, talking about the accelerated English program he was in. On the face of it, an ordinary incident, but why then? why when it happened? and why the way that it happened?

What day was it? The days of the last week of term all seemed to run together. Did Simon King come by on Monday, or Tuesday? Only a day or two after Billy had arrived at the Big Decision (to drop out, to go out to California with Zizi and get a job working for Zizi's brother-in-law at the health food store). It was the day of the big snowstorm. What day was that? Billy wasn't sure whether it was Monday or Tuesday.

He had been sitting at his desk trying to think of a

conclusion for his paper for Russo, but ideas were not forthcoming. He and Zizi had decided that the sensible thing to do was to earn full college credit for the term at Beacham. Who knew? They might want to go back to college once they got to California—Berkeley night school or something. Furthermore, they felt guilty enough when they checked the college red book of rules and regulations to find out that unless a student indicated his intention to take off the second semester in writing, in a letter to the dean received before November 3, the school would not refund any part of the full year's tuition. Billy was pretty sure that his father hadn't gotten around to paying his school bills, but Zizi said her parents had already done so. The cost for the second semester? $3,500. Down the drain.

Studying the handwritten draft of his paper on Sophocles, trying to figure out what it was he was supposed to be concluding in his conclusion, he was surprised when, rising from his desk to answer a knock at the door, he found Simon King standing on the gray slate floor of the corridor, dripping melting snow from his coat and wearing rubber galoshes with buckles unfastened.

Billy and Simon had crossed paths several times during the last three months of the semester. Sometimes they passed on the stairs, Billy going down, Simon coming up, or the other way around. Other times they found themselves using the bathroom at the same time, Billy in the shower, Simon at the urinal, or again the other way around. For the first few weeks of school, Billy had tried to be friendly, giving Simon a hearty "Hi," or "How's it going?" but Simon only nodded and mumbled (a curse? a threat? "fucked-up honky asshole"?) and left Billy standing there, grinning, mumbling, "Okay. See you later, old buddy." Faked out. After a while, Billy soured and from then on he only nodded at Simon, and started mumbling back.

"How you doing, my man?" Simon said, pulling off his head a tight black and orange stretch-wool hat.

"I'm all right. How are you?"

"Not so good, not so good. Mind if I come in?"

"No, come on in."

"See, what it is . . . uh . . . ," said Simon, unbuttoning his huge gray coat and unwinding a scarf around his neck, "like, see, I got to write this English paper. Like I got to have the bitch done tonight . . . ," he said with emphasis, "and I'm having trouble with it, and I was hoping maybe later you could give me some help. Cause I don't know much about writing papers. Like, I don't have what you'd call, it's like a paper-writing intelligence, you know?"

"Well sure, I'll help you all I can. Which may not be much. I'm trying to figure out this paper of my own and it's going really badly. But okay, show me the stuff you have to write about."

"It's this poem."

"What poem?"

"Some bullshit. I don't know. I got it in my pocket." Simon reached over for his coat which he had dumped on the sofa and went through the pockets and the holes in the lining down which the poem, or book of poems, might have slipped before he pulled out a paperback poetry anthology. "I got the page marked in here . . . Let's see . . . yeah, this is it, yeah. It's some poem called 'Dover Beach.' You ever seen it? You know what all this jive bullshit is supposed to be about?"

"Oh I know this poem," Billy said, taking the book; "I had to read it in high school. It's not bullshit, at least I don't think so. Yeah, I can give you some help with this."

"Yeah, help me, you know, just do whatever you

269

can," Simon said, suggesting that if Billy wanted to, or happened to have an old paper lying around from that high school, well, you know . . .

"So what do you need help with?"

"Well, like, can you help me find something to write a five-page paper about?"

"Hmm. Well, okay. Have you read the poem?" Simon nodded. "Okay, then you must know that the action takes place in Dover, England. Right? Dover Beach. The beach at Dover. You know where Dover is, right?"

"Yeah, yeah. White cliffs of Dover and all that World War Two shit."

"Well, right, only this poem was written way before World War Two. But you're right about the white cliffs. So what's across the English channel from the white cliffs?"

"France?"

"Good. Right. And over in France, on the continent, you know, there's a war being fought. Like England, the country of the poet, is fighting a war on the continent, and soldiers are dying and everything's going crazy. Okay? . . . Okay, there's this war going on across the channel and in the meantime, there's this guy, this poet, and he isn't fighting, he's just looking out across the channel and thinking about everything. And he's there with his girl friend, see? Because that's who he's talking to. 'Come to the window, sweet is the night air,' " Billy quoted, almost from memory. "You got it so far?"

"What, like they got a beach house or something?"

"Yeah. Because he's talking about a window, so sure. They live in a house by the beach. They must have a house if they have a window to look out of. So they're in the house, and the night is beautiful, 'the moon lies fair upon the straits.' But across the channel, at that same moment, there's this crazy war being

270

fought, and nobody knows why. It's just some crazy thing that the countries' leaders and generals have gotten the people all mixed up in. So beyond the window, outside, is the crazy world, you see? The world is crazy. You get me?"

"Yeah, yeah. That makes some sense. The world's fucked up, but the dude's in there with some fox, so he don't give a shit."

"Well, yeah. He's looking out the window and he's just thinking to himself, 'Damn. Nothing's the way it should be at all. Everything's going wrong, everybody's acting crazy, shooting at each other, making a mess of everything.' And there's this part about Sophocles." Billy saw that Simon had underlined Sophocles' name in the book and written "Greek writer" in the margin by it. " 'Sophocles long ago heard it on the Aegean, and it brought into his mind the turgid ebb and flow of human misery . . .' Do you understand that part? In other words, Matthew Arnold is saying that it's not just modern-day England, nineteenth-century England that's got things all screwed up. He's saying that that's the way the world has always seemed, especially to literary-minded guys. This crazy world is no different from what it was when Sophocles was writing. People were still fighting and killing each other and acting badly. It was so crazy that even a guy as smart as Sophocles couldn't figure it out. See?"

"Yeah," Simon nodded, "then what?"

In the book, Simon had underlined the word "Aegean" and written by it, "sea near Greece." "Okay, so here's what the poem is saying. The guy's there, right, with his girl friend, and he's just thinking about everything . . ."

"Like getting philosophical?"

"Yeah, that's what he's doing. He's there with his girl, right, who he loves and everything. And he turns to her, and he's all sad about what a fucked-up, hope-

271

less world they live in, and he says: 'Ah love, let us be true to one another! for the world, which seems to lie before us like a land of dreams, so various, so beautiful, so new, hath really neither joy, nor love, nor light, nor certitude, nor peace, nor help from pain . . .' You get that? He's saying that the beauties and happiness and splendors of the world are all illusory . . ." (this word "illusory" was one of the two or three dozen words Billy had learned in Russo's class) ". . . he's saying that life is miserable, like, the world is cruel and it doesn't take any notice whether people are enjoying themselves or not. It just keeps spinning. This crazy life just goes on and on, and there's really nothing anyone can do to change things. There'll always be poverty, and racism and hatred and murder. See? And wars. The only thing he can do, this guy is saying, is if he and his girl can count on each other, and behave well towards each other. Okay? Does that make sense to you?"

"Yeah, yeah, that makes some sense. That poem's cool." Simon said this from sitting on the couch. He was rubbing his cheek and looked digestive.

"I really like that poem. It's really great."

"Okay, so now what do I put?" Simon hung around, drafting his paper, paragraph by paragraph, reading aloud to Billy what he had written, agreeing with every one of Billy's corrections until dinnertime.

Coincidence? It could have been. Certainly there had been earlier times in Billy's life when he had superstitiously interpreted signs to signify this one or that one, good or bad, do it or don't, only to find out eventually that he had read the signs wrong, or that something that had seemed at first brimming with advice or warning was nothing more than gibberish, Rorschach blots of his own hopes, fears, lunacy. But if coincidence this time, why that poem? Why "Dover Beach" and not, say, something by Robert Frost? Was Billy so foolish to interpret this Third Incident in the way he did? As bearing directly and commenting so swiftly upon The Big Decision reached during the Second Incident. Did it not seem that God himself was sticking his nose into Billy's business, sending down godly memoranda to say that he was all in favor of Billy's decision? Because it certainly seemed as if somebody manipulating the cosmic strings was trying to tell him: "This is your big chance. Go, kid. Take Zizi out to California."

Four: Russo called Zizi up. It was Tuesday, 3:30 in the afternoon. He was phoning from his office after she had been absent from his class for the third straight meeting. He suggested they meet to talk things over. He was worried, he said. He was sorry about the way he had behaved toward her, (she said) he said. He had to see her. Would she go out to dinner with him tomorrow night? He'd take her to DiMaggio's and come by her room for her around eight.

Upon hearing about all this from Zizi, hearing that Russo had called her and said all the things she claimed he had said, hearing that Russo proposed to take her out to DiMaggio's, the fanciest restaurant in town, Billy got very upset. He begged her not to go to dinner, told her to "call him up. Just call him up right now. Or I'll call him up and I'll tell him, 'Look, friend, Zizi wants me to tell you she doesn't want to see you . . .' " But Zizi told him that she could handle Russo and that he, Billy, should let her conduct her own life. Then, when she said that she not only had to see Russo again, but wanted to see him, Billy tried sulking, and when she didn't pay attention, he got angry and badmouthed Russo for a full forty-five minutes, threatening, "I'd kill that guy if he were here right now"—until finally Zizi started to cry. She ran

273

into her bedroom and closed the door on him. A minute or so later when he knocked meekly on the door to ask her if she was all right, she told him to go away.

The next day, Billy went over to Zizi's room around five in the afternoon after working on his economics in the library for most of the day. He intended to apologize to her if that was going to be necessary. He hoped that she had calmed down. Bleakly, hopelessly, he hoped that she had thought about it overnight, had decided that Billy was right about it, that she wasn't going to go out to dinner with Russo after all and she had just that second gotten off the phone with the Greyhound bus terminal, having reserved two seats on the bus to San Francisco, California.

He was dismayed to find Zizi in a state of jittery getting-ready-ness: her shampooed hair drying in a towel turban, sitting in a chair in her terry-cloth bathrobe filing her fingernails. A few minutes later, she had disappeared behind her bedroom door and did not reappear for quite some time. But then: skirt, sweater, necklace, bracelets, stockings, perfume. The last sight Billy had of her was when he was trudging down the stairs to go back to his room and turned around for a last look from the foot of the landing: a swirling, ruffly, gaily colored skirt slipping through the bathroom door at the top of the landing.

27

"I DON'T LIKE THE LOOKS OF THIS AT ALL," BILLY SAID
to himself. "I wish I knew what was going on." He
had returned to his room and was sitting now at his
desk. The chapel bell had tolled the hour before: grim,
separate, sonorous clanking. Eight o'clock.

Zizi was where, by now? Still in her room, waiting
for Russo? He pictured her, sitting in her armchair,
getting up every couple of minutes to look out the window to see if he was coming. Waiting for that fucking
bastard. Or was she already sitting in his car? On the
way to DiMaggio's restaurant? What were they saying
to each other? Zizi had told Billy that she was capable
of conducting her own life. She said she could "handle
Phil." All right, fine. But just how was she conducting
that life? Just how was she handling him? And what
did Russo want from her, anyway? Why couldn't he
just leave Zizi alone? Hadn't he done enough?

What would they say? What would they conclude?
Maybe Russo would play it up gallant, maybe offer to
pay for Zizi's operation, or at least go halfsies. "Hey,
look, think nothing of it, Zeez, old girl. Really, it's my
pleasure. I want to pay. After all, it's partly my kid
in there too." But Billy remembered that Zizi had said
that Russo was broke. She said he had been unable to
afford the insurance payments on his car. Alimony, his
son's school bills, psychiatric sessions, a rented apartment in Beacham and steep mortgage payments on

275

the converted barn in Vermont. Maybe Russo wanted to ask Zizi if she could lend him a few dollars until payday.

So what would they say? Would Zizi tell him, "Look, Phil. Before this goes any further, I want you to know that we're through. For one thing, I hate your guts; for another, I've found someone new. The two of us are quitting school at the end of term. In fact, you're lucky you caught me, I was just starting to pack when you called the other day . . . Yes, we're both looking forward to California. Billy has gotten a very promising position with a team of nutritional experts and there's some chance they can place me with the same organization. I think nutrition is a very fast growing field, don't you? Billy and I both agree it's important to commit ourselves now so we can really get in on the ground floor . . . So . . . Do you understand what I'm saying? That you and I are through? Great. Now, if you're still buying dinner . . ."

Billy was sitting at his desk. He had been sitting at his desk for the better part of two hours. He had done a little work and plenty of thinking, most of it speculative, none of it amounting to anything. His stomach hurt, he had a headache, he was wheezing. He had gotten up from his chair only twice; once to go down the hall to the bathroom, where he languished on the toilet seat and where his anxiety seemed to dissipate and his stomach somewhat unknotted. For twenty minutes or so he was content to just sit there, pants down around his ankles, alone. No sooner had he hiked his pants back on and buckled his belt than his stomach began hurting again. In fact all the moving around and the attention it was getting made it hurt even worse.

The other time he had left the room was to slip a

letter into the mailbox in front of the campus post office down the street. The letter was addressed to his father. It was a short letter, saying that Billy was fine, he was dropping out of school and coming out to California. Therefore, he told his father, "If you haven't paid the bill for my second semester's tuition, then don't pay it." He tried to make it all sound very matter-of-fact. One man to another. He wrote that he hoped they could all get together "in the near future."

He had hoped that when he slipped the envelope into the mail slot, the single action would make everything seem more definite. Of course he was quitting school. Of course he was going to California. Of course Zizi was going with him. He had notified his father already. Would he have done something like that if he wasn't sure he was going . . . ? Well? What about it?

Billy sat at his desk, Randy's electric typewriter sitting there before him, a sheet of paper rolled into its carriage, engine whirring. Randy had given Billy permission to use the typewriter to type his paper for Russo (which he had still not finished). Billy had spent at least ten minutes trying to figure out how to get the lousy machine out of its carrying case, then another couple of minutes of trial and error with all the switches, buttons, and levers, trying to figure out which one, or which combination, turned the thing on.

Now, by the time the eight bells had sounded across the freshman yard, Billy had typed two words: "When Sophocles . . ." He was having a hard time concentrating.

"What if Zizi decides to go back to that freak?" he asked himself. "What am I supposed to do if that happens?" He worried the problem for a while, almost positive that if he thought very hard he'd be able to think up a great plan that would fake Russo out, make him look ridiculous, show Zizi what a corrupt fellow he was underneath. Maybe even land the son-of-a-bitch in jail the way it happened on television. But no plan occurred to him. If Zizi went off with fucking David Berkowitz Billy'd be powerless to stop her.

Billy sat back in his chair, stared, glazed-eyed, unseeing, at the blank wall for fully five minutes, not even knowing where he was.

Minutes later, things started to move. Slowly at first, then gathering momentum.

8:15 (approximately): Randy returned with several of his friends from a snowball fight out in the freshman yard. Mel Lavender and Pete and Ron and two other kids whom Billy had never seen before came in with him. They were in high spirits, and Randy stuck his head in through the bedroom door to tell Billy how "it was unbelievable out there" (out in the quad winging snowballs at the upperclassmen). "Everybody was, like, going crazy." Billy had heard whooping and yelling through the window, but he hadn't thought much about it. It could have been Soviet troops, or Martians from space for all he could have known. Mel came into the back room to show off a raw, red bruise under his left eye where he said a snowball had smashed him. Pete and Ron came in to exult over how they had "nailed some asshole" who managed to infiltrate the dorm, with a well-directed squirt in the face and eyes with the fire extinguisher—water and some eye-scalding flame-retardant chemicals. (The end-of-the-winter-semester snowball fight between freshmen, defending their yard and dormitories, and the invading upperclassmen hordes was a Beacham tradition.) Soon Randy's two friends, the two kids Billy had never met before, came into the bedroom to tell Billy their end of the story. There were seven people crammed into one little room, Billy in the center, looking up at them from the desk. Randy and Mel and the rest had all been having a great time when one of the nervous freshmen deans had thought things had gone too far and called in the Beacham campus police force—six officers in leather jackets, with bullhorns, billy clubs, riot shields, and revolver butts protruding prominently out of their holsters. Pete said he had hit one of the cops in the back of the head with a snowball before he ran away.

While Billy was still struggling to complete his term paper for Russo, everyone else had finished the semester's work, or almost finished. Randy's semester had ended that afternoon when he took his last exam (in Sociology 210a: "The Human Experience"). Therefore Randy and Mel and the others are all in celebrating moods. They all wanted to get stoned; Mel had a Baggie-ful of some exotic marijuana (from Brazil, or Tijuana, or Panama, or one of those places). And they tried to coax Billy to take a break—he could finish the paper later.

"Come on, Billy. I think it's fucked up," Randy said, "you sitting in here working all the time. I don't work half as much as you and so far I'm making straight A's. So come on. Party with us."

"Don't be an asshole," Mel said.

(It was true that Randy was getting all A's. He had gotten an A from his introductory Spanish teacher who had never found out that Randy had already studied the language in high school and junior high for five years. Nor that Randy, when young, had had a governess named Consuelo who cooed Spanish lullabies down to him in his crib. Spanish had been Randy's first language, or so he had bragged to Billy. And Randy had also gotten an A on the engineering final exam. Because, sure enough, the exam that Professor Potter passed around on Monday was the same exam Randy had bought from Ron Finkelstein—the same exam Professor Potter had passed around a year

279

ago that Monday, and the year before that.) He was also taking two other courses on a pass/fail option.

"Come on, Billy. Let's get wasted."

Normally an invitation to smoke marijuana would have frightened asthmatic Billy. He and his lungs still recalled that fine ninth-grade spring Sunday when he had gone down to Greenwich Village with Daniel, his friend from school, who said he had heard that you could buy marijuana cigarettes from some guy named Harold who wore a black hat and just hissed at you from a doorway on crowded Eighth Street near St. Mark's Place.

Billy and Daniel walked up the street for a good long hour before they were finally approached by a jangly hippie. He said his name was Montana and he sold them a Baggie-ful of tobacco, oregano, crumpled aspirin, sticks, and ordinary house dust for $25. Whatever it was, it almost killed Billy. He spent the two weeks that followed bedridden with hacking, bucking bronchitis and had to get two shots of penicillin from Dr. Prothero, the family allergist. Daniel, however, said he got "really stoned," and spent most of the afternoon making what he thought were stoned observations. ("Oh wow! Look at that bus. Doesn't it look really surrealistic? Like, look at the headlights. Doesn't it really look like an old man?")

Billy had smoked marijuana a couple of times after that, most notably that time long seasons past, with Zizi when they stayed up all night on the island. Also once or twice with his sister and some of her friends. Also a couple of times with Lulu, once with Lulu's brother Jack in the bathroom of their apartment. It was the night Lulu celebrated her seventeenth birthday with a big party. She invited all her high school friends and Billy was forced to take refuge from her in the bathroom, where he locked himself in and spent a peaceful hour reading the cartoons in the

280

back issues of *The New Yorker,* which Lulu's mother always stacked up on the hamper next to the toilet. Jack and some of his friends knocked on the door and said, "Open up"; they had some hash.

Normally an invitation to smoke marijuana would not have interested Billy very much. But now he dully contemplated Randy and the others from the desk chair, saw little alternative, then switched off the typewriter and said, "Okay. I guess I can finish typing this later."

They herded through the door into the living room and solemnly took their places, grouping on the sofa, pulling up the desk chairs to form a sort of Indian peace-pipe ceremony semicircle. Randy turned on the stereo, selecting for the occasion the most tuneless and violent record in his collection: a postmortem rip-off of Jimi Hendrix tapes (still in his mainlining heroin phase, not yet in his dead phase, although from the sound of the record, he was obviously well on the way).

Pete lit up and passed the joint on to the taller of Randy's two new friends: a skinny junior aristocrat with Gucci loafers and lacquered sandy hair. His friend, fatter, squatter, took the cigarette from there.

When the joint passed on to Billy, he knew enough (from movies and from watching his sister) to swallow rather than to inhale the smoke, pronging the drooly roach between thumb and forefinger (in the high hippie tradition) and sleepily lidding his eyes. He repeated all this a few times, passed it back to Pete, then waited, experiencing nothing other than the rumbling from his air-tightening lung locks.

8:20: The record clicked off. Seconds later, Mel interrupted the peaceful quiescence by asking what time it was.

"Eight-twenty," Randy said, looking at the ruby figures on his digital watch.

Mel said that Master Moss was throwing a Christmas party at his house. It started at eight-thirty. What about it? Anybody feel like going?

Shrugs. "Naw. I don't feel like movin'. Let's stay here."

Mel said that they'd have eggnog and free drinks. Stuff to eat. Cheese and stuff like that.

No one else really wanted to go. Pete said: "Lavender, why don't you go? Go by yourself. Cause I was talking to Mrs. Kandler and I know she wants to see you . . ." (Mrs. Kandler, the dean's wife, was considered by Mel and Randy and Pete and the rest to number among the world's homeliest women—buck teeth, copper wire for hair, 250 pounds overweight, four chins, etc. Mrs. Kandler featured prominently in the jokes they made about each other during the term. In her defense, Mrs. Kandler was very friendly and funny, in a middle-aged-woman kind of way. Many of the girls at Beacham liked her very much. They frequently dropped over to visit her, to drink tea, and to tell her about all the problems they were having.) ". . . We were talking, the other day, and Mrs. Moss told me she has a big thing for you. She said for me to tell you she'll jerk you off in the closet if you show up at her house tonight." Raucous belly-laughs from Randy and Ron at that one. The two strange kids chuckled, a little ill at ease on the sofa. Mel grinned feebly. Billy watched.

At length, they decided that while it was not worth going to the master's Christmas party to get drunk, where they would have to wear jackets and chat with the master about what they planned to do over Christmas break ("Go home, rest, you know . . . Uh . . . take things easy . . . Duh . . ."), it might nevertheless be fun to go out and buy some vodka or gin or something and get drunk right there. The liquor store on Chapel Street stayed open until nine. Pete and Randy put on their coats. Mel contributed the fifteen dollars he had in his wallet. Billy only had a dollar and fifty cents.

8:40 (approximately): Pete and Randy came back with two brown bags full of clinking liquor bottles: vodka, rum, Coca-Cola, orange juice, three bottles of cheap New York champagne which Randy said were on sale.

Billy wasn't very good at getting drunk. That he hated the taste of alcohol always surprised him, considering what drunks his parents were. By the time the others had drained the first quart of vodka, each refilling his glass, Billy had been able to force down only one-third of his screwdriver. He wished that somebody had told him you were supposed to put more orange juice in than vodka, instead of the other way around. He had gotten the ratio reversed: one-quarter orange juice, three-quarters vodka. He wanted to fill up what he had drunk with more orange juice to make it taste better, but he wasn't really thirsty, even for plain orange juice. He felt open-stomached, as though he hadn't eaten anything for months. He had missed dinner that night, but he knew that the feeling had nothing to do with his caloric intake. He knew that the alcohol had nothing to do with it either. It was only a premonition of the hollowness that would come if he lost Zizi, if she went back to Russo, if she decided she didn't want to go to California, at least not with him.

He decided to swallow his drink down as fast as he could—that way it would taste bad only once. After that it would be in his stomach. Randy measured him another drink. Billy swallowed his down,

283

too, in three gulps, interspersed by long, reeling seconds while he clenched shut his eyes and tried not to gag. He poured himself a third drink and put in very little vodka. Not terrible. He hardly tasted anything. He was pleased to notice that while he was not in the lead (Pete was on his fifth glass), he had pulled ahead of Mel and the two strangers. When the vodka was gone, Billy watched Randy uncork the champagne, watched the foam gush all over Randy's lap, on the chair, the floor; heard harsh, hacking laughter. He had two sips of champagne, then put the drink down on the floor while he tried to settle himself. When he reached back down for it, he was surprised to find that it had fallen over. He shut his eyes, and as he did so, the circular swishing in his head, which had been kept at bay while he had his eyes open, rushed in upon him. In the darkness, he felt that his chair had begun to swivel, that someone was spinning him around.

Someone was asking him if he wanted some champagne. Billy tried to say "no more," but he had difficulty getting his tongue to work.

He stood up; the desk chair he had been sitting on fell back behind him, he almost fell over it turning around to reach the door.

The hallway was well lit and that made him feel better. He teetered through the bathroom door, banged into a sink, careened into a toilet stall, then knelt on the floor, neck craning into the toilet bowl. It looked as if he were praying at some altar. In fact he was praying.

"Oh God . . . Oh God. I feel so bad . . ."

But he couldn't throw up. He still felt bad, hot and sweaty. In fact, if anything the ammonia smells rising from the toilet-paper swamp of the toilet made him feel worse.

It occurred to him that what he needed was some

fresh air. He managed to get to his feet and down the flights of stairs, helped by the steel barrier, without tumbling skull-first to the bottom. At the bottom he shoved open the heavy wood door and almost fell into the cold night outside. The quadrangle dormitory roofs and window ledges, tree branches, everything gleamed with snow. The campus walkways were roughly indicated through the white by gray footprint trails. Wind, bearing an occasional snow grain, lashed his face. The moon and stars blazed cleanly in a cloudless, black-ink sky.

Silence. Not a person around. Or in any case, no one that he noticed. Just the humming from the streetlights that lined the walks and illuminated the quadrangle by night. The streetlights had little pyramids of snow on top that made Billy think somehow of yarmulkes.

He stood there in the cold, exhaling steam, his mind gone blank—just the sick juices churning in his stomach. He stood still, trying to straighten himself out, braced by the cold, until he recalled what he had been feeling so miserable about all evening, before getting drunk and sick had made him forget: Zizi— and all that stretched beyond her. Iridescent, tingling feelings, shadowy wishes and more shadowy dreams of fulfillment. If things didn't go wrong. In other words, if some miracle intervened.

Oh Zizi! He turned around to find her window out of the dozens of dormitory windows. Third floor, fourth from the left, the lights were out. Of course they were out. She was gone. Looking up, he wished that the lights would turn on—Zizi returned early! If they went on he could go up to see her. What pretext could he find this time? He could ask her for the address of the health food store where her brother-in-law was the manager—he could ask her how she spelled her brother-in-law's last name (Winks? or

285

Winkes?). He could ask her what she thought, whether he ought to send off his résumé.

He wanted to see her, to sit in her room with all the plants and girl smells. He wanted to talk to her, to use being drunk as an excuse to be bold and to tell her he loved her, how much he cared about her.

Then he began to reconstruct her face in his mind, vague at first, then coming into focus. Her teeth, her nose, her cheeks, her indifferent eyes. The way they all came together to compose—well, her face. Sitting there in the restaurant, listening to Russo. Thinking what? Saying what?

Russo. Son-of-a-bitch. Desperate son-of-a-bitch, what if he decided for some crazy, middle-aged reason that he wanted her back? What if he told her how he had been crazy, he had been wrong, he loved her, his divorce would soon be final, would she marry him?

Oh Christ! What would Zizi do then?

The weakness! How weak he had been to let her go. How stupid. He should have been tough. He should have said no. "Zizi, no. You're not going. No . . . Why? Because I say so. No. Nothing doing." She would have respected that. Felt protected. Besides, what could she have done if he had barred the way? Called the cops? Well, she could have done that . . .

"Stupid. Coward. Weakling. Why didn't you do something to stop her? Why didn't you just say, 'Let's get on the next bus, who cares about finishing the term?' "

The dread that he had lost her now made him say: "I hate you! I hate being you!" to himself. "Stupid idiot!" And he struck himself in the head with his fist. It surprised him how hard he had slugged himself. Two knuckles ached as if he had broken bones, and his skull throbbed sharply.

He didn't know what to do. Everything was out of

control now, going wrong, out of his hands. Like dropping a stack of dishes, having to watch for long, agonized milliseconds as the fancy plates explode all over the floor. Everything going wrong and having to stand helplessly by and having to watch.

That bastard Russo! That dumb bitch Zizi! At that moment he was certain that he hated her. But the passion was indistinguishable from the love he had suffered. It made no difference. Just the other side of the coin. Dualism was what you called the phenomenon, Russo had explained one day in class. Dualism. What a lot of shit.

He felt as if he could start screaming "Fuck! Fuck! Fuck! Fuck!" at the top of his lungs. He wanted to scream, to vent his wrath, or wrent his vath. Take a bath. Oh God. What was that mind of his up to now? "Is this it?" he thought, "the razor's edge? Am I losing my marbles? If I'm not careful, I'm going to be rooming with Henry's kid in the nuthouse." He wanted to scream but at the last instant he realized he didn't want to disturb anyone. He didn't want to call attention to himself, and have someone call the campus cops, so that the dean would have to write home to tell his mother that her son had been suspended from college for standing out in the quadrangle in his shirt-sleeves at approximately 9:30 p.m. December 13, howling swear words up to the cold, impervious moon.

He started to run, diagonally across the yard at first, stumbling in the boggy snow, then cut across to a path that had been cleared with salt and snow shovels, where he got traction and speeded up. Slush sloshed his pants legs and soaked through his shoes. The wind whipping his face and the feeling that he was running very fast, maybe faster than he had ever run before, excited him as he wheeled out the campus gate onto College Street, the campus main drag, running parallel to DeWitt Avenue one block over. He ran to the end of the block, hurdling puddles and drifts and side-stepping pedestrians like a halfback. He didn't stop for the red light at the curb, but took a quick look and chanced the crossing. The glowing face of a bus, the sign SHELTON AVENUE beaming from its forehead, bore down on him and fretted its baritone horn. It missed him by inches. He ran on, leaving street after street behind him, running now to punish himself, to punish himself for everything. His lungs ached and the muscles that lifted his knees had all the con-sistency of jelly, but he kept going, lashing himself onward with inward jeers whenever he begged him-self to stop. "Keep going, goddamnit. Faster. Faster, you clod." And by force of these exertions he ended up far along Webster Avenue, in a strange, dark neighborhood. A block of shabby row houses, fire escapes, graffiti and looted storefronts.

At the end of the block, there was an awning and a window with lights and he made for it. He stopped beneath the awning, put his hands on his hips and tried to breathe. He thought he was going to pass out. Or die there. He sat down on the stoop and put his head down between his knees. He sat there, gasping, for a minute or two, getting cold.

He did not realize that he was sitting in front of DiMaggio's restaurant until the maitre d' rapped angri-ly on the glass door behind him, then poked his gray, oval face outside and said: "Hey, sonny, whatta ya think you're doin'? You can't sit out there. This is a place of business. I got customers going by here."

Billy got to his feet, read the ornate script painted in gold across the glass door: "DiMaggio's"; saw the man's blue blazer, "DiMaggio's" embroided with red thread across the breast pocket.

DiMaggio's. Had God done this? Arranged for him to run down the streets he had run? To stop here, on this stoop, in front of the restaurant where Zizi had said Russo was taking her? Were things going to be all right, then? Was everything under control? Or, if he chose to reject the religious interpretation, had his subconscious guided him here? That was an interesting thought. How could it have known where DiMaggio's was? Billy had never heard of the restaurant until Zizi told him two days earlier that she would be going there. Billy felt that, one way or the other, there were powerful forces at work, helping him out, giving him a hand with his life. Or leading him to disaster.

"I'm sorry," Billy explained to the maître d', who ignored him holding the door open for an elderly couple to pass through.

"Have a good evening now," he addressed the old people as they steeled themselves and readied their canes to descend the first step down to street level, "come back again soon." The old woman trembled, terrified, balancing on the end of her cane. The old man turned to look at the maître d' and mumbled a few words, as if to say: "We'd like to come back. We might die before then, but if we're still around we'll come back. It's a deal . . ." "Come along, mother." The old woman skidded down the last step, looked back at the restaurant and at the maître d' rigidly smiling in the doorway, then turned to look at Billy. Her heart must have jumped with the fear that he was a mugger, for she shook her head and closed her eyes as if maybe when she opened them again, he would no longer be standing there. She stood frozen until her husband caught up with her, then the two of them shuffled off down the street together. The maître d' ducked back inside to bully his waiters and count the silverware. The door closed behind him with a pneumatic hiss.

Snow had begun to fall again and Billy could

289

feel it soaking through his wool sweater to his shoulders and down his neck. He stood there and shivered, pulling his arms tight against his sides.

Zizi was inside. He wanted to walk through the doors and go get her, to see if she needed help, but he was afraid of the maître d' who would throw him out for not having a jacket.

"Oh Zizi," he thought, shuddering with cold and emotion, "are we going to California or not?" But even the question lacked conviction. He imagined the two of them inside, around them everything warm and clean, white tablecloths, candles, baskets of breadsticks, busboys and wine stewards in Nehru jackets cruising around the tables removing plates, and Zizi sitting across from Russo at a corner table, sipping from her wineglass, speaking in low tones about how happy they were going to be. Zizi would lower her head and her hair would glint russet in the candlelight, Irish-setter red.

Billy walked down the block and hid in the shadows of a doorway. He could see the front door of DiMaggio's from his dark hiding place. He watched the glass door, hardly breathing, throat choked, blood on fire, whirling within him, whacking at his temples. What was going to happen?

And then the glass doors quivered, began to open, a flash of a dress. His heart froze for an instant. Oh God—But it wasn't Zizi.

"Oh God." He took a deep breath.

A long time passed. Maybe twenty minutes, maybe an hour. The restaurant emptied, well-dressed diners came through the doors, separated into cars and drove home. Billy wondered whether he had arrived too late. Maybe they had come, eaten dinner, said what they had had to say to one another, and then gone. "I'll wait until three more people leave," he made a deal with himself. He had resolved to stop at nothing, and yet, if they were no longer inside, it made his vigil seem ridiculous. Besides, even if they were inside, he had not decided what he was going to do. When they emerged, if they emerged, should he thunder forth: "All right, you two. What's the big idea? Zizi, are you going to explain all this to me?"

He was chattering and he had lost sensation in his fingers and his toes. Minutes passed and the restaurant door opened and closed several times. An old man and his bimbo, a quintet of rowdy, coiffured hags shrilly griping about the snow: "Isn't this snow awful?" "Too miserable." And the thought began to steal into Billy's brain that it was all pointless. The night seemed to harden around the growing absurdity of a boy standing in a doorway, getting frostbite, watching strangers go home from the restaurant where they had eaten dinner. He thought that if Zizi and Russo were not the next to come through the door, then he would abandon his ambush and go back to his room, get out of his wet sweater and go to bed. But Zizi and Russo were not the next ones out. Nor the ones after that.

Russo appeared first. He sauntered down the steps and stood for a few idle moments on the sidewalk, watching the snow and obviously waiting for Zizi. His hands were in his pea jacket pockets and he was rocking on his heels. Billy was surprised to see his professor in evening dress. Russo had selected his urban guerrilla ensemble for his dinner date with Zizi: Ché Guevara camouflage-pattern safari trousers, French beret cocked at a jaunty angle (probably held in place with bobby pins). Laced-up black paratrooper's boots completed the surprising picture.

Things had gone well for Russo, from the smirking look on his face. He had gotten what he had come for, whatever that was.

He was probably waiting for Zizi to come out of

the ladies' room. Or to get her coat back from the hat check girl. Or maybe he was waiting for her to settle up with the maître d', disgorging her pockets and excavating her linings for nickles and dimes with which to pay the hefty check.

When she finally came through the glass door, she did not look like Zizi. As he watched her tighten the collar of her lambskin, $250 Bloomingdale's coat, do a Walt Disney shiver, then come down the steps cautiously on her spike-heel boots, he felt that he knew no more of her than he could have seen in a photograph. Billy watched Zizi rubbing her lamb-skinned arms with red-mittened hands. He heard her tell Russo that it was freezing and she wanted to go to the car. Hiding breathless in the doorway, Billy thought of Lee Harvey Oswald, and how he must have felt.

Russo put his arm around her and she huddled against his side. They started walking.

The thought "she's gone back to him" raced through him. His heart clenched.

Suddenly he realized that they were coming toward him, that they would walk past him on their way to Russo's car. They would see him hiding there. They would expect him to tell them just what he thought he was doing there, spying on them, wearing only his sweater in the middle of this snowstorm. What was wrong with him? What was his problem?

"What am I going to do?" he asked himself. "Hurry up! Think!" He could make a break for it, but they were by now so close upon him that they would see him, like the hunters training shotgun sights on the single, broken quail. He'd be done for.

Jealous Othello took a deep breath, then sprang from his ambush. He strode murderously up the block toward them, wearing a stern scowl, a frown of cold and concentrated resolution.

"Hi, Billy," Zizi said. She seemed genuinely happy to see him, smiling broadly. For a second it threw him. Then he thought darkly: "She's trying to finesse me. She knows what's going on." Russo did not take his left arm down from around Zizi's shoulder. Both of them pretended that there was nothing unusual about running into Billy on this snowy street, a mile from campus. "Isn't this snow beautiful?" Zizi said.

Knocking back tears, he shoved her and she skittered backward a few steps, trying to right herself on the stilts of her high heels. The slick snow was her undoing, and she went down hard, ass first, a lump of ruffly skirt, lacy petticoat, lambskin coat.

Billy turned to Russo. He was surprised to find (and let the psychologists explain this one) that he no longer bore him particular ill will. In fact the first thought that came into his mind, just before Russo hit him with a roundhouse, was to request an extension of the deadline on his final paper.

Billy felt a black jolt, but no pain. He was surprised to feel himself sinking, his legs giving out. He crumpled to the ground. He wondered where he was. Everything was dark, shimmering cold, radioactive, screaming.

28

Billy regained consciousness to see two large faces looming over him: the first belonged to the policeman who had driven Billy to the infirmary the night he caught chronic bronchitis from sleeping in the closet. Billy recognized him immediately: the uniform, the policeman's hat. Also, his punched-in face and bristly mustache. The cop was slapping Billy awake with flabby fingers.

"Wha—hey! What are you doing? Stop. I'm up."

"Take it easy, Billy," the second face said. It was a long face. A sad face. Beady eyes. Acne scars. Fat, glistening lips. Orange sideburns. Who in the world was that? The face was familiar, but Billy had forgotten whose it was.

"Hi," Billy said, faking recognition, "what are you doing here?"

"I was visiting friends in the neighborhood," Bernie Gould explained, "and I was on my way home when I saw you go down. How do you feel? Don't move."

"I'm okay."

"I can call an ambulance," the cop said to Bernie, "what do you think?"

"An ambulance?" Billy said, "what for? For me? Hey wait—" As he sat up, he realized that a crowd of about twenty people had gathered to watch the drama, intently rubbernecking. Billy spotted Russo among them. And Zizi.

"I don't think he's going to need an ambulance," Bernie said. "Billy? Can you stand up, do you think?"

"Sure," Billy said. He was aware of no great pain, just a dull ache behind his left eye; also the freeze of some snow which had fallen inside his sweater and was melting down his neck.

As he climbed to his feet, he wondered what he was supposed to do. He felt like crying. Instead he tried to play it cool. As cool as you could play it after someone has just flattened you with one punch. As cool as you could play it when the son of your mother's boy friend had seen the whole thing. What if Bernie had already called Billy's mother while Billy was unconscious? What if Bernie had run to the end of the block and called New York collect from a pay phone and said, "Mrs. Wieseltier, this is Bernie Gould. Look, something terrible has just happened . . ." At that very minute she could be hurtling downtown in a taxicab to the train station to be with her boy.

"Oh God," Billy prayed, "please don't have let that happen."

"Okay, people," the cop said, turning to address the crowd, "everything's over. You can all go on home." Two old women looked a little disappointed that Billy wasn't dead after all. "Okay, ladies. Move along now," the cop said. The ladies said something about how they were going to move down to Florida first chance they got, the city just wasn't safe.

"C'mon fellas."

A youth gang of four or five gap-toothed punks told the cop to "take a look at your book of fucking rules and regulations, man. You don't own the street." But they decided to move along when it looked like the cop was going to hit them in the head with his billy club. A group of about six or seven remained, among them two red-jacketed busboys from DiMaggio's restaurant (by way of Greece and points east);

also, Professor Russo, looking pale and unstable in his camouflage; and next to him, but separate, smoking a cigarette, was Zizi.

The cop was trying to make the busboys understand that he wanted them to go back to work. To go away.

"Very sorry," one of the busboys answered, "not speak so much English."

"Look," the officer said, pointing his finger first at them, then in the direction of DiMaggio's restaurant up the street, "You. Go . . . Go. Go, I said."

"Yes, yes," the busboy said, nodding with recognition. But neither of them moved.

"Billy," Russo said, coming forward, "can I talk to you?"

"Sure."

"Look—I'm sorry about what happened. I'm terribly sorry. I lost control for a second."

"I'll say you lost control, Russo," Bernie jumped in, "and you're going to wish you hadn't. Because you're crazy, Russo. You know that? What'd you think you were? Some kind of big man? You're going to settle things with your fists? I'd like you to try taking a swing at someone your own age, someone your own size . . ."

Russo didn't say anything. He waited for Bernie to finish, then said, "Billy, I hope you'll try to understand and accept my deepest apologies."

"You're nothing, Russo," Bernie went on, pointing his finger, "you're a nobody. And you're going to regret what happened here tonight. We're going to prosecute this thing as far as the law allows. You can be sure of that. It'll cost you your job. And a hell of a lot more. You're finished, man."

"Cool off, cool off," the cop said, stepping between Bernie and Russo, "let's just find out what happened first, then you guys can yell all you want at each other."

"Officer, I don't know if this will help," Russo said, "but I'm a professor at Beacham University." Billy watched Russo reach into the back pocket of his camouflaged trousers for his wallet. He opened the wallet and handed his Beacham Faculty ID card to the policeman to prove that regardless of his costume, Russo was not a terrorist, but an English teacher.

The cop studied Russo's photograph on the plastic card, then Russo's face, then the card again.

"I shaved my beard a couple of months after that picture was taken."

"Okay, Professor. I believe you. But that still doesn't explain why you were fighting out here."

Billy was chattering. "If only I hadn't done this, if only I hadn't done this, if only I hadn't done this . . ."

"The kid's going to catch pneumonia if we don't get him indoors," the cop said. "I'll tell you what, Professor. How about if we all go down to the station house. We can get somebody to take a look at the kid's eye, and get him some hot coffee. And I'll take your statements."

Zizi offered to drive Russo's car home for him. She said she'd wait for him at his house. He could drive her back to campus later.

So they all piled into the back seat of the police car, behind the wire mesh—Billy and Russo and Bernie. The cop got in the front seat and radioed headquarters. He talked to the cop at the other end of the transmitter for a minute or two in untranslatable policeman's code: garbled numbers, street addresses, the catalogued code listings for a couple of crimes, victims and perpetrators. Then he hung up the microphone, asked, "Is everybody comfortable back there?" and started the car. Soon they were speeding down the avenue, headed for the police station, and justice.

"Billy, how do you feel?" Bernie asked.

"I feel a lot better."

"I want to talk seriously to you for a second." He wanted to be Billy's adviser. He urged Billy to prosecute. He called Russo "no better than a common thug" and said he should be punished for what he had done. Bernie went on about how, if Billy agreed, the two of them might make legal history. "We could make an important test case. We can sue the school for what happened. We can sue Beacham University, Billy. Don't you understand what this means? We can really go a long way towards establishing a Students Bill of Rights in this country."

An hour and fifteen minutes later, Billy was climbing the stairs, slowly and heavily, to his room. At the top of the landing he sighed and as he did so, he was overcome by a new, unfamiliar kind of misery, as if something inside him were dying. He dragged himself down the hall and pushed open the bathroom door. He almost tripped on Mel Lavender who was passed out on the cold tile floor, oatmeal vomit in his hair and clinging to his fingers.

A few minutes later, Billy returned to his room. He found his roommate sleeping on the floor, in a fetal bundle, and one of his roommate's friends curled up on the sofa. Thoughtfully, Billy turned out the lights for them. Oblivious to the smells of vomit and spilled liquor, Billy sat down on his bed and let the waves of self-pity roll over him. How could this have happened? How could it have happened?

Somehow he managed to strip off his soaking clothes. He cursed meaninglessly to himself . . . "Fuck fuck. Shit fuck fuck," and gasped in breathless grief. He sat there for some time, slumped on his bed, the skin around his eye puffy and discolored, the eye itself sunset red. The radiator clanked and hissed, and he sat there, head in hands, naked except for ragged underwear and watchstrap.

29

RUSSO DID NOT GET BACK FROM DRIVING ZIZI TO HER dorm until nearly 2 A.M. He spent a couple of minutes cleaning up the living room—collecting the balled-up Kleenexes steeped in Zizi's tears and snot and throwing them in the garbage, emptying the ashtray filled with the filter-tipped butts of Zizi's low-tar cigarettes, and carrying the two coffee mugs into the kitchen where he left them in the aluminum sink. Then he turned out all the lights and went into his study.

In one semester, a matter of eleven weeks, Russo had had an affair with a freshman, gotten that freshman pregnant, and earlier that evening agreed to finance her abortion. He had also beaten up another of his students and only avoided being thrown in jail for assault and battery when the student declined to press charges. He was certain that word would get around and then there would be little question, he'd be called onto the carpet and dismissed.

Russo was afraid that the incident might make the *New York Times*. The *Times* would jump for it if they ever got wind that a professor had slugged one of his students. The lead article in the second section: "University Divided Over Russo Incident" in big block letters. Ironic, too, because Russo's book on the Victorian novel had never merited a review in the *Times*.

Russo sat at his desk and examined his swollen knuckles by Tensor lamp. He wondered if any of them were sprained. He thought to himself, with some pride, that he had never belted anyone like that before. Except for his wife. Russo felt Hemingway-esque for a few moments. He sat back in his desk chair.

He had gotten through dinner with Zizi. Everything had been calm and controlled and fairly amicable. No hysteria. He had asked Zizi how much the operation would cost, and when she told him, "About a hundred and fifty dollars," he had assured her, "Of course I'll pay for everything." He had done a pretty good job with her, under the circumstances. She had said, over a plate of antipasto, that she was going to drop out of school and had made plans to run away to California. She had told him some crap about getting a job on her sister's organic farm. Russo had managed to convince her that she was being un-necessarily dramatic. "You're not going to escape your problems," he had told her, "you'll find that they'll come right along with you." And he had gotten her to say that she knew that he was right about everything. She'd stay in school. She even agreed to see a psychiatrist.

If he had been able to get her back to her room without mishap, it all would have worked.

When he got back from the police station he had found her on the living room sofa haggard and in tears. For nearly two and a half hours he listened to her cry shamelessly about what a horrible person he was, and what a horrible person he had made her feel that she was; how she couldn't understand how he could be so cold after what they had shared; she wanted to know how she had failed him; she said she wanted to kill herself, and then two minutes later she said she wanted to murder him; she said that she hated him but would never love anybody else.

Russo had tried to explain to her that he couldn't help it, but something inside him had changed. He didn't fully understand the change, but knew that it was impossible to resist. He could no longer feel about her as he once had. It was not her fault, and he was terribly sorry. "Why don't you let me drive you home? We both need some sleep," he had said.

"I knew it. I knew you'd drop me," she had said, arms folded, resolute beside him in the car. "Alice even tried to warn me that I was getting in way over my head with you."

"Look, Zizi. Get some sleep. We can talk tomorrow if you want. I'll be in my office in the morning." She opened the car door and got out. He braced himself for the inevitable, passionate slam, but when it came, he was nevertheless surprised by her violence.

When he got back to the apartment, he still had a lot of work to do. He'd be up at least another hour. In the file cabinet by the window, Russo searched for the title and mortgage records to his house in Vermont. Tomorrow he would call a real estate agent to see what the house would bring. He had originally paid $45,000 for the old barn and the land, but he had put a lot of money into the property—a new kitchen, new wiring —and besides, the price of land in the country had skyrocketed. Russo would try to get $75,000.

Russo found his bankbook in the top drawer of his desk. He had a little over $5,000 in savings. Where had all his money gone? Car payments, school bills, the mortgage, life insurance, home insurance, car insurance, pyschiatric bills, rent. Tomorrow he'd have to withdraw $150 to give to Zizi.

Russo hoped that $5,000 would be enough to support Thomas and himself until the house was sold. There were ways of cutting costs. The best way, of course, was to go live with his parents in California. There'd be plenty of room for the two of them in that big, old house. And it wouldn't be permanent. Once the house in Vermont had been sold, Russo could buy his own place.

The most important thing was to get as far away from Beacham University, and the bad patterns of his life there, as he could. He had spent enough time on his psychiatrist's couch to realize that the reason he had made such a mess of the semester was that he wasn't very interested in teaching, or in writing his book about Dickens. Obviously being a member of the junior faculty wasn't what he wanted to do. The thing to do now was to get clear.

Furthermore, for several years, almost since his last year in graduate school, Russo had been writing a novel in his head. He'd tried to sit down and make preliminary notes about it, but he'd never had the time to really concentrate on it before. He wondered how much time $5,000 would buy him. He wondered how long he'd be able to stand living with his parents. He wondered if they'd let him move in with them. He'd call them in the morning to see what they thought.

Russo opened a drawer of his desk and took out some paper, then rolled a sheet into the carriage of his typewriter. He began to draft a letter to his editor, explaining that he planned to resign from teaching at the end of the month and then start work on a novel. He asked the editor if he'd be interested in getting together over lunch one day to discuss the project. Russo also explained that he had decided to shelve the Dickens book for the time being.

Then, almost finished, just reading the letter through and making some corrections, Russo opened a seldom-used bottom drawer looking for a gum eraser and found a letter. It had been mailed originally to his house in Vermont, but the village post office had forwarded it to Beacham, as he had instructed them to do with all his mail. It was a letter from Zizi that he had never opened. She had written it several weeks earlier, postmarked October 30. She wrote it one weekend when he had gone up to the house with Thomas and she had taken the train to Princeton to visit her best friend from high school.

Dear Philip,

For some time lying in bed tonight, I've been trying to remember what it feels like to kiss you. I've really been trying to imagine it. Then when I couldn't do that, I tried to remember the way you smell, but I couldn't remember that either. I even got out of bed, turned on the light and got my sweater out of my suitcase, the one I was wearing Thursday, to sniff it, thinking there might be a trace of you left over, but there was none.

What, I wonder, do you feel like? Your hair and arms and face? I still remember how your chin scratches me—my cheeks are still red and irritated. I know what you look like—so handsome and thoughtful and just a little sad around the eyes—because I got back those pictures I took last weekend and brought them with me. I'm looking at some of them now . . . But what is it like to just sit and talk with you? To have you there right in the same room and not some voice carrying across wires telling me to do my work and about all the things you did without me. Maybe Thomas knows what it's like to be there with you. I wish I was Thomas, just for tonight. I feel as if I haven't seen you in a year.

It's funny, too, because when Jojo left last night

303

to go stay in her boy friend's apartment, I sat down here and wrote you an altogether different letter. I've got it in my suitcase. I'll go get it . . .

I wrote: "It is as though normal existence (walking around with Jojo and meeting some of her friends, or being back at Beacham with Alice, going to classes, doing my work) is taking place in another dimension, one in which I am free to join in or not, as I please. I am in a different world with you. It is a feeling, as you would say, 'utterly uncanny,' otherworldly. I feel you there, experiencing what I experience, always observing what I do (teaching me, encouraging me, Professor), always looking over my shoulder. I want to be forever in you presence, which is not the same as being with you, which I like better, but which I understand now that I cannot be, that you need time to think, to be by yourself, to write and work on your book (and you're wrong, your book is really great, it's really going to be a big success) . . ."

But that was last night when I was feeling noble, and tonight is tonight when I have insomnia and feel self-indulgent. What are you doing? I can't sleep here. Can you? All the people at Princeton seem to do is get drunk and yell and scream all night. Are you sleeping alone? Do you miss me as much as I miss you? I know I'm not acting the way that you think I should but just as you have to be what you are, have to feel free to do what you want, to feel honest and unobliged, so do I have to be honest and feel what I feel. Maybe I have a problem.

I love you,
ZIZI

P.S. You should know, however, that when Jojo asked me if I was serious about anyone, I said

"No, nothing really. I've just been into working a lot." I'll see you tomorrow.

Russo crumpled up the letter and threw it in the wastebasket. "What a disaster," he thought.

IT'S THE NEXT DAY NOW AND THE SKIN AROUND Billy's left eye is still discolored, but the swelling has gone down. His vision too has cleared. He no longer sees blurred or doubled. He stands now looking out his open window, cold air blasting his face and exposed neck. He is looking out across the quadrangle, at the kids standing around in the snowy plains. He picks up snatches of their conversations, watches them come and go. His soul is heavy, labored with feelings of chagrin, ennui, and contempt for himself. He is about to pull the window shut and go back to typing his English paper when he sees Zizi walking gingerly across the patches of ice that had formed from puddles frozen on the walks.

Earlier that morning she had paid him a brief visit. He was still lying in bed when she knocked. He had been awake for a couple of minutes, trying to ignore an urgent bladder in the hopes that he'd be able to fall back to sleep. The day would pass, then maybe he'd try to get out of bed tomorrow morning. He'd see how he felt. Randy, hungover, must have lugged himself over to the door to let Zizi in.

"Yeah, he's here. He's in the bedroom. I don't think he's up yet." She stepped over the body of one of Randy's buddies, dozing on the floor, then strode into the bedroom in businesslike silence.

"Zizi?" Billy said, surprised that he didn't feel all that surprised to see her. He sat up in bed, wishing, if only for a second, that he had cleaned up his room. Underwear, dirty socks, Randy's porno magazines, papers, books, junk everywhere.

She closed the plywood door and sat down in the desk chair, on top of Billy's corduroy jacket.

"I want to talk to you," she said. She was trying to be severe, as if threatening imminent legal proceedings. "I want to know why you followed me last night. I want to know why you did what you did. What in the world is wrong with you?"

Billy was surprised to find himself still calm and unfrightened. Or at least not as frightened as he might have been. "I don't know what's wrong with me. I really don't know. I don't know how to explain or apologize for what I did. I guess I just didn't want you to see him again. He's a real creep and——"

"He is not a creep. And besides, who the hell are you to judge my friends?"

"Well I don't know, maybe he's a very nice man, Zizi. I don't really know him. But nice or not, he was taking advantage of you and it drove me crazy that you let that happen, that you'd waste yourself like that . . ." In a quieter voice, he said, "I just think that you're what the whole world wants. I mean you're the girl in all the advertisements and people like Russo are always going to take advantage——"

"Look—no one took advantage of me. And I don't need you to protect me, understand? Do you think you can just——" But then she faltered. It was momentary, and subtle, but for an instant her eyes lowered, her head dipped. Then she pulled herself back together. "Besides, I'm not seeing him anymore. I'm meeting him later this afternoon, he's going to give me some money to pay for the abortion and that'll be it."

Billy opened his mouth to say something, but didn't. No point. "Anyway," Zizi said, "I just wanted to see you because I have something to tell you. And that is that I'm not going to California. I'm willing to write my sister and see if there'd be a job for you on the farm if you're still interested in working there . . . Do you want me to do that or not?"

"No. I mean, thanks for offering and everything. But it wouldn't make sense. It only made sense before. When you were going. You know that. It wasn't just to go to California anyway. What would be the point of me working on some lousy farm?" When she wouldn't answer, he asked her, "What made you change your mind?"

"I'd been thinking a lot about it and I realized that you can't run away from your problems. That they come right along with you and it's best to stay and face them."

Billy was about to say, "Wait a minute. Didn't I say that a long time ago?" but checked himself. There'd be no satisfaction in winning the concession from her. He wished that she would go. He couldn't feel anything with her there. He wished she would go and let him mourn in peace. She told him his eye looked terrible, maybe he should see a doctor. A minute or two later, she left.

Billy stands at the window and watches Zizi walk past the entryway door that would take her, if she wanted, up the stairs to his room. He could easily imagine it: eyes glistening, she'd announce that she has tried, but she can't live without him. Does he still

307

have the money for those bus tickets? Ah, and what would Billy do then? He tries to relish in his mind her hurt when he tells her, "Sorry, baby. No way." But the fantasy doesn't really appeal to him. That's not what he'd really do. What would be the point? What's the point of anything?

Nevertheless he watches to see if she'd flinch as she passes beneath him, if she'd look up, or give any sign; but of course she does not. She is as unflinching, as indifferent to him now, as an army tank. There can be no avenging the looted heart.

He wonders what it all means. When she has passed out of view he is unable to move for some time. He feels that if there were a river flowing beneath his window he would have hurled himself into it with horror, but with no regret. But there are no white currents rushing below him to suck him under to restful oblivion. And he does not particularly feel like jumping out the window and landing on the Wang brothers.

Billy shivers as he gazes across the snow-covered yard, at the skeletal trees, the campus steeple, the imitation medieval turrets and domes of the dormitories and classroom buildings where lights burn; and he wonders, this time out loud, what in the world it all means.

"God—" he says, "I think I'm in even worse trouble than Matthew Arnold."

Later, Billy sits at his desk, chewing on a pencil eraser. He has just finished typing his English paper and now he's going over it. Revisions thus far have taken the form of replacing some of the "ands" with "buts" and the odd "however" with "moreover." He's about to start reading it through for the third time when something bothers him about the first sentence:

"When Sophocles introduced the third actor into drama, he changed the character of tragedy . . ."

On a piece of scrap paper, Billy writes: "When Sophocles introduced a third character into tragedy, he changed the nature of drama."

He decides that the second version sounds better and he pencils in the necessary alterations. But now the first page is a mess and he considers retyping it. He doesn't want to have points taken off for sloppiness. Then he thinks that Russo probably hates him so much already that nothing's going to make any difference.

Billy sits at his desk, proofreading in the half light, when a small red spider appears on the onionskin page, crawling in a zigzag diagonal toward the staple in the top left-hand corner.

"What are you doing here?" Billy asks it, "it's the middle of winter. There aren't supposed to be any spiders left." The spider stands still and tentatively waves one of its front legs. "Hi yourself," Billy says. He's about to flick it off his desk but doesn't. "All right," he says, "go ahead. Be symbolic. I'm watching."

Billy has still not moved when there is a knock at the door. He rises from his chair like an octogenarian and opens the front door to find Simon King standing outside in a football jersey and a red wool hat.

"Hey," Simon says, "you got a phone call downstairs."

Zizi?

He picks up the black receiver.
"Billy?" Not her voice.
"Yeah. Who is this?"
"It's Dad."
"Oh. Hi."
"How's it going?"
"Fine."

"Good. Uh, Billy, listen. Maybe you can explain something to me. I got this letter of yours in the mail today and I tell you, it's confusing the dickens out of me. Now you say here that you're dropping out of school and that you're planning to come out here in January. You said you've gotten some kind of job. But I don't get it, son. I called your mother just now to ask her what she knew about all this. She said she had just got off the phone with you half an hour ago, that she's heard nothing about your quitting school or any job or anything. She thinks I've lost my mind. So I figured I'd better call you up to see if somebody can tell me what the goddamn story is around here, because frankly, I don't get any of this."

The World of
JOHN IRVING

"John Irving's talent for storytelling is so bright and strong he gets down to the truth of his time."—New York Times

"John Irving moves into the front ranks of America's young novelists."—Time Magazine

Discover one of America's most exciting writers with these four books, all published in paperback by Pocket Books.

THE WORLD ACCORDING TO GARP
_____83515-7/$3.50

SETTING FREE THE BEARS
_____82255-1/$2.50

THE WATER METHOD MAN
_____82254-3/$2.50

THE 158-POUND MARRIAGE
_____41402-X/$2.50

POCKET BOOKS